Landlocked

JA Sanchez

@ Julie Ann Sanchez 2014

JS Red Writer Publishing

Dedicated to

Mark Sanchez

For your patience,

Seeing the possibilities,

Thank you for marrying me

Landlocked

You look toward the river,
Your feet locked to the land,
Bound in those
Insignificant grains of sand.
Too afraid the river will carry you
To where you should be.
Always looking but never
Allowing your soul to be free.
Elijhun Cann-Saez- 1922

Chapter One

"I will kill you if you take the girl out of this house."

When Charlie heard his mother's voice downstairs he opened his eyes to stare at the clock reading 7am. He'd be so damn glad when it was summer and his ex-wife, Mariana, wouldn't be at his doorstep to pick up the kids for school. Hearing his mother and Mariana argue was brutal on four hours sleep and no black coffee pumping through his heart.

"Why can't mornings ever go the way they're printed on the custody agreement?" Charlie thought as he stumbled out of bed, stubbing his toe on the bedpost. He held back a few curses so he didn't wake Lisa. He didn't need to put the fiancée in the same room with the two women who knew all the mistakes of his past. Charlie ran toward the stairs, hoping he could reach the front door before the screaming started but it was too late. Charlie could see Brenda bracing the door open just far enough to speak to Mariana.

"You understand?" Brenda said, over-pronouncing each word in her thick, southern accent. "You take the boy. You don't take the girl."

"You don't get to speak to me that way. My English is better than yours and it's my second language," Mariana said, her voice was at full volume and echoing through the front hall, "and the next time you threaten me, I'm getting a restraining order so get out of my way."

"Let the big civil rights attorney inside Mama," Charlie called down the stairs, trying not to wake everyone. He reached the landing just as Mariana charged past Brenda's stronghold. It was a funny visual to see Mariana in the crisp, red business suit and high heels combatting with Brenda's worn pink bathrobe and fuzzy slippers. Mariana moved past Brenda so fast that she looked startled to see Charlie standing there but recovered quickly as she moved downstairs toward the children's bedrooms.

"If you don't give me Oriana, I'm calling my divorce attorney."

"No one's keeping Oriana from you," Charlie protested looking for some help from Brenda. 'What's going on, Mama?"

"The girl's got a fever and spent the night throwing up her dinner," Brenda said, pointing to a stain on the front of her robe.

"If Oriana's sick, just leave her here," Charlie said, pursuing Mariana down the stairs. They both reached for the doorknob of Oriana's bedroom but Charlie got there first and held it tightly shut.

"What are you doing Mariana?" Charlie whispered, "Don't take the judge's ruling out on a sick kid."

"You can't stop me from seeing my daughter," Mariana said heaving her weight against the door to break Charlie's hold. He held her firmly by the arms and prodded her down the hall into the laundry room.

"I'm not having this argument again."

"It is only a week," Mariana said, "if I want to take my children to see their abuelo, then it's my right."

"Not when their grandfather lives in Mexico," Charlie said, feeling the heat rising in his face. He couldn't stop the same tired fight from rolling again. He felt like he was in a car without any brakes and it was heading downhill toward a cliff, "Just last week there was a thirteen year old boy executed when he crossed the border for a birthday party in Tijuana. They blew his brains out while his mother watched."

Mariana grimaced. "The news said his uncle tried to quit the cartel. No one leaves them alive. "

"The cartel never makes mistakes and visits the wrong house?"

My father is a respected businessman. The cartel knows he exports coffee not cocaine," Mariana said, glancing down as her cell phone vibrated, "they have never set foot on Senor's Ranch."

Charlie knew that no one could mistake his former father in law's house for a neighbor. The house was a fortress protected by a hundred feet gate built two miles from the road on a peninsula that was guarded by jagged rocks, isolated beaches, and the Pacific Ocean. It was symbolic of a man so tough that he was known with a mixed sense of respect and fear, by only one name from his business partners down to his children, Senor.

"Bring your father here. I'll spring for the hotel, something with a nice continental breakfast and extended pool privileges," Charlie said with a tight laugh. Maybe it was the fact Mariana was dismissing him with her cell phone. Maybe it was the lack of sleep that heated his irritation. Whatever it was, his ex-wife brought the sarcasm out in Charlie.

"Jokes about Senor were funny when I was a girl in college," Mariana said, bringing her hand up like she was going to slap him but instead she brushed a dark lock of hair from his face, "but that was eight years ago when you were this confident American who made me feel I could make a difference."

"I thought it was because you were tired of being treated like Senor's spoiled little girl," Charlie said, coughing as he averted her eyes but he couldn't avoid her scowl.

"I don't think you're funny anymore," Mariana said, her face leaning close, "and Senor never treated me like a prisoner."

Charlie's ears burned with the accusation that he had any control on Mariana's life. He couldn't keep her from leaving him but that didn't stop her from listing "controlling" on the petition for divorce. Mariana stood fifty feet from Charlie and told the court how Charlie forced her to stay in the house and got her pregnant when she wanted to continue getting her law degree.

The press enjoyed the drama and left a corner of the morning front page and the leading story on the evening news open for Mariana's tearful testimony. Mariana's dramatics angered Charlie but not from the negative publicity which improved business. People wanted to have a drink in the club where the big, bad businessman was courting celebrities while his lonely, knocked-up wife was perched in her golden cage on Mount Soledad. What hurt Charlie was the crap being stored in media archives for his kids. When they were older and had questions, they would get answers from an old People magazine.

In the days of Mariana's public testimony as a lonely bird, she conveniently left out a few facts. She never mentioned the days that Charlie took the kids to the club while she attended her college classes, the nanny hired when she interned at the law firm, and the hundreds of hours she pushed a baby stroller at immigration reform rallies.

Thank God for Remi Parrish, a brilliant attorney, business partner and trusted friend. Remi made sure the media knew Mariana wasn't just a housewife but an accomplished attorney and she quickly dropped the lonely housewife act. To protect the kids, Remi made sure Mariana looked saintly with her devotion to help Mexican immigrants. It even caught the interest of a prestigious immigration right's attorney, Benito

Sanchez, who hired her three weeks before the divorce was finalized.

For Mariana, it was the job of her dreams because she really believed she could make a difference. It was that passion that Charlie loved from the start and the reason he stood speechless even when she was stabbing at his heart.

Charlie picked up her hand and held it tightly, rubbing over the faded line from her wedding ring.

"Oriana can't go to school and you're already late for work," Charlie said, trying to reason with her as he brought her closer to him and pressed her body against the washing machine, "Max can stay here too."

"So you can tell the court and push for more custody?" Mariana said, slamming her shoulder into his chest and pushing past him, "Go to hell."

"Already there." Charlie thought as Mariana charged down the hall and threw open Oriana's door.

Charlie kept a safe distance by leaning against the door. The only light in the bedroom was a soft glow coming underneath Oriana's orange window curtains that fluttered with a blast from a fan covered in butterfly stickers. Mariana bent down and moved Oriana's body so she sat up in bed; her face flushed and eyes squinting.

"It's time to leave, Mija," Mariana said, her voice was calmer as she used her affectionate name for her daughter, removing a skirt and blouse from the closet and putting them on the bed. She picked up a pink canvas bag and started to jam Oriana's school books inside.

Oriana rubbed her right eye and then picked up the skirt.

"You don't look good," Charlie said moving into the room and sitting on her bed. He put his hand on Oriana's forehead which burned to the touch. "Mariana, she can't go anywhere with a fever."

"She's hot because she woke up," Mariana said,

taking a doll's head off as she stuffed it into the bag, "get dressed, Mija."

Oriana stood up and lifted her leg into the skirt but needed to grab for Charlie's hand so she didn't fall over. She looked up at him and swallowed hard. "My stomach hurts, Daddy."

"Get back in bed," Charlie said, pulling back the sheets.

"You'll do what I tell you," Mariana said, dropping the bag and grabbing Oriana's arm yanking her so hard she spun around from the bed, "I said to get dressed."

Oriana opened her mouth and vomited. Her eyes filled with tears as she saw the mess dripping down the front of Mariana's blouse. "I'm sorry, Mommy."

Mariana's face was almost as red as her skirt. She quickly wiped Oriana's mouth with a clean edge of her blouse and forced a smile, "It's alright."

If Oriana wasn't so upset, Charlie would be laughing out loud. He kept the small victory inside and put the sheets over Oriana as she crawled into bed, careful to avoid Mariana's glare.

"I will come back for you." Mariana whispered into Oriana's ear. The girl nodded and was soon asleep. Mariana gave one final look at Oriana and charged into the hall.

"Max goes with me," Mariana said turning quickly and pointing a finger in Charlie's face. He put his hands in the air as if she was robbing him. A raspy cough came from the base of the stairs and they both turned around to see Brenda watching the whole drama. She cast a look at Mariana's blouse and shook her head, "Told you that she was sick."

"Is Max ready?" Mariana said, ignoring Brenda and clutching her jacket around her, "Are his things packed?"

"Sitting at the front door," Brenda said, pointing upstairs, "pick 'em up on your way out."

Mariana eyed Brenda with distrust. "Even his Penguino?"

"Does it look like it's my first day on earth?" Brenda said, clicking her tongue and feigning insult, "Max would be hollering before you left the driveway for that silly, stuffed toy."

Mariana started upstairs without a second glance to Charlie. He could hear Max's happy voice greet her. He climbed to the main floor and reached the front door but Mariana was already outside and clicking Max into his car seat. She slammed the door shut and headed around the car without another word. His four year old son pressed his smiling face to the window and Charlie instinctively started across the driveway. He never liked the kids to leave until he hugged them. It was an obsessive compulsive thing, but without that final goodbye, Charlie always had a shitty day.

Charlie felt a sharp rock poke into his toe and he withdrew back to the concrete. He hesitated at the thought of braving the gravel but Mariana had already turned on the motor and was rolling away from him. Charlie resigned himself that the day was going down the toilet as Max disappeared from view.

Stretching his arms above his head, Charlie let out a loud yawn as he returned inside and let Brenda close the door.

"You yawn like a big, yard dog." Brenda said, placing a worn, overstuffed penguin on the stairwell.

"You told Mariana that you packed it," Charlie said, grabbing the toy and putting it outside the door in case Mariana came back.

"I can't be expected to remember everything," Brenda said with a low grunt.

"Did you do that on purpose?" Charlie said, knowing it was pointless to ask. He couldn't prove it was intentional and she'd never admit the crime.

Brenda ignored him, clutching her bathrobe in the same fist as her oversized ceramic mug and heading back to her room. Charlie thought about going upstairs to close his eyes for a few more hours but knew it wasn't going to happen so he decided to go the club and work on the paperwork he'd avoided. Before he jumped in the shower, he made sure he left his cell phone off. Max would realize that his penguin was missing and the yelling would start. That meant Mariana would be sending a barrage of threats via text and voice mails promising her attorney was getting involved. All for a stupid toy that Brenda didn't include in Max's backpack. Brenda always found a way to make things more difficult. He didn't need a text to remind him that today was already doomed.

Chapter Two

Charlie turned onto Tony Gwynn Drive and pulled into the parking garage across from Petco Park. In a few quick steps he crossed the street and was admiring the entrance to Basin Street Jazz, the pride and joy of his fifty supper clubs. With the brick face, the three story building was perfect to build a little piece of New Orleans in the middle of downtown San Diego.

Charlie entered through the back and cut through the kitchen; slipping unnoticed past the prep cooks and through the dark club into the dreaded office. He had only been in the office three times since the club opened. He hated the thought of wasting his life sitting behind a desk. His business partner, Remi Parrish, would be thrilled that Charlie planned to do some paperwork. They always had the perfect partnership since Charlie preferred to entertain the talent and leave the numbers to Remi but there were still things that needed both of their signatures. He took one look at the stack of invoices on his desk and dusty computer and decided to retreat to the couch and get a few more hours of sleep; dropping his cell phone on the table with the face down so he didn't have to see Mariana's phone calls. The phone had been silent for the last hour but Charlie knew it was a matter of time.

Charlie didn't know how long he'd slept but he woke to the smell of butter and paprika and weight on his legs. Opening his eyes, he saw Lisa straddling him holding a plate of fish. Even in her chef's coat and her hair pulled back, Lisa was so damn sexy.

Lisa pulled a shrimp off the plate and held it above him; giggling as Charlie snatched the meat with his teeth. He pulled himself up by holding onto her waist and kissed her hard on the mouth. "Is that a new shrimp dish?"

"It's something I'm working on for the wedding. I've got to get back to the kitchen but I thought I should wake you up before you slept through dinner. It's already five," Lisa said, squeezing Charlie's thigh and pushing aside his cell phone to drop the plate of shrimp on the table, "after the first dinner service we need to talk about getting a new sous chef. The one you hired is too slow."

Charlie watched Lisa leave and then lay back on the couch.

"What the hell am I doing?" Charlie thought. Remi swore Charlie was making a mistake dating his head chef and he'd regret taking her out of the kitchen. It didn't become a problem until Lisa had a ring on her finger. Now she was charging around the club and making changes like she was the owner.

The cell phone was sitting on the coffee table and Charlie was reluctant to pick it up. He could let Mariana simmer for a few hours but if she thought he was avoiding her for the entire day, Charlie predicted she was going to be a raging volcano. He turned over the phone expecting to see his voice mail was full but there was only one text from Remi. No voicemails should have been a relief but it filled Charlie with more dread.

Charlie dialed his house and after five long rings, Brenda picked up the phone. He didn't give her time to answer. "Has Mariana dropped off Max?"

There was a pause on the line and Charlie could hear Brenda's mind churning with the same tired response, "I told you that she's up to something."

"Is that your way of telling me no?" Charlie asked, her voice grating on his nerves.

"You can't trust her kind to be honest," Brenda said, pausing to clear a raspy cough, "I said that when you got married and you didn't listen."

Charlie hung up on Brenda. A year of divorce hadn't changed the same lecture she'd been giving him since he had married Mariana eight years ago. He called Max's pre-school and caught the owner, Ms. Milligan, before she left for the day. She only confirmed his worst fears. Max never arrived this morning and Mariana told the school he wouldn't be there for the rest of the month. He took a minute to calm down and started to call Mariana again.

The office door swung open with a heavy pounding and Kier, his head of security, charged inside the room.

"Why can't you knock like a real person?" Charlie asked, knowing that Kier was incapable of doing anything that didn't follow with a sonic boom. People only saw Kier as a huge mass of Australian muscle with a crude mouth. He was also a retired colonel who had the best security company in the country so it was a bitter trade.

Kier grunted and headed straight for the shrimp and stuffed a bunch in his mouth, spitting out the tails into his hand.

"Those are for paying customers," Charlie said, unable to pull the dish away before Kier grabbed another handful and stuffed them in his pocket.

"I'm hungry," Kier said, grinning as he sat down

on a chair and propped his feet up on the edge of the sofa, "I've got a new girl, Fiona, who doesn't know that man can't survive on sex alone."

"Am I supposed to feel sorry for you because you had sex all afternoon?" Charlie said, knocking Kier's feet off the couch and hit Mariana's number again, "Shut up I've got to make this call."

Kier winked and popped another shrimp in his mouth. "Yes, master."

Mariana's phone didn't ring but her sharp voice mail connected. *"You've reached Mariana…"*

Charlie threw the phone back on the table in frustration. He snatched a lighter from Kier as he tried to light a cigarette. "You can't smoke in here, you know that."

Kier leaned back and let the unlit cigarette dangle from his mouth, "What's going on, Chuck?

"Mariana hasn't called."

"You bitch that she calls you and now you're pissed when she doesn't?" Kier said, shrugging as he reached for the lighter again. Charlie grabbed the cigarette from his mouth and put it in his pocket.

"Someone doesn't leave ten messages a day for a year and then go silent the next day," Charlie said, "unless they don't need you anymore."

Kier planted both feet on the floor and his expression hardened. "What are you leaving out?"

"She lost the custody hearing," Charlie said, rubbing his eyes," Mariana wanted to bring the kids to Mexico for her Dad's birthday."

"Does she have any idea of the shit going on right now?" Kier shouted, "The cartels are pushing back against the new president they elected. A lot of people are disappearing and the ones that aren't cut into pieces are being ransomed. Do you think she took them down there?"

"No, she watches the news, she knows this isn't the Mexico where she grew up," Charlie said, trying to convince himself, "she wasn't happy when I got engaged and she's trying to make my life hell."

"You better hope not. With the money you make, those kids would be kidnapped the second they set foot off the US soil. I've worked on a couple ransom cases," Kier said, pulling another cigarette and discovering another lighter. He lit up before Charlie could stop him and then grabbed Charlie's phone, "Pretty much just get a stripped corpse back. If they're lucky they just get some fingers chopped off."

"Do you think I need to hear that right now?" Charlie yelled, snatching back the phone, "Put out the damn cigarette before I fire your ass!"

Kier crushed the tip of the cigarette on the plate of shrimp and let it roll inside, "I'm a dick. I don't think about half the crap that falls out of my mouth. Mariana hates you but she loves those kids. She wouldn't hurt Max and she definitely wouldn't leave Oriana here."

Charlie picked up his car keys, "I can't focus. I'm going to find them."

Kier laughed. "You couldn't find your ass cheeks if you were squatting over a mirror. Let me earn a paycheck and I'll bring Max here."

"I think I should go," Charlie argued.

"You're making this too hard, Chuck," Kier said, standing up and slapping Charlie on the back, "I'm going to her house and look in her window. Max will be sitting in the living room watching some cartoons and Mariana will be polishing her nails and will be apologizing because she lost track of time. Stop worrying! Mariana won't get a chance to point that Mercedes toward Mexico."

Chapter Three

An hour passed since Kier left to find Mariana leaving Charlie unable to concentrate. Why hadn't he heard anything yet? It was a twenty minute drive from the club downtown to Mariana's house on La Jolla beach so Kier should know something by now.

Charlie scanned the club and tried to keep his mind off Mariana and his desire to wrap his fingers around her throat. Charlie decided to throw himself into work, and checked with his hostess for the night agenda. He sent a bottle of wine to an elderly couple celebrating their thirtieth wedding anniversary, stopped at a few tables to chat with some patrons and made sure that the bachelorette party at the bar got extra drinks.   It was early in the evening, so there wasn't much to keep him distracted. The club wouldn't find it's rhythm until the night life started around eleven.

Scanned the floor, Charlie noticed two husky Mexican men dressed in matching tan suits and a white kid about nineteen in a crisp, button-down shirt sitting in a corner booth. The "Suits" looked like they should be selling cars in a third rate dealership and were out of place in the crowd. They hadn't caught Charlie's attention until the voice of the older Suit started to rise above the bustle of the club. He was yelling into the ear of the kid who kept his head down and fidgeted with a soda can.

Charlie waited to see if the older Suit would calm down but the man's face was growing red and he was pushing his words out with so much force that he was spitting all over the kid. His anger was escalating and was now causing a couple in the table next to them to looking over their shoulders. Charlie hoped that the argument would fizzle out because he wasn't good with confrontation which is why he paid extra for retired military professionals like Kier's company. Charlie looked for security but the only detail on the floor was dealing with a transient at the entrance which was on the far end of the club. There was rarely trouble this early in the evening so the security detail was light.

Charlie was deciding his next move when the younger Suit grabbed the kid's neck and slammed his head on the table. The older one started thumping the kid in the ear with the bottom of a beer bottle, the alcohol sloshing onto the kid's face.

Charlie caught the attention of a busboy making his way toward the kitchen and directed him to alert security. Charlie walked past the worried couple and gave a smile of assurance that it was under control. The woman relaxed her shoulders but kept her chair angled to observe.

"This is not what I meant by keeping myself busy," Charlie thought, approaching the booth.

"Break it up, Gentlemen," Charlie said, putting one hand on the back of a chair to keep an object in between them, "you are disrupting my guests."

On closer inspection, the oldest Suit looked more out of place. His closely shaved head and a crude tattoo reading, Muerte, was visible on his neck over the stiff collar of a shirt pulled wrinkled out of a package. The younger Suit had an acne pocked face and three tear drops tattooed down the corner of his eye. He snorted and gave Charlie the finger. "Mind your fucking business."

"This is my business," Charlie said noticing two of Kier's security approaching from the other side but not close enough to take over. If the Suits attacked him, he had nothing but the chair between them, "this is my club and I'm telling you to leave."

The younger Suit pressed his arm against the kid's head to keep him from squirming as he emptied the rest of the beer into the kid's nose. He released him and the kid put his head down as he sneezed and snorted. The older Suit pulled the kid by his hair until the kid sat straight up in the booth, the beer dripping out of his nose. "We're leaving now."

The kid's eyes looked wide and frightened at Charlie and then around for an exit but he was frozen in place by the vice grip on his neck by the older Suit. The Suit slammed the kid's face against the table and brought it back up; a fresh cut opened below a welt on his cheek. The drizzle of blood down his cheeks and his swelling nose gave him the appearance of a distorted clown. Charlie needed to buy more time for the security to arrive.

"Kid, what's your name?" Charlie asked, throwing him a napkin to treat the cut on his cheek.

The kid reached for the napkin but his hands were shaking violently and he tucked him into his arm pits. "Jesse."

"Jesse," Charlie said, keeping his voice calm and glancing back at the uneasy couple in the adjoining booth, "do you want to go with these men?"

Jesse swallowed hard as he looked at the older Suit. "I don't know."

Security was now standing behind the booth and Charlie felt a stronger sense of relief over the scene but knew this kid would suffer if walked out the door and he couldn't let that happen. "Jesse, sit there until these gentlemen leave."

The older Suit puffed up his chest, and the younger Suit opened a knife and put it on the table,

"We can take him out peaceful or in pieces."

"Jesse, do you have any ID?" Charlie asked, his hand starting to hurt from the grip he put on the chair.

Jesse shook his head.

"You don't look over 21 and have been served alcohol," Charlie said, "I'm holding you here, until the police come and deal with you."

"What the fuck is this? "The older Suit growled, "Do you know who you're dealing with?"

The younger Suit had moved to the edge of the table and sprang up with the knife in his left hand raised toward Charlie, the security detail swept behind and pinned the younger Suit's arm above his head causing the knife to impale into the table. The older Suit grabbed the handle but released when security slammed an elbow into his throat and pulled him up to escort him out the door. The younger Suit was pulled past Charlie and tried to spit in his face but it dribbled down his chin like a rabid dog. "Don't think you're safe, asshole."

"Don't come here again or you'll leave in the back of a police car," Charlie said, expecting he would back off but the younger Suit laughed until he was out the entrance.

Charlie turned back to Jesse who had cowered deep into the booth, keeping his face hidden until the Suits were gone. He sat across from Jesse and tossed him a napkin. "You want to tell me what's going on?"

Jesse averted Charlie's eyes and stuck the napkin on his cut. "Those guys think I'm someone else."

"Can I call anyone for you?" Charlie asked.

"You aren't calling the police?"

Charlie shook his head. "We didn't serve you any drinks, just those friends. Those guys will be waiting outside so you can go out the back but I think you should have a car waiting before you leave."

Jesse hesitated and then reached for his wallet and handed Charlie a business card.

Charlie ran his finger across the embossed black lettering on the stock white card reading, Judge Robert Andersen, Federal Appellate Court. "You want me to call a judge?"

"He's my Dad."

Charlie noticed a new cut above Jesse's eyebrow and handed him another napkin as he waved over the hostess. "Carrie, please give Judge Andersen a call and see that Jesse gets something non-alcoholic to drink."

Charlie felt his cell phone vibrate and he slid out of the booth. "My hostess will help you from here."

"You saved my ass," Jesse said, his hand reaching up to thank Charlie but put it back on the table when he couldn't steady his fingers.

"You're going to be fine," Charlie said, patting Jesse on the back, and heading away from the stage as the opening band started their first set. He glanced at the screen reading "Kier" and slid on the phone. "Tell me you found them."

The connection was poor and the music was making it difficult to hear Kier's voice.

"I'm at Mariana's house, Chuck." Kier said, his voice fading and then coming back, "She isn't here."

Charlie's heart sank. Mariana always got home early on Friday and she didn't have any friends that she would be visiting. "Wait another half-hour and if she doesn't show, check Mount Soledad Market. She likes to shop before the weekend."

There was brief silence as if the connection was lost but then Kier's voice came through with random words "...it's on the curb... I checked...sign..."

"Repeat what you said," Charlie shouted, plugging his ear to close out the bustle from the club; he moved into the office and shut the door. "What's on the curb, Kier?"

"There's a 'For Sale' sign on the curb, Chuck," Kier said, his voice now coming through loud and clear,

"The house is empty. Mariana doesn't live here anymore."

Chapter Four

Charlie dropped Lisa at the front of the house and drove inside the garage. They had been silent all the way home since Kier confirmed that Mariana's house was vacant. They were both angry but Charlie's anger was directed at Mariana while Lisa hadn't sprung on him the reason for her silence.

Moving swiftly into the kitchen, Charlie threw his keys down on the counter with his left hand and grabbed for a bottle of scotch above the fridge. He pulled two glasses from the dishwasher and poured them half full before sliding one over to Lisa who had quietly taken a seat on a barstool. He threw back his drink and waited for her to pick up the glass. When it sat unmoved, he grabbed her glass and poured it back slamming back on the counter. "Are you going to talk to me?"

Lisa propped her chin up on a fist, her bottom lip jutting out. "You embarrassed me."

"What are you talking about?" Charlie said, her outline was blurring in the darkness.

"You never told me Mariana wanted to take Max to Mexico," Lisa said, her voice high like she was about to cry, "All those people were shocked that I didn't know."

"What a tragedy, how will you ever face them again," Charlie said, leaning to get a better look at her face. There was a flush on her high-boned cheeks but her thick lashes were a canopy for dry, brown eyes free of tears.

"You make me sound shallow," Lisa said reaching for a tissue in her purse. Charlie could hear her sniffing in the darkness; the fifteen years difference in their age was a crevice deeper than the Grand Canyon, "I'm going to be his mother soon and you keep me out of everything."

"It's not always about you!" Charlie shouted.

"Keep your voices down."

A voice came from behind Charlie and the fluorescents sputtered on above him. Blinking to adjust to the light, he turned to see Brenda standing in her bathrobe. She was across the kitchen but Charlie could see her red-rimmed eyes from lack of sleep and inhaling too much smoke.

"Mariana took Max to Mexico?"

"She knows too?" Lisa said, kicking her high heels on the tile so they made a large clatter.

"Keep the whining down, Charlie didn't tell me anything, I heard you yapping." Brenda said, folding her arms across her chest.

"I'm going to bed," Lisa said, hiding her face as she reached over and grabbed her shoes. "Why don't the grown-ups talk and the kids will be in bed?"

Even when they fought, Charlie couldn't stop turning soft as he watched Lisa's body climb gracefully up the stairs. As soon as she disappeared, Charlie had only Brenda's disapproving glare to avoid. "At least the brown one had a brain."

"Don't start, Mama," Charlie groaned.

Brenda shuffled into the kitchen and grabbed a carafe of coffee. She swished the liquid and poured the thick syrup into the mug. "You can't find a nice, white girl? You got to pick a yellow China girl."

"Hush, Mama," Charlie said, peeking to see if Lisa had shut the bedroom door, "you don't know what you're talking about. Lisa is a Filipina not Chinese. I hate it when you start spouting that racist crap."

Brenda grunted and then settled down on a barstool. She took a sip and curled her lip at the heat. Charlie pulled an ice cube from the freezer and splashed it in her coffee. Brenda pushed the mug away. "Why the hell did you do that?"

"It looked hot," Charlie said, "I thought you wanted to cool it off."

"It's not a soda pop," Brenda said struggling to get up and pouring the coffee into the sink, "what does Remi think you should do about Mariana?"

"Remi says I should live with both Mariana and Lisa," Charlie said, opening his arms wide and giving her a big hug.

"Such a mouth on you," Brenda said struggling against him and straightening her bathrobe, "what did Remi tell you to do?"

Charlie bristled. Whenever there was trouble, Brenda always pushed to know Remi's opinion. It was a jab as if Charlie couldn't make a decision without Remi's guidance. Remi was his best friend so it shouldn't be a surprise that he relied on him for help but that didn't make it Remi's decision. Brenda loved to imply that he was castrated without Remi's help.

"He's contacting Mariana's attorney tomorrow to find out what's happening."

"Nothing you can do tonight," Brenda said, yawning, "Get some sleep. I'll wake you when he calls."

Charlie watched Brenda hobble to the kitchen island and brace herself on the corner. Years of cleaning floors on her knees had made them unreliable to hold her up without help. "When are *you* going to sleep?"

"When I'm dead," Brenda said, her blunt voice was the strongest support she had.

"Why don't you take those pills that Dr. Stein gave you?"

Brenda shook her head. "I told you, I don't take

that stuff. It's not natural. When my body wants sleep, I'll get it."

Charlie kissed her quickly on the head before she could protest and headed upstairs. He hoped he'd given Lisa enough time to pretend to be asleep. The bedroom ran the entire third level of the house and the stairs opened up into a landing with a door which was more a formality since it didn't protect for any privacy but it did make a dramatic statement for Lisa to have a door to slam when she was angry and tonight she had closed it tight.

He carefully opened the door and could see Lisa lying with her back faced to the door. He loosened his belt and let his pants fall to the floor, the shirt fell next to them and he climbed exhausted in bed.

Charlie moved beside Lisa and let the sheet delicately drape back over her curves. Her tanned arms crossed over her breasts. He pressed against her and moved his arms to circle her waist but she made no move to edge closer. Charlie kissed her neck and moved onto his back, closing his eyes and inhaled a mixture of Lisa's perfume and a mist from the balcony window. Lisa slid around and nestled into the crook of his arm. He brought his hand down to rest on her smooth flesh and kissed her hair. Charlie did feel bad that she was hurt. Lisa's viewpoint came from somewhere in her twenties with no baggage. Without any children to carry she could leave an ex-boyfriend behind without regret or apologies to hold her down.

"I'm sorry," Charlie whispered, "you deserve better."

"I'm your fiancée, I need to know before anyone else," Lisa said, tracing the curves of his collarbone and kissing his chest, "I know a way you can make it up to me."

Charlie closed his eyes, feeling dread like he was trying to buy him some sleep by rewarding a tantrum with a treat.

Lisa pressed her lips against his ear, resting her

hand on his heart, "You can finally get my name tattooed like you promised."

"I never promised I would do that." Charlie said.

Lisa's hand fell away and Charlie immediately regretted answering too honestly as she rolled away from him.

"A tattoo with a woman's name is bad luck." Charlie said.

Lisa was silent for a moment but then flipped toward him and jabbed her finger into his rib so hard that Charlie gasped as the nail dug into his skin.

"You've got Oriana's name on this bird," Lisa said, her voice no longer silky.

Charlie moved the sheet to show his left bicep and pointed to a lightning bolt, "I've got Max's name on this side and Jackson's name on my right. Having the names of my kids and brother are different than branding a woman's name on me."

"You think I want to brand you like cattle?" Lisa said, moving far enough away Charlie couldn't touch her without an effort.

"That's not what I meant," Charlie said, wishing the day would end.

"I'm tired," Lisa announced, her body turned away, pulling the sheets over her shoulders and was asleep in minutes leaving Charlie struggling to calm down. He finally closed his eyes relaxing his shoulders as he heard the chirping of a bird outside. He had started sleeping when the sun was coming up.

"Charlie!"

There was heavy pounding up the stairs and from the fogginess of sleep he heard his name. Brenda was screaming his name like he had only heard from his mother on the night that Jackson was murdered in front of them. The panic in her voice could stop his heart.

Chapter Five

Charlie barely had time to slip on a shirt over his head when Brenda appeared at the landing, her face pale and her jaw tight.

Lisa grabbed Charlie's pillow and propped it against her shoulder. "You need to knock Brenda."

"Where am I going to knock?" Brenda said, looking at the open door and turning a scathing eye toward Lisa, "I'm not worried about seeing what little you've got."

Lisa turned red and reached for her robe on the floor, leaving her back exposed to Brenda.

"Damn girl," Brenda said, staring at the ridges of Lisa's spine, "maybe you should eat more than just fish heads once awhile."

"Go to hell, Brenda." Lisa hissed.

"Enough Mama," Charlie snapped, "Stop saying things that make you sound racist."

Brenda frowned and turned away. "Come downstairs, you need to see something."

Charlie eyed the bed and thought about crawling back inside but felt his pillow knock him in the head.

"Why do you let her talk to me that way?" Lisa said, sliding from the bed, "when are you going to be a man and stand up for me!"

Lisa ran past him and slammed the bathroom door. Charlie stood still for a few minutes debating what he should say when she reappeared. He decided nothing would make her happy so he headed downstairs. Filling the house was a comforting smell of coffee mixed with frying of andouille sausage. Charlie entered the kitchen as Nola was pulling biscuits out of the oven. Brenda expected them to be fresh which meant Nola was up before the sun rolling dough.

Nola's batter streaked face looked up at Charlie and he couldn't help but smile before he kissed the top of her hair which smelled like sweet strawberries and flour. Every time he looked at his sister, Charlie imagined that was how Brenda looked when she was in her twenties if she hadn't been struggling to feed kids as a cleaning lady. They had the same dusty, blonde hair and big green eyes but Nola's face wasn't creviced from worry, her hands weren't calloused from scrubbing floors and her skin wasn't ashy from living on a diet of cigarettes and coffee. She was a fresh sixteen year old girl trapped in the body of a twenty-seven year old woman. Nola's mind slowed the day that the drug addicted bastard of a father known as Sam threw her against a wall; slowly robbing her brain of oxygen. It didn't rob Nola of the knowledge that she was different and could see it as she compared the rubber of her sneakers to Lisa's expensive high heels. Nola knew that Lisa was the woman she was supposed to be.

Nola removed a second baking sheet of biscuits but lost her footing and they headed for the floor.

"Watch what you're doing," Brenda snapped as she saved the tray with her bare hands and threw it on the counter.

Lisa sulked into the kitchen and ran her arm across Nola's shoulder. "Did you make my coffee?"

"Nothing with white fluff on it," Brenda said jiggling a set of car keys, "drive over to get your gourmet goop."

Nola cast her eyes down to a cabinet and pulled out a small French press. "I'll get some ready for you."

"Thank you, Nola, at least someone loves me," Lisa said squeezing Nola's hand causing her to blush, "Not all of us want to be sucking on water soaked in that chicory wood."

"This isn't a party," Brenda said, pushing Charlie toward the living room, "Come look at the big TV."

On the screen was a middle-aged Mexican with thinning hair and kind eyes surrounded by a cluster of children. Charlie recognized him as Jimenez Delgado, the key note speaker for a rally that he attended with Mariana for human rights in Tijuana. Delgado was a reporter campaigning against the high percent of Mexican citizens dying as innocent bystanders from the cartel. The president of Mexico called him the "voice of the people," until he started campaigning to run against him at the next election.

The screen flashed to Delgado speaking to a crowd of thousands from a balcony. A reporter's voice talked over the images:

Jimenez Delgado was vacationing with his family in an undisclosed location following a recent conference in Tijuana, the largest city in the Baja peninsula plagued by violence from the cartels. He had recently assisted making good on his promises to expose corrupt officials with ties to drug cartels which led to the recent arrests of the Tijuana police chief and dismissal of his entire department.

The screen cut to a speech of Jimenez Delgado in front of a crumpled building on Revolucion Ave in Tijuana's tourist district.

"We can no longer ignore that our people are suffering from the criminal actions of people that call themselves patriots. To continue forward is accepting

the genocide of our citizens..."

"I met him once at a fundraiser." Charlie said, "What's he got to say that is worth cutting my sleep short?"

"He's got a permanent sleep." Brenda said, her face still turned toward the TV, "he's been murdered."

Charlie's heart lurched. "What?"

"Assassinated," Brenda said, turning up the volume, "along with his wife and five kids last night."

Charlie stared back at the TV screen as the pictures continued to loop underneath the reporter's anxious words over Delgado's face and a heap of bodies covered with a waterlogged tarp. There was blood smeared on a white wall and then dozens of police standing outside entrenched in thick mud.

"Why would anyone do that?" Nola asked, dripping Lisa's coffee onto the tile as she stared at the screen. She cowered back and handed Lisa the mug.

"I'll explain in a minute, honey." Charlie said, trying to gather the information on the screen.

"I just want to know what happened!" Nola said, her voice drowning out the reporter on the TV.

"Hush," Brenda said, her head snapping around, "we're trying to listen."

Nola cowered down and dabbed the coffee from the tile on the sleeve of her sweater.

Brenda turned up the volume and the reporter's voice was the only thing that could be heard in the room.

The entire country is saddened and stunned by this tragic loss but it appears the country has no time to mourn.

The screen cut to a wide-eyed reporter, clearly picked because she was the only one in the area not her experience on the field, stood next to a group of

Mexican Federale soldiers who were setting up several military jeeps.

At the announcement of Delgado's death, the Palacios Nacional in Mexico City was besieged in a riot and key members of parliament have been taken hostage," the reporter said pausing to look behind her and then gripping the microphone with white knuckles, "Reports of violence are breaking out in Mexico City, Tijuana, Guadalajara and Monterrey..."

A crack of thunder came from behind and the reporter screamed as she threw her hands up. The camera blurred and then the details reappeared but appeared lying on its side. The reporter's voice was muffled and then the soldiers began to scramble like ants into the jeeps as they drove away from the camera toward a barrage of gunfire.

"He's not breathing," the reporter screamed, abandoning the fact that she was on live television, "Jack has been shot! Oh my God, get us out of here!"

The feed dropped and a surprised anchorman scrambled to his desk trying to regain control. "As you can hear from the gunfire in the background, our reporter is an area of Tijuana that is changing its condition rapidly. If you are just joining us, we have received confirmation that Delgado Jimenez has been assassinated. This tragic loss occurs at a time when the cartels have made a strong presence on our border cities. We need to take a quick commercial break and we'll be back with complete coverage."

Brenda grumbled and began to change the channel.

"We need to keep watching," Charlie said grabbing the remote and moved away from the couch.

Nola brought Lisa back a full cup of coffee and looked at the clock. "Mariana is late. Is Oriana staying with us?"

"Don't ask the grown-ups, they'll never tell you anything," Lisa said into her coffee. She moved to the couch and kissed Charlie. "I'm going upstairs to take a shower. I've got to be at the club at ten."

"I want to know," Nola said, curling next to Charlie on the couch and leaned her head against his shoulder.

"Nola, honey," Charlie said, trying to find the right words, "Mariana was supposed to bring Max back last night."

"She wasn't supposed to bring Max back," Nola said, "she's taking the kids to Mexico."

Charlie and Brenda sat up at the same time.

"How do you know that?" Charlie asked.

"Oriana told me," Nola said, noticing that Brenda was glaring at her.

Charlie felt like shaking Nola by the shoulders, but knew she would only withdraw from him if she was scared, "What did Oriana tell you?"

"Mariana told Oriana that she was going to live with her grandpa. Mariana said she was going to take her and Max to ride horses on the beach every day," Nola said, eyeing Brenda who was now standing next to the couch, "Why don't they allow horses on the beach here?"

Brenda grabbed Nola by her arm and pulled her to her feet causing her to cry in pain. "You knew she was going to kidnap the kids and you said nothing?"

Nola pulled her arm free and threw herself on Charlie and looked up at him, tears welling in her eyes. "She didn't kidnap them. It was supposed to be a surprise."

Charlie's heart was beating wildly and he tried to keep calm so he didn't frighten Nola.

She sniffed and buried her head into his arm. "I didn't mean to spoil things."

Charlie exhaled. "Don't keep a surprise next time."

"Next time! Like hell!" Brenda yelled causing Nola to fall off the couch, "There won't be a next time!"

Brenda pulled Nola to her feet. "Go to your

room until I tell you to come out."

Nola rubbed her eye and silently made her way down the stairs.

"Don't be hard on her," Charlie said, "You know she can't understand."

"Mariana is waving her middle finger at you from the border right now. You're not going to get any news," Brenda said, her voice crackled as she coughed roughly into the sleeve of her robe, "But you can bet there is one little safecracker of a little girl that knows Mariana's plans."

"What about Mommy?"

Oriana ran into the room and slid onto Brenda's lap. Charlie quickly snapped off the TV before she could see the violence.

"Where is Max?" Oriana said, squeezing Brenda tightly around her middle. Despite Brenda's vinegar toward life, she had sweetness for Oriana. She was the only one that got treated like a human being.

Brenda stroked a strand of hair from Oriana's face and kissed her forehead. "Are you feeling better, Baby Girl?"

Oriana nodded as she curled into Brenda's arm. "Is Max with Mommy?"

Charlie couldn't be sure if Nola had been confused about what was going on. If Oriana knew anything, he would need to draw it out her. "Max was too sleepy so he stayed with Mommy last night."

Oriana frowned. "I don't get to go with them?"

"Go where?" Charlie asked.

"I'm not supposed to say anything. It's a surprise," Oriana said sliding off Brenda's lap and skipping to the kitchen. Charlie eyes met Brenda. It was a look that they had shared since he was a kid and he needed help. Brenda always knew what needed to be done.

Brenda followed Oriana into the kitchen and picked up the cereal box and guided her to the barstool. "Sit here, Baby Girl and I'll get you a bowl."

Setting two bowls and a spoon beside Oriana, Brenda carefully poured the milk into the bowl and picked up the cereal box.

"Your Daddy will be so excited." Brenda said, pouring some cereal into the second bowl and sat next of Oriana.

Oriana's ears perked up and stopped stirring her cereal. "Did Mommy tell you the secret?"

"She told me yesterday," Brenda said casually pouring cereal into her bowl.

Oriana grabbed a flake and crunched her cereal. "When is Mommy coming back for me?"

"Not when you're so sick," Brenda said, pushing the cereal box to the side, her eyes focused on a newspaper sitting on the table.

Oriana's lip quivered. "But I wanted to see Senor too."

Senor was the name everyone called Mariana's father. For as long as Charlie had known him, he'd never been called Grandpa or Papa directly. Even his wife on her death bed called her husband, Senor. It was a sign of respect that also evoked fear for the powerful owner of the most productive coffee plantations in Mexico.

"No, Baby Girl," Brenda said turning to cough, "You can't get him sick. He's too old."

"I'm not sick anymore." Oriana said, thrusting her spoon in the bowl with an unsettling clack.

Brenda looked down at her own bowl. "I forgot my spoon."

Standing up, Brenda turned her back to Oriana as she fiddled for a spoon in the drawer. She took her time scanning the drawer before she slid it closed.

Oriana pounded the table. "It's not fair! I feel okay now!"

Brenda put her hand to Oriana's forehead. "She does feel cool Charlie. What do you think?"

Charlie hated looking at Oriana. It was like they were pulling a scam and a wave of guilt swept over him. "I don't know Mama. I don't know where she wants to go."

"Maw Maw," Oriana whispered to Brenda, "Maybe we can tell him? Then he could take me?"

"I don't know," Brenda said shaking her head, "Won't your mommy be mad?"

"Not if Mommy said you said it was okay," Oriana pleaded.

"I guess if your mommy left it to me then I guess you should tell him." Brenda said, picking up her cup of coffee and took a deep swig at the lie.

Oriana ran to Charlie and climbed into his lap, clapping her hands unable to contain their excitement. "We're going to live in Mexico and be Mexicans!"

"Don't think that way, Baby Girl," Brenda said, blowing out a gust of air and pulling Oriana onto her lap, "You're lucky to be an American. You don't have to be Mexican."

Oriana looked hurt at Brenda's reaction. "Mommy is Mexican."

Charlie couldn't look at his daughter. It was Oriana's happy, child voice but it was Mariana's angry words spilling out of her mouth. Charlie suddenly felt a bolt of lightning surge through him and he jumped from the couch. He picked up the last family photo on the mantle and stared at his stupid grin. He despised that his face look clueless as his hand rested on Mariana's shoulder; her smug face was mocking him as she clutched their children on her lap. He should have known that she wouldn't be happy with just taking them to a party; Mariana had distracted him in court with every intention of stealing his children.

Charlie felt a warm hand touching his fingers. He looked down at Oriana's face and saw Mariana's eyes looking at him. "Don't be sad, Daddy. Mommy said you can live in Mexico with us."

Oriana threw her arms around his neck and kissed him. Charlie forced a smiled. "We live in San

Diego."

"No," Oriana said, her lips pressed firmly, "If we live in Mexico, we can live in Senor's house in Rosarito. You and Mommy can be married again."

When the divorce was final, Oriana tried to find reasons for them to be together, insisting Mariana and Charlie take her for a celebration dinner after a dance recital and refusing to share her report cards unless both were present. For the first few months, he was rooting for her to win until it became clear that Mariana had moved on leaving Oriana and Charlie as the losers. "What about Lisa, honey? Where would Lisa live?"

Oriana bit her lip. "If we live in Mexico, she can't stop you from loving Mommy."

"That's not true," Charlie said, grabbing Oriana's arm causing her to cry out and he quickly released his grip, "did Mommy tell you that?"

Oriana stepped away and he wanted to beat himself for making her look afraid. He took a deep breath and tried to find his patience, "Lisa isn't the reason that Mommy and I aren't married anymore. Nobody, not you, or Max, Nola, or Maw Maw. Sometimes, people don't agree and everyone is happier if we just stay friends."

"I have friends," Oriana said, her chin pinched and mouth quivering, "I want my family again."

Charlie couldn't stop Oriana from running down the stairs to her room. She left him with the picture of his family when things were still in his hand. It was taken a week before Mariana announced she was leaving him. Behind him, Charlie could feel the pressure building inside Brenda like a powder keg of disapproval waiting to explode. She was kind enough to wait until they could hear Oriana's door close.

"What kind of man lets his wife drag his children to live as bean farmers?" Brenda muttered.

"Christ, do you ever shut up, Mama?" Charlie shouted, letting the picture of Mariana and the kids shatter against the wall.

Chapter Six

"You've got responsibilities here." Brenda said, sitting on Lisa's side of the bed.

"It's just three days," Charlie said, grabbing a bottle of cologne before it tipped over on his nightstand. He shoved his wallet in his pocket and stuck his hand in the top drawer and shut it in frustration, "where the hell are the keys to the Range Rover?"

Brenda reached across the bed and removed a gold keychain from under Charlie's coat. She held onto his hand and forced him to look her in the eye.

"Why three days? They've got cars down there don't they?"

"Don't be ridiculous, Mama." Charlie said, pulling his hand away.

"How am I supposed to know?" Brenda sat on his bed and stared at her son. "For all I know you could be riding a donkey back."

As soon as he announced he was going with Kier to Mexico, every female in the walls of his house went into hormonal imbalance. Each one had something different to corner him about.

Lisa cried that Charlie was going to get killed and make her a widow before they even got married. Oriana said she hated him because he refused to let her go. Nola remained frightened, sulking like a lonely puppy with mournful eyes every time he walked in the room. Brenda was angry that Kier couldn't do his job if he was protecting Charlie.

"You know it's only fifty miles from the border," Charlie said, pointing to a picture next to the bed. It was a group photo taken two years ago in Puerto Nuevo for an anniversary party for Mariana's brother, Alejandro. Everyone was happy and smiling except Brenda who sat stiffly between Oriana and Mariana's mother, Lourdes, "You've been there for God's sake."

Brenda grabbed the picture, laid it flat and put her coffee mug on the glass. "That doesn't explain why it takes three days. Make her bring him back."

"With the border closing, she can't get back that easy." Charlie said.

Bringing Mariana back was debated for days mostly between Kier and Remi. Kier made it clear he wanted to leave her there. It wasn't just because she "was the bitch that caused this mess" but from the logistics it was easier to bring one boy back. Remi disagreed. Max wouldn't be distressed with both his parents safe. They didn't know what was going to be waiting for them; Mariana was Max's mother and deserved to be saved.

The decision was made for Charlie when President Walden called a press conference for the US response to the "disturbances" in Mexico. Overnight, the border from Texas to California was militarized to deal with massive rush of refugees trying to flee the country. The United States made an official statement that they couldn't be sure if terrorist organizations wouldn't use the chaos to enter the country so no one would be allowed to come through. Charlie wasn't concerned about a terrorist but it meant that Mariana's Mexican citizenship left her with no escape.

As soon as Remi heard the news, he started working on connections to slide across the border and bring them back. It didn't come without a cost.

Charlie would get no support from the US if there was trouble. He was given a document that was vague enough to include his "family" to be brought through which meant he could slide Kier, Mariana and Max with him provided he got them to the US Embassy before it's closure in seventy-two hours.

"Send Kier by himself. He's man enough to kick some ass." Brenda said.

"And, I'm not?" Charlie asked.

Brenda stared down at her mug and slowly stirred the coffee with her finger, "Its cold."

"You really have amazing timing." Charlie said.

Brenda grabbed her cigarettes. "Come back in one piece."

"Priceless!" Charlie muttered, watching her disappear from view, "Love you too, Mama!"

Charlie sat down on the bed and ran his hands through his hair. He wanted Mariana to know that he wasn't going to let her take their son without a fight. He couldn't make Brenda or Lisa understand it was a matter of pride for a man to protect his family. Who would have thought this was the one time they agreed?

Charlie headed toward the kitchen to the sound of a witch's cackle and a cranky motor. Around the corner was Kier's burly frame hunched over the kitchen counter talking to Nola. Although Remi told him to dress conservative, he still chose to look like he was breaking out of his clothes. His jacket had the sleeves cut off revealing a glaring eagle with an Australian flag carried in the talons. His worn utility shorts were clean but had tell-tale stains that never went away. There were always cuts on his legs but he chose to dress one up with a bandage two sizes too small.

"Morning!" Kier reached a hand out and slapped Charlie on the back, "Just talking to my girl."

Nola grinned at Charlie, her eyes brighter than usual. "When Kier was a boy he had a kangaroo in his backyard."

Kier suppressed a smile under his hand and winked at Charlie.

"Don't believe this one, Nola," Charlie said, "He exaggerates."

"What's exaggerate?" Nola asked.

"Your brother thinks I like to make things up," Kier picking up a cheese Danish and tearing it in half with his teeth, "where's the Queen?"

Kier worshipped Brenda like she was royalty. He respected that she spoke her mind even when no one asked for an opinion. They were the same jagged pieces of a broken glass.

"She's pretending that she doesn't smoke on the patio." Charlie said.

Kier grinned and pulled out a stub of a cigar. "Mind if I get one last light up before we go?"

The world could be falling around him on fire and he'd still have time to light one last cigar off a burning building.

"We're leaving in fifteen minutes." Charlie said.

"You stay pretty," Kier said grabbed Nola's hand and kissed it gruffly, "I'm going to say hi to your Mom."

Nola giggled as Kier leaped over the counter and knocked a boot on the pans above.

"Hey!" Charlie warned, "Don't tear down my house!"

"Stop the worries. I'll still have energy to knock about some Taco Heads if needed." Kier grinned and bounded toward the patio.

Charlie went to the fridge. He pulled out a carton of orange juice. Nola was waiting with a glass.

"Why doesn't Kier call them Mexican?" Nola asked, pouring the orange juice and putting it away.

Charlie shrugged. "Who knows with Kier. He's got his own strange language for things."

"If Mama had said that, you would be mad." Nola said.

"Mama knows better." Charlie said.

"You shouldn't let him say things like that." Nola said into the fridge.

"It's not our place to change people even when they say stupid things," Charlie said, feeling like this was a conversation that should come from a father. In so many ways, he was that role for his little sister, "But as long as you know the difference. Don't say those things. Okay?"

Nola looked down and stared at her hands. "I wish you weren't leaving."

Charlie put his arms around her and hugged her tight. "I've been gone before."

"But Mama says you're going to a place where people kill each other." Nola said.

Charlie silently cursed Brenda. "I wish she hadn't told you that."

Nola nodded and slipped her arms around him. "It isn't always the bad people getting killed."

"I've got Kier with me," Charlie said, hugging him tight, "You know that Kier will keep me safe right?"

Nola smiled. "I will keep everything okay around here."

Charlie knew that Nola's pride in the house it gave her a sense of purpose. "Of course you will. While I'm gone, you're in charge, okay?"

Heavy shoes clumped through the living room and Kier peered around the corner. He looked for a grin from Nola but she glared at him.

"Where's the smile?" Kier asked.

"I don't want you to say Taco Head in this house anymore. Charlie and I don't like it." Nola said.

"I'm very sorry, darling," Kier said, pulling Nola into a hug and extending the middle finger to Charlie, "I didn't mean to hurt you."

Charlie rolled his eyes, knowing he'd catch hell from Kier all the way down to the border. "Just get the car."

As soon as the Range Rover pulled up, Charlie climbed inside and didn't look back. He barely had time to click his seatbelt before Kier peeled out of the driveway and charged down Mount Soledad Road.

Kier waited until they had pulled out of Pacific Beach and on to Interstate Five South. "So when did you grow a pussy?"

"I hate that you spout that racist bullshit!" Charlie yelled, punching the dashboard, "My kids are half-Mexican, so don't think its okay to come in my house and disrespect them."

"If I don't watch my mouth are you going to cry to Nola?" Kier said, cowering as if he was about to be hit but then punched Charlie in the arm, "You know I love those kids like they were my seed. I don't have a filter on this mouth and I forget you look at the world in a happy rainbow of color."

"I have to hear that hate coming out of Brenda's mouth day and night, but it doesn't mean I have to hear it from you. Can we just talk about what to expect down there?" Charlie said, wishing he could actually hit Kier, "This is a paying job, remember?"

"Right," Kier sobered quickly, "I picked up the papers from Remi this morning. That man has got a lot of pull. Mexico is sucked up tighter than your pucker hole. No one but military personnel allowed inside too bring the embassy out."

"It isn't really closed, is it?" Charlie muttered, "Isn't that what everyone is complaining about, the border is just a line drawn on a map?"

Kier nodded, "The military has a fortress all across the border. There's never been a country in revolution so close in a hundred years. It's about time we took Mexico seriously. This century has cartels and terrorists shitting across our borders like a public restroom, with the world watching the show. It's an embarrassment to the US if one fart squeaks across."

Kier reached behind the backseat and threw

Charlie the briefcase Remi had given him. "We need to travel light so get the papers out."

Charlie pulled an envelope thick with transportation papers and saw a glassy eye staring from the briefcase. "You brought Max's stuffed penguin?"

"The Queen said it would reduce Max's fear," Kier said, "we don't know how long it will take to get home so anything to help move him along the better."

It hadn't occurred to Charlie that they might not get all the way to Senor's Ranch today. If there was too much violence, they would need to wait. Nervous energy shot through him as he pulled a second envelope thick with a wad of bills. He started to organize them in his jacket.

"Shove all the money and passes into your pants." Kier said

"They're going to get trashed." Charlie said.

"Stop your whining," Kier said, "You need them on you in case we need to make a quick exit."

"It's fine in my jacket!" Charlie said.

"If it gets hot and you take it off," Kier said," then we're screwed."

Charlie laughed. "These are the things you think about? What I'm wearing?"

"You pay me to keep us alive." Kier said.

Charlie looked at the bulky papers and then thrust them into his jacket. "I will not take my jacket off."

"Even if the temperature is one million fucking degrees?" Kier asked.

"I'll be sweating buckets and I will ask you to turn the heat up." Charlie said.

"That jacket better stay like a second skin." Kier threatened.

Charlie stared out the passenger window to Mission bay. A slight breeze was blowing over the palm trees. Clusters of beach houses lined the beach in a half moon on the beach. A few lone water skis were bouncing behind khaki and orange boats. The Hilton stood like a magical castle with its red tiled roof and sand colored shutters. It was the same coast and yet existing an hour away was a war zone. The hills were the same and yet Charlie's home was fortified with steel, a view of gentle breaking waves in the Pacific. There was a Mexican man with that same view except his home was a shack constructed of sheet metal and chunks of wood. It was strictly luck that Charlie wasn't sitting in a shack and that scared him to death.

"Hey, pay attention," Kier clicked his fingers and pointed to a map on his phone, "we stop at the Border Patrol site in San Ysidro. They'll take us through to the Mexican side.

Kier swerved between two lanes as he became distracted by searching through his phone. Charlie closed his eyes to keep from throwing up.

"After we get there we'll meet some guy named General Carvajal," Kier said, glaring at the phone and then throwing it on the dashboard, "He's supposed to escort us the rest of the way."

Charlie waved his hand and leaned back into the leather. "Whatever it takes, let's just get down there."

"Hey-" Kier punched him the shoulder, forcing Charlie's eyes back open, "It's going to be fine. We'll be back by tomorrow at the latest."

"Would this really go faster without me?" Charlie asked.

"Maybe, but you need to go," Kier scowled. "It's your kid down there. You letting the old Queen get to you?"

"You'd already be back by now." Charlie found a lighter in his jacket and began to click it open.

"You think I'm going in there guns cocked and create a little war?" Kier shook his head and jerked the clutch. "This is all about you, Chuck. I'm just the muscle getting you there."

"What am I going to do? Put a pistol to Mariana's head and drag her out?" Charlie said.

"I'm hearing the Queen talking right now. You let her leave little knives in you," Kier complained, "Pull them out, man! Don't you know most rescue missions are all talk and no action? If you say the right things, you won't even need me."

Saying the right things was what worried Charlie. He didn't know what he was going to say once he saw Mariana. Any conversation between them never ended well. How was he going to face her when she had the strength of her family behind her? She usually won and that wasn't even on her own turf.

"I don't want to talk anymore." Charlie said, leaning his head against the headrest and was silent the rest of the drive to San Ysidro.

Chapter Seven

Charlie felt the irritation growing when he saw the city green sign reading San Ysidro, the last US city before entering into Tijuana.

A Texas Congressman, Stormy Chandler, was an advocate for shutting down the borders. He was quoted off-camera calling San Ysidro and El Paso the country's "Sewer Grates" leaking out sewage in the form of drug dealers, convicts, slave traders, and illegals who corrupt and burden the economy.

The desire to cross has caused people to attempt more dangerous and desperate ways. A three year old was recently found dead pressed into a gas tank. To his parents it was a better alternative to inhale fumes in a modified gas tank then to spend days surviving rattlesnakes, dehydration, hypothermia, and drowning.

Charlie distinctly remembered the last time he'd stopped at the border to enjoy Tijuana. It was nine years ago on his fifth date with Mariana. They walked across the border into Tijuana because Mariana wanted to dance at the night clubs on Revolucion Ave. The bridge was crowded with loud shouts and celebration of party goers. The energy was filled with tourists drinking outside the bars, dancers waving from clubs and peddlers holding out souvenirs; each trying to make a connection with your eyes to part with the money in your wallet.

Charlie's eyes were always looking down, he was afraid to step on the people sitting in his path. They were usually mothers sitting at the opening, a baby at their chest wrapped in tattered blankets, holding out disfigured arms looking for money. Tiny children with toothless mouths selling gum, their clothes soiled with dirt and barely holding on to skeleton rib cages. Charlie tried to follow Mariana's lead when moving through the open poverty in the streets. She knew where to step and moved around them quickly like she was avoiding trash in the road. Charlie was bothered that it was easy for her to ignore the problems. He'd grown up poor but Mariana never knew the meaning to go hungry.

Kier cracked his knuckles and brought Charlie's attention to their destination. Through the windshield he was shocked at the transformation of the crossing station. It was no longer visible because the Border Patrol had shut off Interstate Five at the Camino de la Plaza exit. Lines of familiar white and green trucks of the Border Patrol lined the overpass. To the right the Las Americas Outlets parking lots had been taken over by the Marines. A week ago, the mall was filled with shoppers looking for designer deals, Coach and Old Navy stores thrived in the warm brown Mercado with lights strung from the rafters. Now it was confiscated by military green trucks stacked in the parking lot facing the familiar rust metal fence that stood up the embankment from the last parking aisle. Watch towers had been built with a clear view into Tijuana and the channel of water that moated the modest homes lining the Tijuana freeway.

Concrete barricades that used to line the border lanes channeling traffic now faced front and lined with soldiers who stood vigilante for an order.

Kier slowed at the first barricade with the trained barrels of three rifles aimed at his head. A border patrol agent with the name Rickel stitched on his uniform motioned him to move to the side and park on the shoulder of the freeway behind a dented, Econoline van and a generic government issued Crown Victoria.

Charlie heard the shouting as soon as he stepped out of the Range Rover. He didn't see any crowds but so many angry voices were all shouting out of unison.

"You aren't losing it, sir," Rickel said, noticing Charlie's reaction, "The voices are all around you."

"What is that?" Kier asked.

Rickel pointed to the rumble behind them in the northwest. "Those are protestors against the US closing the border. People complaining they've been shut off from their relatives, their homes and jobs, especially the ones that work at the outlet. We can't let them go back and most are going to get laid off."

"Over there," Rickel said, pointing to the East County, "they don't think we're doing enough to keep the border secure and they want tighter control. Pretty much want us to nuke the border."

Charlie could now see a small cluster that was standing at a chain link fence at the edge of the compound with signs reading, '51st State.' "And them?"

Rickel laughed. "Those guys want us to invade Mexico."

Kier grinned. "Good idea."

Charlie pointed to the loudest set of voices coming from the south in Mexico. Rickel nodded. "Those are crowds of refugees. Since we shut the border they're stuck in Tijuana and caught in the middle of the fighting. They can't go home so they come here in case we change our minds."

"How do you not go insane?" Charlie said, tormented by the shouts and it had only been five minutes. The border agents were exposed to listen for hours. "Can't something be done to help them?"

Rickel shook his head. "We keep our distance, sir. When the riots settle and we see what happens with the Mexican government we can try to set up communication."

You'll follow orders and watch everyone die, Charlie thought, wanting desperately to turn around and never come back. Instead, he held back his thoughts and followed Rickel and Kier down a line of barricades toward the border and through a crowd of border patrol agents who eyed them with distrust as they stepped back just far enough they could squeeze through until they reached a white mobile office. Entering through the door led a vacant room lined with metal cabinets and a stark fluorescent bulb; the only color in the room was stamped on a sign at a single door at the far end. Charlie couldn't stop feeling dread as they got closer to the bold red print:

Beyond this point, you are no longer on US soil. Enter at your own peril.

Chapter Eight
Mexico- Tijuana Border Crossing

General Carvajal was an imposing man with shoulder blades straight and heavy. His neck protruded from his collar and formed an apron around his chin. Carvajal's thick mustache was a bristled broom, neatly trimmed around his upper lip but his cheeks were bristled as if he had been interrupted on his daily grooming. His eyes, swollen and red from exhaustion, were now casting disapproval at another task added to his list. He was being pulled away from restoring order to his beloved Baja because his superiors were punishing him with an exercise in humiliation.

The General had been given strict instructions to escort some rich American down to Rosarito. Help him pick up his brat. Find him a lobster and get him back over the border. This was the last thing he should be doing. He had always been there for his country and now he was glorified tour guide.

Mexico had worked so hard to find its ground again. Since that business with the towers in New York, the tourism trade had left Tijuana a ghost town. Parents didn't want their kids dancing on Revolucion. Cruise ships wanted to keep sailing like the whole damn country was on quarantine. All the Mexicans owning shops, restaurants, and hotels, suddenly left with starving children and business gone. Just as things started turning around and now they weren't going to recover. Not this way.

"Sir, they're here." A soldier said tapping on Carvajal's door.

Carvajal coughed and sharply pulled down his uniform and charged down to the room. He took his time, let them sweat a little. He paused at the door and observed them through a slotted window.

Of the two men, he picked the Rich American from the herd. From his dark hair, tan skin and casual demeanor passed him as a native of Southern California possibly living on one of the Naval ships in Coronado or maybe he was a biker living in Lakeside. He was dressed in a basic leather jacket with a cream button down shirt and jeans, nothing you'd imagine millionaire would wear unless you were Carvajal, the son of a tailor. Carvajal knew that every piece was custom-made for that Rich American, the seams perfectly fit the lines of his body. Each piece probably cost more than what he made in ten years. Carvajal didn't need to meet him to know he hated him.

The older guy looked like a worn guard dog. He had a sharp look like a hawk surveying his surroundings, definitely old military. His clothes were probably what he found on the floor that morning a wrinkled shirt torn on several seams. Carvajal could smell this one as he opened the door and acknowledged him first as a courtesy because he was military and to piss off the rich American.

Carvajal extended his hand, "General Carvajal."

The military guy didn't look him in the eye and ignored his hand. "Kier."

Carvajal gritted his teeth. He was taking his valuable time away from his country and couldn't even get respect of a proper greeting. "The area you wish to travel is not very stable right now. We cannot guarantee your safety."

The men continued to look at him if they were

waiting for him to finish his sentence. Alarmed at their silence, General decided to continue and looked at the rich American. "I would suggest that I send a few of my men down to pick up your wife and son. You can sit here if you'd like but I think you'd be more comfortable returning to your home and we will contact you to pick them up."

After looking briefly at each other, Kier coughed and then glared at Carvajal, resembling an attack dog.

"Look, General Corvel-"

"Carvajal."

"Yeah, right, Carvajal," Kier said, continuing, "I know you don't give a shit about us. We just need a quick ride down there and we'll come right back. We know you got better things to do. Give me a Humvee and you'll have us out of our hair."

Carvajal's eyes narrowed and his face grew very hot. He was about to have them thrown back on their side of the border.

"He's not paid for his personality," the rich American said, sticking his hand out, "I'm Charlie. I want to thank you for helping me out here."

Carvajal shook his hand reluctantly and caught sight of the thick watch on his wrist. There were at least ten diamonds encrusted on the face, the gold gleaming off the fluorescents made his eyes hurt.

"Nice watch," Carvajal said, walking down the hallway with the men following behind, "I believe it's a Sauger?"

Charlie looked impressed. "You have a good eye for watches."

Carvajal smiled at the compliment. "There are no two alike, customized by Sauger himself."

Charlie shrugged. "You know more than I do. It was a gift."

Kier coughed loudly. "Can we get on with this? Just give me a key. We'll go down and pick up his wife and son. We'll be back before you can order a burrito."

"What did you say?" General wheeled around abruptly. Kier smirked and Charlie looked uncomfortable.

"Sir," Charlie coughed, "We appreciate what you are doing for us-"

"What I'm doing is wasting my time with you." General interrupted, "Time that could be spent keeping my country together has been bought by your American dollars to make sure your heads don't get blown off in the fifty miles it takes to get to Rosarito. If it were up to me, I'd let you go. You'd be dead before you left the city limits. Then I could go on with more important things."

Charlie looked nervous and started to open his mouth but Kier's laughter cut him off.

"You do have a pair of huevos," Kier said, slapping Carvajal on the back, "Let's get going."

It took all of the Carvajal's strength to not shove the Sauger still attached to Charlie's arm down Kier's throat.

The Carvajal escorted them through the compound to a loading dock filled with tanks and dozens of SUV's all fit for military use. A low roar was heard over the south wall.

"It sounds like we're standing outside of the Sports Arena," Charlie said, referring to the coliseum in San Diego which caused the General to hold back a smile. Even rich Americans couldn't buy themselves out of fear.

"There are several...protests going on right now," Carvajal said calmly, going down a flight of stairs and headed toward a bank of SUV's, "They'd love to tear apart some Americans right now."

"What did we do?" Charlie said, "This isn't our problem."

Carvajal ignored the question and stopped at a long black armored car. "Let's get on our way."

Kier let out a low whistle. "Not in that piece of shit. That's a glorified prom limo. We'll be a moving target."

Carvajal's face reddened. "It is completely secured."

Kier shook his head, "No fucking way."

"Then you'll wait here." Carvajal said relaxing his shoulders and turning toward the compound.

Charlie looked at Kier. "Don't fuck this up."

"Charlie, this whole plan rots," Kier paused as a loud scream came over the wall. He banged his hand on the passenger panel causing Carvajal to turn around, "Come on, let's get going."

"What the hell," Kier said, opening the door for Charlie, "We're going to die someday. Might as well be today."

Chapter Nine

Carvajal started to move into the cabin of the limousine but Kier put his arm across the door.

"I get we need an escort, Kier said gruffly, "but we don't need a chaperone. I promise to be a real gentleman."

The color filled Carvajal's face. He stepped back and surveyed the situation. Finally he nodded but then leaned on the ledge preventing Kier from closing the door.

"Keep the curtains closed. Do not look out." Carvajal said.

Kier grinned. "Afraid it won't look like the travel brochure?"

"A lot of protesters are outside the gate." Carvajal said, matching Kier's grin, "I'm sure they would love to tear up some Americans."

Carvajal slammed the door hard, pinching the side of Kier's thumb before he pulled it way with a yelp. The cabin was sealed off from the drivers giving a false expectation of privacy. Charlie could hear the front door open and the weight jostled on the right side before it settled unevenly.

"Think they'll need to pry Carvajal out of that seat with a crow bar?" Kier laughed, he quickly sucked on the gash on his thumb, "fucking prick."

"What did he mean about Americans?" Charlie asked.

"There's a group down here that blames the US for this mess. Can you believe that? You don't need to worry, the Mexican government knows better than let anything happen to you. They need the US support." Kier snorted and opening the door to the mini-bar. "They couldn't even leave us with any liquor in this heap?"

"I've never seen a limo strapped with armor like this one," Charlie said.

"They don't know what the fuck they're doing down here," Kier said, slamming the min-bar door, "Seriously? What better moving target than a limo? I checked they fixed it up with bullet-proof glass and armor. We wouldn't be in here if I didn't think it was safe."

The limo lurched forward and Charlie pressed his shoulders into the seat. Charlie could tell by the shadow falling into the window that they were passing the gateway outside the compound. The rumble he had heard before was starting to grow louder. At first Charlie thought it was just machinery but then he started to be able to separate sounds. The low guttural sounds were human. An occasional cry rose above a jarring repetition of gun-fire and the scraping of metal. It was out of joint and Charlie had no desire to see what was behind the curtain.

Kier, however, was vigilant. He peeled back the curtain to a small shaft of light left a rectangle on the floor.

"Idiots, do they think a few people are going to make the Federales worry?" Kier muttered, "They're going up against guns with hammers and garden hoses."

Charlie leaned forward, his eyes trying to adjust in the small shaft of sun. The happy Tijuana from his memory was now a war zone. There were glimpses of buildings, the store fronts blackened and burned out. Occasionally tumbled blocks of cement blocked part of the street. The limo heaved forward and jerked as it maneuvered around. Jolts and chunks of dust and debris would run from the side. It reminded Charlie when he went off-roading in Ocotillo. He glimpsed a street that he recognized just off Revolucion. There used to be a bakery on the corner that Mariana liked to pick up thick empanadas stuffed with cream. Metal gates were partially torn from the entrance. A spray of red graffiti on the wall and a pool of red had dried onto the sidewalk.

The gears ground and the limo struggled around the time that the rumbling grew louder. The window shadowed like the sun passing behind a cloud. Kier ripped more of the curtains back and a wall of faces hovered over them. Distorted faces jammed against the window, trying to press into the car. The limo rocked with the weight and the engine whined as it pushed forward, starting to gain speed. The cabin shocks forced them into the air and Kier and Charlie ended up on the floor as the limo launched over a series of bumps. Loud screams came from underneath them and Charlie's stomach lurched.

"He's running them over!" Charlie yelled as there was a quick jolt and Kier fell toward him and they both knocked on the floor. He was alarmed that Kier pulled himself back into his seat and stared blankly ahead.

"We've got to help them," Charlie said, grasping the door handle but it just flipped back and forth in this hand, they had been sealed inside. Kier pulled at Charlie's arm and guided him toward the seat.

"There's nothing you can do for them!" Kier shouted at him. Charlie shoved his arm away and began throwing his weight on the door. Kier grabbed him again and threw Charlie to the floor of the limo. He straddled Charlie and held him by the throat. "Are you crazy?"

"We're killing them!" Charlie choked, grabbing at Kier's hand as he gasped for air.

"And you think you can save them?" Kier yelled back, "What do you think they'll do to us if they get in here? I'm getting off you and you're going to sit down. If you try to open that door again, I swear to God, I'll knock you so hard you'll sleep through this whole fieldtrip."

Charlie pulled himself back off the floor and helplessly stared at the faces still pressed against the window their eyes scared and pleading. He couldn't look away.

The loose strands of hair ran like a ribbon through the mesh of faces. He followed them until he found their owner, a woman who might be twenty. Her mouth pressed against the glass, distorting her lips and forcing her to keep her mouth parted, her teeth scraping the window leaving spittle and blood. Her eyes stared into Charlie and for a moment he felt as if she was asking only him to save her.

A cracking sound thundered and the repeating drum of bullets was heard above. The faces fell away except the woman. Her coat had attached her to the armor. She ran along the limo as it gained speed, her lips moving rapidly as she continued to plead. A crack echoed in the air and smatters of red smeared against the window. Someone had pierced her neck. Before Charlie could comprehend what he was seeing, he heard another crack and her head came apart onto the window, the sound of her body banging against the side before it hit the ground.

"Jesus Christ," Charlie whispered, unsure if he was praying for the woman or calling out for help.

Kier pulled the curtains closed and shook his head. "Maybe I should have come by myself."

"And you can handle all this? This is okay to you?" Charlie shouted.

Kier eased himself into the seat. "I can't let my heart bleed for everyone."

Even with the curtains closed, Charlie could still see an imprint of the woman's blood. He turned toward the interior and closed his eyes, the image burned into his memory.

The limo was now moving to smooth road and gained speed. Charlie was left to wonder what he would find when he found Mariana.

With some distance between Tijuana, they slowed to a crawl, moving smoothly onto the freeway south. Kier had left his gun at the border but produced a thin machete from underneath his pant leg and laid it on the seat. They hadn't heard any sounds for over half an hour so he pushed the curtain away. Charlie saw the serene Pacific looking like a picture postcard. Gone was the violence that had surrounded them. The dried blood and bits of brain on the window made sure it was not forgotten.

Charlie checked his watch, they had been in Mexico for three hours which meant Lisa would be heading into the club. He checked his phone. Two bars. Enough to call her and let her know he got through okay. Lisa didn't answer right away. On the fourth ring, she caught the phone.

"Are you already there?" Lisa asked.

"Not yet, we're through Tijuana," Charlie said, trying to talk over the loud grinding gears, "It's going slow but we should be there soon."

"I still don't understand why it's going to take you a couple days." Lisa said.

"It might not. We got through a lot of the red tape early." Charlie said.

"Is it as bad as they said it is down there? The news makes it look terrible," Lisa said.

Charlie tried to avoid the window. "No, it's been smooth so far."

Kier shook his head and chuckled.

"Good. When you get back, come to the club. You can pick me up and we can-" Lisa started to speak.

"-I know I said getting here was smooth but it's going to be awhile," Charlie interrupted, "I'm not going to be home until very late. Don't wait on me."

Lisa's car door slammed and Charlie could hear the radio pop on. She turned it down but the connection was still hard to hear.

"So you *are* going to be a couple days," Lisa's voice was tight and accusing, "look, if you and Kier want some sort of guy's weekend."

Charlie almost dropped the phone. "Yeah, a guy's weekend in the middle of the week in a war zone. Lisa, you can really say some stupid things sometimes."

"Me? I just don't understand-" Lisa's voice was static and then suddenly it was silent.

"Lisa?" Charlie said.

"She thinking you caused a war to get a night out?" Kier smirked, "I'm surprised you had any reception this long. You're cut off now."

"In more than one way," Charlie sighed. "How much longer?"

"We should be hitting Rosarito soon." Kier said.

"I didn't think it would be this quick." Charlie said.

Kier nodded, his eye brows scrunched. "It should be more of a problem."

"You mean other than trampling over innocent people?" Charlie said.

"Oh stop being such a fucking patriot." Kier grumbled.

The limo started an incline. The move was a familiar tilt up toward a winding pathway and it wasn't long before they could see the Ranch in the distance.

Charlie remembered Mariana's stories about the Ranch. It was her favorite fairy tale complete with a fortress and her role as the princess in distress.

Mariana's mother, Lourdes, told her husband, Senor Mendoza Jimenez, she wanted to build a vacation home to bring their large family. It had to be a place grand enough that her four sons and two daughters were going to bring their own families someday. There was also an ulterior motive. She wanted somewhere that was far enough from Senor's coffee fields in Mazatlán so he would pay attention to her.

Lourdes bought acres just past the tourist town of Rosarito in Baja. It sat upon a strand of land that was its own peninsula with three private beaches. Once the priest had blessed the land, she christened the building of Paradise de Dios, God's Haven.

It took two years to build. Lourdes changed the plans three times before it was right. When she was done there was a mansion with twenty bedrooms, a library, pool cabana, stables, and three separate casitas each large enough to fit a family of four. The gardens overlooking the ocean were featured in several travel magazines.

Mariana had a lot of memories of happy summers spent with her family. In those summers, Lourdes took her shopping in San Diego and it made the decision to go to college there.

As grand as it was, Lourdes was only able to get her husband out a few times. He preferred to spend his time in his coffee fields. He was only interested in controlling his business.

Mariana would tear up about her mother's struggle with Senor; her loneliness and hardship to keep the family together. Charlie had a hard time feeling any pity when his own mother struggled to keep her kids together and Brenda didn't have a vacation homes or servants. Lourdes had many rooms to grow her children instead of a dank, hotel room. Lourdes had a husband that gave her money instead of stealing all she earned.

Charlie didn't feel sorry for Lourdes but he did like his mother in law. She didn't speak any English but she never let that stop her from making him feel welcome. She made sure that he felt accepted.

Lourdes died on Charlie and Mariana's fifth wedding anniversary at Paradise de Dios. It was a cancer that took her quickly while Senor was negotiating for a site for his new processing plant. It took Mariana two days to tell him because he never returned her phone calls.

The guilt made Senor set his headquarters at Paradise de Dios and got out of his fields. Before he moved his head operations to Baja, he built a large wall around, brought some of his security and shut of Paraiso de Dios off from the world.

The irony wasn't lost on Mariana. It burned inside that after her mother's death, her father finally settled in the haven Lourdes had built for them.

Over the last years, Lourdes' paradise ceased to exist. It became less of a retreat and more a fortified compound. Mariana started to call it the Ranch after the vaquero-like security guards that roam the grounds like they were rounding up cattle.

The limo approached the thick, wooden gate that surrounded the property and came to a stop as twenty men blocked the opening. Charlie quickly pushed out of the back, anxious to breathe fresh air, careful to avoid the blood on the outside.

A thin, muscular man in his twenties approached. Charlie recognized him as Mariana's brother Alejandro. He couldn't remember all of her family but Alejandro's light eyes and flowing hair made him look like he belonged in a Mexican TV novella.

Alejandro tapped on the car's hood, eyeing the General and slowly walked around the passenger side. Carvajal stepped out and let his arms stretch wide. Charlie wasn't sure if he was trying to show that he was unarmed or as a sign of friendship.

"Is there something you need?" Alejandro asked. He showed no sign that Carvajal was welcome.

"You better get up there," Kier said prodding Charlie forward.

Charlie stepped out. Alejandro's eyes left the General and took a few minutes to adjust to Charlie's face. His eyebrows raised and he motioned over to Charlie.

"What are you doing here Charlie?" Alejandro said.

Charlie moved cautiously past the General and stood next to Alejandro.

"Just needed a little help getting down here," Charlie said, flashing a smile, "You know how hard it is getting through San Ysidro around rush hour."

Alejandro didn't smile. Charlie forgot that he never understood his sense of humor. Alejandro glared back at Carvajal. "Is the military just a bus service now?"

Carvajal shifted his stance and leaned on the limo. "I wanted to come down here personally to make sure your family was alright. We hadn't heard from Senor. Since your brother in law needed some help to gather his family, I thought I would check on you."

Carvajal's words only angered Alejandro. He slammed his hand down on the car. "Senor is fine. He's alive. Why don't you do something useful and get this country stable?"

These words seemed expected. The general smiled a politician's grin and shrugged his shoulders. "As soon as we go inside and get Mr. Thibodeaux's family."

Alejandro stared down the roadway. "And you needed all those trucks to transport them?"

Charlie looked down the driveway. He hadn't been watching behind them but in the short distance that there were four SUV's sitting down the road."

"It's not safe to travel light these days." Carvajal said.

"No. It isn't." Alejandro said.

The two men stared at each other in silence and Charlie found himself standing awkwardly between them. Kier had gotten out of the car by now and was surveying the situation. He stared over at the SUVs and exchanged glances with Alejandro.

"When are we going up?" Kier finally said.

Alejandro nodded. "You can go up. But not that caravan."

"Good, we'll be gone soon," Carvajal said turning to get in the car.

"Not you, Carvajal. You stay here."

Carvajal heaved his weight back around and now looked irritated. "We need to gather Mr. Thibodeaux's family."

"Charlie and his friend can go," Alejandro said, "You aren't welcome here."

Charlie knew that the Ranch was another two miles up the hill. They still needed a ride to get to the main house. He turned to Carvajal. "Can we just drive this thing up there?"

"You are not authorized to drive a military vehicle." Carvajal growled, losing some of his composure.

"This is a glorified prom limo with some hunks of metal attached," Charlie retorted. It was an impulsive reaction and Charlie knew it was out of place.

Kier snorted back a laugh and the color rose in Carvajal's face again. "No."

Kier peered in at the driver's seat. A skinny soldier who looked no older than eighteen sat nervously behind the wheel. "Then let this guy drive us. He looks harmless."

"No military!" Alejandro said, now the one irritated.

"Why don't you just bring down Mariana and Max?" Charlie suggested, feeling a growing uneasiness as dusk was starting to shade the air. The yellow headlights from the SUV's behind them began to gleam like eyes of a predator.

"What are you hiding in there Alejandro?" Carvajal said, he started to walk toward him, "If I want to go in there, do you really think you can stop us?"

Alejandro spat on the ground at Carvajal's feet. "I know a call to the governor will, he's our family. Remember?"

Carvajal stepped back from the spit and forced a smile. "Why don't you just make this easy on your brother in law? Let Manuel drive them up there?"

Alejandro eyed the boy who was staring down at the odometer, nervously clutching the steering wheel. Alejandro sighed and waved his arms up to allow the men to clear a path. "Fine. Just the boy can drive them."

Carvajal looked disappointed. He patted Charlie on the back. "When you are ready to leave Manuel will bring you back."

Carvajal turned his back and the lead SUV pulled quickly up the driveway and opened the door.

Kier and Charlie hopped back in the car and offered for Alejandro to join them.

"I will see you for dinner," Alejandro said and waved for the gates to be opened. The heavy wood creaked and reluctantly swung open. From the top of the arch, Charlie noticed several men sat on its crook. Manuel slid the limo under the arch and passed Alejandro.

Alejandro kept his eyes fixed down the road as they passed him. He didn't look like the college kid that crashed on Charlie's couch a couple weekends, now he was militant and suspicious. Charlie noticed that the steadiness of Alejandro's jaw couldn't hide that his hand was shaking as it clutched the side his pants.

The twists and turns up the driveway were filled with exotic plants and trees. It was a scenic paradise and calmed Charlie's nerves from the gate way.

The warm glow from the Ranch appeared above the trees until the rounded the corner and it came into view. It was like arriving at a five star resort with a circular driveway leading up to the stone walkway that was lined with several of Mariana's "vaqueros." Kier didn't wait for Manuel to stop and moved quickly out of the car to speak with them.

Charlie sat staring at the front of the cabin. It allowed too many thoughts to go through his head. What if Mariana knew he was coming and didn't bring Max? Would Kier have to get involved? What would he say to Oriana if he couldn't bring her brother home? What if Brenda was right and he screwed all this up by not letting Kier to go alone He was about to lose his mind and jump out when Kier opened the door.

"Max is in there," Kier said, "go get him."

"Wait, here okay?" Charlie tapped on the windshield which startled Manuel. Charlie headed up the stone steps but Kier leaned against the limo.

"I'm staying here," Kier said, lighting a cigar.

"It could be hours." Charlie said.

"Bring me a tortilla," Kier said, flicking ash on the windshield, "I want to keep an eye on Mannie here."

"What's he going to do? Wet the seat?" Charlie said.

"Don't underestimate anybody." Kier stared into the windshield at Manuel who swallowed hard and squirmed in the seat.

Charlie looked toward the door. It had been opened for him to move through but there were shadows looming on the inside, not a place he wanted to go alone. He needed to convince Kier to go with him. "Patricia will be there."

Kier's ears perked up. He always had a small crush on Patricia but he never acted out of respect for her. "Give her right tit a squeeze for me!"

Charlie rolled his eyes. "You're a class act."

"You got to face Mariana," Kier said, his hands giving a wave like he was pushing him forward, "The sooner this is done then we can go home."

Charlie walked through the trellis walkway. The thick wooden beams adorned with jasmine that perfumed the night air with every step.

Inside, the scent of roasted meat filled the air. Two boys were standing in the hallway. They looked uneasy at him and then walked the other direction. To his right was a large living room, the high ceilings were decorated with three large rod iron chandeliers. There was a scatter of stiff leather sofas and wooden tables. The large room was meant to be a reception to hold hundreds of people. There used to be a lot of parties before Mariana's mother died but now the room stayed quiet and the family spent all their time in the back rooms beside the kitchen.

The centerpiece was a fireplace made of white stucco that reached up to the ceiling. Tonight it was lit with flames licking up the chimney making the room heavy with the scent of pinon wood and sage. No other lights or life inhabited the room and it reminded Charlie of a doorway to hell. He felt uneasy and moved through a hallway behind the giant staircase. Voices told him that he was on the right track and he found his way into the large dining room. The ceiling was three stories above with thick vigas that held up smooth adobe walls.

In the center was a wooden table wide enough and stretching in length to accommodate at least fifty people. The room was still large enough to accommodate five smaller tables and three small card tables close to the kitchen. Each was decorated with crimson runners down the center and set with silver and teal table plates and casks of wine.

Charlie thought of the first time he had eaten in the room. He remembered being overwhelmed by how large Mariana's family each knowing their rightful table. Even making room for Mariana's new husband did not upset anyone's rightful place, there was always room to fill more. It gave him the strange sensation of belonging to something bigger. It was a great contrast to sitting with Brenda and Jackson in the hotel room where his bed was also his dining table.

Charlie was alone in the room and it surprised him that he was able to walk this far without getting spotted. The large army outside made him think this would be a place preparing for war. The warm sage from the fire, the smell of preparing food and the polite boys made him feel that strange sensation of a family celebration, a feeling completely foreign to him.

"Hello Charles."

A voice from behind startled Charlie. He turned to see Mariana's sister, Patricia, following with two men.

Patricia was his favorite member of Mariana's family. She was five years younger than Mariana but they could have been twins. Deep chestnut hair, high, honey-kissed cheekbones and almond shaped eyes. Except Patricia's eyes were always bright and kind and Mariana's were always burning with self-righteousness.

Charlie was quick to give her a hug. She smelled better than the flowers outside.

"You look good." Charlie said.

Patricia smiled and nodded at the two men. "It's alright."

The men eyed Charlie and then moved down another hallway toward a familiar oak door.
It opened and Charlie glimpsed a cluster of men busy in what used to be a family room.

Patricia pointed the other direction toward a thinner door. "She's in the kitchen."

"What can I expect?" Charlie asked.

Patricia placed her hands up. "This is not my business. You need to talk with her."

"Where's Max?" Charlie asked.

Patricia shrugged. "He's playing with his cousins somewhere."

Charlie kissed her cheek. "Wish me luck."

"Here goes everything," Charlie thought. He took the long walk past the table and pushed past the wooden door.

Chapter Ten

Charlie paused at the doorway to survey the situation. Mariana was alone in the kitchen chopping vegetables, her hair was piled on her head, a loose curl had escaped and fell across her cheek. Her thick lashes weren't matted with mascara and her lips were absent the thick, wine-stained gloss from all her expensive cosmetics. If she wasn't the mother of his kids, he'd think she was the college girl he met nine years ago. She looked fresh and domestic in a yellow sundress and a light green apron that draped her curves. In California, she only passed through the kitchen to get to the garage. Charlie wondered if she ever looked that peaceful in their home.

"I didn't know you knew how to cook," Charlie called out, immediately regretting the words chosen to announce his arrival.

The chopping came to an abrupt halt. Mariana's eyes never looked up as she grabbed at a loaf of bread and began to tear into large pieces and throw into a bowl. "I didn't think you'd come here yourself."

Charlie thought he heard Max's laughter in the courtyard just outside. He stepped out of the entryway to get a better look and glimpsed three small heads run past a glass door.

Charlie suddenly felt a need to hold his son. A pain stabbed at his heart when he realized that only a glass door divided them.

"We need to get out of here." Charlie
said, hearing that he was backsliding into that tone of
voice he knew she hated, it was commanding and
fatherly. He couldn't help what came naturally. He
was trying to hold back the desire to push past her and
grab Max.

Mariana's eyes flashed with a familiar hatred.
Gone was the tranquil woman preparing dinner and in
her place stood the familiar wife. The angry one that
had told Charlie she was suffocating with his control.

"You've come to save us?" Maria challenged. "Has
the great Charlie Thibodeaux jumped over the border
on his white horse?"

"I didn't say it that way." Charlie grumbled,
growing irritated with her dramatic overreaction.

"Are you going to save Mexico too?" Mariana
smiled as she picked up a small Mexican flag that was
sticking out of a plant. She waved it around the
kitchen.

"Cut the sarcasm!" Charlie snapped, failing at
any attempt to keep things civil. He felt as if he was
transported back to a year ago when fighting about
the trouble in Mexico was the only way they seemed
to communicate. "I never said I was here to save you."

"Don't tell me how to sound! You don't tell me
that ever again!" Mariana's voice continued to grow
louder with every word. Her voice was only half as
animated as her arms that were thrashing about as if
looking for something to throw. "You came here to
bring me and Max back to the US. How is that not
saving us? "

Charlie felt there were eyes staring all around
him. From the corner of his eye he looked at the
courtyard. The glass door was crowded with concerned
faces from Mariana's family but no one that he
recognized.

Charlie knew only a small cast of Mariana's
family. He'd never met two of her brothers and there

75

were so many cousins and uncles and nieces that lived all over Mexico. If Charlie hadn't convinced Mariana to elope to Vegas, there would have been a guest list of a thousand on her side. It would have been ridiculous to his guest list of thirty and that was if he packed the guest list with his staff. Right now, all of her family stared in, some looking concerned and others looking angry. He knew he might have some reasons to worry but that was why he brought Kier.

Mariana followed his glance to the door and actually smiled. "You can see I have plenty of support. Let me ask you, surrounded by all my family, who is going to save you, Charlie?"

Charlie sighed and tried to find a calmer voice but it wasn't happening.

"Mexico is exploding," Charlie said, "There are people killing each other out there!"

Mariana brushed the hair from her face. "Open your eyes Charlie! How is that new?"

"Mexico is on the verge of a civil war."

Mariana forced a grim smile and nodded, "It's been at war a long time but now we are preparing for a revolution."

"Call it what you want! War, revolution, protest all mean people are dying!" Charlie said holding up his hands in frustration, "You can't seriously want to be here!"

Mariana shook her head. "I need to show support for my father and my country."

"Even if that means you could die?" Charlie asked.

Mariana lowered her head and began to chop vegetables again. Charlie started to feel her shutting down.

"You need to support, Senor," Charlie said quickly, "I understand that it's important to you. That doesn't mean you have to let Max suffer. He needs to come home and he needs his mother with him." Charlie said.

"I am many people at times in my life. I am a daughter, a mother and a lawyer. I was even your wife once," Mariana said, "But I've always been a Mexican first. I'm not looking to die, Charlie, I just can't ignore anymore. If things are going to change then it has to start with me."

Chapter Eleven

After Mariana's outburst, Charlie left the kitchen and stayed in the safety of the dining room. He wanted to take Max now but it was smarter to wait until after dinner. In the thick of her family, he could quickly slip out before Mariana realized what happened.

Heavy laughter came from down the hall. Charlie decided not to venture any further. Mariana's brothers would be clustered in a back room intended as a family room but had been transformed into a trashed Man Cave. They brooded and huddled inside, claiming the room as their own.

All the fine leather couches were scuffed and worn from boots dug in to watch the soccer games. The walls pitted with careless scuffles. Charlie had brought an antique pool table direct from New Orleans when Lourdes wanted something for the boys to play. He remembered Lourdes' smile as her fingers traced the claw and ball legs. Charlie was thrilled that she appreciated the gesture. He even had custom made pool cues designed with the family crest engraved in the handle. Lourdes shared his appreciation for fine things. Now those cues were splintered and dulled as they lay scattered across the felt. It made Charlie sick.

Lourdes' sons came from the coffee fields that built Senor's business. They were a rough cut like their father. When Lourdes was alive, they watched where they treaded. Now they didn't care when the mud caked into the fibers of the hand-woven rugs and there were chunks in the paint and chipped tiles. It was a work room when Lourdes had wanted a room of art.

Charlie heard Max first, his laugh was imprinted on him and he could pick him out of a thousand kids on a playground that was five miles away. Max bounced around the opposite side of the hall holding hands with an older cousin. Mariana had dressed him like all the boys in a starch white shirt and black pants that hung a little too long over patent leather shoes. The boys looked like they were going to church and Max looked like a little businessman with his hair pulled back from his face.

As soon as Max saw Charlie he broke his hold and ran to him, narrowly missing Patricia who was bringing in massive bowls of meat.

"Papa!" Max's voice echoed in delight up to the vigas as he saw Charlie.

Charlie bent down to Max's level and almost fell over as Max hit him with the force of a line-backer.

"Maximus! Whoa!" Charlie said, bracing back against the wall, his arms circling the boy in a fierce grip. "What are they feeding you, kid?"

Max pulled back and extended his arm to make a muscle. "Senor says that I am going to be a football player someday!"

"Well, Senor is right."

Max scrunched his face. "He's talking about soccer. That's what they call football here."

"You'd be a good soccer player." Charlie tugged on Max's leg, "You've got a great kick."

Max shook his head. "I want to be a Charger! Or maybe a Saint!"

Charlie smiled. That was one battle that he had won. Mariana wanted to introduce Max to soccer but Charlie loved American football. Mariana was not willing to allow both. Charlie didn't even kick a soccer ball until he had come to California. One of his first jobs had been playing a saxophone for money outside of Saints games in the Quarter. He brought Max to his first Charger game at Qualcomm Stadium. The first time Max heard the roar of the stadium and the fireworks at a touchdown, Max was entranced.

"Where is Orrie?" Max asked, looking around Charlie. "Didn't she want to come?"

Charlie shook his head. "Not this time, Maximus."

"Was it because I spilled milk in her room?" Max's eyes looked sorrowful beneath his thick lashes, "I said I was sorry."

Charlie smiled. "No, she knows it was an accident."

"I miss her." Max pulled up his sleeve to show a temporary tattoo, "I want to trick her and Tia Nola."

"You'll see them soon." Charlie said, tousling his hair, "We're going to eat dinner and then head back home."

A bowl clattered drawing their attention to the heavy wood table and Charlie saw Mariana staring down at them.

"That was loud!" Max said, holding his ears, "Did you break the bowl Mama?"

"Why don't you go see Kier?" Charlie suggested, "He has Penguino in the car."

"Kier is here!" Max clapped his hands in excitement.

Mariana quickly moved around the table and put her arms around Max. "Go find your cousins."

"I want to see Kier!" Max protested.

"You'll see him later." Mariana said turning him toward the kitchen.

Max's shoulders slumped, "Okay Mama."

Max began to move but then hung his arms around Charlie's neck.

"You won't go home without me, right?" Max whispered into Charlie's ear.

Charlie pulled the boy so close he could hear feel his heart pounding and kissed his head. "I'm not going anywhere without you."

As soon as Max rounded the corner, Mariana stuck a finger in Charlie's face.

"Nice try!" Mariana hissed.

"What did I do?" Charlie protested.

"Get Max out with Kier and he throws him in the car," Mariana turned and began to fidget with the bowl, "Keep your wolf outside!"

"Did you really think I would pile him in the car and take off?" Charlie asked.

Mariana turned back to him and gave a familiar look. "I know what you would try."

"This place is a fortress." Charlie said waving his hands around at the massive house, "How am I going to get Max past your brothers? Throw him in the trunk?"

Mariana rolled her eyes and began to walk back toward the kitchen.

"We'll stay for dinner. But then we're going." Charlie said, trying to keep a lid on the anger as she turned her back on him.

"You can go now," Mariana said, "Not Max."

Charlie caught Mariana's arm and he pulled her backward. "Today I saw a woman blown up. Blown up! How can you think this is the right place to be?"

Mariana pulled back her arm. "I don't see anyone being hurt here."

"Are you going to keep him in this bubble until he's eighteen?" Charlie challenged her, "He can't hide in Senor's house."

"Not today," Mariana said, "The violence will calm down. It always does."

"When will I get to see him?" Charlie yelled, "We have joint custody!"

"We have joint custody in the US," Mariana said, quietly, "We will see what a Mexican court has to say."

Mariana's words struck him like a bolt and he was seeing what was really going on. Mariana could give all the speeches about wanting to drape in the

Mexican flag but the reality was that she didn't like losing full custody. She had taken her toys and was going to fight on another playground.

Charlie felt a little of the air go out of his lungs, "Do you know what you are putting our kids through?"

"I am doing this for my kids," Mariana said, "I want them to grow up knowing their culture."

"Bullshit," Charlie shouted, his patience lost, "just stop with the good Mexican act."

Mariana's eyes narrowed. "You better buy a house down here so you can see Max."

"Will you really separate Max and Oriana?" Charlie said, sitting down and rubbing his eyes, "How cruel can you be?"

"How is she?" Mariana asked, her voice now sounding like a worried mother, "Did her fever go down?"

"Come home and see for yourself."

"Charles!"

"The fever is gone." Charlie said, "She went back to school on Monday."

Mariana's shoulders relaxed. "She's a strong girl."

"She's not going to understand that you and Max are living here." Charlie said.

"Max stays here," she said, waving her hand as if the discussion was over, "You don't separate a mother and her children and that is why you'll bring Oriana. You'll come see them one weekend a month. You'll go live in that big house with Brenda and Nola and marry that little girl of yours and get her pregnant. Start again."

"I'm taking Max." Charlie said, his voice threatening, "Don't try to stop us or you'll never see either of the kids without an armed guard."

"You're in my father's home. Just try." Mariana called as she disappeared into the kitchen, "you won't get out the door alive."

Charlie stood up and started into the kitchen door but Patricia was coming through with an arm full of plates. A bowl began to slide but Charlie grabbed it before it fell to the floor.

"Thank you Charlie," Patricia gasped, "you are always saving me."

Charlie rolled his eyes and placed the bowls on the table. It was always the wrong woman who thought he was a hero. Patricia smiled and kissed his cheek.

"You don't believe me." Patricia said, placing a stack of plates onto the table and straightening the runner, "but you are always there to help when someone needs you."

"Brenda would have skinned us if we didn't do our share," Charlie lied, taking the plates from the stack and handing them to her. Good manners were something he learned from watching old TV sitcoms.

Patricia waved her hand toward the hallway were you could hear the call of a sports announcer from the TV and husky laughter. "My brothers would never help."

Patricia looked toward the kitchen and then motioned for Charlie to hand her more plates. "You know Mariana means well."

"Yeah, practically a saint," Charlie snorted," ready to save the world, accept the Nobel Peace Prize and then beat me to death."

"She goes after what's important to her," Patricia said in a whisper, "sometimes she forgets that people might get hurt."

Charlie leaned over the table and grabbed her hand. "You know Max needs to come home with me."

Patricia stared at Charlie's hand. She gently moved her hand and began to place more plates on the table.

"When Mariana and I were kids, she would argue us down until we were tired of her. She always liked Alejandro's bedroom. It was in the third tower, with rounded walls and a balcony that reminded her of the fairy tale, Rapunzel. One morning, she marched into the room, put all of her things inside, packed Alejandro's clothes and stacked them at the bottom of the stairs. Alejandro was furious. They went back and forth for hours. Yelling and screaming. In the end, Alejandro picked up his clothes and started to bring them to the smaller bedroom on the ground floor. When Senor found out, he demanded that Mariana move Alejandro back into his room. After so many fierce hours of fighting, Mariana didn't even let out a whisper."

"Even when she was a little girl," Charlie said, "she was full of piss and vinegar."

"Not as a little girl." Patricia said, shaking her head, "That was a week ago."

Charlie felt like he was hit in the head. Patricia stood there with a knowing smile. "If I want to take Max, I need Senor on my side."

"It won't be easy." Patricia warned, "All her strong-will comes from my father. Senor has enjoyed having his grandson around. He believes that things are safe here."

"You don't think they are, do you?" Charlie asked.

Patricia hesitated before answering, "No."

Charlie realized that his focus was only on Max but in reality no one was safe. "Come with us Patricia. We'll get you through."

Patricia shook her head. "This is my home."

"Come back when it's safe," Charlie said, scrambling to think how he'd explain this to Kier. He wouldn't object to passing her through as Mariana.

"Decide what you are going to say to Senor," Patricia said, putting her hand on his arm. "If you can't make it clear to Senor that he doesn't make the decisions for your son, then you'll never get out of here in one piece."

Charlie headed toward the front door. He

wanted to update Kier on what he already knew that Mariana was going to be difficult and Patricia offered him some hope to go through Senor.

The front door opened and a large group of women flew inside like an agitated nest of birds. A dozen men followed and turned the front hall into chaos. A silent bell had rung and relatives were coming from all directions toward the dinner hall. It was the perfect confusion to move Max out the door. Charlie let the crowd guide him back to the dining hall. Each one broke off in happy chatter and settled down at the numerous tables. The kids bounced into the hallway and their mothers moved them toward the tables. Charlie spotted Mariana in the kitchen when the door swung open. He only had a limited time to grab Max but with dozens of kids running around, he couldn't find him. His covering crowd was also working against him.

Max spotted Charlie first and attached himself to his leg. Charlie pried him loose and picked him up.

"Want to sit with me?" Charlie asked.

"Uh-huh," Max said rubbing his eyes and resting his head on Charlie's shoulder. He was getting tired which meant a smooth drive with him in the back seat. The front hall, once full of family was starting to thin. His window was closing. He took three steps forward into the hallway when Alejandro entered the front door and looked directly in Charlie's eye as he moved toward him and motioned toward the dining hall.

Charlie spotted a bank of empty chairs at a table close to the front hall. When everyone started eating then he could make it toward the door. He scooted Max into a chair and was about to sit down when Mariana pulled his chair away. She grabbed Max's wrist and helped him up.

"Go sit with your cousins," Mariana said.

Max looked at Charlie in confusion. He put his hand on Charlie's leg.

He wants to sit with me," Charlie said, putting his hand on Max's head and got a small delight at Mariana's reddening face.

"Why? So you can sneak out when my back is turned?" Mariana hissed through her teeth, "not a chance."

Charlie picked Max up. "I haven't seen him in days. It's the longest we've been apart. Can't you let us just eat a meal together?"

Mariana looked at Max's face leaning against Charlie's neck.

"Please Mama?" Max asked, reaching out to touch her face.

Mariana's eyes started to mist and she turned away. When she looked back she gave a big smile to Max and took him from Charlie's arms. She kissed his head and squeezed him tightly. "Of course, Mijo."

The motherly love drained as she looked back at Charlie. "Come with me."

Mariana moved deep into the heart of the floor, weaving around several tables and chairs blocking the aisles. Any chance of an exit would require moving through a maze of relatives, carts of food and strollers with sleeping babies.

Mariana brought them to the main table close to the head. She motioned for a curvy woman who Charlie thought might be Alejandro's wife, Grisella, to move down a few chairs.

Grisella jutted her chin out indignantly but moved over so that three chairs were vacant close to Senor's chair. Even during happy times, Charlie would never have sat this close.

"Are you seriously sitting us next to Senor?" Charlie whispered, "Is he going to be our babysitter?"

Mariana smiled and settled Max in the chair next to her. "I'd understand if you wanted to leave now. Max and I will manage if you need to get back over the border."

Max patted the chair next to him. "Sit next to

me, Daddy."

Bitch. Bitch. Bitch. The words repeated over in Charlie's head like a broken record. No sooner had he sat down when the chairs began to scrape on the tile and everyone stood up.

Stand back up, Daddy," Max's eyes looked down at Charlie and pulled his hand, "Senor can't see you sitting down."

Charlie pushed his chair back to move up but by then it was too late. Senor rounded the corner, escorted by Patricia. He caught sight of Charlie sitting down. Now, even when Charlie stood up, it looked like an act of reluctance and not respect. Mariana looked gleeful.

Not a good way to start out," Charlie thought, "I just made a touchdown on Mariana's team.

It had been a long time since Charlie had seen Senor. He looked the same just a little older, maybe more tired. He forgot that it was a sworn secret that he wore women's boots because they had a higher heel. For such a powerful man, he was very short. The time spent in the field had left his skin like a worn leather of a deep couch. Wrinkles from his cheekbones left deep creases when he shifted his jaw. The creases in his forehead stopped at a widow's peak from slick, deep brown hair. Even at seventy five, his hair didn't have a single, gray strand. The only tell-tale sign of his age was a small patch of white in his neatly trimmed moustache that hung like a heavy curtain above his lip. His eyes were squinty when he spoke. He was too proud to wear glasses which left him blurry and blinded most of the time. He spent longer looking in one direction and was intimidating with his unyielding stare. It gave the impression he was always angry.

It was that stare that focused disapproving at Charlie right now. Charlie nodded at Senor and forced a smile. Senor nodded back and surveyed the table.

"I am a lucky man to be surrounded by so many.

A strong family," Senor said, glancing over at Max. "I am so glad to see my grandson, Maximillian."

Max beamed between his parents and squeezed Charlie's hand. Senor paused before sitting down at his chair.

"I have something to ask Charles." Senor said, nodding to his daughter. "Patricia, translate to him."

"Actually Senor, I-" Charlie started to explain he already understood Spanish if he spoke slowly but Mariana interrupted.

"I can translate for him, Senor." Mariana said, starting to stand up.

Senor shook his head. "I don't want your words coming out instead of mine."

Mariana's face reddened and she immediately began to arrange Max's napkin.

Senor turned to Charlie and motioned for Patricia.

"I will translate for Senor," Patricia said, "if that is alright?"

"Of course," Charlie said, he understood Spanish if spoken slowly but having Patricia move things along was an advantage for him. He wouldn't have trusted Mariana to be fair.

"I want to thank you for allowing Max to come here to spend time with me, Charles," Senor's words were low but Patricia was quick to translate, "I am curious why you did not allow Oriana to join her cousins. We have missed her bright smile."

Charlie looked over at Mariana who avoided his gaze. The entire table was aware of the fight an hour ago except Senor. Could it be that he hadn't been told the truth?

"To be honest, and with the greatest respect to you Senor, I didn't allow Max to come here," Charlie said, watching Mariana's shoulders stiffen, "Mariana brought him down here without my knowledge."

The entire table grew quiet. All small chatter had subsided and Charlie felt a strong desire to drink at that moment.

Senor shifted and leaned over on his arms. "Is this true Mariana?"

Mariana nodded.

Senor's voice was sharp. "Answer when I ask a question."

"Yes, Senor."

"You told me that Charles would be joining you with Oriana later." Senor said.

"Yes Papa." Mariana said, glaring up at Charlie.

"Charles, for what reason did you not want Max to come here?" Senor asked.

Charlie fought the urge to yell the obvious. "There is a lot of violence in the country. The border has closed. It's not safe."

"I can understand your concern. But Max came here days ago," Senor countered, motioning for Patricia to give him a piece of fish. "The borders were free for travel. This cannot be your only reason."

"Senor, the border closing was not the beginning of the trouble," Charlie said, "I have to think of the safety of my-"

"Nonsense, you have your gangs that shoot at each other" Senor interrupted, "There was a little girl that was just run over in a police chase in Chula Vista. This does not bother you?"

"Of course there is violence on each side, Senor but-" Charlie said, wishing he'd been better at debate in school.

"You have seen my home. I provide safety for my family," Senor said calmly, "Nothing gets in without my permission." Senor motioned to pass a pile of tortillas.

"Yes, it's safe."

"Do you not see children playing?" Senor asked.

"Yes- but" Charlie started.

Senor continued to talk over Charlie. Patricia was having trouble keeping up.

"Answer the question," Senor said, "are children happily playing?"

Charlie sighed. "Yes."

"Well then you have nothing to worry about." Senor said, dismissively. He sat down and began to reach for his napkin.

"Senor, the cartel is taking on the government directly. Just to get here was a risk. We saw many people suffering."

Senor frowned. "Things need some shaking sometimes."

"There is danger for your family and all around here."

Senor shook his head and motioned for Grisella to pile some carnitas on his plate. "The cartel does not bother us. The government leaves us alone. Let them fight it out and we'll have a new government more willing to work than the last. Max is safe here."

The family grumbled and nodded in agreement. They kept their heads focused on their plate in front of them but occasionally an eye would look up at Charlie with accusation.

There were a lot of bad things happening every day on both sides. There was no winning on domestic affairs. But Charlie needed to get his point across. He needed Senor to see his point of view otherwise Kier would take over. People were going to get hurt.

Senor looked up and waved his hand toward Charlie, "Sentado... sit."

Charlie gritted his teeth. He wasn't a loyal dog lying down by his side. Senor continued eating his food. His daughters catered to him and his son sat with their wives on further down. If he was going to leave tonight without trouble, he had to establish his own place at the table. Kier wouldn't just stand there. He'd take all the space and get the attention of everyone in the room.

Charlie pushed himself back from the table causing the chair to scrape along the tile. The clatter from plates and whiny babies drowned out the effect.

"You don't get to tell me how to raise my son."

All eyes lifted and moved to Senor. Senor stopped his knife in mid-air and then slammed it down on the plate, tipping his beer into a plate of carne asada. Patricia tried to save the flow but Senor swung her away as if he was waving away a gnat.

Senor glared at Charlie. "You are a guest in my house."

Senor's voice startled Max and he grabbed onto Charlie's hand.

All eyes were a spotlight on Charlie. He felt the tension rising hot against his neck. If he backed down now, he would lose all respect. If he didn't back down he was going to get a beating from Mariana's brothers. Charlie tried to think about what Kier would do at this minute.

"Do you really think I would let a dirty bean herder raise my son?" Charlie said, hearing Brenda's voice spewing out of his mouth. Kier used racial slurs and Charlie dismissed him as ignorant, coming out of his mouth they sounded unnatural. Why did he think it made him sound in control? It was too late to take it back, the damage was done.

The color in Senor's face told him that Charlie's words didn't need to be interpreted. He knew enough English to know when he was insulted, if he didn't, Mariana's brothers didn't have any problem with their English. They moved quickly from their chairs and were quickly behind Charlie, shouts roared around him.

Charlie felt his legs go out from underneath him and he was pulled by his neck and arms away from the table. Senor was yelling rapidly, too fast for Charlie to understand.

Charlie reached down for Max but he was gone. From underneath an arm circling his head he could see Mariana was carrying Max into the kitchen. Patricia was following behind them but looked back at him.

"Get Kier," Charlie gasped, as the arm tightened. He couldn't be sure if she heard him. His focus was on the searing pain of his toe crushing against the tiles and he wasn't walking with his own power. Arms and hands were grabbing him and pulling him out down the hall, he felt a punch to the back of his head.

It could have been comical, the beginning of a funny story you would tell at a bar except these stories always ended with a release from jail or the hospital.

Heavy feet and curses rumbled in Spanish seemed to be carrying him into the ruined family room Lourdes used to cherish. Charlie was able to look up when he was thrown onto the floor. There were at least ten men around him and several more that were gathering at the openings. A short, but solid man held him by his neck. He had a thick goatee and steely eyes that fixed on him. It was difficult to be sure but Charlie thought he recognized him as one of his former brother in laws. Oscar? Oscelio? He couldn't be sure. Charlie was surrounded on all sides by angry eyes looking at him. Hands grabbed at him as if they each wanted an opportunity to beat him. There was a lot of indecision about what to do with Charlie. The Spanish was rapid and hard to keep up but from what he could determine, no one knew what they should do with him. Some insisted they send him back to the US, others wanted to beat some respect into him but most wanted to do both.

What Charlie knew for certain, he needed help. When the hands began to shift, he gasped for a much needed breath but spent it on preservation. "Kier!"

"Shut up, pendejo," the brother in law who might be named Oscar said. He grabbed Charlie by the neck and pulling him toward the edge of the couch, landing on the couch and tumbling to the floor. Charlie quickly scrambled toward a wall and braced against as he was surrounded by dozens of boots.

A rumble came from the back and voices began to rise higher a familiar voice broke above them all.

"Get the fuck out of my way!"

A large arm pulled through and Kier's face, fierce with frustration, floated between the bodies until Charlie felt a release on his arm and was then being pulled up by the Aussie.

"What did you do to these people?" Kier yelled, trying to be heard over all the chatter.

"Later," Charlie said, rubbing the growing welt on his arm, "Mariana doesn't want to release Max."

"Well he ain't fucking staying here," Kier grumbled, "What direction did they take him?"

Kier slid back his vest to show the glint of a smuggled knife. Charlie put his hand up. "No, there are kids and women back there and you'll scare them."

"Got any other brilliant ideas?" Kier growled, "Each of these bean planters wants to refry your head."

"Will you stop with the bean jokes? It's your fault I got in this mess to begin with."

"Me?" Kier protested, "I was minding my business at the limo."

"You filled my head with too much of that racist crap," Kier shouted, "I couldn't think straight and I called Senor a bean herder."

"I don't know if I should laugh or kill you," Kier shook his head. "I may say a lot of things but I don't have the balls to call the head of the family a bean herder in front of his own kin."

Charlie spotted Alejandro coming into the room. He knew that this one familiar face was the only thing that could save him. He nudged Kier to try to move him through the crowd. In the arguing, no one was paying attention to what he was doing. With some carefully planned maneuvers from Kier, Charlie was still not in close distance to reach Alejandro.

"This is the closest I can get without really hurting anyone. They ain't letting you go any further." Kier yelled, "if you got a plan, you better do it now."

"Alejandro!" Charlie's voice barely carried over

the crowd," I need to speak with Senor again."

Alejandro shook his head. Charlie felt the crowd shift again and Alejandro's face disappeared.

"That is your big idea? You want another chance to insult his Old Man? Brilliant." Kier said, moving Charlie out from the middle of three more cousins, "If all you want is to talk to the Old Man, I can make that happen."

"He's not going to listen to me if you storm in there." Charlie argued, "I need someone close to talk with him."

"Alright," Kier said, "stay here."

"Where the hell are you going?" Charlie yelled as Kier disappeared into the crowd. Charlie found himself pushed back again and flipped onto the couch. His head rested on the lap of a large bellied relative with a tattoo of the name "Al" on his neck.

"What the fuck you doing, cabron?" the relative growled.

"I'm leaving...really soon, Al." Charlie said, trying to roll himself to the ground.

"Al? Al's my brother."

"Oh, you both look so much alike," Charlie said, trying to move quicker, "I get you confused all the time."

"I'm Norte. Al's been dead five years, mother fucker." Norte pushed Charlie by the face and he fell hard on the floor, narrowly missing his head getting smashed by a boot. A hand pulled hard on Charlie's arm and he was able to get his head above the crowd only to be face to face with Norte.

"Max belongs with Mariana," Norte said, his hand pushed Charlie back and he cracked his knuckles, "What kind of man takes a kid away from his mama?"

"He's not the one that kidnapped him," Kier's voice shot over Norte's meaty head. Norte turned his head so that Charlie could see Kier standing on the other side.

"We'll start by beating the shit out of you,"

Norte said to Kier, "You don't come into Senor's house and disrespect him."

The more Norte spoke, Kier grinned wider with every word.

"Something wrong with your face?" Norte snorted, "You some sort of retard?"

Kier laughed and started to rock on his heels. Charlie knew that wasn't a good sign. He shot him a look to keep calm. Norte intercepted the exchange.

"Yeah, that's right," Norte said, leaning on Charlie's shoulder," Keep your wolf on a leash."

Kier's lip curled and he snarled. He tilted his head and howled.

"Kier," Charlie warned, watching as ten other men entered now filling the entrance.

"I see them," Kier said, "I've got it covered."

That wasn't what worried Charlie. Kier could handle himself but Charlie hadn't had to hit anyone since high school. It was easier to talk his way out of things. If Kier started something, Charlie had only two fists to back him up. There were one hundred other pairs in this room.

"Guess we know your breed," Norte laughed and settled his large belly on the arm of the couch, "Charlie's got himself a bitch."

That was all Kier needed and he swung forward and his right fist hit Norte's fleshy jowl, knocking him off balance. Norte's feet flew upward and kicked a cousin in the neck.

A warrior cry came from the corner and soon Kier was being pounded by three of the larger family. Charlie jumped to his feet before a fist pounded the wall near him. Charlie raised his arm to fend off any blows and then reached for one of the hefty arms flying up to punch Kier. He held the left arm back but then felt tight knuckles meet with his jaw. The pain made his skull shake and he felt a burning coming from another blow to his back. Charlie started to swing and landed a few punches.

A high pitched whistle shot through the room and everyone froze like some school playground shuffle.

Alejandro was standing on the landing. He glared at everyone in the room. It was enough to make family back away. Kier shot up, his lips bloodied and left eye half-shut. He poked at his left temple which was already discoloring. He stumbled but was able to steady himself.

Alejandro shook his head in disgust. He motioned to Charlie. "Go down the hall and first door on the right."

The crowd protested but Alejandro put his hand up. "Get him up here. It's over."

Charlie was pushed forward until he faced Alejandro. "Thanks for the help."

"If it were up to me, you'd be beat and dumped out with your General friend," Alejandro whispered into Charlie's ear, his fist balled and sticking in Charlie's side, "Senor told me he wants to see you. That's the only reason that all your ribs aren't broken."

Any sign of friendliness toward Charlie was gone from Alejandro's face. Charlie just insulted his father and was trying to hurt his sister. No words were going to change how he felt. Kier started up to the landing but Alejandro put up his hand. "Alone."

"I'll be back," Charlie said.

"I think this is a shitty idea," Kier warned.

"It's the only shitty idea we've got," Charlie said and continued up. Kier stopped and leaned against a wooden viga.

"Get him something to clean himself up." Alejandro motioned to someone to bring Kier a towel for the cut on his head. He observed the band of men still piled on the floor." What's wrong with you? We don't do this in Senor's house."

Chapter Twelve

The study was a place that Charlie had only heard about. It was built in the north tower. Books circled up three stories to a huge atrium carved with wood stairways. Lourdes had been an avid reader and had insisted all of her children read all the classics.

When most of his kids were in high school, Senor became disgusted with their poor grades and brought the sons to Mazatlán. Senor had left school in eighth grade. If his sons weren't going to learn, then they would work. Lourdes kept the girls with her and hired a tutor. They spent an entire year learning from the library that Lourdes had collected.

Senor was staring out a stained glass window. It looked just like the ones that lined the back stairway in the house in La Jolla. It had been a request to the decorator that Mariana would not compromise when building their house. Charlie and Mariana had fought over every detail of the construction. The cost was ridiculous and Mariana could not come up with a practical reason. She had managed to put some part of her childhood in the house. If she had told Charlie in the first place, they could have saved an argument.

Patricia sat in a chair next to the desk. She smiled when she saw Charlie and motioned for him to sit down. Charlie looked over at Senor to make sure this was permitted. Perhaps it was a test for control and he would lose ground if he didn't stand. Senor lifted his head slightly and sighed. He waved his arm toward the chair in front of a large wooden desk. Patricia gestured again, impatiently. Charlie eased himself in the chair which forced his back to stiffen with the uncomfortable wooden spine.

"Senor asked me to interpret for you," Patricia said, patting her father's hand, "he asks that you will listen to what he wants to say."

"Of course," Charlie said, shifting his weight to rest a shoulder on the back of the leather, "but I would like to say something first."

Patricia hesitated but then nodded.

"Senor, I apologize for disrespecting you. I did come to your home. I don't know where those words came from." Charlie said, wishing he could stand up from the horrible chair, "I am not a man who believes in labeling people and I was frustrated to get your attention. That was wrong of me."

Patricia repeated the words. Senor nodded as he listened, his expression never changing. The words hung in the air and silence was filling up the room. Charlie wondered if Senor was looking for more. He was about to open his mouth when Senor began to speak.

"I accept your apology," Senor said, "You do not come into a man's house and give him orders at his own table. I can forget that for now. I want to talk with you about your family. I imagine with all the trouble you have changed your mind about living in Mexico?"

Patricia looked down at her hands as Charlie tried to process what Senor was asking. Had Mariana been telling the same lie to everyone? That the whole family was just packing up and moving down here to live in the Ranch? What Charlie wanted to say was that he never would live in Mexico but he had to think what was going to get him out of here with Max.

"That is correct, Senor. I do not think it is safe to live here."

Senor nodded. "You Americans always think that things are so much better in the North. Mexico is a beautiful country. We have so much to offer and yet all you want to do is use our beaches, buy a few souvenirs and then head back with some survival story. My country is filled with proud people. We have fought off European domination just like the Americans. We have pyramids as reminders of civilizations that were beyond their years. Yet... all you see are a violent and backward people."

"Senor, I don't know what Mariana has told you," Charlie said, "I am only here for my son. I am not passing judgment on Mexico or its history."

"Mariana is my daughter. So I know she is stubborn," Senor said, pausing to cough, "She is difficult to steer in another course other than the one she wants."

Charlie didn't bother to nod. His opinion, even if he agreed, did not really matter right now. It might even provoke an argument if he was too enthusiastic. Senor was going to sit there and lecture him like a punished child. Charlie didn't care as long as the end result was Max leaving.

Senor coughed again and then continued.

"When she was seventeen, Mariana insisted that she wanted to go to school up North. I refused. I did not want her so far away. I was born and raised in Mazatlán. That is where my children were born. She didn't belong in another country. Mariana wanted to be on the coast in California. I wanted us all together and forbid her to leave. Soon, Mariana had all my children rioting at my door to grant her the chance to go. Even my wife insisted on a vacation home in Baja. I could not refuse my wife. By September, Mariana was living with a family friend in Tijuana and going to college in San Diego. By December, she was telling me about a man she had met. A year later she is letting me know she intends to marry this man. Not ask me. Tell me. And he is not Mexican. He is white but that is okay because he is Southern.

Senor paused to glare at Charlie. He reached for a crystal cask of tequila and poured into a ceramic cup. He took a quick gulp and continued.

"I did not know what Southern was. What I learned was a trouble part of your country's history where white men fought to secede against their country, who kept slaves and segregated the blacks."

Charlie shifted uneasily in his chair. He stared at the cask and wished he could down the whole thing.

"Well, that isn't really true about today, Senor-" Charlie said, "I can't be responsible for something that happened before I was born."

Senor raised his hand up in irritation and continued to talk over Charlie. "So I was extremely upset to think that my daughter was going to go with such a man to live."

"Senor," Charlie tried to interrupt, "I am not a slave owner. Your daughter didn't leave you to be pampered on a plantation. You know your daughter would not allow that to happen."

"And yet, she has been sitting in your home having babies and doing nothing with the education she earned. It is only in the last few years that she has begun to use that degree to help her people." Senor yelled, slamming his fist down on the desk. The rumble echoed into the rafters. Charlie gave up and settled back in his chair. "I was very upset by what I heard. I asked Lena to find out some information about this man. Maybe I will have him killed and then he can't keep my Mariana."

Charlie boiled at the words. Senor was making Mariana look like she was a helpless prisoner kept in his house. Was he serious about wanting him killed? He looked up at Senor whose eyes were serious but he had a slight smile curl under his moustache.

Senor continued. "But then I learned that this man my Mariana loves put himself through college and started his own business when he was only twenty, that he had been living on the streets making a living as a musician and turned his talents into one of the ten most successful businesses in the country. This was a man who worked from nothing and built it into everything. He had worked hard for everything in his life. Nothing had been given to him. I knew that for such a man to want my Mariana then he had worked hard to deserve her loyalty. He also knew she was valued because her love was not given easily."

Senor paused and picked up the cask again. He poured more tequila into his ceramic mug and then grabbed a glass. He handed Charlie a deep curved azure glass filled to the brim and raised his mug before tilting it back. Charlie eyed the glass filled with the equivalent of five shots of tequila and looked at Senor. Senor waited for him to catch up so raised the glass and felt the cool liquid set fire to his throat. It settled in his stomach and burned like a fireball.

Senor nodded with approval and reached for the glass back to pour again. "My daughter does not want to part with her son." Senor said.

Charlie sat straighter in the chair. "Senor, I am not here to negotiate about Max."

Senor handed him another full glass. "I do not want to part with my grandson."

Charlie placed the glass down. He did not want to be unclear about his intentions and he could already feel warmth obscuring some of the edges. "Getting me drunk isn't going to change my mind."

"My grandson needs to go back with you." Senor interrupted and tilted back the mug again.

Charlie thought he had heard wrong. "Are you trying to confuse me? You say Max needs to be here but then needs to go?"

Senor frowned and stroked his moustache. "Things are bad right now. Mariana was unwise to come. She came because I told her I needed her and I was selfish. I wanted my children with me. Since my wife died, I have missed their company."

Charlie sat in silence afraid to say anything that would change Senor's mood. He watched the old man's eyes become soft and red as the tequila revived a memory. Senor moved his sleeve over his eyes and turned away. "Mariana is not going to want him to go. She will not go herself. Max will be brought to you and then you must leave. No goodbyes. I will handle Mariana. When things are more settled here, then you will consider bringing him back?"

No chance in hell, Charlie thought. He'd never give her a chance to keep him but tonight he would keep the peace. "I will consider it."

Senor nodded and motioned to Patricia. "She will bring Max to the side gate. Get your dog...or wolf... out of here and tell him to drive straight to the border."

Patricia helped Senor stand, the tequila now taking its toll. He reached for Charlie's hand and gave it a firm squeeze.

"Thank you Senor," Charlie said, trying to think of the right words to say. He reached for the glass of tequila to give him inspiration.

By the time Charlie thought of more, Senor was already out the door.

Patricia turned to Charlie and breathed a sigh of relief.

"I know you had something to do with this." Charlie said quietly, "you saved me from making this a real mess."

Patricia shrugged. "I did nothing."

Charlie stood up and leaned into her. The tequila was now making his tongue loosen. "Mariana may get her way but you are the old man's quiet voice. I know he wouldn't have agreed to meet me without your help."

Patricia pulled the door closed to shield from any unexpected guests in the hallway. "I am sure that Mariana will not forgive me."

"She'll understand," Charlie said, at a weak attempt to be reassuring, "eventually."

Patricia frowned and bit her lower lip, repressing the urge to say something more. She pointed to a small door near the windows. "There's some stairs on the right. They'll take you to the outside to a path by the garages. I'll tell Kier to bring Max there."

Charlie gave her a kiss on her cheek and waited until Patricia closed the door behind her. It was almost over. Just meet Kier and Max and head up the coast. His watch read 9:30. There would be some processing of the paperwork but that would be in the safety of a border station. It was going to be early in the morning to get past the border but he would be home in time to put Max in bed and then take Lisa for an early breakfast.

He checked his phone. The signal bars were gone and it was running out of juice but he had enough time to see the smiling picture of Oriana and Max blur at the edge of the screen. He noticed Mariana's arm holding Max and he remembered the day it was taken. It was the last Fourth of July they spent as a family and he felt an old familiar pain hit his chest. It had dulled through time but occasionally it could still poke through his ribcage. He watched the picture disappear as the energy finally drained from the phone. Allowing for air to expand his chest, he headed through the door. Things were definitely blurring but he found there wasn't a pain that didn't dull with the right amount of tequila.

It's almost over.

Chapter Thirteen

Charlie opened the door into a path covered with hanging trellis of bougainvillea. Their pink and peach flowers peeked from the thorns but it was the jasmine that filled the air. The thick leaves and delicate white blossoms clung around the shrubs that led toward the coast. A memory of meeting Senor for the first time came forward. Mariana had brought him back through here. She wanted him to wait in the backyard until she had time to talk to him. Charlie remembered thinking it was a bad idea to meet on the ledge. If Senor or her brothers didn't like the situation, it would be easy to just throw him off. There had been some joke that Charlie would only fall on the beach and it would be too messy to clean up.

Charlie looked down the path toward the garages. He paused and looked out toward the sky, the clouds covering the sky were too thick to just be marine layer. A chilling wind was coming from the ocean that made the hairs stand on end. He began to feel along the wall toward the garages. This area was only lit by small lights to accentuate the plants. It was always meant to be an area to be seen and not traveled.

Where is Patricia? Charlie thought, tapping at the wall. The tequila had already taken him beyond comfortable and now he was starting to feel paranoid. Maybe Senor had changed his mind? What if Mariana had found out and had left with Max? He was about to pull open the door when he heard crunching on the gravel. The shadows grew darker and then took shape. Max stumbled slightly and a tattooed arm steadied him. He felt immediate relief when he saw Kier.

Max's face came closer and Charlie could see a watery trail reflecting down his cheek. "You okay, Max?"

"I thought you left without me," Max said, his voice full of tears.

Charlie knelt down and pulled Max close and whispered. "I'm not going anywhere without you."

Max smiled and pulled at his back pack. "Kier brought Penguino."

Charlie nodded. "I told you he was here."

Max squeezed the stuffed penguin and tried to control a sniff as he looked up at Kier. "I'm cold."

"Yeah, there's a storm coming," Kier said, fidgeting in his jacket and pulled out his lighter and a pack of cigarettes.

"Senor said to take off and he'll deal with Mariana," Charlie said. Kier nodded but his head was glancing all around.

"What's in your head?"

Kier sighed and gave a low whistle. "I'm just keeping my wits. There are some strange things going on around here."

"Yeah, we're in the middle of a war zone."

Kier shrugged. "That's just it. All the security that was up front is only about half now."

"Maybe they wanted to give us a show when we got here but now they've backed off."

Kier blew smoke up in the air and seemed deep in thought. "Let's get the fuck out of here."

Max looked up at Kier with surprise. "That's a bad word Uncle Kier."

Kier looked down at Max and tousled his hair.

"Sorry Little Man. I forget sometimes. I'll wash my mouth out with soap later."

Max scrunched his face. "Why don't you just stop saying that word?"

Kier laughed and picked him up. "You've got a real smart one on your hands, Chuck."

Kier carried Max ahead of Charlie and they made their way around the back of the garages. Kier moved easily through the path. Charlie had fifteen minutes to get his eyes accustomed to the dark and he still clutched the wall.

"You know Little Man, I think you're getting too big to carry," Kier said, he hoisted Max down so he could walk on his own, "do you weigh five hundred pounds?"

"I'm getting big!" Max said proudly, "It's my birthday in five days!"

"How old you going to be? Eighteen? Twenty-five?" Kier teased, he scanned the next part of the path and seemed pre-occupied by the upper rim of the wall.

"No!" Max said, giggling, "I'm going to be five!"

"Five? No way! Kier said, taking Max's arm and leading him to his side as they rounded the corner of the garage. "You're as big as—"

Kier stopped and pulled Max so hard that he jerked back like on a short leash.

"Uncle Kier-" Max cried out but Kier put his hand over his mouth and picked him up in his arms. He backed up so quickly that Charlie fell back against the wall, knocking his head on a planter.

"Get back," Kier hissed. He pushed hard past Charlie and began to move quickly down the lane, "Now, damn it!"

Worry was something that Charlie had never seen on Kier before. Within a few seconds, Kier had rushed them around the back of the house, past the trellises and down the pathway. Kier pushed through the bushes and past the fence that Senor had put up to keep the children away from the cliff. They traveled along the landscape until the smooth grass no longer blended with the dirt and weeds. Kier pushed Charlie toward the edge of the bluff almost knocking him off balance as he peered over the edge.

"Get down on that ledge and wait."

"There isn't a ledge down there," Charlie protested, "What's going on?"

Before Kier could say anything, he had picked up Max by the arm and was lowering him off the side. Max shrieked in fear as he fought to come back up.

"Jesus Kier! Hold on a minute!" Charlie yelled, holding onto Max's legs and awkwardly feeling for a hole or something for Max to put his feet. Max began to cry.

"It's just a game, Little Man. Like hide and seek, Kier whispered and gave a quick smile, "You're going to stay down here until I come back for you."

Max sniffed. "Daddy, are you going to stay with me?"

"Yeah Max, I'm coming down." Charlie said, turning to face the house. The music had stopped and there were lights turning out upstairs.

"Kier? What is happening in there?"

Kier shook his head. "There's no time. Get to the ledge. Don't say anything. Keep Max quiet. I'll be back soon."

Kier looked over the cliff again. "Change of plan. The beach isn't that far so climb down and start walking north. I'll get a car and come find you."

Charlie peered over the rounded lip of the cliff. Despite a ledge that seemed to leave footing for a small child, it was a sheer drop to a pocket of sand that was losing ground with the waves. "What the hell are you talking about? That's almost fifty feet down!"

Kier grabbed him hard by the arm and pulled him down. "Don't fuck with me right now. Do what I say. Keep your feet digging into the dirt. They'll provide you temporary balance and then grab onto the rocks as they come by. Keep Max tight on your left leg and he'll anchor you. It's the only way."

Charlie felt a chill run through his neck. "What did you see Kier?"

"This is a set-up. I don't know what's going to happen in there. Do what I say and I'll meet you up the way."

It occurred to Charlie that he wasn't the only one at risk. He had pulled Mariana's family into this. "I need to stay and help."

Kier shoved Charlie so hard that he lost balance and teetered over the edge of the cliff. Charlie looked backward at the black liquid of the ocean as his sky. Charlie felt his arm wrench as Kier pulled him back up to clutch the cliff. Max clung to Charlie's leg and let out a small cry as his arm got pinned against the pressure.

Charlie peered up to the top and could only see Kier's head. "Damn it Kier! If I caused this I need to help."

A woman's scream echoed from the house and suddenly several pops pierced the air. A growing wall of fierce cries and angry shouts as Kier's face peered down. "No one can be helped right now. Just survive."

And Kier was gone.

Charlie clung to the cliff and stared out at the black water moving parallel to him. He listened to the heavy fall of Kier's feet crunching above him until they faded into the sound of the waves. The wind gave a sharp blast and Max shivered.

Charlie carefully touched Max's head. "It's okay Max."

"I don't like this game. I want Mama."

"I do too," Charlie said softly. He felt frozen and foolish as he tried to figure out what to do. Kier knew best but how was he going to climb down a cliff with a four year old in the dark? Maybe he could inch up to the top and keep heading down the coast. But what was happening up there? Was he putting them in danger to be seen?

There had to be an easier answer.

The waves had increased and the wind was making it difficult to hear anything. An angry howl would fill his ears but he couldn't tell if this was just the wind. What seemed like an hour, Charlie heard the crunching above. Some gravel slipped onto his head. He tried to move his head up to see, "Kier?"

"Did you say something?" A deep voice came from top in Spanish. Charlie's heart stopped. Was it Alejandro? It wasn't Senor. Charlie put his hand over Max's mouth.

"What the fuck did I say?" A higher voice returned in Spanish.

Charlie looked up to see two forms directly above their heads on the ledge.

"Hate the wind out here. Makes it sound like there's some ghost. We need to finish up and go."

There was low laughter. "You scared of ghosts?"

"Yeah, I'm scared of 'em," Deep Voice said defensively.

"You think that Dracula going to suck your blood too?"

"Hey- they're real!" Deep Voice said angrily, "I fucking see them everywhere."

"Bullshit."

"That kid on Ave. Remember the one with the tattoo of that girl with the bird?"

"Rogelio's cousin, Norberto, the bug eye kid."

"Yeah, well he was waiting for me in bathroom two nights ago. I got up to take a piss and he was lying in my bathtub. His throat cut exactly like I left him."

"You're hallucinating pendejo! You need to stop smoking so much shit before you go to bed!"

"No! He was there! Staring up at me! I fucking pissed all over the floor. I could hear him gasping out of that hole- trying to breath- he was trying to pull himself up on the faucet and he knocked over the soap onto my foot. He was close to me I could smell him! Reached to grab my knife and when I looked up he was gone!"

"See! It was just you dreaming!"

"No because the soap was still lying on the bathroom floor next to the toilet."

"How would you know what soap looks like? You ain't had a bath since your baptism."

"Fuck you."

"No! Stop this shit. You start talking like this around anyone else and they're going to put a bullet in your empty skull. Fucking junkie. No more talking about Norbert, got it? Anyone else out here?"

"We're done," Deep Voice grumbled.

"No, we can't find them. They might have gotten out."

"Where? In the ocean? What'd they do? Fly away?"

"You better hope we can find them. If someone killed them on accident. Don't want to be them."

"Well no one out here."

"Then come back, we need to finish up. There's still some work to be done."

"Orders are no one else left alive. Come on, take pride in your work."

The voices laughed and the crunching faded.

Chapter Fourteen

Charlie inched Max down on his leg and steadied him on a precarious clump of sand and rock just below him. Once he was sure that Max was not going to slip, Charlie slid down, reaching up and pulling Max down. Charlie started the process again. Moving Max down his leg, blindly finding a clearing to keep Max secure enough that he could move past him and begin again. Charlie could hear the waves crashing but there was no way to know what was below them. If he dropped Max he could cut himself on a pile of jagged rocks or a strong wave that could pull a small boy out with the tide.

Time passed in agony. The air carried sounds to Charlie's ears. There was suffering going on above. He dared not look up to confirm the reality. His imagination was torturing his mind with images that he couldn't let go.

Charlie put his foot down into a wet pool of sand that filled his shoe. A layer of cloudy marine film cloaked them from the landing above. It shielded more than a few feet ahead of them on the beach. How far did it go? It didn't matter, Charlie need to put as much distance as possible between them and the Ranch. He needed to find a place to hide where Kier would find them. Charlie grabbed Max's hand and plunged them into darkness.

Charlie and Max moved quickly down the beach. The only sounds he could hear were the waves and a hum. It was a piercing sound like a tuner that grew louder in Charlie's head. It tilted his head up like a marionette as his rubbery legs flopped in front of each other.

Max looked up at Charlie and then back to the Ranch. He pulled on Charlie's leg and was speaking but all Charlie could hear was the piercing sound. He felt panic begin to rise from his feet and paralyze his body. It seized his chest-pumping his heart, ferocious and raising it into his throat. The screams were coming back in a mad rush. They rose to his stomach and hurled the tequila around like a hurricane.

Charlie looked down at Max's face, his eyes fearfully looking at him, his mouth moving but Charlie's ears were deaf. Charlie squinted at his moving lips, trying to read them. He pieced the words together and they came screaming at full volume.

"What about Mommy?"

Charlie felt something break and he ran toward the ocean- he felt his stomach lurched and all the tequila spilled out into the foam.

"Daddy, you're hurting me!"

Charlie tried to release his grip but Max was the one that pulled his hand away. Charlie reached for him and picked the struggling child into his arms as he felt his chest heave and then fell to the ground.

"Are you okay, Daddy?" Max asked his tiny voice breaking," Where's Mommy?"

Charlie stared at the sky and then back at the fear in Max's eyes. What was he supposed to say? What if she had gotten out? Kier was with her. He may not care for her but he could protect her, couldn't he? He couldn't release images of Mariana hurt. Her eyes exposed and dress covered in blood. It struck him cold and he began to shake his body to release the chill.

"Mommy is going to catch up with us," Charlie said, straightening Max's shirt as if it even mattered right now, "Kier and Mommy are together and will come soon."

Max strained to look down the beach and pointed his finger. "I see them."

Charlie looked in the direction of the Ranch. Two beams of light floated on the marine layer like combatting lighthouses on the beach. Ten more appeared at the top of the bluff. He picked up Max and began to run down the beach.

"Wait! Daddy! Mommy's behind us!" Max protested.

"We're playing a game, Max," Charlie gasped as he sand shifted beneath his feet, "Kier and Mommy are trying to catch us!"

"I don't want to play right now" Max said.

"Just for a little bit," Charlie huffed, "I don't want to be "It.""

Max's weight grew heavy as he struggled to get down. Charlie lost his grasp and Max slid down his leg. He tried to grab his hand but Max broke free and began to run back toward the Ranch.

"You can't catch us!" Max yelled, raising his hands and jumping around.

Charlie caught up with him and covered Max's mouth, dragging him the other direction. Max's eyes were wide and Charlie gasped to catch his breath. "More like Hide and Seek. We have to be quiet."

"Okay," Max whispered,

Charlie picked up Max again and began to run forward. He glanced only for a moment behind them. The beams of light were dancing above the sky. It seemed like they were getting two steps closer with every step they moved away.

Charlie and Max kept walking until he couldn't see any lights behind him anymore. Kier had said he'd find them but so could anyone else. The beach was foggy and black but no place to hide if someone came close.

A glimpse of a wooden plank in his right eye

made Charlie stop. He almost missed the washed out stairway leading back up the bluff. Its bottom steps had worn away from the tide. Charlie grasped the rickety outline of the rail and heaved Max onto the landing, a chunk of wood splintered into his palm forcing him to regain position.

"I don't want to play anymore," Max grumbled, "I'm cold."

"Just a little longer Max," Charlie said, his voice catching with a bitter sweep of wind, "We're going to win right?"

"They can't find us," Max said, straining to look down the beach.

"They'll be up on top?" Charlie picked up Max again and he rested his head heavily on Charlie's shoulder. "I know you're tired Max. I am too."

"I don't want to walk anymore," Max said, yawning.

Charlie scanned. "We need to find Kier."

"My feet hurt." Max whimpered.

"Pretty soon, we'll be in a nice warm car," Charlie said, rubbing Max's back, it always calmed him as a baby, "You can sleep all the way home."

Max nodded and snuggled deeper into Charlie's neck.

The landing came out into a gravel lot with an abandoned horse rental shack. The door to the shack was open and Charlie considered it as a place to hide but it was too obvious.

Charlie made his way across the gravel and toward the buttress of the highway overpass. It wasn't the best but he could see down the singular road that led from the Ranch to get on the Highway. Anyone returning to Tijuana had to pass through here. The highway supports were pocked with chunks of missing concrete. Charlie couldn't tell if the rubble left on the ground was from decay or violence. He found a "Y" shaped crevice that was smooth enough to lay a sleeping child. With a clear view of the road, Charlie placed Max in the crook of the Y buttress and tried to get feeling in his arms. They throbbed from Max's weight and he cold. It didn't feel anything like the ache tearing into his heart. He could keep a look out of anyone coming to the south.

Come on Kier, Charlie thought, unable to stop feeling anxious.

"Where is Kier?" Max asked, he lifted his head, rubbing a left eye with a clutched fist.

"He'll be here soon," Charlie said, noticing Max was shivering. He put his jacket on top of him and gently pushed Max's head onto the plank, "it will be over soon."

Max cried out and tried to scramble off the buttress. "Penguino's gone!"

Charlie felt the tension rise in his voice, "We can't get him right now!"

"But he needs me! We must have left him on the beach!" Max whimpered.

Charlie felt his nerves rubbed raw. "Max, someday you're going to have to learn that we can't always have our way! We can't get him right now!"

Max's eyes started to water.

"What?" Charlie yelled.

"He's scared and cold," Max whispered.

Charlie looked blankly at the frightened face. He put his arm around Max and hugged him tightly. "Mommy will bring him okay?"

Max sniffed but was pacified for now. He squirmed in the space but soon had closed his eyes and had fallen asleep.

Charlie slid against the wood and tried to keep his eyes from closing. They had been walking for hours or it could be minutes but his customized, expensive watch didn't come with a light or GPS. He felt his eyes grow heavy with every blink but he was afraid he might miss Kier passing on the road, so much depended on him keeping his eyes wide. He tried to scan each direction of the dark road and keep the beach stairs in view, from every angle could be danger or salvation but two eyes were impossible to watch every direction. Charlie could no longer tell if his eyes were staring at the back of his lids or into the dark sky. He found himself leaning against the wall and his eyelids unable to deny him sleep.

Chapter Fifteen
Basin Street Club- Downtown San Diego

When Remi Parrish walked in Basin Street, it didn't take long to find Lisa. He looked for where all the men could get a full view. It was not a surprise that she sat at the bar, like a center spotlight was shining on her. Her muscular legs were bronzed and perfect as they crossed on the bar stool. Her face was turned to look at the TV above, all the curves were partially hidden by ebony silk that encased two of the most perfectly firm breasts that rested above a small waist; she was a supermodel jumping off a magazine with not a strand of her shimmering, black hair out of place as it hung down her toned, bronze back. If this was the first time they had met, he would have invested heavy charm and every minute up to last call to make sure he was the one to take her home, but Remi didn't lock eyes with Lisa in a bar and they weren't strangers that could overlook imperfections.

Two years ago, Lisa walked inside Basin Street. She walked past the hostess and found Charlie and Remi enjoying drinks at the bar. Flashing a "Pick Me" smile, Lisa put the resume in Charlie's hands. Her breasts were bursting out of a green low-cut sweater that showed a flawless bronze tan. The girl knew how to work what she had.

Lisa wanted to be the head chef for Basin

Street. She expected an interview with Charlie personally. It was cute actually, Charlie was amused at the twenty-something girl that looked like a super model standing there with all her confidence. Lisa's looks made her the poster girl that drew you inside for the real attraction. Charlie got serious when he read her resume.

Lisa's first job was working in her father's popular Filipino restaurant in National City when she was seven. She was running his kitchen at twelve. At sixteen, she graduated high school and went off to chef school in San Francisco. She spent three years working as a sous chef for Bobbie Flay. Charlie hired her on the spot.

Remi knew Lisa liked Charlie but he was married and even though Mariana was making Charlie's life hell on earth, he'd never cheat, so Remi asked her out. He took a chance that she would be impressed by his successful attorney practice and co-ownership of Basin Street.

Lisa didn't want to go for dinner or a walk on the beach. He drove her to Barona Casino and gave her a stack of cash to play Blackjack which she doubled and didn't share in the wealth. He took her to see the view of the Coronado Bridge at his downtown condo and she gave him the most mind blowing sex he had ever thought possible. Without a doubt, the best lay he'd ever had in his life but it was only going to be one date.

Lisa put the Basin Street kitchen between them with no apologies or polite excuses. She didn't want to get tangled with someone who wasn't going to give her what she wanted in life. She didn't see a future with him.

A long weekend and a very expensive call girl later, Remi recovered. He figured it wouldn't matter anymore since she was always in the kitchen at Basin Street and never came out once the dinner started and he never showed up at the club until after ten.

That was when Charlie was free to sit back and survey the club. They could sit in the office above the VIP lounge and survey the floor below. Charlie could vent about Mariana while Remi staked out which girl would be ready to take home.

The day came that Mariana walked out on Charlie. She said if he ever loved her then he wouldn't have kept her a prisoner in their house, he was stopping her from defending the rights of her people. Charlie was torn up and confused. There was no doubt he loved his wife and was worried how the kids would feel with two separate houses, Charlie wanted to keep everyone together.

Lisa barely waited for Mariana's perfume to clear the club. She wanted to review new menu ideas with Charlie, showed up with dinner at his house for the family and took Nola for a pedicure. Lisa wanted to show she was committed to his whole family.

Everyone loved her except Brenda. Good, old, reliable, racist Brenda. She had hated Mariana and every tortilla she flipped instead of a pancake. If it hadn't been for giving her Oriana and Max, Brenda might have tried to kill Mariana in her sleep. Remi imagined one of Brenda's best days was when Mariana filed for divorce and was followed by the worst day when Lisa moved into the house.

Remi knew exactly who Lisa was. Lisa wasn't interested in history unless you called it vintage. She didn't like pretty, expensive things; she wanted to be the only pretty, expensive thing. Lisa knew there was something that was more important than money, she loved power. Power brought money and opened doors. It didn't matter how much money Remi had in the bank, he was just an attorney who had one powerful connection in his best friend, Charlie. What did Lisa need Remi for if she was Charlie's wife?

"What took you so long?" Lisa said, her eyes watching Remi in the mirror behind the bar.

"Just can't move fast enough for you," Remi

grumbled, "You summoned me, mistress?"

Lisa rolled her eyes and didn't answer. She tilted back her scotch and finished the glass. She never drank anything but fruit juice unless Charlie was out of town or if she was stressed, in this case both.

"Charlie hasn't called yet?" Remi asked, sitting down at the stool next to her. He felt a certain satisfaction that every man wished they were in his place.

"I got disconnected when he was moving through TJ." Lisa said, she was staring at the TV above Remi's head. He turned to watch three boys pull a bloodied body off Revolucion. It used to be a street for tourists to hit the dance clubs and bars, now the army was using it as a strong hold for refugees. Since the assassination, Mexicans were scrambling to find a way out, a sea of hopeless faces desperate to be out from the fire storm between the cartels and the federal troops.

Remi noticed the two empty glasses next to the one Lisa was finishing. Remi signaled to the bartender, Jamey, to bring his standing order and motioned to cut Lisa off from the booze.

"You don't decide when I've had enough," Lisa said, emptying the scotch from the glass, "I'm just getting started."

"How long have you been here?" Remi asked, "About an hour?"

"I don't know." Lisa mumbled, "I don't have a watch."

"Measure it in drinks." Remi said, tilting his own scotch back.

"Fuck you."

Remi knew Lisa only cursed when something was bothering her and that was usually her future mother in law. "Trouble with Brenda again?"

Lisa looked up as if Remi had been reading her thoughts. "What am I supposed to do with her?"

Lisa slammed the glass down and adjusted herself on the barstool. It exposed a great deal of her left breast leaving Remi to focus at the liquor lining the back wall.

"She absolutely hates me. The piece of trash is so wrapped up on the fact that I'm not shining white," Lisa said, sliding her empty glass into Remi's scotch causing it to slosh, "like her family sailed over on the Mayflower. They probably paddled out of a swamp on an alligator."

Remi smiled and tilted back his drink. He loved Lisa's humor, it bordered on inappropriate. "Brenda is born from another time without a filter on her mouth."

Lisa waved Jamey over for another drink. When her face was turned, Remi held up his fingers to Jamey to only give Lisa half.

"I don't know why you're looking at him, Jamey, I'm the one that ordered the drink," Lisa said, glaring at Remi in the back mirror, "I'm the one that's going to be your boss, the ambulance hijacker isn't going to get you promoted."

Lisa drank this one faster. "If I'm going to marry Charlie, what's it going to be if Brenda becomes my mother in law? Am I going to lose my mind like Nola? I understand that Nola can't live by herself but he could put her in a place with other special people. Charlie could buy Brenda a house in Lakeside but he will never kick her out. Why the hell does he want to live with her?"

"What did you mean *if* Brenda becomes your mother in law?" Remi asked, a small smile crossing his lips.

Lisa pointed a finger at him. "Do you know why he keeps them around? What does Brenda hold over him?"

Remi raised his glass and finished the scotch.

"Well?" Lisa's voice began to rise above the customers. "Do you know?"

121

Remi looked back at the TV and then back at Lisa. He liked having her full attention. "I know a few things."

"And?"

Remi picked up his glass and clinked the ice in Jamey's direction.

"Remi," Lisa said his name more as a curse. She moved her chair to face the bar again.

"When Charlie's ready, then he'll tell you," Remi said quietly.

Lisa's face crumpled. "He never opens up. I get only so close and then this door shuts in my face."

Remi was surprised that she seemed sincere, perhaps there was a part of her that cared about Charlie, whether she loved him was another story.

A customer behind Lisa asked Jamey to turn up the TV. A loud barrage of gunfire could be heard and then the scream of a reporter who had gotten too close to the fighting.

Lisa began to weep, the alcohol was taking toll. Remi waved at Jamey to lower the volume and shot a look at the customer who was about to protest but he shrunk back in his chair.

"Charlie is in that hell hole!" Lisa said, looking up at the TV,"I need him here!"

Remi put his arm around her and slid her off the stool. "Charlie will be back soon. Mariana's ranch is only fifty miles from the border. He's got an armored guard and Kier is with him. He'll be back in the morning with Max and Mariana. Let's get you home."

"What home?" Lisa said grabbing his arm and looking into his eyes, "Please don't make me go to that house."

Lisa's eyes pleaded with him. He sensed opportunity in her desperation which was more temptation then he wanted. Remi grabbed her purse and forced it into her hands.

"You have to go home sometime," Remi said looking her directly in the eyes. He wanted so desperately for that home to be with him tonight. She chose her fate. She wanted Charlie not him. No matter how much he wanted her right now, he could never do that to Charlie.

Lisa slid her hand around his back and pressed her head on his chest. "I just need to wait for Brenda to go up to her room. I can slip in and get to Charlie's bedroom. I can hide out there until he gets back tomorrow."

Remi wanted to take her over to Horton Plaza, purchase a movie ticket, send her into a dark theater and then run like hell. So many options other than the one mistake he was about to make. "My condo is just a block away."

"I remember where you live, Remi." She slid her arm away from him and grazed his inner thigh. Remi caught her hand.

"For an hour," Remi said, gruffly, "Then you go home."

Lisa leaned in and kissed his cheek, smelling like scotch and perfume. She smiled and he felt like he was having a cardiac attack. As her curves slinked through the club and out the door, there wasn't a man that didn't feel his heart skip a beat.

Chapter Sixteen
Rosarito Mexico

The sound of crunching gravel woke Charlie. He hadn't realized he had fallen asleep and was dreaming about panhandling on Bourbon Street and was now trading one nightmare for another. He couldn't tell what direction the shoes were coming from except they didn't hesitate; whoever wore the shoes knew their way in the dark.

Charlie wearily moved up against the wall and checked on Max. He hadn't moved his position. Charlie tried to look at his watch but could barely make out the oval of the glass when he heard the footsteps coming directly toward him. A silhouette formed from the shadows and stopped on the path.

"Kier?" Charlie called out. The figure hesitated but continued moving without a word. Charlie tensed as he leaned his back to hide Max from view.

Soon the figure took on definition, his clothing were camouflage, his hand firmly on the gun strapped on his belt. Charlie saw the glint of something on his belt shining like authority.

Charlie felt relief lessen the strain in his shoulders when he saw the uniform of the Mexican soldier.

"Hablo ingles?" Charlie called out. "I'm sorry I don't speak Spanish very well."

The soldier didn't seem surprised to see him and didn't make any reaction at first except to cock his head and looked at Charlie.

"You don't speak English," Charlie said, trying to think out loud, "Okay, we can make this work."

Charlie debated to wake up Max to help translate. The things he needed answered were not questions he could bring his son to ask right now.

"Okay, I need help!" Charlie stepped forward which prompted the soldier to pull his gun and aim it toward his head. Charlie stumbled back, "Whoa, hold on. I'm not causing trouble."

The soldier advanced in a semi-circle around Charlie. It forced Charlie to press his back against Max. He found himself stuttering over his words over and over, tumbling and twisting his tongue over his teeth, unable to find anything else to say, "We don't want trouble! We just need some help!"

The soldier raised the gun again. Charlie was horrified at the realization he and Max had escaped death to be killed under a freeway ramp. He could not stop the sadness from overtaking him that he didn't know what was going to happen to his son. He pulled out a wad of bills from his jacket with a desperate appeal. "I've got money....dinero...I'll pay anything you want."

Charlie inhaled as the soldier put his finger on the trigger. He turned toward Max and focused on his sleeping face, trying to memorize his thick lashes, the curve of his cheek and the color of his hair.

"I'm sorry," Charlie whispered, leaning his head over the boy, "I love you."

Charlie covered his son and waited to feel the pain, instead he heard a sharp cry from the soldier and the thud of the gun dropping to the ground. Charlie brought his face up to see the solider shielding his face with his arm. Out of the corner of his eye, he saw a jagged chunk of concrete strike the soldier's cheek and knock him to the ground.

A surreal vision of a woman and girl appeared from the shadows. There was no reason for them to be there and yet they appeared like angels from a Bible parable or the haunted vision of a ghost story. Charlie couldn't be sure if he was hallucinating.

The woman's face was painted like a warrior. She struggled to bring her arms above the soldier with another chunk of concrete. Her eyes met Charlie and she paused. He was staring at her face which was red and sweating from the weight in her arms.

Charlie's fogginess lifted into hard reality when the woman released another rock with a fury that crashed down onto the soldier's chest.

Chapter Seventeen

Charlie move forward and stood with the soldier's body separating them. The woman had reached down and picked up the soldier's gun. She hesitated as she looked at Charlie and tucked it into a sash on her skirt.

"Were you following us on the beach?" Charlie asked.

The woman was staring at the soldier, her breath ragged. She looked up at Charlie and fixed on his face as if she was trying to understand what Charlie had said.

It occurred to Charlie that she didn't speak English. He repeated the question slowly, trying to think how to ask in Spanish.

"Donde esta... I don't know what the hell I'm saying," Charlie spoke out loud, running his hands through his hair.

"We were at the Ranch," the woman said gaining her breath and to Charlie's relief in English, "we came up from the beach."

Charlie tried to recall where she had been at the Ranch. There were so many people running in and out. What once might have been a cream silk dress was wet and streaked with red. Sand dragged at the lining of the "V" neck. The green beaded sash where she had tucked the gun was like a dozen of expensive ones he had seen in Lisa's closet. She was not a cleaner or security who worked on the Ranch. Charlie admitted that he didn't know all of Mariana's relatives but he knew she wasn't family. The wives who married into the family were short, domestic birds that hovered over their children. This woman was taller and despite her wild appearance, possessed something graceful. Charlie could only assume that she had been a guest at Senor's party.

The woman, aware that Charlie was examining her, moved back and covered herself in her shall. Charlie had forgotten about the girl until she moved from behind the woman. She was wrapped in a cloth that Charlie recognized had covered a kitchen table at the Ranch. She stared at him with eyes hollowed and unfazed by the bleeding soldier at her feet. Charlie didn't want to think what this wasn't the worse that this little girl had seen.

Charlie and the woman stared at each other unsure what to do next. So many questions were filling Charlie's head.

"How did you escape?" Charlie didn't know how to ask.

"We were in the kitchen," the woman said, her voice cracking pushing a fallen strand of hair back in her braid, "I was pushed back when they struck Patricia. We lay under her body and they assumed we were dead too."

"Patricia is dead?" Charlie asked, his heart beating fast. The words he spoke didn't sound real, "Did anyone else get-"

"I know you have many questions," the woman interrupted, "but we need to move away from here. There are others who are coming."

"Who is coming?" Charlie asked looking at his watch. It had been two hours since this nightmare had begun.

"We need to go." Lena said.

"Mariana," Charlie said, ignoring her, "did she get out?"

The woman glanced at her daughter. "I do not think we should talk about this now."

Charlie had the sickening feeling he got in his stomach as a child when he knew something violent was coming. He still felt like the helpless kid, someone else was holding back knowledge that was going to change the direction of his life. He hated having no control.

Max sat up and rubbed his eyes and let out a cry. "Daddy, that man is bleeding!"

"Don't worry about him," Charlie ran back to Max and shielded his body with his jacket. "Turn over on your side and close your ears until I tell you it's okay."

Max started to whimper but stopped when Charlie leaned into his ear.

"Remember the game we play when we see something that kids aren't supposed to see?" Charlie said, the words spitting out like he had cotton stuffed in his mouth. He also didn't want him to hear what he was going to ask, "This isn't something you should see."

"Is he going to be okay?" Max asked, trying to see above Charlie's shoulder.

"Yes, Max, please," Charlie gently pushed him to face into the concrete wall and placed Max's hands on his ears, "Squeeze them tight."

Charlie went back to stand near the soldier. He felt sweat trickle down his hair and chill his back. "Okay, now please tell me."

"It's really important we begin to move." The woman said, looking quickly down the road toward the Ranch.

"Goddamn it! Please just say something," Charlie found himself yelling, his hands starting to shake. "Is my wife alive?"

The woman sighed and drew the girl close to

her. "Mariana is...gone."

The woman hadn't moved a muscle but Charlie felt like she had just carved into his chest. He put his hand on his heart and then looked back to make sure Max was still holding his ears.

"Gone?" Charlie said, hoping he had misunderstood, "She got out?

The woman bit her lip and her eyes looking at him sadly. "Please don't make me say what you already know."

Charlie jerked back. He was starting to have visions of Mariana lying hurt but still alive. Maybe she just needed help. "I need to know, did you see her?"

The soldier began to moan. His left arm swung over and landed on the woman's foot. She was startled and immediately reached down to the ground and picked up a jagged chunk of cement with both arms.

The woman stumbled trying to steady herself with the block of cement above her head. It was almost half her size with strips of rebar that flailed like octopus tentacles. She began to heave the block toward the soldier's head.

Charlie grabbed at her arms, steadying the block between them. "What are you doing?" Charlie exclaimed.

The woman struggled to not lose grip of the block. "Let it fall!"

"You hit him hard enough," Charlie said, "He's not going anywhere."

The sadness was gone in the woman's eyes. His appeal was only making her grip the block harder. "We must kill him."

"He doesn't have to die!" Charlie argued.

"Then it will be your son that dies." The woman said.

Charlie couldn't be sure if she was threatening Max. He positioned himself so he could grab her if she tried to run at his son. "Drop the block!"

The woman sensed his fear. "You do not

understand. He will come after you again!"

The soldier began to move between them and his legs twitched. She tried to force the block to fall on the ground. Charlie gripped harder and his foot kicked the soldier involuntarily while trying to gain his balance. The soldier groaned and held the back of Charlie's calf, almost bracing him.

"This man cannot be saved," the woman continued, "He is a murderer."

Charlie looked for signs on the soldier that she was telling the truth. His camouflage jacket was covered in blood. Had it been there before he was on the ground? It was too dark to be sure.

The woman tried to shake the block to keep his attention. Charlie looked back into her eyes, trying to find some possible truth. "Your son is currency. He can be traded for money."

"But-" Charlie stared down again. There was a badge reflecting on his belt and the crest was reflecting in the dim light.

The woman shook the block again with impatience. "We don't have time for this! There are others! They are searching too. They will be here soon."

The soldier's boot twitched but he rolled to his side and grew still. Charlie made one more stretch to get a grasp on the block, "He's going nowhere. We don't have to kill him."

"She was calling for Max."

"What?" Charlie said, unsure what he had heard.

"Mariana was calling for Max," the woman said, swallowing hard, "One of them followed her out and slit her throat."

The words were like huge hands wrenching loose the block from Charlie's hands. She pulled free, knocking Charlie's balance. He fell over the soldier's arm and back onto the ground.   The woman raised the block and smashed it down with a final crack on the soldier's skull.

The grip loosened on Charlie's leg. Charlie stared at his pant leg and noticed a deep cut on his ankle and he couldn't feel anything.

The woman stepped back from the blood that flowed freely from the soldier's head. "If you don't take the chances when God gives them to you, they will take you instead."

The woman looked quickly down the road and reached for his arm. The sharp pain had come back to his head. Her touch stuck him like electricity.

"There are more!" the woman shouted, pointing down the road, "Move with your son or you will both die too!"

Chapter Eighteen

The woman guided them to a frontage road that ran parallel to the highway. The hope was that whatever was coming up from the Ranch would take the highway. Charlie took comfort that they could hide in the darkness but it also meant that they couldn't see what was waiting ahead of them, for all Charlie knew, they were walking off a cliff into the ocean.

Charlie felt the crumbling road crush under his feet and looked down at his son's scuffed shoes. They wouldn't make the journey. He reached down and picked Max up. Normally, Charlie would have loved these moments. He knew that pretty soon, Max would rather run ahead than be carried. But for now, the walk was going to be hours and the extra thirty five pounds was going to grow heavier.

The wind was picking up and carried a voice, like a fifth traveler even though he knew it was impossible, he felt like he could hear the loud wail of the soldier. Charlie wondered if they would ever put enough distance between themselves or the death that was left in their trail. The image of the crushed skull underneath the rock wouldn't leave his mind.

Charlie tried to focus on the woman who walked three steps ahead of him. Her face was hidden but when she glanced down at the girl Charlie captured a look. He wanted to know anything to learn more about this stranger who appeared from the darkness. Her face was streaked in blood like war paint and it was difficult to tell her age. Whatever she had gone through in the last hours had taken several years away. He would get a better look in the daylight. For now, she was a ghost-like face with eyes looking straight into the darkness Charlie cast a glance down at her hands clasped with the little girl.

The little girl caught his gaze and her eyes peering at him, wide like an owl. She had grown accustomed to the darkness and seemed to recognize every detail of his face. Charlie quickly looked ahead. He felt like he was walking in a nightmare. He clutched Max tighter and the boy shivered trying to burrow under Charlie's coat. Charlie struggled with his right sleeve trying to remove the jacket and cover him but he suddenly felt a thin braid slap his face. The woman had placed her shawl over Max. It wasn't very thick but it calmed the trembling boy. He glanced over but it was as if she hadn't made any changes, she continued to look forward, never losing her directed pace.

Charlie debated if he should give her his jacket. It was the right thing to do. She only had a thin blouse, the wind blowing from the ocean was beginning to bite and howl. At least Max's warmth would keep him from freezing.

"Take my jacket." Charlie offered.

The woman continued to look forward. "I do not need to be warm."

"But it's cold out here and you've only got a blouse." Charlie tried again, the conversation was not going like he imagined in his mind.

The woman did not pause. "The children need to stay warm."

Charlie noticed that the little girl was dragging the heavy table cloth

"This will be easier to wear," Charlie said. He put Max down and began to slip off his jacket.

"No," the woman argued, 'Don't stop, we need to keep moving."

"It will just take a moment," Charlie reasoned, "That sheet can't be keeping her warm."

"I said no!" The woman yelled. She was irritated to take the steps back. "We must keep moving forward!"

Just as she moved toward him, Charlie soon understood why she didn't want her daughter unveiled. Underneath, the little girl was dressed in a thin pink, dress. Thick pockets of blood covered her front and caked her neck.

"Were you hurt?" Charlie asked, trying to check the little girl. The woman grabbed his arm and pushed it away.

"Don't touch her!" The woman was alarmed and clutched at the girl.

"I just wanted to make sure she is alright!" Charlie yelled back, "Is-any of that- her blood?"

Charlie looked at the little girl, her owl eyes looking clearly at him and she shook her head. He did not want to upset the woman again by reaching for the girl and he had a vivid memory of the last person that had tried was lying under an overpass with his skull crushed.

Charlie handed his jacket to the woman. She snatched the clothing and wrapped it around her daughter. She picked up the girl's hand and began to charge down the road. Charlie moved quickly to keep up with her.

"We must keep moving. It isn't safe here," she said.

"Daddy, is Giselle okay?" Max whispered into Charlie's ear.

"Is that the little girl's name?" Charlie whispered back.

Max stared down at the girl and she looked up

at him.

"Are you okay?" he called down.

"She only speaks Spanish, remember Max?" the woman said in Spanish.

"My son speaks perfect Spanish." Charlie said in English.

The woman looked surprised that Charlie answered her. "Hablo espanol?"

Charlie shook his head. "No, I understand most words but I've never been very good at speaking."

"Never bothered to learn?" she said with a slight edge.

"No," Charlie said, "I have an accent to begin with. I have trouble rolling my "R's."

The woman smiled, "I wondered."

"My wife would tease me." Charlie stopped himself at the thought of Mariana. Her face laughing as she listened to him read a menu in Spanish. "I've gotten good at hearing the words but just can't roll them around my tongue."

Charlie realized that he didn't know her name.

"What is the name of the lady," Charlie whispered to Max.

"The lady is named Lena," the woman answered.

"I feel like I'm the stranger at the party," Charlie said, embarrassed to be caught, "I just wanted to know the name of the person to thank for saving our lives."

Lena continued to walk in silence.

"So... thank you," Charlie said, feeling awkward, "we are in your debt."

Lena stopped walking. "That makes what I am going to say easier."

It alarmed Charlie that she had stopped walking since she had been so anxious to move forward. "You need something? You can have anything you want as soon as I get across the border, I can send you money.

Think of a number and I'll double it. I'll triple it."

"I don't need money," Lena said quietly.

"No money?" Charlie said, in disbelief, "I don't believe that, everyone needs money."

"You have something I want more," Lena said, turning toward him.

Charlie looked confused. He had money, other than that, he couldn't think of anything that he had to offer. "What do you want?"

Lena paused, looking down the road again. "We can discuss later."

Charlie started to feel the same feeling of dread and loss of control again. "No, tell me now."

Lena turned to him and sighed deeply. "I want you to take us across the border."

"And you think I can take you?" Charlie said, he threw his hand up and circled the air, "If you haven't noticed- I can't exactly get myself there."

Lena looked behind them down the road. She nodded impatiently and began to move them forward on the road. "I will get you there. You do the rest."

"What rest?" Charlie laughed, "Dig a hole and we can crawl under?"

"I know you have papers that will get your family across."

Lena's words surprised him. Only Kier knew that information and had made it clear that anyone that knew that information wasn't to be trusted. Now he was staring at a slender woman and passive little girl that hardly looked like the enemy.

"Yes. I have papers. But they are only for my family," Charlie said cautiously, "For my son and me."

Lena's expression darkened and she now looked at him with disapproval, "You have two more."

"How did you know that?" Charlie asked.

"Your friend was talking outside," Lena said, "he said you planned to bring back Mariana and there was one made for your daughter by accident."

"Kier wouldn't talk to anyone," Charlie argued,

his distrust now making him angry, "you're lying."

"Do you not have the papers? Lena demanded.

"Even if I do- I can't get you over," Charlie said, "You don't look anything like my wife."

"They do not have any photos," Lena argued, "Giselle is close in age to your daughter. She could be your own."

Charlie glanced at Giselle and felt a sting of remorse. He wanted to see Oriana again and he tried to imagine this girl was his daughter. When he stared down at Giselle, her skin was lighter than Oriana. She was a couple years older and taller. The almond curve of her face was like Lena. Oriana's face was heart shaped like Mariana. The deep thickness of Giselle's hair shined like the moon reflecting on a dark river. Oriana's hair was the color of chocolate cream. These all would be okay because there were things that Charlie could see in a daughter. But he couldn't accept the eyes. Oriana's were hazel and shaped just like Charlie. They crinkled and laughed the same. There was also a sprinkle of freckles that crossed over the bridge of her nose. There was no doubt that Oriana was his child but Giselle's eyes were large and hollow like an owl. These were not the eyes of his happy daughter and there was no part of him that could pretend. If he couldn't believe Giselle was his daughter, why would anyone else? What would happen if they didn't?

"No, I'm not risking my life or Max," Charlie said, "If they find out, they could keep us all back."

"You are assuming that you can make it there." Lena said.

"Are you threatening me?" Charlie asked.

"I'm saying you need help to get there," Lena said shaking her head, "and you won't survive the night."

Charlie put Max down and leaned against a road sign. "We're going to wait here for my friend. Thank you for your help back there but I can't give you what you want."

Lena sighed, frustrated at the delay. "Your friend is dead."

"You don't know that!" Charlie shouted, his words not even convincing himself, "If a little girl and a woman can crawl out then he can make it! He's a military beast, for God's sake."

Lena looked toward the ocean. Her silence was more than Charlie wanted to hear.

"What?" Charlie said, "What are you not saying?"

Lena stood silent for a moment and then turned to face him. "I saw them kill your friend."

The words Lena spoke were matter of fact. They rang of a truth that alarmed Charlie.

"You'd say anything right now to get me to agree with you." Charlie said, trying to find any fault to prevent the panic from overtaking him.

"The first bullet hit him on a tattoo. I think it was of an eagle on his left arm," Lena said pointing to her bicep. She then touched her neck. "The second went through his throat on a place he already had a scar."

"Don't do this! They don't need to hear that!" Charlie yelled, pointing to the kids. "I'm not helping you!"

Lena shrugged and pulled Charlie's jacket from Giselle and placed it around Max. She turned her back and began to move down the road.

"Where are you going?" Charlie called after her. He felt stupid as soon as it came out of his mouth. It didn't matter because she knew this strange place.

Lena and Giselle began to gain momentum and Charlie lost them up ahead in the darkness.

Charlie couldn't think fast enough and had nothing to defend himself. No car. No weapon. He was thinking of a word that he despised, helpless, a fear that had plagued him all his life. Having children only charged the fear even more.

Stuck in Mexico, he didn't know where to expect the danger. How could he protect Max when he couldn't defend himself? Charlie didn't speak Spanish. His very skin would expose him as a target to be ransomed or killed.

Charlie started down the road at Senor's Ranch. He sure as hell couldn't go back and he had no choice except to move down the same road. His eyes were accustomed to the surroundings and he could dismiss a passing bush or a broken pillar. He couldn't teach his ears to do the same. He heard every snap of a twig. The fall of their feet or skip of a breath made him wonder what followed behind. How could he travel forward when he was always looking back?

Charlie hated the silence of being in nature. He had tried camping once with Remi and left after one night. He preferred a crowded street in Manhattan. The crowded sexual bustle of Mardi Gras or a packed Padres game at Petco Park. All had more potential for someone to steal from him yet in a sea of people he never felt like he was surrounded by sharks. He had lived all his life knowing how to survive in an urban ocean.

"Can we get Mama now?" Max rubbed his eye and yawned, "I want to go home."

Survival out here was something else. He didn't know all the things to expect. If Kier was really gone, Charlie needed someone to help and Lena was offering help he needed.

Charlie's heart began to race, it was the loudest thing he could hear in his head and he felt blinded by hesitation. "She's going to catch up later, Max."

Charlie scooped him in his arms and walked quickly down the road after Lena. If he hadn't been heavy with Max in his arms, he might have tried to run.

"Wait!" Charlie called out but only heard the echo of his voice. "Hey! Can you hear me?"

Charlie continued forward, there was nothing

up ahead but the sounds around him seemed louder than ever and his mind was playing tricks on him. Red eyes were in the darkness, demons waiting for the moment to devour them.

"Hey! Wait!" Charlie yelled.

"Shhh!"

Lena's voice was just ahead. He kept moving forward until two forms took shape in front of him. Charlie felt and instant feeling of dread and relief.

Charlie could soon see Lena's face which appeared unsmiling before him.

"Thank you for stopping!" Charlie panted, releasing Max from his arms as he tried to catch his breath.

"You need to be quiet," Lena whispered.

"I just..." Charlie gasped and grabbed at his chest, "I didn't want to lose you."

Lena shook her head, "You are too dangerous. Someone else could have heard you."

Charlie looked around and the demon eyes had disappeared. "It's dark as hell out here. There's no one around us."

"There is a lot you don't see."

Charlie nodded, "I don't want to fight about this. I just need your help. Please."

"We need your help too." Lena whispered, her voice so soft that Charlie barely heard her.

"I understand you want to get across but I don't think that this is the way," Charlie reasoned, "I can get across and then help you get assistance over. I have plenty of connections."

Lena frowned. "If you want my help then you know my terms."

Charlie's business senses started to take over. "What are you offering me? How can you really help me?"

"I can get us shelter in Rosarito," Lena said, "Transportation can be arranged. We could be at the border by late tomorrow."

Charlie looked at Max. The desire to already be on the other side and safe was rushing through him. "Get us to the border and I promise to get you both across."

"Say with the papers."

"With the papers," Charlie repeated, carefully picking up her hand and transferring some blood onto his wrist.

Lena grabbed Giselle's hand. "You will not leave us."

"Lady- Lena, there is one thing you should know about me." Charlie said picking up Max, "Charles August Thibodeaux doesn't leave anybody."

Another mile was spent in silence. Charlie was left to his thoughts which were like having a nightmare with your eyes open when you only had your fears to walk with you. Hell wasn't forged with fire and sin and it was built on quiet contemplation of a violent past and a future that was certain to hold more fear.

"Where do you live?"

Charlie's heart lurched. Her voice came out of nowhere and unnerved him. Lena was looking at him. Her face indicated she was lost in the hell of her own thoughts. "I am supposed to be your wife and they may ask things I don't know."

"Oh, right," Charlie said, coughing to give his heart a chance to calm down, "I live in La Jolla."

"Where in La Jolla?" Lena asked.

"It's a city north of San Diego," Charlie said, just up the hill from Pacific Beach."

"I know about La Jolla," Lena said with an edge of irritation in her voice. I asked where in La Jolla you lived. Do you live in the Village or near Torrey Pines Golf Course?"

Charlie was surprised at her knowledge of the area. "I live a few blocks from the monument on Mount Soledad."

Lena thought for a few moments. "Can you see

the ocean?"

"We can see the ocean from all three floors of Daddy's house," Max said. "You can see Mama's house on the beach."

"Mama's house?" Lena said, confused. "You have two houses?"

"We're divorced." Charlie said, feeling like the questions were somewhere between a first date and filling out a loan application.

"Divorced?" Lena said, turning to look at Charlie directly, "Mariana didn't mention you were not married."

How could Mariana hide she was divorced? Charlie thought. Maybe Lena wasn't that close to the family. "How did you know Mariana?"

Lena ignored the question. "You are divorced. For how long?"

"A year." Charlie said, "How did you know Mariana?

"Senor Mendoza did not know." Lena said, talking to herself, "He would never let her come through the door. Did Patricia know?"

"Hey!" Charlie stopped to get her attention. "You don't get to ask all the questions."

Lena reached back and grabbed his hand. "We must move."

Charlie pulled his hand away. "Start answering some questions."

Lena began to plead. "Please, I will answer all your questions but we must move."

Charlie stared into her eyes. She was nervous.

Lena pointed to the sky in the East. It was turning a soft grey.

"In the daylight, we are not safe," Lena said, grabbing his hand again and pulling him again, "We have a long way to go to reach Rosarito. I will answer all your questions as long as we keep moving. Please."

Charlie nodded and started to move again but she didn't speak again for twenty minutes.

"I worked for Senor Mendoza."

"Doing what?" Charlie asked. Now he was sure this was a first date.

"Foreign relations."

"Foreign relations?" Charlie said, "He sells coffee beans. He's not a UN representative."

"He sells coffee in the north," Lena said, giving a small smile at Charlie's attempt to be funny.

"So, it's interesting that you judge me for not learning Spanish," Charlie said, "but you work for a man who refuses to learn English."

Lena looked surprised. "I was not judging you."

"Yes you were. I could hear it in your voice," Charlie said, "you thought I hadn't made an effort."

Lena shrugged. "Well you haven't."

"I tried to learn."

"You didn't try," Lena said, taking his hand again and pulling him beside her, "If you had, you wouldn't care if your "r's" rolled perfectly. I am speaking to you in English right now. I speak slowly and I don't always say the right way but I try and you understand me just fine."

Charlie knew she had a point. He still carried the memory of Mariana laughing at him. He disliked being mocked. Eventually he just stopped trying to speak and let Mariana translate when he visited her family. Charlie felt remorse the closest moment he had spent with his father in law was the fifteen minutes in his study.

"Just because Senor didn't learn your language doesn't make him hateful of all Americans," Lena said, "He's Mexican and proud of his country. Senor felt if Americans come here then they should learn the language. Why is it that Americans always think that everyone should learn English?"

"English is the accepted language." Charlie said.

"Go to China," Lena said, quickening her pace, "See if they think the same."

Charlie liked her sense of humor. She was smart

and not afraid to give an opinion. Mariana was always yelling what she thought. If he didn't agree, then she just yelled louder.

"I've never been to China." Charlie said, trying to break conversation into a new direction.

"I went once."

"Really?" Charlie said, not meaning it to sound as a surprise.

"Why do you think I haven't seen the world?" Lena asked.

"No, it's just that you want to go to the US. That shouldn't be too hard if you've been to China," Charlie said, kicking a rock and feeling his toe swell. It didn't feel as big as the foot he was putting in his mouth. "You know, for a world traveler."

Charlie started to think following Lena was a mistake. Could she be leading him into a trap? Why didn't he remember her from the Ranch? His senses were tingling that he had no reassurance that he should trust this woman.

Charlie debated whether he should pick up Max and hide until daylight. Someone would come along that he could trust but that thought filled him with more fear. Why would the daylight make it any easier? He wanted to trust a soldier because of his uniform and it almost got him killed. Charlie was following a crazed woman caked in blood and mud who smashed a soldier's skull without hesitation. He was walking blind without any sign that she was the one to trust.

"Keep moving with me," Lena said, "don't let your feet lock on the land."

Charlie's head snapped up at the phrase. Those were words he hadn't heard in thirty years but he'd heard every day until he was twelve. That was Jackson's favorite thing to say and he said it ten times a day. Charlie could hear the words as he pictured his brother standing above him with his sideways smile, his eyes adjusting to the sun on Bourbon Street. He tried his best to keep a happy image of Jackson smiling and push the thoughts of Jackson crying as he lay broken and bleeding at the feet of their father, Sam.

"Why did you say that?" Charlie asked, his heart beating loudly.

"It's a poem I read once from Elijhun Cann-Saez," Lena said, "I don't know why that came to my mind."

"My brother always said that," Charlie said, almost imagining his brother standing beside him, "I don't think he knew what it meant. He just liked the way it sounded."

Lights flashed from the highway coming from behind them. Lena pulled at Charlie's arm.

"Don't let them see us," Lena said, almost stumbling as she moved them off the road and into a ditch.

"Maybe it's Mama." Max whispered.

"No Max," Charlie said.

"I want Mama," Max said squirming, "We need to get her."

Max pushed hard against Charlie. The lights were now forming into distinct shapes. Five SUV's with a search light scanning ahead. Charlie tried to hold Max tighter but he cried against the pressure.

"You need to control him," Lena whispered, pushing away a thin strip of metal so they could lie down.

Max broke Charlie's hold to run up the embankment but Lena grasped onto the boy's shirt causing him to scream as she dragged him back, cradling him like a baby and whispering into his ear. Tears streamed down his face but his voice lowered. Lena looked over at Charlie with desperation. She waved over to Giselle who stared unfazed at the growling motors that were approaching. Charlie put his arms around Giselle and moved her toward Lena. A small brush and one concrete beam provided the only cover to hide as the engine grew louder. They moved swiftly through the roadway, their lights flashing over them.

"Keep your faces away," Lena whispered, "Don't move until I say."

Charlie remained quiet but could have sworn that his heart would betray him. As the trucks rumbled past them the silence began to restore, Charlie's lungs exhaled the fear. He almost forgot Lena's words and started to stand up until he heard the branch crack near his head. From the corner of his eye was the thick sole of a boot only five feet away. Had the heel lost footing or just stepped into the air, it would land on top of his head. Charlie suddenly realized there wasn't just one but several dark forms moving on the road, their treads moving systematically through the roadway.

All this time Charlie thought there a storm carrying them, blowing behind them and they were only keeping a few steps ahead. Now the wind that had carried up the soldier's moans was joined by the screams and howls of the dead. Charlie was sure he was going mad, hearing their demands lift high in the air. The loudest was Mariana's voice, it's tone thick with venom screaming at him, "Who's going to save you Charlie? Who is going to save you?"

Chapter Nineteen

Max struggled like dead weight in Charlie's arms that had grown numb from holding him. Max would close his eyes for a few minutes but a quick stumble or an uneven part of the road and Max's eyes would pry open, red from exhaustion. He would mumble and squirm as he tried to find some way to relax.

Giselle continued to walk silently next to Lena. She never made a single noise and fell into a rhythm with her mother. When Lena stumbled, Giselle's pattern faltered as well. It was as if she copying every move.

They hadn't seen anyone on the road since the caravan had come through. Lena didn't need to explain who they were searching for in the middle of the night. They were moving too slowly, pausing with their lights flashing around them at the slightest movement. All they had to do was stoop down for an untied shoe to see four bodies crouched in a ditch by their feet. Lena seemed to know they would be looking to the left, searching the beach, perhaps they didn't think that they would be willing to lie down in a brush damp with brown liquid, the overpowering stench of something rotting in the shadows.

The sound of their vehicles and crunching of their feet had been still for what felt like hours.

Charlie didn't dare move until Lena began to rustle

Clouds were forming and the sky was changing to a Dresden blue that was defining the hills, taking shape above them as the sun prepared to rise. Lena's steps quickened and she glanced around at the slightest sound.

"The sun will be up in another half hour. We need to get to town. We cannot be out in the daylight," Lena said quietly. Charlie said nothing but when he stepped on a branch, the crack sent Lena into a panic. She moved them off the road and they were forced to walk through a poor walking path for the beach. Charlie kept looking for signs of the town. The building would continue to appear in view but then hide behind the bluffs.

The buildings were deceptive and Charlie gave up on all impressions that they were close. In reality, they walked another forty five minutes before they would get near. By now the sun was heating the ridge making it clear how vulnerable they were to discovery.

Charlie felt like he was going to stumble with exhaustion but now a fear stood in back of his neck, as if small fingers were touching every hair on his head, he was naked and exposed.

Approaching the edge of the town, Lena moved them toward the protection within the landscape of the wall for a hotel, its three towers stood on the bluff overlooking the ocean and a slice of beach below. In the darkness, it looked like a touristy, beachfront hotel. Charlie noticed how quiet things were for a popular tourist town like Rosarito. This early in the morning, there should be vendors bustling to get souvenirs ready. There should be farmers and fisherman bringing their food to the restaurants and no trucks carrying supplies. There should be lights in the windows but it was abandoned of any signs of daily life.

"Where are the people?" Charlie whispered.

"The good people are gone," Lena said quietly,

"they are getting out of the way for what is coming."

"What about their business and homes?" Charlie said, staring at a shuttered window to a tangerine colored restaurant. He remembered bringing the family on a warm summer day. A chubby woman with a sweet smile brought plates stacked with lobsters, stacks of hand-made tortillas and bowls of beans. Mariana and Charlie had toasted with margaritas and the kids drank frothy, glasses of horchata. Now it stood quiet, a ghost house haunted by happier days.

"They will come back when they know their family can be safe." Lena hurried them toward a stone wall before the gate-way into the hotel. She knelt down and took Giselle's hands in her face, "Stay here and do not move."

"Do you have any money with you?"

Charlie pulled out his wallet and found a stack of crisp, twenty dollar bills. Remi must have put them in his wallet because he never carried money. Lena took all the bills and noticed his watch.

"Give me your watch."

Charlie's heart sank as it slipped off and she snatched it quickly, "Are you robbing me now?"

"I need to get us shelter and he'll want a bribe," Lena said, her arm pressing Charlie's chest against the wall, "Do not move until I come back."

"Wait, where are you going?" Charlie could feel the fear creeping back, by now a sliver of sun light was peering like a searchlight into the road. The shadow and safety of the hotel wall was starting to shrink.

"I need to get permission to enter the hotel."

"Who gives you permission to enter a hotel?" Charlie said with irritation, "there's nobody here?"

"We don't have time for questions," Lena snapped, moving away in the shadow toward the corner onto the main road. "Just stay quiet against the wall."

Charlie put Max onto a planter box, the boy groaned and then rested against the coolness of the wall. His arms felt relief but weak and drained of blood, unable to gain strength. He looked at Giselle who had blended to the side of a tree, she stood fixed just as Lena had instructed, like a tiny statue in a haunted garden.

Charlie kept his eye on the sunrise, losing their cover by the second. After twenty minutes, Lena had not returned and they were exposed to sunlight. The blue glow was now turning into a bright, rose building. While things were still, he could now hear rustling, like cockroaches that scurried out of plain sight.

"Where the hell is she?"

Charlie looked at the children lying on the planter boxes, exhausted with no strength to go anywhere. Charlie moved along the shadow and peered over onto the road. It was still abandoned of cars or life. There was a tourist bar across the street that looked abandoned but Charlie could see someone inside the entrance. Charlie inched around the corner, still safely within the ledge of shadows. Closer to the entrance, he noticed the flash of a muddy skirt that could only belong to Lena. Straining inside, Charlie could see a huge Mexican with a fleshy face and serious scowl propped up on a barstool talking to Lena. Charlie watched the Mexican reach toward Lena and she pushed him away, backing out the door followed by a deep, booming laughter from inside.

Before Charlie could move from the shadows, Lena spotted him and ran quickly to him. "You don't leave the children."

"I'm ten steps away." Charlie said as she pushed him around the corner and relaxed when she saw them, "Who was the guy in the bar?"

"Jaime keeps an eye on this area. He's the person who arranges things that you aren't able to find... legally," Lena said, picking up Max and putting him in Charlie's arms. She took Giselle's limp hand and moved along the shrinking shadow along the wall, "nothing happens in Rosarito that he doesn't control."

"He's going to drive us to the border?"

"He uses a courier, Estrella, to move things for him," Lena said, "we can wait in the hotel until she arrives."

"Can we trust him?"

"Barely," Lena muttered, "but he knows you're not a threat and he can make some money off you."

Charlie stared over at the bar. "You didn't tell him why, did you?"

"I told him your wife left you and the kid down here and you're too stupid to get back to the border." Lena said.

"Oh," Charlie felt his face color with embarrassment. She pressed Charlie's watch into his hand.

"Put the watch back on, we don't need it right now," Lena said, "and that way you know I'm not robbing you."

I don't know why I said that, I make stupid jokes when I'm stressed," Charlie said, sliding the watch back on and feeling embarrassed for the second time in a matter of seconds, "what does Jaime think you're getting out of the deal?"

"I told him that you are paying my ride into Tijuana." Lena said.

"Why would I pay him to take you with me?" Charlie asked.

"He thinks that I'm giving you sex," Lena said, now the one looking embarrassed.

"Oh," Charlie said unable to stop a smile. He found her response so ridiculous it was funny. Lena was caked in mud, blood and stench and there was a fat man in a bar who thought someone was desperate enough to pay for sex while hell was breaking loose. In tense situations, he couldn't help but have the wrong reaction. It always got him into trouble and this time was no different from the look on Lena's face as she pushed past him to open a metal gate on the side of the hotel.

The side gate led to a service corridor that reminded Charlie of a hospital ward. It turned abruptly to an alcove with a man blocking a large, generic door. His eyes were covered by a furry brow and his nose protruded over his mouth which exposed a sharp incisor causing a permanent sneer. He reminded Charlie of a "wolf" in the children's book he read to Oriana.

The Wolf put a hand to Lena's collar bone to stop her and then looked down at Giselle. His hand moved to touch her when Lena slapped him away and held up a chain in her hand.

"Jaime said to give this to you and tell you there better not be any trouble," Lena said, allowing the chain to dangle in front of the Wolf's face. He sneered and snatched the chain but as he opened the door he waved his arm like a courteous bellman, allowing Lena to pass but not without giving another lingering glance at Giselle and sneering at Charlie.

As soon as Charlie and Max entered, the Wolf locked them inside. Charlie started to feel his heart rise in his throat at the realization they were being entombed in pitch black. His only guide was the sound of feet heavy on a metal floor and the labored breath of Max in his ear but nothing to show his hand in front of his face.

"We are in the emergency stair well. Your eyes will adjust in a moment," Lena said, her voice giving him relief as he reach out and felt a railing, "We're climbing to the tenth floor."

"No elevator?" Charlie said gasping as he took a deep breath, feeling his muscles in his back tense with anticipation of forging up several flights of stairs with Max in his arms.

"There's no electricity," Lena said, her voice was now above him as she had begun to climb, "but you can wait down here until it comes."

Charlie smiled in the darkness knowing he was free of judgment. Lena did have a sense of humor even when fear was entombing them in a metal mausoleum. They finally had something in common.

Chapter Twenty
La Jolla- Charlie's Home

Lisa entered the darkness of Charlie's bedroom and stared at the smooth bed. She pulled out her pillow and bed spread. As she wrinkled the sheets, she tried to push back the guilt she'd been feeling since she had gotten in a cab downtown.

"Didn't you wear that yesterday?"

Lisa jumped as she saw Nola standing in the doorway. "Nola, don't ever sneak up on anyone!"

Nola leaned against the doorway and stuck out her lip. Lisa never liked being mean to Nola. It was hard to remember that she may have the body of a thirty year old but mentally half that age. Lisa had to be nicer to her future sister in law.

Lisa slid off her stilettoes and put them carefully on the floor. She patted the bed. "Sit down."

Nola sat down next to her but not before noticing the bed hadn't been slept inside. She pulled one Lisa's heels from the floor and ran her finger across the delicate beads.

"Are you getting home now?" Nola asked slipping off her sneakers. She started to wedge her sock inside the heel.

"Where were you?"

"I had some work to do," Lisa said pulling

the heel from Nola's hand and placing it gently next to its partner.

"I had to work on the dinner menu," Lisa said slipping off the shimmery fabric and putting it gently on a hanger. She chose a black robe from the dozen hung carefully and slid it over her, "with your brother gone, I need to make sure things runs smoothly.

"You worked in the kitchen dressed like that?" Nola asked. Lisa's shoe was straddled again in her hand. The corner of her sock was wedged in the opening toe, "Your dress would get dirty."

"You're going to break them," Lisa said snatching the shoes and sliding them on a rack in the closet. The right one slipped off the rung and fell onto the floor. She groaned as she reached down and grabbed it by the strap.

"It's lonely without you and Charlie here," Nola sniffed. "Do you have any more chocolate?"

"Chocolate?" Lisa said, she turned around to see Nola reaching into Lisa's purse.

Lisa snatched the purse from her hands. "Don't look through my things!"

"I saw this sticking out from the top," Nola said, picking up a torn wrapper that lay on the bed. "I just want some chocolate."

Lisa eyed the foil packet of a condom in Nola's hand and without thinking slapped it away. Nola's startled eyes looked up and she let out a small cry as Lisa pulled Nola up from the bed by her arm and pushed her out the door. "Go downstairs. I'll be down in a minute."

"What did I do? I'm sorry for whatever I did," Nola protested as Lisa shut the door. Lisa stood still against the door and listened to Nola sniffle as she went down the stairs.

Why couldn't she stay out of my purse? Lisa thought. She stared down at the torn wrapper in her hand. The word Trojan flooded her with memories of regret and pleasure. Rather than throwing it in an open waste basket, she stuffed the wrapper down deep into her purse and flung it far into her closet.

She hoped that once it was out of sight she'd forget but the feelings still remained.

Lisa ran into the bathroom and sat inside under the shower water until she could no longer stand the heat on her skin.

Chapter Twenty One
Rosarito, Mexico

Groping in the darkness, holding Max with his left arm and his right arm clutching the railing, Charlie felt they'd been climbing for an eternity. His eyes had adjusted to the black and relying on the pounding of feet up the stairs had been his only guide so he was blinded when Lena pulled open the door to the tenth hall. Charlie surveyed the tenth floor which consisted of one leg of a hexagon built with an atrium in the center of the building and clear view of the floors below. Charlie put Max into the hallway and felt the hairs stand on the back of his neck at the silence. He hadn't thought a hotel had a heartbeat until it was drained of life. There was no murmur of guests walking through corridors, no televisions humming through thin walls, no swift bustle of maids with stacks of towels, and no bell boys struggling with the squeaky wheel of an overloaded luggage cart.

Peeking over the side of dusty, limp foliage clumped in planter boxes, Charlie could make out the first floor where the reception desk stood deserted. He tried to imagine that it wasn't abandoned but late at night and all the guests were sleeping. He smiled at the thought of the Wolf downstairs sitting behind a counter with a gold name tag clipped to his crisp, brown uniform. Charlie got pleasure at the thought of the Wolf leaning on his arm; stripped of the smug sense of power he had controlling access to the building.

Lena noticed that Charlie was searching for life. "The hotel was evacuated a week ago. A group of German tourists was abandoned by their travel guide."

"What happened to them?"

"I don't know," Lena said, pushing on the hotel doors, "They fled in the middle of the night so fast they left their luggage."

Pushing on the seventh door, the lock hadn't been shut completely and it opened. Charlie walked inside a suite large enough to hold a queen bed and living room couch on a Saltillo tiled floor. Without electricity, the only light in the room came through strips of cloth partitioning a balcony.

Charlie put Max down on the couch where his heavy eyelids closed without a fight. Lena guided Giselle toward the bed where she tucked her feet underneath, her expression unchanged as she looked through Charlie.

Lena motioned to Charlie toward a stack of luggage sat in a corner. She pulled the first one down with a low thud. Digging through, she held up a pink T-shirt with a cartoonish monkey on the front.

Charlie lifted a small piece of luggage with a broken zipper. He stuck his fingers inside until the metal teeth fell apart revealing a hair drier and several bloodied towels.

"Something bad happened in here." Charlie said, brushing away the clumps, "they got attacked."

Lena pushed the luggage with her foot. "Nothing happened on this floor."

"How do you know?"

"We're on the top floor and the elevator is out," Lena said, handing him a brown leather carry-on, "no one would have breath or energy to attack them and there is still luggage, nothing has been scavenged."

Charlie nodded at the logic and started to check a brown leather carry-on.

Lena handed Charlie a stack of clothes. "These will fit Max."

Charlie overturned the last suitcase which held a child's swimsuit and a leather belt. He crossed the hall into another room but found Lena had already emptied the suitcases and folded stacks on the bed. Charlie was about to leave when he heard the shower in the bathroom and noticed Lena's muddy clothes laying in a pile on the floor.

"There's no heat." Lena called from the bathroom, the door was wide open but she was concealed in the darkness by a shower curtain.

"I'll check on the kids," Charlie said.

"Please don't leave," Lena called out, "Look on the bed, I found some clothes that might fit you."

Charlie found a stack with jeans and a stack of shirts from tourist traps and bars with the tags showing his size. He started to pull off his jacket and heard Kier's voice screaming in his head.

Never take off the jacket even if it's a million fucking degrees!

Charlie felt a twinge of remorse as he pulled the papers from the side pocket and laid them on the bed. They made him nervous so he folded them and shoved the bulk into the back pocket of the new pair of jeans. Unbuttoning made his fingers ache and it slipped off the torn, shredded rag that used to be his favorite shirt. Kicking off his pants, he breathed a sigh of relief and wondered why it felt liberating to stand in your underwear.

"You look relaxed."

The shower was no longer running and Charlie hadn't realized that Lena had stepped out of the bathroom and was standing behind him. Her voice so close to his ear that he fell forward onto the bed. "Jesus, you scared me."

Charlie turned to look at Lena and the irritation

of being exposed disappeared as he looked at a stranger. The crazed woman had washed down the shower drain. She was now wearing a blue skirt that hugged her curves and a black, silk blouse that wrapped tightly around her breasts. The mud-caked braid had been released and dark, silky ringlets cascaded around her face and down her back. The chalky ghost had come to life with smooth, olive skin and lips the color of a deep wine. Her eyes captivated his attention; they were grey like an approaching storm cloud rolling from the Pacific Ocean. He was meeting the real Lena for the first time and a lump of nerves was building in his throat like a school boy at his first dance. He looked down at the toned muscles in Lena's legs and frowned at the dingy hiking boots on her feet. "Nice boots."

"They're the only ones that fit me," Lena said, staring down at her feet.

"They really add some class." Charlie said, holding his thumb up.

Lena raised her eyebrow in amusement. "Wait until you see the hot pink stilettos I found for you. It's your turn to clean off the dust."

The water from the shower was a cold, electric shock that struck Charlie's head and charged him with a pain that elated him. He scrubbed with the disk of soap until it was a sliver and once his skin was completely numb, he jumped from the shower and threw on the jeans and a black T-shirt bought in Ensenada at a famous bar, Papas & Beer.

Charlie found Lena sitting on the floor between the sleeping children, her eyes focused on him and he could tell she was seeing him for the first time as well. She nodded in approval and reached for his hand as he slid next to her. She gently ran her fingers on his knuckles, the sensation causing a tingle at the back of his neck. Shifting her weight, she pressed her head into his shoulder. "We're safe for now."

"How can you be so sure that Wolf watching the

door downstairs isn't going to rob us?" Charlie asked.

"Jaime would skin him alive."

"Jaime has my money so he doesn't give a damn. How do you know he's not going to have us killed?"

"He's a thief but Jaime keeps his promises," Lena said pulling a plastic shopping bag beside her and giving Charlie a bottle of water, "and he's my husband's brother."

"Brother in law?" Charlie said, taken by surprise, he hadn't thought about Lena having a husband, a life with routine problems like what to have for dinner or meeting Giselle's teachers for a parent conference. He felt guilt that he was so selfish to think that Lena only existed to save him from his nightmare.

Charlie sat with Lena in silence listening to the children breathing. The wall was keeping him from falling over. Lena's head had slipped to his chest and was rising with his breath. The last time he had laid so still was when Max was just a baby and would fall asleep, comforted by his father's strong chest keeping him close.

"We need to talk about Mariana," Lena said, her soft voice made his stomach quiver.

"Did you live in Rosarito?" Charlie said, moving Lena to sit up, "Does anyone actually live in Rosarito?"

"They may separate us and ask questions." Lena said tilting his head toward her. He could see the sadness in her eyes and he felt her pain because it was his own.

"Does your brother in law just sleep at the bar? It's six in the morning and he's propped up on a barstool." Charlie said, coughing and sliding away, "He looked big enough to be the bar."

Lena picked up his hand and pulled him back to her, "Get all the jokes out now."

Charlie swallowed hard as Lena squeezed his hand. "We can't possibly know what they're going to ask."

"We don't have a lot of time," Lena said, raising herself up to look him in the eye," How old was I when we met?"

Charlie stared at her and felt anger rise in his throat. "This isn't some acting class. I'm not pretending you're Mariana."

Lena's eyebrows furrowed into a deep frown. "This is our lives. You must look at me with love of husband and wife. You must believe I am Mariana."

"Mariana's dead," Charlie said, his voice breaking as he said the words, looking over at Max sleeping on the couch, "Yesterday, she was alive. Now all that is left is her smile on my son's face. Every time I look at him, it's like looking at Mariana."

"You still want to love her." Lena said.

Charlie would always love Mariana for giving him Oriana and Max, they gave his life purpose. There was a part of him that wanted Mariana but not the woman. He wanted her to be the girl he saw eight years ago on the college campus that looked at him with love in her eyes.

"You don't get to mourn right now," Lena said pulling Charlie's face back to see her desperate eyes, "Do you understand we need to look in love?"

Charlie pulled back. "You think it's so easy to pretend?"

"We die if you don't." Lena said, pointing to a doll with a cracked porcelain face lying on the floor, "Our children are better than money. They can be sold to perverts who hunt black markets for lost children. They can be strung out on drugs so they can peddle them in the streets. If they are sold then death will be what they pray to end their suffering."

Fear clutched Charlie's stomach. He fought back the desire to vomit. He closed his eyes and tried to squeeze out the world. "Just give me a minute."

Lena grasped his hand and rested her head back on his chest. "I wish I can say I am sorry. I just need you to understand and we have little time."

"Where do I even start?

"Tell me like a story," Lena said, gently, "Start with the day we met."

Charlie thought about the day he had first seen Mariana. She had split the side of her skirt which exposed her thigh. Mariana had caught Charlie's gaze as she tried to adjust the seam. This time, it was Lena's face that looked up at him and smiled. Already, Mariana's image was fading.

"We met at USD. You were nineteen years old."

Chapter Twenty Two

It had been three hours and Lena pressed Charlie about the dates that mattered. The first date on a cruise around Mission Bay, weekend trips to Vegas, honeymoon in Brazil, children's birthday parties in Balboa Park and all the happy memories that filled eight years of a marriage. Lena listened and asked many questions as simple as what toothpaste Charlie used and as technical as the time and manner that Max was born. It was the questions about his marriage that weren't easy to answer. What did Mariana find annoying about Charlie? What were fights about? How many times a week was sex? The questions were not just as easy as a day on a calendar. They dug deeper started to feel like daggers tearing into fresh wounds.

"Did you ever cheat on Mariana?"

Charlie shifted off the floor and felt an ache in his legs that was matching his mood. "They aren't going to ask that."

"We don't know what they will ask," Lena said, "They might want to rattle our cage to see how we react."

"Fine," Charlie sighed. "I've never cheated."

"Never?" Lena said, the tone in her voice and frown on her face was proof she didn't believe him.

Charlie had been asked this question many times by Remi and Brenda. It was true that he had never cheated on Mariana. He didn't want to be with anyone else.

"I was married eight years and I had opportunity but I never did," Charlie said, "I didn't want to be with anyone else."

"Who is Brenda?" Lena said as if he had caught him in a lie.

The question was unexpected and it took Charlie by surprise. "Where did you hear about her?"

Mariana mention her name." Lena said, her jaw hardening and her eyes look accusing, "Mariana said you were always putting the other woman above her."

"I'm sure she did." Charlie said with a low laugh.

"So you admit you have a mistress." Lena said, folding her arms and waiting for an answer.

Charlie was amused. He leaned back and allowed her to enjoy a few more moments of satisfaction. Charlie leaned forward and gave a slow grin. "Brenda's my mom."

Lena sat up straight, her cheeks were reddened. "I didn't know."

"It's not a secret that Mariana and Brenda fought. Brenda is the world's worst mother in law and Senor gave Mariana everything she wanted," Charlie said, "a spoiled rich kid was never going to get along with poor, white trash."

"I don't know what that means."

"White trash is a phrase for people who are white that don't have any class," Charlie said, cringing at the bare branches of his family tree, "Combine that with the fact that Brenda's a raging racist and she's like a powder keg with Mariana as the spark."

"You call yourself racist, white... trash? "Lena asked, her face looked like she had tasted something bitter.

"I *do* come from white trash but I'm not a racist," Charlie laughed, "I hate everybody."

Lena's mouth dropped open.

"It's just an expression." Charlie said quickly, "I don't have a problem with anyone. I've met a lot of people in this world who do bad things. It didn't matter if they were black, white, green or purple. They share one thing in common. They think they have the one reason that makes it okay to treat someone like they are shit. You can't rationalize hate."

"So you don't call yourself a racist," Lena said slowly, "but you call your mother one?"

"We've talked enough about this, "Charlie said, her focus making him uncomfortable, "Let's turn the magnifying glass on you. Let you fry like an ant for a little."

"Ants and magnifying glasses?"

"It's just a stupid expression."

"Charlie Thibodeaux, you say some really strange things sometimes."

"Why aren't you already in the US with your husband?" Charlie said, throwing the question at her.

"It's complicated."

"Is he waiting in San Diego?"

"He was working in a restaurant in a part of your country called Oregano," Lena said.

"Oregon." Charlie corrected.

"Oregon?" Lena said confused, she looked suspicious. "Are you sure it's not Oregano?"

"Pretty sure," Charlie said looking amused, "unless your husband worked in a spice used to make tomato sauce."

Lena gave a real laugh. She had a beautiful smile, her face looked soft and gentle with thick lashes covering deep, questioning eyes. It was as if her soul was looking directly at you. Normally he didn't search out women unless they were younger. Younger women were easy to impress. Lena wasn't the kind of woman who wanted to be entertained; she wanted someone who could hold up their part of a conversation. She was closer to his age, maybe in her middle to late-thirties. If she had sat down in his club, Charlie would have looked right past her and what a shame to miss her.

"When did he go to the US?"

"Three years."

"Three years?" Charlie said unable to hide his surprise, "You haven't seen your husband in that long? Marriages begin and end in less time than that."

"He always sent money and would call every week until eight months ago," Lena said, her smile fading, "That is why I must go find him. I don't know if he is alive or dead."

"Have you cheated?" Charlie asked.

Lena's eyes darkened. "Of course not."

"Don't act offended," Charlie said, "That's a valid question. I'm supposed to believe you haven't been with anyone else in three years?"

Lena was growing irritated. "We have talked enough about me. Let's talk about your family. Do you have any siblings?"

"Do you really think they are going to ask all these questions?"

Lena looked around the room. "Is there something else you need to be doing right now?"

Charlie shrugged. "I have a sister Nola and I had a brother, Jackson, but he was killed when I was twelve."

Lena did not seem fazed. "And your sister? Is she older or younger?"

"She is ten years younger than me."

"Is she married?"

"Not in the cards for Nola," Charlie said, tapping his fingers on the floor. He never liked talking about his family, "she and Brenda live with me."

Charlie wanted the subject to end. "What about you? Any brothers or sisters?"

Lena hesitated. "I had twelve brothers and sisters."

"Twelve? Damn, that's a big family," Charlie said, always feeling a little envious to have so many siblings to depend on, "Are you the oldest?"

"I am now the youngest." Lena said, "They are not going to ask about my family."

"They aren't going to ask about my sister either," Charlie said, his voice raised high enough that he caused Max to stir. "Let's talk about something else."

"What's your father's name?" Lena asked.

"Something else other than my family."

Lena continued to stare at him and wait for an answer.

"Samuel Dooney Thibodeaux," Charlie said, "the last bastard child born on Bourbon Street."

"How did he make money?"

"Sam... he scraped by on whatever he could pick up," Charlie said, the memory of Sam standing over him, a crooked smile chewing on a tooth pick with the smell of cheap bourbon and teeth not brushed in a week, "I don't know if he ever had a legitimate job. He loved the summer season because he could work on a tourist who wanted some local color. Lift a wad of cash and make it last a few days for drugs and women but he'd never think to spend a dime on the family unless we wanted a cigarette."

"What about your mother? How did she raise three children with no money?"

"Brenda worked as a cleaner," Charlie said, "She scooped up trash and swished toilets at a hotel in New Orleans. The owner took half her pay in exchange for letting us live in a converted janitor closet with a drain for a toilet. Brenda squeezed a bed in there and we had a fucking palace."

"Why do you call your parents by their first names?"

"We're not a real close family."

"You say that, but when I ask about your sister-" Lena started to speak but Charlie was finished with the happy family chit-chat.

"Nola's a fifteen year old in a grown woman's body," Charlie interrupted, "she'll never have kids or a husband. She'll never own a house, never have a career... there is always a 'never' that begins and ends any sentence with Nola's name. She's a lost little girl who will never grow up."

"Charlie..."

Lena's voice softened as she reached for him but Charlie moved away from her touch and jumped to his feet.

"No, more," Charlie said, heading out the hotel door, "this is over. No Mexican soldier gives a shit about the questions you're asking. Knowing everything about me isn't going to turn you into Mariana."

Chapter Twenty Three

Charlie's head felt foggy and he stumbled around the hall. He leaned over the planter boxes and stared down at the lobby. Lena followed him out and rested her head on his shoulder.

"You are right, knowing about your sister isn't going to make me like Mariana," Lena said, stretching so far over the planter that Charlie thought she might fall. He put his arm across her back to brace her. Lena leaned back into his arm and smiled, moving a lock of hair from his eye.

Charlie felt something break inside. "I haven't slept in twenty-four hours. When I close my eyes, I just see Mariana dead. I see Kier trying to save her."

Lena took Charlie's hand and headed back to the hotel room. "We need to rest."

"I can't rest," Charlie protested, glancing at the exit door, "Anyone could rush through and rob us or worse. There is still someone out there looking for me after murdering a family and because you are helping me, that puts you and Giselle in danger. God sent you a curse when you met me."

"I want to show you something," Lena said, pulling Charlie back into the room and down to the floor. She reached inside a shopping bag and pulled out a green, tattered book. The jacket cover was gone and the smelled of mildew and glue residue on the back reminded Charlie of a forgotten overdue library book. Lena opened up the book to the middle pages which were threading away from the spine and pointed to the title of a poem, "I found this book in one of the suitcases."

Lena's finger stopped on the word, *Binnen*, which meant nothing to him. He scanned the poem for help but it was written in German.

Lena tapped the word. It's German for *Landlocked*."

Charlie shook his head and she pointed to a stanza, *In das Land gesperrt*.

"You read German?" Charlie asked, not surprised.

"I speak six languages," Lena said and tapped her fingers back to the book, "and this says *locked to the land*. It's the poem by Elijhun Cann-Saez that you said your brother liked to quote. It's what I quoted to you on the road. The poem is about taking risks to find happiness in your life."

"It's a coincidence," Charlie said, "It means nothing."

This book is sixty years old and brought thousands of miles for us to find," Lena said, her eyes brimming with tears, "it means you and I are meant to be here."

"Where did you come from?" Charlie whispered, stopping a tear from falling down her cheek, "When you speak, it makes me feel things are going to be okay."

"I came to save you and Max," Lena said, "and Giselle and I won't survive unless you bring us across the border. God doesn't curse, Charlie. He's brought us together when we need each other the most."

Chapter Twenty Four
La Jolla- Charlie's House

The only sound was the TV in the kitchen. Nola sat with her back hunched on a bar stool, a bowl of popcorn in her arms. She was intently watching some ridiculous show that splashed between a cartoon and some really energetic woman.

Lisa placed her hand on Nola's back, she jumped and some popcorn slid from the lip of the bowl.

"Sit straight Nola."

Nola slouched back over. "It hurts my back to sit that way."

"But you look taller and it makes you look thinner."

"Oh," Nola looked down and then shifted herself to move straight.

"Hey," Lisa reached over and touched her arm, "I'm sorry if I got upset with you earlier. I was just tired."

"I just- I wanted to see what you're doing."

"Where's Brenda?"

"She's asleep." Nola said, her face brightening, "Do you want to go swimming?"

"No, Nola, I'm going to go to Fashion Valley and pick up a dress," Lisa said picking up her purse.

Nola slumped back over the counter and placed

the popcorn on the counter.

"Why don't you go swimming?" Lisa asked.

"Mama and Charlie say I can't go by myself." Nola grumbled, "I can't even take Max and Orrie in with me."

Lisa listened downstairs. The murmur of Brenda's TV was the only thing. Otherwise it was quiet.

"Nola, do you want to come with me?"

Nola's eyes brightened. "Really?"

"Sure," Lisa looked at her watch, "go change your clothes."

Nola looked down. "Why?"

Lisa surveyed Nola's loose fitting jeans. Her sneakers were splotched with mud and there were crumbs on her button down red cardigan. "Don't you have a dress?"

"Mama won't buy me any," Nola said, trying to brush the crumbs from her cardigan.

"How about we go pick you a dress?"

"I can pick out a dress?" Nola's eyes beamed, "I'll go tell Mama."

"Let's let her sleep," Lisa said, gently pulling Nola toward the door, "she doesn't get a lot of time to rest."

Chapter Twenty Five
Rosarito Hotel, Mexico

Charlie propped himself on the floor with his back against the wall and faced the front door. There was a wind chime that beat a metal clink on the balcony. Charlie closed his eyes and tried to sleep. At his side, Lena had fallen asleep against him. He inhaled her scent of hotel soap and felt his shoulders relax. Giselle let out a soft cry and Charlie watched her try to sleep with her eyes clenched tight. Charlie could only imagine what nightmares were running through her mind. It made Charlie want to comfort her and he felt the ache to be with his own daughter.

Thick, meaty palms circled firm on Charlie's throat pressing him against the floor. Hot breath exhaled on him that reeked of sour beer and onions and he was now staring at Jaime, the large Mexican from the bar and Lena's brother in law.

Jaime pounded a heavy fist into Charlie's chest. "Vacation is over. It's time for you to check out, cabron."

Jaime's fist turned to fingers struggling to pull Charlie's zipper. Charlie lurched forward, using his weight to break their hold, putting his arms between them, ready for defense.

"Relax," Jaime said with such a hard laugh that he struggled to catch his breath, "If I wanted to rape you, it ain't like you could stop me."

Charlie looked for the kids. He caught a glimpse of Max now sitting up with his eyes wide with fright.

"Kids are safe" Jaime growled, "but you're in trouble."

Lena was still lying on the floor near Charlie. She was looking up at the man and appeared startled but did not look frightened.

"Jaime, what are you doing?" Lena said, pulling at the giant's pant leg to get his attention.

"Tourist, my ass," Jaime spat in Spanish, "I knew you were up to something when you wanted to start making money. What do you think I am? Pendejo?"

Shoving a fat finger in Charlie's direction, Jaime switched back to English. "Everyone is looking for this rich guy."

Charlie responded by slamming his fist into Jaime's nose which was answered with Jaime's fist hit the side of his face.

"You're worth money as a corpse or just bruised," Jaime snorted back blood trickling from his nose, "You tell me how you want to go."

Charlie reached for Lena but she was no longer next to him. A crack came from behind Jaime weakened his grip on Charlie and he dropped him back to the floor. Jaime straightened up and Charlie caught a glimpse of Lena holding a lamp before Jaime swung his large arm behind him and hit Lena square on the cheek. Lena let out a small cry as she staggered from behind and dropped the lamp. She tried to place her footing but stumbled and fell to the floor as Jaime dropped on top of her.

Charlie scrambled to his feet unsure how he was going to move Jaime off Lena. He raised a fist toward Jaime's neck when he realized that Lena was upright and Jaime hovered over her like a protective brother.

"Why do you make me do that, Lena?" Jaime asked transforming from the heavy giant into a large child. He gently moved Lena on to the couch which gave Charlie time to look for something to defend himself. He reached for a curling iron lying underneath the night stand. Grasping at a hard lump sticking into his back, he pulled out a shampoo bottle. Sizing up the large width of Jaime and the strength of his fist, Charlie felt ridiculous grabbing hair products and dropped them to the side.

Lena pushed Jaime's arm away as he tried to hug her. "You promised Antonio that you would protect me."

"I'm sorry that I hurt you." Jaime said softly and then darted his eyes like a guard dog back to Charlie, "Eulojo has sent the word he's looking for a white guy and boy. If I give them up then I'm protecting you."

Lena shook her head, "I won't let them be harmed, they're too important."

Jaime's face clouded over and he sneered in disgust. "You cheating on my brother with this gringo?"

"You're such a hypocrite, a few hours ago you wanted me to sell my body to him," Lena said, cringing as if she'd smelled something foul, "How does that honor Antonio?"

Jaime's face was turning bright red. Charlie wondered if he was forgetting to breathe. "Don't avoid the question! Selling your body isn't the same when it's for survival."

Lena leaned back and rolled her eyes. She was gathering strength from his anger.
"He's getting Giselle and me across the border."

Jaime laughed. "Him? He's got something that can get across? How's he going to protect you? What's he hiding in the shampoo bottle, a grenade launcher?"

Jaime's moved toward Charlie. "What you got Vidal Sassoon?"

Jaime grabbed for his leg but Charlie broke the grip and kicked Jaime's hand popping his knuckle. Jaime howled with laughter. "You should have tried to launch the shampoo bottle."

Jaime lunged for Charlie but not before Lena got between them. She intertwined her legs with Charlie and used the weight to anchor against the floor. Her arms pushed up against Jaime's chest. "Don't touch him!"

"But if he's got papers," Jaime whined, trying to figure out how to move her without harm, "That could be a lot of money! We could give him to Eulojo and then sell the papers. You can get you over no problem with the money we get!"

Lena reached inside Jaime's shirt and grabbed a lock of hair.

"You've told me that before." she whispered and then twisted her fingers until he howled. He turned away from her but she continued to intertwine fingers. His fist was clenched but he pounded the floor instead of her. "Remember your promise to your brother."

"I remember, now let me go, Lena," Jaime whimpered, moving away once Lena relaxed her hold. He spoke to Lena in Spanish but kept one eye on Charlie, unaware Charlie was following every word, "What am I going to tell Eulojo?"

"You haven't seen us." Lena snapped.

Jaime snorted. "Eulojo knows that no white man is going to get past Rosarito without me knowing."

"You were drunk. You're cabrons were celebrating with some whores. I don't care what you tell him."

"He'll make things hard around here," Jaime said, lowering his voice, "I say that we turn over the gringo and I'll have a buyer for the papers by tonight. With the money, you can get across and I'll still make some money on the deal."

Lena pointed to Giselle on the bed, by now awake and staring at Jaime. "Antonio said that Giselle looked like her Abuela. Is that true? Does she look like your mother?"

Jaime shifted his weight to look at Giselle and shrugged.

"I never got to meet your Mama," Lena said, watching Jaime squirming, "she was killed before I met Antonio, but you know that, don't you?"

"I don't want to talk about this."

"You were fifteen, right?" Lena continued to press, "She was a few years older than Giselle right now, at least they didn't shoot your Mama in the face, so you could have one last picture in her casket."

"Stop saying that!" Jaime yelled, struggling to get up from the floor as if he was in physical pain.

"If you give the gringo to Eulojo, just put us in the grave with your Mama." Lena said, her voice full of venom.

Jaime struggled to his feet and lumbered toward the hotel door nearly taking it off the hinges. He paused to glare at Charlie and Lena. "Estrella's coming down. You better be ready when I call you."

Charlie listened to Jaime's heavy steps lumbered down the hall. He chose to not move until he heard the stairwell door slam shut.

Max ran quickly to Charlie and clung to his neck.

"Are you hurt, Daddy?" Max whispered, squeezing Charlie on his chest which ached from Jaime's fist.

"I'm fine, "Charlie said gently pushing Max away and forcing as big a smile as he could pretend, "You were so brave."

Max's eyes filled with tears. "I was scared for you."

"We were playing, he didn't hurt me at all," Charlie lied kissing Max's cheek which took a streak of dirt away, "I found a clean spot. We'd better wash the rest of you."

Charlie picked up Max and moved him into the bathroom but kept his eyes on Lena. She avoided his stare and moved Giselle into the room across the hall causing Charlie's blood starting to boil. She knew he understood the conversation with Jaime. It was clear she did know who was following them. If she was keeping secrets, how could he trust her with anything else?

Wondering what else Lena was holding back made it difficult for Charlie to concentrate on bathing Max and the boy shrieked and howled at the cold water. By the end, Max sat scrubbed and miserable on the edge of the tub while Charlie towel-dried his head. Charlie was pretty sure that he had missed Max's left leg but he could worry about that when they were home.

"I'm hungry," Max grumbled.

Charlie left the bathroom and spied Giselle huddled on the bed again but this time she was washed and dressed in the pink T-shirt and jeans Lena had found. Charlie sat Max down next to her. "Stay with Giselle and I'll find you food."

Entering the hall, Charlie searched for Lena. He was too angry to be afraid what was lurking around the corners. Lena had torn him open about his life, bringing up personal details about Mariana that would pain him under the best of circumstances. No one was going anywhere until she answered his own questions.

Charlie found Lena at a bank of vending machines stuffing a shopping bag full of chips and sodas. "The tourists pried open the machine but fled before they could grab them."

"Who is Eulojo?" Charlie shouted, "why don't I know about him until now?"

"I couldn't be sure until Jaime said his name," Lena said, wiping her eyes, "I had to be sure."

"What would he want with me?"

"He kidnaps important people, infamous for brutal murders when their families don't pay the ransom," Lena said, picking up the bags and sliding them onto Charlie's arm, "because he is loyal to the cartels in Sinaloa, they gave him control of the drug corridor that moves through the Baja border. Nothing happens within a thousand miles that Eulojo doesn't control. Someone must have told him you were coming and knows you are worth a lot of money."

"Jaime said that you were in danger if Eulojo was looking for us."

"Eulojo is like Diablo, the devil," Lena shuddered, "you are in danger the moment he knows your name because he won't stop until he possesses your soul. Jaime knows he can't protect us if Diablo wants to own us."

Lena's hands were trembling. In the bleak hours, Charlie had seen her afraid but the thought of Eulojo gave her a look of terror. Keeping silent wasn't deception; she was praying that she wasn't right. He felt the anger draining and pulled her toward him feeling a crunch on his hip. Pulling back, the bags on his arm, swung from between them. "Now we have chip dust and sodas for our dinner."

Lena laughed and Charlie felt thrilled that he had brought her happiness when she was so frightened.

Going back inside the hotel room, Charlie and Lena found Max had piled postcards on the bed and Giselle was helping him stack them into a house. Giselle was breaking through her zombie-like paralysis.

"Sit with me," Lena said, waving toward Max and then pulling him up on the couch, "let's put something in your tummy."

Max stuffed his mouth and grinned as he made a loud crunch. "I can have chips for dinner?"

"They're great for your eyesight," Lena said, pulling out a chip and crossing her eyes as she made a loud crunch.

Max laughed. "Lisa doesn't like me to eat junk food."

"Who is Lisa?"

"Daddy's finance," Max said.

Lena frowned as she looked at Charlie. "Do you mean fiancée? Lisa is his fiancée?"

Charlie felt a sinking feeling in his stomach as Max nodded. In all the hours, discussions about every detail of his life and he had not put Lisa in a single memory.

"We're not getting hitched next week," Charlie said realizing that was a stupid thing to say, it didn't matter when he was getting married, that wasn't the point.

"Congratulations to you," Lena said as she stood up, her back toward him as she headed for the door, "Estrella should be here by now."

"Where are you going?" Charlie asked, but she was out the door. Charlie scrambled to his feet and headed after her but she was already at the stairwell, "Lena!"

Lena looked toward him, her face shadowed in the hall. "We need to get going."

"You're acting like you're-"Charlie started to say but hesitated.

Lena had moved into the stairwell but paused with her foot propping the door. "Like I am what?"

Charlie wanted to say she was acting like a jealous girlfriend. He wanted to shake her and tell her that grown women don't play these games. "You're acting like... your upset... about Lisa."

"You did not mention her."

"I didn't think about her." Charlie said, knowing that was the worst thing to say but it was the truth.

"You gave me the name of the street you buy groceries," Lena said, her voice accusing, like it had been with Jaime, "but you don't mention you're going to be married?"

"You wanted to know Mariana. That's the wife of my past," Charlie said, charging down the hall and grabbing the exit door, "you didn't want to know about my present life."

"What else are you keeping from me?" Lena said, moving down a flight of stairs, keeping a distance between them, "how do I know you'll really get us across?"

"I am putting my life and Max in your hands. All I know about you is that you are willing to lie that you're my wife to get across a border and that you don't have any problem killing someone if they threaten you," Charlie shouted not caring that his voice was echoing on the first floor, "How do I know that you're going to deliver what you promised? How do I know you're not bringing me to Eulojo to save yourself?"

"You need to find a way to trust me because I am all you've got right now," Lena shouted back, "if I wanted to sacrifice you to Eulojo, why didn't I let him murder you on the beach? Why didn't I leave you on the road for him to take you?"

"I'll go look at your damn green book, maybe God will teach me German and I'll find another clue." Charlie said, slamming the exit door leaving Lena in darkness.

Chapter Twenty Six

Lena had been gone for over an hour, by now the sun had come down and the room was as dark as the stair well. Charlie would have feared that Lena had abandoned them except that she wouldn't leave Giselle. Max was irritated from sitting still and squirmed to move around but Charlie needed to keep him close. The hotel was no longer a haven but the beginning of any ghost story with dark corners and dozens of halls to get lost and never be seen again. Giselle lay motionless on the couch staring at the wall.

Charlie groped in the darkness through a suitcase and found a jacket, possibly a tourist that had planned to go back to a colder climate. He put it aside to wrap around Giselle. A smaller jacket, possible for a woman would dwarf Max but he ripped at the sleeves to make them easier to roll up.

"Daddy, when are we going to see Mama?" Max said, bouncing on the bed, "You said she would be here. I'm bored. Can't we turn on the lights?"

"Mama is-" Charlie said, grasping for the right words to quiet him, "Mama will be seeing us later."

Max rubbed his eye and yawned. "Where is she?"

"Muerte."

Giselle was now sitting up, her figure an outline in the darkness.

Max looked up at Charlie. "Muerte? Who's dead? Mama?"

"No, she's not Max," Charlie said hoarsely, trying to reach for the edge of the bed, "Mama just can't.... be here right now."

"But," Max said, his voice wavering in belief, "why did Giselle say that?"

Charlie stared over to the couch, "Giselle was talking about someone else."

"The man on the road?"

"Yes, Max." Charlie lied, looking in Giselle's direction. He was afraid she was going to speak again and he couldn't have this conversation now. How do you tell your son that his mother is dead?

Max squeezed his arms around Charlie. "I want to go home Daddy."

Charlie sighed. "Soon, Max. Be patient. Are you still hungry?"

Max threw an empty bag on the floor. "I want a hamburger."

"When we get home, we'll have all the hamburgers you want," Charlie said, putting aluminum can in Max's hands, "drink some soda."

"It's warm," Max whined, "I want some ice."

"There isn't any," Charlie said, his teeth gritting as he tried to decide if Max was too young or too spoiled to understand, "now quiet down."

Max settled back on the couch, his fists balled against him. Carlie waited until his breathing become heavy before he moved from the couch toward Giselle. He hated himself for what he was about to ask but he knew Giselle had answers locked in her nightmares and he needed to know without waking Max.

Charlie slid a bag of chips next to Giselle and then slowly moved to the floor next to the bed, afraid she would scurry away like a cat. "What happened at the Ranch? What did you see, Giselle? Did you see what happened to Max's Mama?"

Charlie watched for a reaction, a nod of her head, a sigh, or a tremble from a finger. Anything that would let Giselle find a way to let the truth surface but nothing could break the frozen statue.

What the hell am I doing? Charlie mumbled, "even if you told me, it doesn't help us right now."

Giselle lowered her face and whispered into Charlie's ear the one word that needed no explanation.

"Muerte."

Charlie wasn't sure if she was talking about the past or predicting their future.

The sun had been down for an hour. Charlie sat in the doorway with his eyes fixed on the opening in the exit stairwell. Occasionally he would hear a clang echo from inside but he was too tired to be alarmed. Lena had been gone for hours and Charlie held on to the fact she was coming back because she wouldn't leave her daughter with a stranger.

Unable to sleep anymore, Max found a pen and was drawing over the walls above the bed while Giselle lay watching him, only blinking when necessary. Charlie thought about stopping Max but figured it didn't really matter right now. He could lecture him when they got home about defacing a wall. For now, it was keeping him entertained and he had nothing else to keep his mind distracted from his Mama and losing his stuffed Penguino.

Time only gave the demons a chance to fill Charlie's mind with questions. Would they make the border before the passes expired? Would Jaime betray them? Was it dishonest to leave out that he had a fiancée? Was it worse that he hadn't thought to mention Lisa at all?

When Lena did return it wasn't a loud clang, she slipped inside and floated in the darkness toward him. She was so graceful that Charlie wasn't sure if she was an apparition until she lowered herself beside him and her hands touched his face.

"I was jealous," Lena whispered, "I don't have

a reason."

Relief washed over Charlie. "I should have told you about Lisa-"

Lena put her fingers on his lips. "You owe me no excuses. I got caught up in the moment. We've gone over so many things about each other. I felt like..."

"Like it was a first date?" Charlie interrupted.

Lena looked caught off guard. "I suppose."

Charlie leaned toward her and rested his head on her knees. "Was that our first fight then?"

Lena gave a faint smile. "Are you saying more strange phrases that no one understands except you?"

Charlie grinned. "I've got a million of them."

"If you keep speaking in your own language," Lena said, pulling him off the floor, "no one is going to ever understand what you really mean."

"Is it time to go home?" Max asked, moving by Lena's side and grasping her hand.

"We have one more ride," Lena said, kissing the top of his head, "but very soon."

Max looked toward the emergency door. "Did you bring Mama?"

Before Charlie could say anything, Lena pulled Max into her arms and hugged him, "Your Mama loves you very much. Can you be strong for her?"

Max nodded. "I miss her."

"Grab Giselle's hand," Lena said, releasing him and wiping her eyes, "it's time to go."

Lena stood in the hotel door and stared at the walls. Above the bed, Max had drawn many things, a ship sailing on a giant wave, a dinosaur fighting with a sharp-winged bird, and a monster with three eyes. In the center was where Max had taken his time drawing a woman was reading a story to a boy holding a penguin. On her throat was a jagged, dark line that dripped onto the boy's head creating tears from his eyes.

"I know you must wait to tell Max about Mariana," Lena whispered to Charlie, "but you are running out of time."

Chapter Twenty Seven
Fashion Valley Mall-San Diego

Fashion Valley was the first outdoor mall that Remi had seen when he had arrived from Loyola. He was fresh out of college and met his father, Dale Parrish, in San Diego for a quick vacation. Dale was heading overseas for a few months and let Remi stay at his girlfriend's house in Mission Bay. Remi liked the mall with its sunny sky for a ceiling and airy inlet of stores.

Remi thought it might impress his mother, Nance, when she flew down from Seattle for a visit. She was not amused that he expected her to stay in the house of her ex-husband's girlfriend and that he thought this was a place she would consider shopping.

"It's a glorified strip mall," Nance sniffed outside the Farrell's Ice Cream Parlor sitting in the corner of the parking lot. She refused to step out of the car and insisted Remi turn back toward the freeway and head north. She spent her visit checked into the Westin and canvasing the vast shopping mecca of South Coast Plaza. Remi left her to the closed off mall and went back to the perfection of Fashion Valley. There were young college girls that didn't have to bundle themselves up in heavy coats and sweaters. They were running with bright eyes out of Nordstrom's carrying big bags full of summer dresses and tiny shorts and it was only October. It made him call his college dorm mate, Charlie Thibodeaux and convince him this was the perfect place to start that club they dreamed about opening. What was not to love about San Diego? There were beautiful beaches, active nightlife in the Gaslamp District, major sports teams, and an open air mall with girls in shorts.

The love Remi felt for Fashion Valley was diminishing today. He moved his way from the square cobble stone and smooth cream walls bathed in sunlight to a sterile hallway that smelled of plumbing and trash compactors encased in florescent light. His shoes echoed on the linoleum that was left over from the years before the remodel. A brown wood door out of place in the sterile white hallway read security. Opening the door, was not the place he would expect to see long tan legs with delicate size five Jimmy Choos. Lisa sat legs crossed and tapping her polished nails on the metal of a folding chair. Her eyes brightened as the door opened but then settled once she recognized him.

Lisa stood up and rushed toward Remi, her arms reaching around him.

"Oh thank God you're here," Lisa said, pressing her head into his chest, "Maybe you can get something done."

"Have you heard anything new?" Remi asked.

Lisa shook her head and glanced back in irritation at the security guards. "They should have found her by now! This is ridiculous!"

"Calm down," Remi pulled her aside, "Tell me what happened."

"I took Nola to get a pedicure," Lisa said, holding out her perfectly polished crimson nails, "then we went to do a little shopping."

"A little shopping?" Remi asked.

Lisa glanced down at her bag and pulled it up to show Nola's sneakers, "She liked my shoes so I thought I would buy her some pretty shoes."

"Didn't Brenda tell you that she wanted you to stop dressing her up?" Remi said, glaring at Lisa, "She's not a doll for you to play with!"

"No, she's not! But she isn't five years old either," Lisa protested. She tossed the bag into his lap, "She looks ridiculous always wearing those sweaters and jeans."

"So you thought you'd give her a make-over?" Remi said, trying to keep his voice down but couldn't help feel angry. He always felt territorial like a brother when it came to Nola.

"It's not like you are making it sound!" Lisa protested, "She wanted to look different and asked me to help her. If you give her some make-up, Nola can be gorgeous!"

Remi had lost all patience. "Does it ever occur to you that it isn't always about the outside?"

Lisa pushed back from Remi allowing the chair to make a loud scrape against the floor bringing the attention of the guards.   "Stop yelling at me!"

"Okay...I'm not yelling," Remi said as he inhaled and gripped his hands on the counter. "How far did you dress her up? Was it just the shoes?"

Lisa's eyes narrowed and she snapped her fingers at the head security guard. "Why don't you talk to him? He's just going to keep yelling at me."

The guard flipped through his notepad, "The girl is wearing a blue and green mini dress and black heels."

Remi flipped back to Lisa who refused to look at him. He picked up the bags and recognized the red cardigan and blue jeans folded neatly in the bag. "Jesus, Lisa. Don't you understand why you can't do this? It's like letting out a little girl. She can't handle the attention."

Lisa bit her lip and stared silently ahead.

"Where's the last place you saw her?" Remi demanded but Lisa continued to stare silently, he gripped her arm and squeezed, "Damn it Lisa! Talk to me!"

Lisa squealed and pulled her arm back. "We were at Neiman's. I was paying, turned my back and she was gone."

Lisa's explanation didn't make sense to Remi. Anytime he had been outside the house, Nola she always followed closely to Charlie or Brenda. "She wouldn't just walk away."

"She didn't like that I was using Charlie's account."

"You use Charlie's cards all the time, that's not a reason she'd leave." Remi said, irritated that he was asking full questions and only getting half the truth each time.

Lisa was starting to look less indignant. "I may have said that our job is to look pretty and for men to pay for it."

"You said that about her brother?" Remi demanded.

"Oh, I was only joking." Lisa scoffed.

"She's not your best friend," Remi exclaimed, "You can't say things like to your future sister in law!"

Lisa started to pout. "I know I can't change her. It's just-"

"Bullshit!" Remi yelled, "You always want people to fit your mood!"

Lisa put her finger to his lips. "No! She wanted me to do it."

Remi had now lost all patience and started to mock her. "Nola came to you and said, "Please put me in a tight dress and paint my face?"

"You aren't listening," Lisa said, her voice became weepy, "you didn't see her face. Nola stared at herself in the mirror. She was so excited until she started to speak and she scared herself. Like she couldn't believe she wasn't looking at a stranger."

"She couldn't understand what was happening to her."

Lisa shook her head. "She understood just fine. This is how she should look. She knows something isn't right.

"You better hope you're wrong," Remi warned, "that brings a whole other problem and no one is prepared for that."

The door opened and the sound of awkward clicks came through the door and two guards came through the door followed by a woman. Remi didn't recognize Nola. Her hair had been straightened and given a fresh cut. The thick eye shadow and blush all perfectly placed to the contours of her face, making Nola's ordinarily fresh face looked sexual.

The mini dress showed off Nola's toned, long legs, her sneakers replaced with black stilettos. It was hard to deny that she was a woman and Remi couldn't help feeling guilty looking at her like a woman.

Nola spotted Remi standing there and her eyes filled with tears. She was so anxious that she stumbled to over her feet and Remi had to catch her before she fell.

"Remi!" Nola grasped him tightly, "I'm being arrested."

"No sweetheart, you didn't do anything wrong." Remi said, softly, his heart swelling as the gentle girl he loved like a sister revealed herself.

Nola steadied herself and smiled at him. "Look how pretty I look! Lisa bought me some clothes!"

Remi glared at Lisa. Clearly so much more had been done than putting a new dress on her. Lisa averted his gaze and looked only at pride at her creation.

"You look so pretty!" Lisa stood up and avoided Remi's eyes. She hugged Nola tightly. Together, they looked like they could be old sorority sisters, "we were so worried about you!"

The head of security moved past them and

clunked down a clipboard on the table to get their attention. "We found her in the food court."

"Can we go home, now?" Nola asked Remi, wiping her eye and smearing a pool of mascara. Lisa tried in vain to dab away the damage.

"Of course," Remi said, ushering her to the door.

Remi extended his hand to the security guard. "Thanks for your help."

Nola and Lisa started down the hall but the head of security stopped Remi. "I think you should know that we did find her in the food court but she was heading toward the parking lot. She was leaving with three men."

Chapter Twenty Eight
Rosarito Hotel- Mexico

Lena led them out to the other side of the hotel hallway and down another stairwell that was darker than the last. Cool air rushed inside as Lena finally pushed open the ground exit door and Charlie felt a rush of freedom. The day had passed into night and Charlie's comfort in the anonymity was short-lived. There were now more people around making Charlie nervous. It would be difficult to know what direction trouble was coming from. A crowd of men cut them off and Charlie clutched Max to his side. A woman ran behind them. She chattered rapidly in Spanish as she ran to catch up with the men. No one was interested in them as they hurried across the street. Crowds were all gravitating toward the bar which was like a neon flame that drew out the shadow figures. A band played from the inside and poured out a voice that called them to disappear inside. It occurred to Charlie that they weren't the only ones who had been kept captive in the light of day.

Lena led them across the street with the crowds but then broke away to the alley to the right. The alley opened to a small parking lot in the back of the bar. A battered white pick-up parked at the base of a wooden flight of stairs leading up the stucco wall to the bar's backdoor.

A woman pulled herself out of the driver's seat as they approached.

"That's Estrella," Lena whispered when Charlie hesitated. She prodded him forward when he stood frozen in surprise.

Estrella's thighs were stout like an exaggerated cartoon of a cowboy's chaps. They strained against faded and dusty jeans that frayed open at the bottom for flip flops. Her fat, pudgy toes were caked with mud and gave her feet the look of yellowed clay. Her belly strained against a plaid button down shirt that was two sizes too small. When she shifted her weight she exposed a rose tattoo rising up near her pelvis from two stretch marks that seemed to encase it like garden wire. Her hair had yellowed from being over colored. It reminded Charlie of the scarecrow in Wizard of Oz as it stuck in random directions from a hasty bun. A dark bed of roots were like the pitch of a thatched roof sitting squat on a brown stucco house baked in the sun. Her skin was broken and blotched from too much time in the sun and her nose was a bulbous tomato that was clipped with a single gold ring.

For some reason, Charlie had imagined Estrella as a stealth woman, tall and lean. His imagination built her as fearless and full of courage. In his mind she was a rugged beauty that withstood a tough life as a courier. It was the fault of all the movies he had to reference. He decided that this woman had never been called beautiful in her life. She was a beaten pack mule who had been dragged a few times but this didn't stop her from getting in a few kicks of her own. She had toughened her callous and made her so mean that she stepped on everyone's heads to give her height. This was the woman he was supposed to trust with their lives?

Lena sensed his concern. She put her hand firmly on his arm and whispered into his shoulder. "This is the only way."

Charlie nodded and placed his hand on Max's head. The boy looked up at him with wide eyes and he tousled his hair to get him to smile but Max turned back to Estrella.

Estrella counted everyone and stared at the wad of money in her hand. She frowned and then counted again. A small man, a wisp of his partner sat wiping his hands on an oversized white T-Shirt that was gray from dirt. His thin legs violently swung on the tailgate and stared at Lena, chewing absentminded on a toothpick with a slow smile. Estrella noticed his looks and her pleasant frown turned into a deep scowl. Despite her weighty arms they were quick and she punched the man on the side of his head, nearly swallowing the toothpick.

"Keep your head," Estrella's lips were fleshy and pushed out every syllable into his ear. He nodded meekly and jumped off the tailgate, pulling some tarps and trying to look busy.

She glared over at Lena and squinted as if she was looking at the sun.

"I know you," Lena said, pointing her finger at Lena.

Lena shook her head and looked down at Giselle.

"No, I know you!" Estrella said, but this time with a bit more anger, "What's your name?"

"Mariana." Lena said, looking quickly at Charlie.

Charlie tried not to look surprised at the lie. It was too soon to start. Was she afraid that Estrella would turn them in for more money?

Estrella started to walk towards them. "What'd you say?"

"Mariana," Lena said softly, her eyes locked on Giselle who looked up at her, "Mariana Thibodeaux."

Estrella got a closer look. She lifted Lena's chin and put her face within inches. Charlie smelled her foulness which reminded him of onions and sour milk. "That's not your name."

Estrella started to back away. She looked edgy and angry. "Something isn't right here."

Charlie stepped forward, "Ma'am. This is my wife. These are our children- we-"

Charlie heard a click and noticed the small man had produced a shot gun aimed at Charlie's head. He instinctively put his hands in the air. "Look, we don't want any trouble."

Estrella laughed. She displayed a mouth missing a front tooth and sputtered in English, "He stupid but he's quick."

Lena was spared more attention by the approach of three shadows coming down the alley from behind. Two men appeared with a thin, teenage girl between them.

"We're not the only ones?" Charlie whispered.

Lena shook her head. "I don't know how many she's taking."

The men were heavily dressed, their arms thick from multiple shirts, they bowed and prevented them from falling naturally to their sides. Estrella poked them and nodded in approval. "Gets cold up north, don't it? You got any dollars packed inside?"

Estrella took interest in a younger girl. Charlie guessed she wasn't older than sixteen. Unlike her traveling companions, she was only dressed in a thin white dress as if it was decided at the last minute to leave the country. She glanced nervously at Estrella who was enjoying taunting her. Estrella put her hands on the girl's waist and tugged at her skirt. "What you dressed for? Is this your Quinceanera?"

Charlie remembered seeing pictures of Mariana's own Quinceanera. While American girls had Sweet Sixteen parties, a Mexican girl dreamed of their coming of age party. It reminded Charlie of a southern tradition of a debutante ball. Many of the parties cost more than weddings and this girl looked like a party was out of the question. Charlie found Estrella's cruelty a new reason to not like this woman.

The men, Charlie assumed were a father and brother, stepped forward protectively to surround the girl but the small man who was acting like Estrella's side kick raised his gun again. The men retreated but were careful to leave the girl in between them.

Jaime's heavy steps pounded inside and he appeared at the back door of the bar. His massive frame allowed shafts of light to peer through. "Ain't you gone yet?"

"This one," Estrella said pointing to Lena, "I don't like her."

Jaime shrugged. "She too pretty for you?"

The small man let out a low laugh but sucked back his air when Estrella glared back at him. "What's her story?"

"Ask her yourself." Jaime snorted.

"She just lies," Estrella shouted and kicked up dirt at Lena.

"She's just a whore wanting to get her kids across." Jaime yelled.

Estrella looked at Charlie and spit on the ground. "The gringo is going to take her?"

"What am I, a fucking resume? What do you care why? He's stuck here and lost his passport," Jaime yelled, leaning against the railing causing it to groan in protest, "No help from the North anymore. They cleared out this morning."

Lena and Charlie exchanged glances. The Embassy was gone. All help was going to depend on the papers and a border agent. Charlie swallowed nervously feeling his throat stick. He wished he had brought a few more sodas with them.

Estrella waved her hands up and shoved the money into her pocket. "I'll take the Gringo and the kids to the border."

She began to slide some tarps from the back of the truck but then formed a fist at Lena. "But that bitch stays here."

For the first time Giselle stirred and looked

frantically at Lena. The whine of a feral cat rose from her body with no movement of her mouth. Lena knelt down and kissed her cheek as she swept hair from her face. "It's okay. I'll be on the next one."

Giselle's feral sounds lowed to a hum and Lena put Giselle's ice cold hand into Charlie's. She smiled nervously at Charlie and kissed Giselle's cheek again.

"I'll be there soon." Lena said in a voice that convinced no one.

Giselle closed her eyes and grasped hard at Lena's waist. Lena pried her arms loose and wrapped them around Max. She knelt down and forced them to look her in the eye. "Protect each other."

Charlie's heart was sinking. He couldn't just leave her here. "I- maybe we can wait."

"I can take care of myself," Lena said shaking her head, her hands pressed into his arm, "I'm trusting you with all that matters to me."

Charlie stared into Lena's eyes. She represented the strength, sorrow, courage and heroism that he expected from Estrella. His hand reached behind her head and he drew her face toward him, kissing her impulsively. Lena stiffened in surprised but then allowed his arms to circle her waist. She gently reached up and touched his face as she pressed into him. He tasted her lips, they were not sweet or glossed, but smooth and salty.

The flutter of tarps breaking in front of them broke the apart. Estrella's small man was prodding the two other men to pull rocks from the back of the truck. Charlie started to move to help but small man raised his shot gun.

"I want to help," Charlie said, pointing to the truck.

The small man nodded but Charlie didn't move until he had lowered his weapon to the ground.

Jaime looked over at Lena and drummed his hands on the railing and then back at Estrella, "You serious, Este?"

Estrella continued to look busy pulling the tarp from the truck, "About what?"

Jaime took another step down. The angry giant that Charlie had seen hours before was starting to appear. "You aren't taking the woman?"

"I'm not taking her." Estrella mumbled.

"Well then give me back the money," Jaime growled.

"No!" Estrella grunted, dropping the tarps, "You owe me from the last one."

"I don't owe you shit," Jaime spat on the ground, "We're square. If you thought I was short, you should have settled earlier. I collected money for six people. Give it up."

The small man raised his shotgun defensively as Estrella began to heave her weight up the stairs to talk to Jaime. Jaime leaned on the doorway and laughed. " Lower that shotgun before I hurt you, Jorge."

The shotgun stayed raised and Jaime pounded the side of the wall. It shook like an earthquake and rumbled pebbles off the roof, skittering and landing at Jorge's feet. He slowly lowered his head and the shotgun. Jaime nodded. "Don't ever point a gun at me again or I'll shoot that stick up your ass."

Estrella reached the landing with difficulty. She paused and released her breath in a series of grunts. "You going to pinch me because I won't take one stupid whore?"

Jaime eyed Lena and then folded his arms. "I'm done with her. Don't need her around her taking up business. Take her out of here."

Estrella looked over at her and then whispered hoarsely toward Jaime.

Jaime looked disgusted at her. "Don't even think about it!"

Estrella mumbled and started back down toward the truck but Jaime grabbed her by the neck and pushed her to the side. Estrella struggled to break free but couldn't get her arms around to reach him. He pushed her face into the stucco, her cheek folding into her lips like an accordion.

Jaime leaned in toward her. The vicious menace and growl was almost spitting on her. "I mean it Estrella. Don't need more orphans running around here."

Jaime looked over at Jorge who had jumped off the tail gate but stood motionless. For a moment, he seemed to be hesitating to bring up the shotgun but decided to leave its nose buried out of their business and facing the ground.

"Get off me!" Estrella screamed.

Jaime leaned into Estrella's ear. "Do we understand each other?"

"Go fuck yourself." Estrella said, her arms trying to swipe at Jaime.

Jaime pushed harder into the wall and Estrella squealed in pain. He continued to press until she lowered her arms. "Okay!"

When Estrella lifted her face off the wall, it was pocked with blood. She swiped absently at her face and glared at Jaime. Jaime nodded at her and headed back up to the door. "Now get the fuck out of here. I've got business."

With that, he slammed the door and the only light came from a small rectangular window from a bathroom and the glow of the back door. Music began to come from a band inside. It made the whole building rattle.

"Bring the kids here!" Estrella yelled over. Giselle looked up at Lena who nodded it was okay.

Estrella looked down at Max and eyed the spare tire well. "Crawl in there."

Charlie looked over at the wheel well. It barely hung on the side of the truck. The slightest bump and the wrong weight, it would fly off the truck.

"He can't fit in there," Charlie objected.

Estrella squinted at him, trying to figure out the English. She ignored him and grabbed Max by the arm, pulling him up with her left arm and trying to catch his legs under the flesh of her right. Max squirmed in protest and she let go, he tumbled hard onto his back.

"He can't fit in there," Charlie said again. Estrella ignored him and continued to struggle with a .squirming Max. She grunted to keep her arms around him. She pinned him with one arm and raised her hand slapping him hard across the face. Max's leg swung up and smashed her hand against the truck. She dropped him and he fell hard on his back. She raised her hand again.

"Get off him!" Charlie yelled. He didn't care if he had ten shotguns pointed at his face; he moved underneath Estrella and picked Max up. Max's face turned into his shoulders, a large red welt on his cheek and his eyes liquid with tears.

In a flow of cursing and frustration, Estrella howled and held her right hand. "That bastard kicked me!"

"Can't he stay next to me?" Charlie said, trying to hide an overwhelming desire to smash her in the face. He looked over at Lena who translated for him.

Estrella continued to violently rub her hand and then pounded it against the spare wheel casing, it groaned and shook with her weight.

"Put him in there or he goes in pieces!" Estrella screamed.

Charlie looked down at his son. Max looked up at him fearfully, his chin quivering. Charlie tried to calm down. "We're going to go for a quick ride. You get the best seat. It's in a circle."

"I don't want to go in there Daddy." Max sobbed.

Charlie sighed heavily as he glanced over at Estrella who was impatiently pacing. She would not wait forever and whatever Lena knew may be coming was going to be here soon.

I'm sorry to do this to you, Max, Charlie

thought. With a heavy heart and harshness turned on his son. "Do what I tell you!"

"But, Daddy..." Max whined.

Charlie moved him over to the wheel well and lifted Max's legs so they fit up the south wall of the tire. Max's back curved under leaving the top of his face to press against a hole of rusted metal that opened into the bed of the truck. It was just big enough to see his left side of his eye. The boy cried out in discomfort as Charlie placed a canvas cover over the outside.

"Shut him up," Estrella said, her fist gripped the edge of the tailgate.

Charlie peered inside the bed and tried to find the hole. A shiny wide eye stared up at him.

"You need to be quiet, Max." Charlie said.

"This hurts! Max said, struggled to get his foot from the wheel," I don't want to be here."

"You'll stay in there until I tell you to get out!" Charlie barked. He looked away before Max could see there was pain in his face.

The sobs were almost muffled but Charlie could still hear him softly whisper. "Mommy..."

Estrella was now lining everyone by the tailgate. She motioned for the two men to lay down with their backs on the bed. Charlie was then waved over to lie next to them. With the bulk of their shirts, there was barely room for Charlie to fit but at least he was pressed near the hole with Max. He could hear the boy's breathing but could no longer see his face without having to turn to his side.

Jorge lifted Giselle onto the bed, her feet trying to not step on the men but she slipped and fell back with a thud. The older man let out a gasp as he lost his air. Eventually, she crawled between their heads and curled into a fetal position into a small pocket of unused space. The teenager was lifted onto the younger man and stacked between them, her head resting on the older man. Her eyes, were wide and nervous. Charlie tried to smile with some reassurance but she slid into the shadows of the truck and turned her back.

Jorge helped up Lena but not without trying to reach up her skirt. Lena's face remained emotionless as his hand slid inside. Jorge grinned as his hand passed up and down until he saw Estrella move around the side and he immediately pushed Lena up onto the tail gate. When Estrella began to make her way back into the bar, Jorge grabbed Lena firmly by the hips and pulled her toward him. He looked back for Estrella as he started to pull at his buckle.

Charlie lifted his foot and shoved it hard into Jorge's crotch causing him to groan and steady himself on the tail gate. He pulled a knife from his pocket and raised the blade to stab Charlie's leg but changed his mind when Estrella's heavy feet kicked open the bar door. He pushed Lena so she fell on top of Charlie.

Lena closed her eyes and leaned her head onto Charlie's chest.

"This will be over soon," Charlie whispered.

"You shouldn't have done that," Lena said softly gripping onto his arms.

"Like hell I didn't," Charlie said, feeling a little satisfaction at Jorge's pained face.

Charlie felt a hard, fragment rock fall near his face. Soon there were several more. He looked into the sky and saw a flood of rocks, some large, some pebbles, rain onto his face.

Jorge peered over with a sneer. Charlie began to feel pressure on his leg, hard and sharp, he wasn't able to look up but felt the weight grow, his fingertips felt the jagged tip of a rock.

"What the hell are they doing?" Charlie yelled.

"They need to hide us."

"Why can't they just put the tarps over us?" Charlie grimaced as a heavy rock pressed against his arm. "This is ridiculous! We're not even close to the border. What are we hiding from?"

"There are checkpoints all along the route," Lena paused as two pieces of granite rolled onto her shoulder, narrowly missing her face, "they aren't going to remove the whole tarp but they may peek inside.

"If it's the military then they can take us the rest of the way," Charlie complained.

"There are all kinds of checkpoints." Lena said, "most people have abandoned their cars. Estrella has to have a reason to be moving around. She's only protecting herself from the risk."

"You almost sound like you respect her," Charlie whispered.

Lena paused. "I understand her."

The boulders were continuing to bear down heavier and heavier. Pressure on his skull, afraid to move and send them crashing on his face.

"We're being buried alive," Charlie said, barely able to get the words out from the pressure.

Lena's breath was labored as she tried to respond. "Can...you... hear Giselle?"

Charlie tried to shift his head but it was firmly encased. He listened for any sound and tried to call out her name. "Giselle?"

He strained to hear sounds against the rolling of the rocks.

"Giselle, honey, please try to let us...know you're okay?"

The rocks continued to shift over them, Charlie starting to feel a growing sense of fear. That if this didn't crush them, it would smother them. Don't panic. Don't panic, Goddamn it. "Giselle, please?"

The rocks suddenly shifted from his head and he felt push on his right cheek. From the corner of his eye the rubber canvas under sole of a sandal.

"She's okay, Lena." Charlie called out, spitting out dust from a fragment of rocks falling in his mouth.

Lena didn't acknowledge. By now her body was only visible by a strand of hair that flicked upward from the rocks like a struggling plant.

"Lena!" he gasped before he felt the rocks roll onto his mouth. He squirmed to keep his nose in line with a gap.

"Please be okay," Charlie thought, "Please don't leave me Lena."

The rocks no longer clanged and the tiny crack of light now darkened blue. Jorge was pulling the tarp over them. The strain caused the rocks to lock in place. Immobile, murmurs from Estrella's voice in the distance and then the closer grumbling of Jorge, cursing as he tore his finger on the rope bindings. Charlie strained to hear a sound from Max.

A grumbling noise came from beneath and the truck roared reluctantly to life. There was a lurch forward and Charlie felt rib cage crack. A sharp burn seemed to radiate from his left side. He did his best to not inhale but found himself squirming to alleviate the pain.

The truck began to move slowly. It would stop and turn, shifting them around in a rocky coffin. It was difficult to tell how long they had been trapped inside. Charlie tried to count seconds but gave up when he'd reached a thousand. Twice the engine stalled but soon they were moving again. What air was left under the tarp was hot. It reminded him of Jackson trapping him under the blankets of a bed. The air seemed to grow stale and the feeling of panic as he punched to get out. Except this time, there was no mercy and no help from a fist. The movement shook the rocks around his face and he feared that they would cover his nose. Instead they seemed to give him a pocket of air and free his mouth.

"Max! Can you hear me?" Charlie was grateful that Max had been placed on the side of the truck and not buried under the weight. This would easily have crushed him.

Charlie listened but did not hear any sound. "Max, speak to me!"

"I'm scared Daddy."

Charlie felt relief at his voice even if the words were what every parent dreads to hear.

"I'm scared too Max," Charlie said as loudly as he could over the wail of the engine, "but it's going to be okay."

The truck jerked again and Charlie struggled to keep the rocks from his mouth. He knew he may not have much time.

"Giselle, if you can, let me know you're okay," Charlie called out. He felt pressure on his shoulder. Giselle must be in a better position since she was in the corner.

Only one more left. Lena was baring most of the weight and he had not heard anything from her in a while. Charlie silently prayed, "Please God, let her be okay."

"Lena!" Charlie called out.

Only silence. Charlie tried again and strained to hear her voice. He thought her heard her once but had it been the wind? Was it the engine?

A few minutes passed like hours, the truck began to heave upward and groan. This sent the rocks toward the tailgate and heavier on Lena's body.

He was not a religious man and even in the darkest hours, he had not asked for help but today, he was finding a voice. "God, please let her be okay, this was not how anyone should die."

Eyes closed with a shooting pain from a rock on his left eye and his right pressed against the tarp, he strained to listen for any sounds. The growl of the motor, Max's breathing, from the left he heard one of the men cry out and a tethered rope that slapped to gain freedom against the truck's bed.

Charlie felt something on his chest. A tiny tap that could have been the shifting of a rock but it continued to play a beat over and over. It never gained strength but seemed to repeat itself in a rhythm. Tap-tap Tap- Tap-tap.

Chapter Twenty Nine
La Jolla- Charlie's Home

Nola slipped out of the car, slamming the door and running up the driveway. The straps of her new shoes were interwoven with her fingers and clunked against the wall as she disappeared around the side entrance to the garage.

Lisa flinched as if she had been hit directly in the face. "Those are five hundred dollar shoes."

"When you can, rescue them into your closet," Remi said dismissively, "She'll never wear them again."

Lisa sighed. "She wears three sizes bigger than me."

Remi stared at the ignition. He thought about turning it off but was afraid he would startle her out of the car. "Have you heard from Charlie?"

"Not since yesterday," Lisa said, her hands wrapped tightly around the straps of her purse.

Remi carefully reached for the ignition and switched it off but didn't remove the keys. He noticed she didn't make any move to leave; her eyes misting. She was lost in her thoughts.

"He's going to be okay down there. Kier won't let anything happen," Remi said gently.

Lisa looked up as if she had just realized he was still there. She stared at his face, her eyebrows curved into a frown.

"He promised me he would be back before the governor's party at the Dell," Lisa sniffed, "I'm beginning to think he isn't going to make it in time."

Remi bit his lip and smiled. "And I almost thought you were worried about Charlie."

Lisa sat up straight and clicked off her seatbelt. "Of course I'm worried about him!"

"Right," Remi said, a low laugh escaping his mouth, "I'm sure you are."

Lisa balled her hand into a fist and punched him on his arm. It didn't hurt but it was unexpected and he moved back in his seat. "You are the biggest asshole sometimes."

Remi put his hands up in an apology, "I know, I know. You're worried about him."

Remi had been sincere. For Lisa, life was event to event. There wasn't a place for sentiment. It was one of the things he liked about her. She never seemed caught up in emotions, only planning the moments of her life. They sat in silence and she still made no move to leave. He felt bold to bring up the night before. "You got home okay."

"Obviously."

Lisa's silence continued to make him bold. "I didn't hear you leave."

"I'm going to go now." Lisa cracked the door and slid her legs out. Remi gently put his hand on her arm.

"You don't have to go." Remi said, softly to not startle her further.

Lisa nodded, "I can't sit out her forever. I've got to face Brenda sometime."

Remi started to feel a little rise of panic. His words drowning him but he couldn't seem to stop. "Why don't you come with me? I was heading to Del Mar for some dinner. How about some pasta at Il Fornaio? We can go to Zecote's for happy hour first? Watch the tide come in. I'll bring you home later."

Lisa didn't smile but she leaned in and kissed his cheek. Her lips felt cool on his skin that burned with embarrassment. "Sweet Remi."

Remi felt like he had discovered a deer and watched with disappointment as she startled toward the house. He sat in the car for another twenty minutes hoping she would return before he drove away.

Chapter Thirty
Mexico

With no way to tell time, Charlie relied on a rhythm to the truck and constant creaks to give him a sense of safety. It was ridiculous to say he felt secure entombed in rocks but Charlie was tired of feeling exposed. He was falling asleep but jolted when he heard the high pitched screech like a tea kettle he knew they were going to crash. The truck lurched with a heavy jolt toward the right. The left tires tilted up and could have flipped if the weight didn't throw them back to the road. Three pops like a gun sounded just above the tarp and Charlie heard the back window shatter.

The truck slammed to a halt, the rocks shifted again, Charlie struggled to spit out a mouthful of pebbles. Angry shouts were close and Charlie's heart stopped as three loud bangs pounded next to Charlie's head on the side of the pickup; close to the wheel where Max was trying to hang on.

Charlie heard Estrella's muffled voice was unmistaken in its hoarse pitch but had something he never heard before; it was timid and polite.

The square of tarp visible in Charlie's sight lifted to a shot of sunlight. The tail gate slammed down and rocks trembled like an earthquake and scraped his face. Charlie felt a hand firmly grab his legs and he slid helplessly down and out of the tail gate and onto the ground.

There were sixteen men with guns pointed in his direction. Behind them, Charlie could see they were no longer in a city or even close to the ocean. They were on a dirt road surrounded by mounds of dirt and brush. Several trucks were blocking the pick-up.

Charlie found Lena laying at his feet and holding her chest as she gasped for air. He felt immediate relief that she was alive even if it was in pain.

The sound of Giselle sliding on the tail gate made Charlie reach his hands up to brace her fall. She landed hard on his left arm and rolled to her side scrambling into Lena's arms.

"I want my Daddy."

Charlie heard Max's voice call out at the same time he saw his frightened face streaked with dirt and tears. He pulled Max close to him, closing his arms around his head, silently swearing he would never curse at his son again. It would have killed Charlie if the last words Max heard were of anger.

Three more heavy thuds between pelts of rocks and Charlie saw the two men groan as they hit the ground face first. The girl slid easily onto the ground next to him but her head never moved. She rolled beside him, her fingertips delicately touched Charlie's arm.

A stout gunman struggled to step over Charlie and prodded the girl with the barrel of his gun. She rolled onto her back, her face gray from the dust, eyes staring up at the sky, unshielded in the sun.

"This one's dead." Stout One called out and looked toward a man leaning on a truck just up a small embankment. Charlie could see he was physically set apart as the leader. The other men had hair cut short, fleshy arms and thicker middles and carried guns. Leader looked like a model from commercial, similar in age to Charlie, muscular and toned arms with his tailored hair waving in a breeze, his eyes shielded by dark glasses sat on high cheek bones. He needed no gun to show he was in control.

"Too bad," Leader said his voice was casual and indifferent as if the girl had declined to show at a party, "we could have used her."

"We can still take her with us," Stout One said, picking up her arm and measuring its length on his chest, "the guys are tired of practicing on dogs."

The older man from the truck let out a sob and lay his head on the dead girl overcome by grief. Leader observed him with interest. He snapped his fingers to get the attention of the younger one. "This was his daughter?"

The younger man nodded, his chest slumping over as he looked away but Stout One put a muzzle under his chin and forced him to look at Leader.

"What's your name and how old are you?" Leader asked, leaning in to look at him.

"Twenty."

The younger one swallowed hard, his throat touching the muzzle of Stout One's gun as he was pulled to his feet.

"Your name," Leader said snapping his fingers again in irritation, "What is your name?"

"Donato."

"Donato." Leader repeated as he eased his way down the side, "why are you hiding like a coward in a pile of rocks?"

Donato looked down at the older man and remained silent. He flinched as Leader got close and slapped his face. "Mexico is being re-born! You could be writing its history but you cower with an old man and a girl?"

Donato's expression changed to anger causing Leader to laugh. "So there is a man inside of you after all."

Leader patted Donato's arm. "I understand. You are loyal to your family. It's more important to you than politics. I like that. It's the quality I look for in my men."

Donato looked confused as Stout One pushed him back down. Leader wiped away dust from the tail gate and sat down. "Relax, Donato. This is a job interview. I'm offering you a chance to work with me. I only offer once. You will have all the money and women you can ever want. You can be the one that people fear instead of old, fat Paulo."

Leader motioned to Stout One now identified as Paulo who chuckled, not caring that he was being insulted.

The older man shook his head but Donato turned toward Leader. "I will work for you if I can have a safe place to keep my father."

"You didn't hear me. I only make one offer," Leader said, taking a gun from one of the men and shooting the older man in the chest. The older man spit out blood as he clutched his chest and reached for Donato just as the second bullet hit his head and he crumpled on top of the girl.

Donato cried out and lunged toward Leader as Paulo bashed him in the head until he crumpled over the older man.

"He's no use to me," Leader said putting the gun in his pocket and waving his hand. Paulo pulled Donato by the arm. A second henchman, with a bald head and a tattoo on his cheek kicked the father out of the way and picked up the girl by her torso, she folded, limp in his arm. He followed after Paulo dragging Donato by his jacket and disappearing around a dune.

Lena jumped at the sound of two shots echoing in the air.

Max squeezed tightly into Charlie's arms. Leader pointed at him. "This is your son?"

Charlie swallowed hard. "These are my wife and children."

Lena looked up, her eyes wild, placing a hand to her mouth. Charlie had said too much.

"This is your wife and children?" Leader asked

and spun around to look at Lena, "That is interesting."

Leader produced a machete and spun it around like a game of spin the bottle, the pointed curve landed on Lena. She let out a nervous cry when he brought the machete to her throat. "You are a seductive beauty, aren't you?"

Charlie tried to crawl toward her but lay on the ground when he found four guns pointed at his head.

"You don't like me admiring your wife?" Leader asked watching Charlie halt on the ground. Leader let the machete drop from her throat and trace along her left breast and down her stomach until he dropped it away. His right hand reached up and unstrapped her hair until it fell around her face in a wild, untamed mane. "Do you go to sleep at night and think of all the dirty things you'll make her perform? She's your wife so if you demand a blow job she better fall on her knees."

Leader pushed Lena's shoulders down until her head was bent forward.

"You can't take him in your mouth looking at the ground," Leader said laughing. He grabbed her hair until Lena's head tilted back and she cried out.

Charlie wanted to scream and wrap his hands around the monster's throat but he stayed silent. He didn't know what answer would be the one that could get her killed. For now, humiliation was keeping her alive. Leader was not pleased that Charlie didn't react and he looked over at Giselle.

"Or maybe you like the young one?" Leader said reaching over to caress Giselle's arm, "Your *daughter?* Do you prefer that young skin?"

Lena brought her face forward and bit his arm until he pulled back. Leader cursed as he rubbed a red welt just below his elbow and then laughed as he poked her with the tip of the machete.

"I just want my family safe," Charlie said, swallowing hard, "I've got money and I can get you whatever you want."

Leader stood over Lena and watched her clutch onto Giselle. He picked up a piece of her hair into his fingers and then tapped the top of her head.

"What do you think you can possibly do for me that I can't do myself?" Leader asked Charlie as he tilted Lena's face until she looked up at him. A single tear fell from her eye and splashed onto his shoe. Before Charlie could answer, Leader waved his hand to dismiss him.

"We shall talk about what you're going to do for me, but first I have business to finish."

A yelp came from the truck and Jorge stumbled to the ground. He grabbed onto Leader's leg and reached his hand up. Leader looked down in disgust, removed a gun from his pocket and fired a shot into Jorge's head.

"We are losing time," Leader said shaking his leg from Jorge's body, "Where is the bitch?"

Paulo returned from the dune and scrambled with the Bald One to drag a screeching Estrella onto Jorge's body. She scrambled away as her hands soaked in his blood, trying to move off her knees but the Bald One nudged her head with a muddied boot.

"You work for Jaime?" Leader asked.

"I work for no one." Estrella whispered. Bald One stomped her back, cracking could be heard and she rolled onto her belly as he kicked her in the mouth causing her to sputter blood and bits of teeth, "I was helping Jaime."

"I said no crossing over until things settle down," Leader said, his voice condescending like speaking to a child, "Jaime knows that."

"No, no," Estrella begged, "I'm just supposed to bring them there, not take them over."

The Bald One fired a shot into Estrella's neck. Charlie turned Max away from Estrella, the boy's arms pushed against him and Charlie realized he was smothering him into his leg. Charlie moved his arm and Max's face tilted with a gasp for breath.

Leader stood over Charlie, his foot pressed down on his groin. Charlie felt a heavy cloth envelope his head, the rough burlap suffocating him. He struggled against the cloth but heavy arms pulled him down. Max's voice called out as his weight was lifted off Charlie.

"Relax," Leader said, "If I kill you, it won't be like this. Keep still and everyone will be fine."

Charlie could hear Lena's voice in rapid Spanish. The words were coming too fast to understand but he was able to understand one phrase, 'don't hurt us, Eulojo.'

Leader's mask had been removed and revealed the devil that had been chasing him since Senor's Ranch. Charlie didn't think it was possible to feel more horrified. He felt another sharp blow to the head and everything went dark.

Chapter Thirty One
La Jolla- Charlie's House

"Jesus, you always have to take your sweet time," Lisa said as Remi walked through the door of Charlie's home office. She wouldn't look him in the eye but stared out the window toward the pool with arms crossed tight against her, "What kind of watches do assholes carry?"

Remi felt his face flush hot with anger. He had given the car to the valet at the restaurant when Lisa called him and begged him to come back, refusing to say the reason. It was only a fifteen minute drive from the beaches of Del Mar to the hills of La Jolla but Remi was growing weary of her drama.

"I let you stay at my condo so you don't have to go home to Brenda. I help you find Nola when she gets lost at Fashion Valley and offered to buy you dinner to recover. I have been a moment away when you need me and you're going to call me an asshole?"

"It took you so long to get here," Lisa said, glaring at the clock on the cable box, "I thought you said that you cared about me."

"When you summoned me, I was about to get intimate with a large bottle of scotch and cigar and I'm too tired to deal with your next drama. I'll be back tomorrow if you haven't figured out that the world still rotates whether the spoiled brat gets her way," Remi said turning his back and walking out of Charlie's office.

"Kier is dead."

Remi spun around so hard he almost hit the door frame, feeling the wind knocked out of him. "What are you talking about?"

Lisa pulled the small TV toward him. CNN was blazing about the latest Breaking News, a tired warning that took an ominous tone when it became personal.

Remi's face was frozen on the TV screen. A flash of three fleshy figures strapped over a graffiti strewn wall. A poorly edited splice cut over to a swarm of military buzzing around three bloodied white sheets just below in bold, letters read, AMERICANS BEHEADED.

Remi felt his heart race faster. He looked at Lisa's face which was paralyzed in fear. She had applied new mascara but her eyes were rimmed red. His held back his first impulse to want to hold her and he found his way to a chair before he lost all strength in his legs.

"Those sheets could be any American," Remi said, the lawyer side trying to find the logical reason and irritated that Lisa was overreacting, "we don't know that is Kier. Did they show a jacket or something that made you think it was him?"

Lisa held up her phone. A female voice that Remi recognized as one of Kier's girlfriend, Fiona, was screaming on the speaker:

"His body is hanging on the wall! Look at the TV! Kier is hanging like a piece of meat on the wall!"

Fiona continued for a few more seconds of incoherent gibberish and wailing before Lisa closed the message. "She goes on for a while but doesn't make any sense. I called Kier's brother and he said the border patrol notified them an hour ago."

"What else do we know?" Remi stammered. He was fearful to ask the real question. "Is Charlie... one of the other men?"

The sentence hung in the air, afraid to be answered by either of them.

Lisa's shoulders began to shake and travel down her arms until she looked like her whole body was having a seizure. Remi leaped up from the chair and grabbed Lisa. "Is it Charlie?"

"We don't know yet," Lisa whispered as she leaned into Remi's chest, "We haven't gotten any calls."

The sound of the sliding door could be heard from the living room and Brenda's heavy feet were shuffling through the kitchen.

"Have you told Brenda and Nola yet?" Remi asked.

Lisa shook her head and Remi gently put her down on Charlie's overstuffed business chair before he headed out the office door, "Remi, please don't leave me here."

"It's going to be okay," Remi said turning at the door and trying to give a reassuring smile, "We don't know anything yet. I'm going to let the girls know."

"I'm sorry I called you an asshole," Lisa said dabbing her eye gently with a corner of a tissue, "I know you are always there for me."

Remi made his way across the living room, his feet working without his assistance as he gone numb everywhere except his heart that was exploding out of his chest. He found Brenda and Nola in the kitchen. Brenda was staring at the TV and Nola was working with some soup on the stove. Remi snapped off the TV and sat down next to Brenda. Yesterday, Brenda would have grumbled at Remi about politics and Nola would have looked at him with a dreamy-eyed sweetness but today everything was changing.

"We need to talk."

Brenda looked offended at the dark TV and she

snapped it back on. "Nola, take the soup off the stove and go to your room."

Nola groaned. "But I'm hungry."

Brenda snapped her head around sharply. "Damn it girl, do what you're told!"

Nola's lip curled into a pout as she snapped off the stove and lifted the soup off the burner.

"I think that Nola should stay." Remi suggested.

"I know what you think," Brenda said, "and I think you don't know anything."

Brenda waved at Nola. "Go on."

Nola grabbed an apple from a bowl and dragged her feet as she examined three water bottles on the counter.

Brenda grunted in irritation. "I didn't say you can't come back. You don't need to supply yourself for the night. I'll call you when we're done."

Remi flinched at Brenda's sharp edge and didn't know how Nola wasn't crying every minute of the day.

Brenda made sure she heard Nola's door close shut and turned back toward Remi. This time the caustic bitterness was gone and replaced with a look that appeared chiseled in stone. "Is one of those corpses my son? Is my grandson dead?"

"I don't know yet," Remi said, trying to put a hand on Brenda's arm before she pulled it away, "but I know someone who can help find out."

Chapter Thirty Two
San Diego

Remi accessed a random number on his speed dial that he thought was Clef in the Justice Department. Instead he dialed Mariana's employer.

"Benito Salazar, attorney at law."

A breathless voice on the other end answered abruptly. Benito's' assistant, Angela, always sounded liked she was juggling which was true. Keeping two steps ahead of her boss' social calendar was a circus act.

"How are you Angela?"

"Hello, Mr. Parrish." Angela said, her voice relaxing as it came over Remi's car speakers.

No one except Remi asked about her and wasn't just going through the motions. It had given him an edge when he needed a favor.

"I would do better if I could get Mr. Salazar off the phone," Angela said, "he was due at a rally an hour ago."

"Has he talked to Mariana?"

Angela paused. "Why do you ask?"

"Benito told me she was still in Mexico," Remi lied, "I wanted to make sure she's okay."

Maybe he could get some information about where she had taken Max and find out if Charlie ever got there far.

"I just transferred her to Mr. Salazar," Angela said, "she sounded shaken."

"Benito is talking to Mariana?" Remi's heart stopped and he almost slammed the brakes to a complete stop on the freeway.

Angela's voice lowered. "I can't say Mr. Parrish. Please don't cause me to say something I don't have any business about. She got very upset with me when I gave you the number in Mexico."

"No, Angela, it's..."

"I will tell Mr. Salazar you called but it may not be for a few days," Angela said, her voice turning professional, "He is very busy with the protest rallies."

"Angela, wait!" Remi said scrambling to find the right question, "I need to talk to Benito, how long will you be at the office?"

"We'll be leaving at 4:30," Angela said abruptly, "Thank you for calling, Mr. Parrish."

The phone disconnected and Remi slammed on the gas, gunning down the freeway glancing at the clock. It was already 4:20 and he was twenty minutes away if the freeway was clear.

The Audi swerved across the four lanes of traffic, narrowly missing an old VW bug full of surfers that were trying to merge from Sea World Dr. After a few honks and the finger from a soccer mom in an SUV. Remi was rushing down past Interstate Eight. The downtown skyline still ten minutes away. He glanced at the dash clock. 4:30.

"Shit," Remi thought, "They're going to leave." He had called everyone he knew. His contacts at the Border Patrol said it was out of their hands. His friend at the embassy wasn't answering his phone. There was something on the news that the embassy in Tijuana fled overnight, using an old trail with the help of a couple coyotes. A little ironic, he couldn't imagine Dylan trekking through the brush in the mountains or crawling under wire like he was an illegal immigrant.

The last chance he had was Mariana's lawyer, Benito Salazar. Things between them hadn't been that friendly lately. Benito used to stretch out his right hand for a firm shake and slap Remi's back with the left. That was when Benito dismissed Remi as a corporate suit with ego too big to admit he hadn't practiced in family law. Benito should have dug deeper into Remi's background. He would have found out that Remi got his first look at the family court system before he passed the bar. He had cut his legal teeth on his parent's divorce, two re-marriages, a custody battle for the dog, Sprinkles (who died two weeks after the settlement) and his brother's failed petition to emancipate from their mother. Remi was an expert at divorce law and a worthy opponent.

Benito was caught off guard and embarrassed when he couldn't strip Charlie of his custody rights. He acknowledged he had been practicing immigration and civil rights issues for the last twenty years but he had gotten his start working in divorce hearings.

At 4:35, Remi rounded the corner of First Street, expecting to cut off Benito as he was pulling out of the parking garage. His office was actually in a modest store front on India St but he always parked his customized Lincoln far from sight. Remi liked that about Benito. He was sincere and passionate about helping the rights of Mexicans sort through US red-tape. Benito was smart enough to know that Benito needed the image of a simple man suffering for the people and that didn't come with air-conditioning and leather seats.

Remi saw Benito's Lincoln was barricaded by ten cars parked tight against the curb. Some were double parked and jammed up on the apron of the structure. Remi slowly turned the corner and had a clear view of Benito's' office. A crowd had gathered at the entrance and was continuing to fill the sidewalk. Remi drove past and squeezed behind a supply truck and moved toward the group.

The gathering was an eclectic mix of short men in neatly pressed button down shirts and brimmed cowboy hats, twenty-something's wearing campus shirts, women holding babies that leaned sleepily on their necks and clasping hands of children overdressed in frilly dresses and Sunday school black polished shoes. The group was mixed in emotion from the charged electricity of the college students, chattering between themselves like a network, moving around the passive frowns of men staring into the office window and the mothers trying to focus on the movement of their kids in a crowd that could ignite with one spark.

Remi inched his way through a narrow gap as the crowd shifted to allow a heavy set delivery man to move out. Inside was more congested when you add furniture to fit everyone around. He inched along the back wall ignored, unable to see glimpses of the receptionist desk but could see Angela's face. Her voice was desperately trying to rise above the speakers.

"I can assure you that Mr. Salazar is just fine." She said, strands of blond hair falling from the comb in her hair.

"My sister isn't fine. She can't get back!" screamed a thin girl with thick black hair and a bright red Aztec shirt. He didn't hear the comment but could see that Angela's attempt to be professional was souring.

"I don't know where this started but it's just a rumor," Angela called out, "Mr. Salazar is dedicated to your plight."

"Our plight?" A petite man said in khakis and a plaid shirt leaned over to an older grandfather, "Who does she think she is?"

"You don't know shit about our *plight*," a voice piped from the middle, "They rounded up my grandson and three of his friends this morning!"

A thin voice next to Remi whispered behind him. "They took my Blanca last night."

"Mr. Salazar will answer all of questions, but for now, I need to ask you to go home," Angela shouted, "If you don't disperse I'll have to-"

"Have to what! Call the police?"

The anger in the room rose and more people started to press themselves inside. Angela reached for her cell phone and moved herself into a side room, her hand pressed to her ear to block out the shouting. Remi noticed a shadow move under the door leading to Benito's office. As the crowd began to shift, he quickly opened the door and slid inside.

After the stifling chaos of the lobby, Benito's room seemed a blast of fresh air and quiet. Benito sat in his leather chair turned away from his heavy oak desk, he stared through the slats of a blinded window at the glow of light. He glanced up when the door opened, startled by the interruption but unaware of the growing riot outside.

"Remi," Benito's voice was quiet, much softer than his hearty boom that filled up a room. He rubbed his forehead. "I was going to call you."

Remi moved around the desk, noticing that Benito's free hand rested on his leg, shaking violently. He knelt down and grabbed his arm, "I'm calling an ambulance."

Remi reached for the desk phone but Benito placed an unsteady hand over his, pulling it away. "No, please don't. I'm not sick."

"What the hell is going on in your lobby?" Remi said.

"Police took a group of college students into custody last night," Benito said, his voice gaining its trademark strength, "they're supposedly part of the conspiracy to kill the Mexican president. The problem is they're also on a list of kids belonging to illegals who brought them over when they were seven. They're honor students at colleges all over southern California. They don't know any other life and now they're suddenly masterminds that caused a civil war? It's just the US government trying to look like they're doing their part for Mexico."

The voices started to rise in the lobby. "I think Angela could use some help out there."

"She may look timid but she worked for a civilian contractor in Iraq. Nothing rattles her," Benito said, going back to look out the windows, "They heard a rumor that I was injured trying to stop the arrest. There was supposed to be a rally today against immigration reform but with the unrest, it had turned into a protest."

"So go out there and let them see you." Remi said, reaching for the door.

Benito held up his hands which were shaking violently. "I can't let them see me like this."

"Benito, it's really important I speak with Mariana."

Benito started to open his mouth but he shut it quickly and moved his chair back.

Remi pushed Benito's chair with his foot to call his attention. "I'm not asking you to violate client privilege. I only need you to call her and make sure that Charlie and Max are with her. Just make a call."

Benito's eyes glazed over. He snorted and swallowed hard. "I don't know if Charlie got there. I hadn't talked to Mariana four days."

"I'm not here as a lawyer, I just want to know that my best friend and his son are safe," Remi said, throwing his hands in frustration, "Angela just told me she transferred Mariana to you half an hour ago."

"The call was from Mariana's aunt that came up from Monterrey. The whole family was going to hold up there. More secure. Better security," Benito said, his voice choking in his throat, "They got there and found Senor's Ranch was attacked and burned."

Remi felt the air go out of his lungs and he braced against Senor's desk. "When?"

"Last Wednesday," Benito shook his head before Remi could even find the question, "They found Mariana on the back lawn."

"I'm sorry, Benito."

"She's the closest I ever had to a daughter," Benito said, "part of my heart was taken today."

Remi could barely ask the question he knew had to be asked. "Did they find Charlie and Max?"

"There were one hundred adults and over twenty children that have been counted so far," Benito said, "I'm sure Max was there."

"But we don't have proof." Remi countered.

"Remi," Benito said, placing his hand on Remi's arm, "stop thinking like an attorney and start thinking like his friend. Max was with Mariana. If Charlie had taken Max he would be home right now. You need prepare to tell the little girl that her family is dead."

Chapter Thirty Three
Mexico- Eulojo's Compound

It wasn't sleep that kept Charlie frozen on a worn blanket. His body surrendered and lay there motionless. The darkness covered any memory of what happened. One moment he was grasping tightly to Max and the next he was lying in some kind of stall, broken and with a sharp, stabbing pain in the back of his head.

Charlie's left eye was blurry but he could see a bale of hay and several crates stamped with a flower were stacked in the corners. He recognized them as a wine imported to the club.

He studied the wood of the shack. It looked rotted and the slats provided no shelter- the air blew cold through them. He didn't bother with the door, from one of the slats he could see there was a chain holding in place. It didn't matter if it was wide open and could walk away.

Where would he go? He had no idea where they were. It was hard to tell where Estrella had taken them. She had driven for hours. They would be so far from the border and he wasn't going to leave anywhere without Lena or the children.

Charlie started to think about the fate of the men and girl in the truck. The group of men had lurched around doing anything that Eulojo commanded like mindless henchmen. They didn't have the brains to think for them themselves. Could they kill Lena and the children in the same way? Anxiety filled his heart and it began to pump furiously at the thought. He tried to move onto his side but found his body fighting to stay on his back.

Soon the soft light through the slats began to grow brighter and fill the barn like a strobe in a disco. The shafts of light started to heat the ground and Charlie began to wish for the wind again. He lay sweating, paralyzed by his body, left with demonic thoughts he couldn't escape. He was alone to replay the past three days in his mind like a movie projector that would flash on screen. All the horror and fear fresh on the faces of the children and Lena, buried alive in the truck.

Charlie had barely thought about the killing of Mariana and Kier. For the entire families that were murdered. It seemed years since they had been gone and yet this time last week, they were all alive and moving through their days toward the finality of their lives. There were other nagging questions. Why did they kill the whole family? They could have come in and dragged him away? They had opportunity before he had even gotten into the ranch? Had they used an opportunity to settle old scores while they were working on new ones?

Charlie wished he had not come to Lena for help. Not because he didn't need her, there was no doubt they would be dead by now but he felt guilt for getting her mixed into his problems. She had been desperate to get her daughter over the border. Maybe she would have quietly gone into the darkness, waiting to find another opportunity. She took a risk knowing there were men out to capture him.

Now the guilt was pouring into Charlie's mind and drowning him.

Charlie only wanted to marry a girl, have a few

kids and live happily ever after. It was a simple wish to not repeat his childhood with a drug addict father, a beaten mother, a murdered brother and lost sister. It was a family of dysfunction and sadness. For all of Charlie's money and success, it couldn't stop him from screwing up his own chance for a happy, normal family.

Lying on his back gave Charlie time to wonder about those waiting for him in California. Who would explain the loss of her family to Oriana? She was losing her parents and brother and left to be raised by Brenda and Nola. She'd never want for money but there was so much more she will be without. She would carry the loss with her but find a way to cope and build her life. She had Mariana's fire in her soul.

Brenda and Nola needed him. They needed to be protected. Remi would make sure that they would be looked after. To lose another son and brother was cruel.

Lisa. It occurred to Charlie that he had not really thought about her. Everyone else had come to mind but not her. Not until Max and brought up getting married. Lisa never really needs him. She was young and would move on.

The door latch groaned and a shaft of bright light shot blinded him and left him paralyzed to the ground. A shadowed form moved into the barn and knelt by his side. He heard the barn door swing closed and he felt a cool hand touch his face.

"Open your eyes, Charlie."

A voice was like a cool balm. His eyes eagerly adjusted to Lena's face staring down at him.

Charlie tried to sit up but fell back, feeling every muscle in his body ache. "Did they hurt you? Where are the kids?"

All the words came out so fast that he began to choke. He didn't know when the last time he had anything to drink. Lena pried a crate open, took a nail to the cork and put a bottle to his lips. The liquid was warm and fermented.

"The children are in a safe place." Lena said.

"I want to see them!" Charlie managed. Lena glanced at the door and shook her head.

"They let me check on you." Lena said putting her hand on his chest, "but you can't see them right now."

Where are we?"

Lena confirmed his fears. "We're on a farm outside Tecate."

"Estrella was going to rob us," Charlie said, fueling anger but then remembered that Estrella was lying on a dirt road with her head blown off.

Lena patted his leg and helped him sit up. She put her arm around him to support his back and put a wine bottle in his hands. "No, I think she was trying to do what she promised. Eulojo was waiting on the hill for her."

Charlie thought about the stranger who had been chasing him for days. He killed without thought and went to great lengths to humiliate Lena. All these things while Charlie was a captive audience. He should be dead but there was a reason that he was still here. He needed to know why. It was the only leverage they had to keep them alive.

Charlie listened to Lena's steady breathing and stared at the rafters as he opened his mouth to speak. Lena had to know the answer.

"I've been thinking about your mother." Lena said out of the blue.

Charlie was caught off guard, "In the middle of this hell and you are thinking about Brenda?"

"She must be worried about you," Lena said.

"I'm not a good son," Charlie said, "Brenda has survived bigger tragedy."

"How can you say that about yourself?" Lena exclaimed.

"I am weak when it comes to being there for the women in my life. I was a weak son and terrible husband," Charlie said, turning to look at Lena, "I didn't care that Mariana was unhappy. She only wanted to prove she was smart enough to stand on her own. The more freedom she wanted, the more things I bought to keep her playing house. Now that I'm figuring it out, it's too late to tell her."

"Stop talking like it's you're giving up. If you think you can do better, you will get a chance with your mother and children," Lena said, gently brushing hair from his forehead, "As for Mariana, she is with God where she won't hurt anymore, she knows what you feel inside."

"I'm having a hard time believing in a heaven right now, "Charlie stared at the slats in the wood where a soft glow was coming through, "what kind of God takes their mother from her kids? Brenda lost Jackson. Mariana was a good mom and now Oriana and Max have lost her. All she wanted was to be with them and I couldn't handle them living in Mexico so I charged down here."

"We aren't meant to understand God's plan for us," Lena said, her voice so soft that he almost missed her words.

"How do you know that His plan isn't to pick us off one by one?" Charlie asked, "Maybe He enjoys that we suffer."

"God sent you to save us," Lena said taking Charlie's hand, "the book of poems was a sign. If God did not send you, Giselle and I would have died at the ranch."

"So I can bring you to a farm to die?" Charlie argued, "Even if we do convince that psycho to let us go, those passes are expired. I don't think you can hold a little, green book up and they'll let us through. Unless Elias-"

"Elijhun Cann-Saez."

"Yeah, your great poet," Charlie said, "is he going to come down here and tell the nice border people to let us go?"

234

"He lived over one hundred years ago," Lena said, shrugging her shoulder, "Why don't you use a secret phone to ask the US to send a helicopter. Isn't that the way all American movies end?"

"I'm starting to rub off on you," Charlie said sitting up and kissing her hair, "You're getting sarcastic."

"Why did you kiss me?" Lena asked, frowning.

"I'm sorry." Charlie said, searching for a reason but all he could think was how natural it felt.

"Not now," Lena said, "before we got in Estrella's truck."

Charlie studied her face. Her lips were pressed together as if she was angry. In her eyes he saw something else.

"I kissed you."

"Yes," Lena said, looking for more, "I'm a married woman. You are a divorced man who is engaged to another.

Charlie smiled softly. "Are you angry for that?" Lena's eyebrows arched. "I should be."

Charlie leaned toward her, afraid she would pull away but she did not move. Her hair had fallen into her face and there was a streak of dirt on her chin. He didn't want to take his eyes away from her.

"I thought we were going to die," Charlie said, feeling no humor at the moment, "I had to know how kissing you tasted."

Lena tried to stop herself from smiling. Charlie brushed her hair onto her shoulder and turned her face toward him. "You should never stop that smile. It's beautiful."

Charlie was warmed by her blush.

"It's been a long time since I've heard that," Lena pressed her hand onto his arm, "but you shouldn't say those things. I am married and you are engaged to..."

Charlie didn't allow her to finish as he leaned in and kissed her lips. Lena tried to pull back but Charlie slipped his hand around her neck and moved her closer, "Don't lock on the land."

"I don't know what is right anymore," Lena whispered. She pressed herself into Charlie's chest and let him kiss her again.

Chapter Thirty Four

The sun had turned the barn into a sauna. Reluctantly, Charlie released his hold on Lena and was leaning with his back toward a draft that allowed him some relief. Lena had moved toward the corner with the crates pulled out two more bottles, she placed one next to Charlie. She studied his face as she tilted her bottle toward her lips making it hard to focus. He needed to know why Eulojo was keeping him alive.

"Why hasn't Eulojo killed us?" Charlie asked, "Is he going to hold us for a ransom?"

Lena stared at him with her mouth twisted in a frown.

"What?" Charlie asked, "What are you not telling me?"

A sharp crack on the door sent a flash of blinding light and Paulo and the Bald One charged inside. Lena dropped the bottle and ran for Charlie. He was able to wrap one arm around her waist when a hand reached over and grabbed Lena's leg.

"Wait," Lena shouted, her voice cracking, "Not yet."

Charlie moved his face as the large one smashed him in the forehead. He felt his head spin but he struggled to keep his grip, "Don't take her."

"Just give me one minute with him." Lena

pleaded.

"Times up," Paulo said, nodding to the Bald One, "Go with Facundo."

The Bald One now had the name of Facundo. He grabbed her left leg with gruff hands but Lena's right leg swung up and hit him in the stomach. He bowled back for a moment, trying to keep his balance as he cursed under his breath.

Lena strained to move closer to Charlie's ear.

"It's okay," Lena whispered, "They are going to bring me to the kids. Be strong and we won't stay locked on the land."

"No, no," Charlie argued like a child, flashes of Mariana crying for Max flooded his head. He gripped her hard on her thigh but Lena moved his hand away.

"I will keep the children safe," Lena said.

With that final breath, Facundo grabbed Lena by the hair and her head flipped back, a large knife against her throat.

"You bastards," Charlie shouted, "don't hurt her!"

A deep, rumbled chuckle came from Facundo as he removed the knife and slid it back into a holster. Lena stood up and Paulo grabbed her arm, pushing Lena out the door but not before he began to yell at Facundo. "Are you fucking crazy?"

"I know what I'm doing," Facundo grumbled.

" He would carve out your eyeballs if you cut her. He won't care if it was an accident."

"Shut the fuck up, Paulo."

Lena and Charlie kept their eyes focused on each other until the door closed shut.

Chapter Thirty Five
La Jolla- Charlie's House

Whenever Charlie went on trips, Brenda tried to imagine that he was still bustling around in the house. It gave her a sense of comfort that he had never really left. She nestled into the lounge chair and stared at the ocean. Soon, the sound of the screen door slid open and Orrie's smiling face blocked the view. "Was school good today?"

Orrie nodded. Brenda patted the side of the lounge chair. "Stay with me, Baby Girl.

Oriana curled up next to Brenda on the lounge chair. They lay in silence for a few moments.

Oriana ran her fingers on Brenda's left hand. She tried to reach for the cigarette but Brenda switched to the right and tapped the ash into a groove on the balcony.

"Not for you Baby Girl."

"This looks like it hurts." Oriana asked.

Brenda looked down at her hand. Oriana was running her fingers on a bunched scar on the fleshy part of her thumb. It was gnarled and turned into her palm.

Brenda took another puff on her cigarette before she answered. "I cut that on a fishing boat."

"You go fishing?"

"Long time ago, my daddy worked on a fishing

boat." Brenda said, flicking the thick, knotted flesh, "I wasn't listening and a hook came up and got me instead of the fish."

"That was a big hook."

"It dragged me into the water," Brenda said, "My daddy had to dive in to save me."

"Did it bleed a lot?"

"A bit. Daddy tied it together with some fishing wire," Brenda said, remembering the steady stream of blood dripping off the boat, "That's why it doesn't look so pretty."

Orrie flinched. "Did that hurt?"

"Still does sometimes."

"Why didn't he take you to the doctor?"

"Didn't have money for that."

"You didn't have money for the doctor?"

Brenda felt relief that Oriana didn't know a world that people suffered without a doctor but it also irritated her. "Never forget you are a lucky girl. Most people don't have a daddy that makes money."

"And this?" Oriana held Brenda's hand and examined the smooth patches across her top knuckles.

"That's where some soap ate away at my hands."

"Soap doesn't eat your hands!" Oriana said, frowning as if she was being fooled.

"There are some strong soap that clean floors," Brenda said, the memory still felt real, "My skin didn't like the chemicals and didn't heal real fast."

Oriana looked horrified. "Why did you keep putting your hands in there?"

Brenda patted her lap. "Come sit up here, Baby Girl."

Oriana leaned against Brenda's chest as her hair was gently stroked. She purred like a kitten as she waited for Brenda to continue. After a few moments, Brenda took a deep breath. "I hope in your life you don't know what it's like but when Maw Maw grew up, there wasn't a lot of money around. You had to eat so you took what job you could get."

"Why didn't you become a singer or a doctor?"

Brenda smiled. "Those would have been nice jobs. Maw Maw can't sing and she didn't go to a fancy school. I knew how to clean."

"But you didn't have any money," Oriana asked, tilting her head up, "How did you know how to clean?"

"Being poor doesn't mean you're dirty, Oriana," Brenda said, bristling at the accusation and trying to remember that Oriana was young, "I kept house for my family. My Mama and Daddy worked. I was the oldest so I made sure the house ran okay. When I moved out, I didn't know how to do anything else. So I worked cleaning houses and hotels for a real long time."

"You were a maid?"

"Yes."

"Why did you want to that?"

"No one wants to be a maid. But sometimes you need to be one." Brenda said, pausing to inhale on her cigarette and blowing the smoke into the air. "I had your Daddy and your Uncle Jackson and Nola to feed. If I didn't work they would starve."

"Did you get that scar from cleaning too?"

Oriana reached up to the moon crested lump near her collar bone. Brenda swallowed hard and looked away. "No."

"Well, how did you get that one?"

Brenda kissed the top of Oriana's head. "How old are you?"

"Maw Maw, you know I'm eight. You were at my birthday party."

Brenda crushed the cigarette and circled her arms around the tiny girl. The breeze from the ocean was no longer warm and she felt the little girls flesh turning prickled with goose bumps. "Well, I guess if you're eight then I suppose that makes you a big girl."

"Maw Maw, you haven't told me about the mark on your neck."

"I'm getting to that, but you need to listen,"

Brenda said in a tone without any softness always kept for Baby Girl. Oriana stiffened slightly but then rested her head against Brenda's chest. "What I'm trying to say is that you're a big girl now. So I think you're old enough to understand some things that maybe a seven year old would not understand."

Oriana nodded and pressed closer. Brenda felt her heart quicken. She knew that Charlie would have already whisked the girl out of the room. If he had his way, Oriana would know nothing about his past but that meant that all that died would be lost and Brenda wouldn't allow that to happen.

"I have that mark because someone shot me."

Oriana lifted her head in surprise. "You were shot?"

"Yes."

"And you didn't die?"

"I almost did."

"Who shot you?"

"Charlie's Daddy."

"Grandpa shot you? But why would he do that?"

Brenda closed her eyes. "Your Grandpa was sick. He had taken some drugs that made him act strange."

"If he was acting strange, why did anyone give him a gun?"

"I don't know Baby Girl."

"But did he think you were a bad guy and shot you by accident?"

"Your Grandpa was sick. He hurt your Daddy and Nola. He -shot me and your Uncle Jackson."

"He hurt everybody?"

"He got very mad and did some bad things."

"What did he do?"

"Nola... he threw against a wall. Your Daddy... he beat him with his gun."

"Why didn't they fight him?"

"Uncle Jackson tried but he wasn't strong enough. Nola was just a baby so she couldn't defend herself."

"Why would a Daddy hurt his kids?"

"Sometimes adults do some real stupid things. He took some drugs and he didn't know he was hurting everybody."

"But if you love somebody, you don't hurt them."

"It's not always that easy, Baby Girl."

"And he shot you and Uncle Jackson?"

"Yes."

"Why didn't he shoot Daddy and Nola?"

"I was lying on top of them." Brenda, said feeling like her throat was going to close up,

The words were gone as the memories came back of the deafening sound of the bullets, Jackson and Charlie crying in terror, and Nola limp beneath her. Brenda forgot that Oriana was still lying on her until she asked another question.

"How old was Uncle Jackson?"

"Fourteen."

"I wish I got to meet him."

Brenda smiled. "You would have liked him. He was smart and handsome. He liked to tell jokes and loved music."

"Just like Daddy," Oriana said.

"Jackson and your Daddy were a lot alike," Brenda said, remembering they would play their instruments on the street for money, "They had the same green eyes but Jackson's hair was darker. Sometimes looking at your Daddy is like looking at your Grandpa."

"Is Grandpa still alive?"

"Yes," Brenda said, gritting her teeth at the thought of Sam smiling at her.

"Could he come back and try to hurt us?" Oriana asked.

"No Baby Girl," Brenda said, patting her leg, "He's in prison in Louisiana and is too old to get out of there. If he tried to get out- an old guard alligator would bite him."

Oriana giggled. "Maw Maw!"

Oriana sighed and tilted her head again, "I miss Daddy, Mommy and Max. I wish they had taken me with them." Oriana said.

"Soon," Brenda said with no idea if that were true, "Why don't you get working on your homework?"

"Okay Maw Maw," Oriana said reluctantly, she reached up and kissed her cheek. She slid off her lap and headed toward the screen door. It magically seemed to open for her and Oriana slid her arms around a shadowy figure inside.

Brenda grabbed another cigarette and searched impatiently for her lighter. She was going to catch hell from Charlie for talking about the past. But he was going to have to come back first. She deserved to know about her family.

Oriana's eyes and skin may be her mother's but the blood in her veins was Thibodeaux. She was the past living in the future. Her smile was Jackson. It made Brenda ache for him. It had been over thirty years and she still wanted him there with her.

Oriana went inside and took the sunshine. Just inside the door, Brenda could see a living shadow. Nola stood at the entrance, afraid to step forward, trying to blend into the wall, a dark reminder of the Thibodeaux past. If Oriana was the living joy of the future then Nola was the dying shame of a tragic past.

Brenda picked up her glass and shook it in Nola's direction, grabbing attention of the sad eyes staring in the corner.

"Make yourself useful," Brenda ordered. "Get me more sweet tea."

Nola never said a word and left Brenda alone with her thoughts. Soon the empty glass was replaced and Nola was gone again.

Nola was always going to be lost. Now Charlie was missing and never coming back from that wasted land, lost with the grandson she didn't get to know. It made Brenda wonder why the men always have to leave.

Brenda felt a tear wanting to rise. She didn't cry anymore because it never got her anywhere in life and didn't make her feel better. The only thing that was comforting was the smoke from the cigarettes that she created with her lungs. It was something she could control even if it didn't replace the feeling of dread. Only God could replace that when he took her life. If He was merciful, she would be dead before she exhaled.

Chapter Thirty Six
Mexico- Eulojo's Compound

Charlie didn't wait long for them to come for him. Unlike before, the barn door opened and he wasn't wrenched out by his arm and dragged across the ground. Paulo stood alone and patiently at the door and waited for Charlie to get to his feet.

Struggling to his feet, Charlie's body was screaming to sit back down so he took his time and got a better look at the one they called Paulo. He struck Charlie as comical with a full lion's mane of hair and poch-marked cheeks. He looked like assembled parts of left over pieces, an odd but friendly sidekick in a cartoon. Looking in his eyes, Charlie knew different. They were black, no spark of a soul.

Paulo's head tilted as a signal for Charlie to follow him.

It was late afternoon, maybe five. The sun met Charlie square in the eyes. He adjusted as they started moving over gravel into a surreal place that he never expected to see.

Charlie assumed the barn was just a random building like so many unexpected places that didn't have any reason to be there. Rather than a dirty compound that he imagined, it had green vegetation and three rectangular barns that sat at the base of a hill. Just across on a slope stood a house that was well cared for with a vine climbing up a trellis and open windows balancing a red door. Beyond a fence was a swing set. Not the place that a ruthless killer would be living. That thought sent a chill through Charlie's body. Eulojo wasn't hiding. He was living in plain sight among the people.

Walking toward the barns, Charlie sized up Paulo. He was stocky which gave him weight but it made his walk labored and sluggish. They walked freely toward the barns with no other henchmen around which almost gave Charlie a false sense of security. Paulo walked with a confidence that showed Charlie they weren't alone on the path. Somewhere there were eyes watching and waiting for him to make a mistake.

Paulo and Charlie reached the middle barn and Paulo thumped his chest to stop him. The middle barn door was opened big enough for someone to pass but small enough that he could only see the glow of light in the rafters.

"I want to see my wife and kids," Charlie said, his stomach turning at the realization that he might not come back from the barn.

"Your wife and kids?" Paulo said as he scratched his nose and shrugged. He pointed to the barn door.

A voice came from inside. "Hurry the fuck up Paulo, he's waiting."

The face of the bald henchman, Facundo, peered out and Paulo puffed up his chest.

"He's standing right here." Paulo growled pulling Charlie's arm and pushed him forward.

"Paulo, if I'm going to die," Charlie said pausing at the door, "I've got to know they're not hurt."

Paulo sniffed. "Can't tell you what I don't know."

He pushed Charlie thought the door with a hard shove and the barn door closed behind him.

The bales of hay stacked high and three singular lights hung the length of the rafters. It looked like any barn that Charlie had seen in a picture except for what was set up on the far end. Several henchmen leaned against the posts looking hot and irritated as their attention focused on Charlie.

In the center, like a king holding court, Eulojo sat on a red blanket draping over a chair propped up against bales of hay on a raised platform. He was groomed in a new tailored suit, looking refreshed compared to the stained shirts on his henchmen sweating like peasants as they followed behind Charlie and perched on bales of hay.

Charlie didn't care anymore about being outnumbered because his focus was on the guests next to Eulojo. Sitting on the ground at Eulojo's feet was Lena with Giselle sitting stiff as a board next to Eulojo. Her hand rested on Lena's shoulder but no Max. Charlie's heart beat faster as he scanned the corners but no movement. Where was his son?

"I found him!" Max's voice broke from behind a bale of hay and ran around to Eulojo's knee.

Eulojo put Max on his lap as naturally as an uncle picking up his nephew and gazed up at Charlie. He smiled as his attention turned to Max. "I told you he was hiding."

Charlie couldn't force any words to come out. He stared at the scene, paralyzed in his tracks.

"Daddy!" Max's happy voice echoed in the rafters, "Look who Eulojo brought me!"

Penguino had suffered a lot in his travels with his white belly stained brown and one eye missing but now he sat worn on Max's lap. It could only be rescued by someone who saw it abandoned on a beach in the dark of night. Charlie had no illusions that Eulojo had been the one hunting them. Max's hero had been watching from the killing field of Senor's Ranch and was sitting on the lap of his mother's murderer.

"Come closer," Eulojo called casually waving his hand, "I've been waiting to talk to you."

Moving forward, Charlie kept his eyes on Lena who wouldn't look at him. It had been only a few hours since he had held her and now she had been changed. All the color was drained from her face except a sliver of blue underneath a swelling left eye. Charlie felt anger begin to boil.

As Charlie got within twenty feet, Eulojo held up his hand and Facundo held a machete to his neck. He moved Charlie to sit on a bale of hay in front of Eulojo's throne.

"You like my office? It's what I am forced to use right now," Eulojo said pointing to the stacks of hay. "I'm sure you're used to fancy marble floors and air conditioned palaces that are thirty stories off the ground. Personally, I agree with you. Dirt and sweat ruin all my good suits. Right now I am stuck here while my home is being defended by troops against civilians armed with rocks and pipe bombs. Can you believe that? Do you have any idea how much damage that is going to cause? War is a hell of an excuse to redecorate."

Eulojo's left hand pinched Max's stuffed penguin from behind and made its wings dance. Max laughed and tried to grab the penguin but Eulojo held it out of reach. Max squirmed to reach him but Eulojo's grip tightened, pressing Max against him and forced him to put his arms down.

"You like this penguin?" Eulojo asked.

Max nodded and reached again but Eulojo pressed his arm tighter against him.

"Don't you speak?" Eulojo asked.

"Yo habla," Max said.

Eulojo smiled and shook the penguin, "Your mother's language."

"You know my mommy?" Max's eyes brightened.

Eulojo kept his eyes on Charlie as Max lowered to the floor. "Of course I know your mommy."

"Where is she?" Max's eyes brightened.

Eulojo looked at Lena and nudged her with his foot. "You don't see your mommy?"

Max frowned and Charlie's heart jumped in his throat. For all the preparation to fool the authorities they didn't prepare Max.

Eulojo gently putting the penguin down beside Max who reached for its wing but Eulojo stuck his leg between them. "No, no Max. We're going to play a game."

From the side of chair Eulojo pulled a thick Bowie knife and steadied it on his thigh. "Max, do you think it's okay to lie?"

Max shook his head.

"Have you ever told a lie?" Eulojo asked.

Max eyed Eulojo rubbed the blade on his thumb creating a thin red mark on the bed.

Max looked at his feet. "Yes."

Eulojo stopped rubbing the knife and thumped it against his leg. "You are a little boy. What have you lied about?"

Max's cheeks reddened and he cast his eyes through a veil of lashes. "I said I like sushi."

"That is a terrible lie. When you say you like sushi, you are stuck eating raw fish instead of eating what you want," Eulojo said, clicking his tongue and spinning the knife on his knee, "liars are always doing things they shouldn't because they don't just tell the truth. Sometimes I cut a piece of their finger as a reminder."

Max's eyes widened. His lips quivered and he stuck his hands in his pocket.

"I'm not going to cut you little man. You are part of my family," Eulojo laughed, pulling Max close and rubbing his belly, "but you must promise to never lie to me."

Max's face lifted and a single tear ran down the side. He looked over to Charlie but Eulojo pulled his chin toward him. "Say you promise."

"I promise." Max whispered.

Eulojo's face darkened. "Max, someone has lied to me."

Max's shoulders shook. "I didn't lie to you."

"Oh I know," Eulojo said tilting the knife, "you wouldn't be part of my family if you weren't honest."

Eulojo slowly swung the handle so it tapped Max's knuckle. "I need you to punish a liar."

Max stared at the knife. Eulojo nudged the handle into his hand. "Have you held a knife before?"

"No," Max picked up the handle and it dropped his hand to his side.

"How does it feel?" Eulojo asked.

"Heavy."

"Can you lift it?"

Eulojo smiled as Max lifted the blade and patted him on the head. "Good. Strong boy. What do we do to liars?"

"We cut their fingers."

"Max, I want you to cut your Daddy's finger."

Max's eyes widened as he stared at Charlie. He put the knife back in Eulojo's hand. Lena shifted closer to Max. She motioned for Max to come to her. "He's just a little boy. Don't do this to him."

Eulojo's eyes narrowed and he held Max by his arms. "Shut your mouth."

Eulojo turned Max to face Charlie. "Do you think your Daddy only tells the truth?"

Max nodded and glanced nervously at Charlie. Charlie smiled at him.

"He said your mommy would be here," Eulojo said, glancing at Charlie, "where is she?"

Max's smile faltered and his face turned so he could scan the barn. Eulojo lifted him down from the bales. "Maybe she is hiding? Why don't you look for her?"

Max checked behind the doors and the Henchman parted so that Max could walk through their legs. They lifted some bales of hay for Max to check.

251

Max sat back down next to Eulojo; his chin tucked into his chest. "Where is she Max?"

"She's not here," Max said, his lip quivering.

"Of course she's here." Eulojo said leaning back and smiling.

Max's chin lifted as Eulojo grabbed Lena's face and pulled her onto her feet. "Here is your mommy."

Max's eyes watered. "She's not my mommy."

Eulojo squeezed Lena's face tighter. "But your Daddy says this is your mommy."

Max sniffed and wiped his nose on his sleeve. He tried to look down again. Eulojo reached for Max, dropping Lena to the floor causing her to fall onto Giselle. Eulojo's face reddened as he pushed out spit onto Max's face. "Your daddy is a fucking liar and you need to cut him."

Eulojo shoved the knife in Max's hand and pushed him toward Charlie. The boy stumbled with the blade toward his chest and was about to impale himself. Lena grabbed the edge of Max's shirt pulling him toward her. She circled her arms around him, the blade catching her on the arm. She pulled it from Max's hand and threw it to the floor. "Enough!"

Eulojo laughed so hard he had to steady himself on the bales of hay.

"What kind of sick fuck gets off hurting a kid?" Charlie yelled.

Charlie felt a blow to his back and his knees buckled. He drew his hand back toward his head catching a second blow on the back of his hand. He withdrew it back to brace him on the ground, a stream of blood grazed from the top of his knuckles. The Henchmen wiped the blade onto Charlie's shirt.

Eulojo observed the beating and then cast a glance at Max who withdrew his face into Lena's shoulder with a heavy sob. He pressed his foot on the penguin lying below him. "I'm not going to hurt you Max. But you did break a promise to me."

Eulojo's hand circled the penguin's head and he squished the face. "And there are consequences for breaking promises."

Eulojo pulled the penguin's head and it tore free from the body under foot. With a quick movement he stuck the Bowie's blade into the penguin's torso and ripped at the seam. Stuffing flew in the air like clumps of snow. He threw the carcass toward Lena, a black wing touched Max's foot and he recoiled with a loud cry.

"Get them cleaned up," Eulojo yelled, shoving Lena with his foot. Clutching Max in her arms, she moved quickly off the bale of hay and looked back at Charlie. She opened her mouth to say something but was distracted when Facundo grabbed Giselle by the arm.

"Don't touch her," Lena snapped as she slapped his arm away. Facundo moved his hands away and ushered them out a side door.

"Your wife is feisty." Eulojo said, his eyes meeting Charlie. "You better stop lying or I will gut your son just like that penguin."

Chapter Thirty Seven
La Jolla- Charlie's House

Brenda always felt Charlie had always been swimming in luck, more than one life preserver thrown his direction and now it appeared he was going to drown. A mother should never feel satisfaction at the downfall of her children. Brenda had a sickening feeling of satisfaction that washed over her. Her anger was usually projected at everyone else. She'd always relied on it to give her strength and now it was being turned inward.

Brenda reached down underneath her bed for the pack of cigarettes she had dropped this morning. After a few grabs with her fingers, she crushed the box with her palm as she dragged it from underneath. It had one single stick with a filter stuck straight in the air. She picked it slowly from the pack and threw the carton on the floor. Normally it would nag at her until she put it in the trash. She may be white trash but she doesn't live in trash and she always kept herself and the kids real clean.

Brenda thought about leaving everything in a pile. Let is stack and rot until it covered her body, paralyzed under the weight of her own decision to be buried under it all.

Brenda placed the cigarette gently on the table and closed her eyes as she lay down on the bed. She had already turned on the two TV's on the left wall with a braille she had created in her sanctuary of TV. All those voices chattering about their important worlds, the commercials telling her what she couldn't live without, and her favorite were the rich bitches on the reality shows. All the plastic surgery, everything given to them, their husbands older than their fathers, buying them everything their manicured hands wanted just to avoid a temper tantrum. It should be the farthest thing from entertaining but it was the confirmation that she was right that was soothing. No matter how much money, you can't be happy. Everyone has that one crack in their soul that cannot be filled with things. We spend our lives trying to find the glue to make us whole again, everyone except Charlie.

Charlie had come from nothing. She knew that because she and Sam were nothing. Charlie never asked for anything to be given to him that he didn't work for, only took what he had earned but it takes more than a good work ethic.

People can work hard their entire lives, their bones aching from the effort, sleep tightening every muscle only to be stretched again every morning in their routine. Charlie's hard work didn't make him climb out of poverty. He was just one lucky son of a bitch.

Brenda blamed herself. With all his success, turning trouble into trinkets, she started to believe he escaped the Thibodeaux curse. Brenda knew it hadn't been broken. If it had, her daughter wouldn't be an idiot child. She hoped his luck had allowed him to be passed over.

Sam wouldn't admit there was a curse, too blind or proud to admit that he was a loser. She didn't know about it until she had fallen hard for him. She had been so stupid in love and didn't know anything about him or his family except from fragments of his family history blurted between his binges.

Brenda figured the curse had been bought by his coward of a great, great granddaddy, Jeb Thibodeaux, when he turned and ran from a Civil War battlefield after shooting his general by accident.

The army found Jeb hidden under the bed of a farm house belonging to another soldier where he was dragged out and hung. He had been hidden by Liza Cather who should have been executed as harboring a traitor but was four months pregnant when her husband hadn't been home in a year. She left the farm house before her husband returned, taking the Thibodeaux name and gave birth to a son who would live long enough to be shot robbing a grocer in Baton Rouge. He left two sons that killed each other in a bar fight when Sam's daddy was three. Sam's daddy killed his wife and daughter by driving drunk into the Mississippi. And then there was Sam who managed to stay alive only to be penned up in a prison. He was given his life by the mercy of the good people of Louisiana who felt a child murderer should live with his conscience then die for his sins. Brenda would have begged them to strap him into a chair if they had let her speak at the hearing but they blamed her for what happened. She was a bad mother for letting a monster near her children.

Brenda knew she wasn't a bad mother. She was just a weak woman who made bad choices. And for that, she was just like Liza Cather. Their sons lived under a death sentence because of their bad choices.

Of all Brenda's hopes for her kids, she would have put her bet on Jackson. That just showed her the horrible luck she had at picking the right man, it's just that her Jackson was strong. He had her ability to push through all the storms. He took care of the little ones, found food, brought home a little money and he was actually a good student. Jackson liked learning but he'd never let anyone know that. Maybe that's why he had to die. God couldn't have the son of cowards, robbers, and murderers rise above. Bad breeds can't be redeemed and even God must rectify his mistakes.

Now Max was gone before Brenda even got to really know her grandson. When he was born, she wouldn't allow herself to hold him until she couldn't bear to not hug him. She didn't want to love Max too much.

Now all that were left were the Thibodeaux women. They were not survivors, just living with their own obligations under the curse. She had been a stupid girl that followed a quick wink and belief in some drunken promises for a better life. Nola was damaged goods and never going to have a life that wasn't clinging to Brenda's hip like she was still a babe. The biggest blessing was she couldn't marry and have a son of her own to die.

Oriana, a half-breed branded with the name of Thibodeaux and her mother's Mexican blood. It was just a matter of time before her fate was decided.

A black reporter on CNN was recapping the week's events. Chaos collected in a few blurs of the assassination, Mexicans crushing themselves in a panic in Tijuana, the burning of the embassy and finally the bodies hanging from the wall. Brenda sat up and snapped off the TVs on the wall.

"Damn you Charlie," Brenda thought, eyeing the unlit cigarette on the table, "couldn't just marry one of our own kind?"

"Don't like me smoking in your house Charlie?" Brenda said out loud. She moved toward the window and slid it wide open with a large screech. "Why don't you come here and stop me?"

A blast of wind pressed a mist through the mesh. Clouds were darkening to the south. Brenda sucked smoke deeply into her chest and blew her own cloud in their direction, keenly aware the storm was hovering over Mexico. Somewhere under that storm, her babies were trapped underneath.

"You let them kill you." Brenda inhaled again and held back as long as she could, her lungs begging to release and finally forcing a cough high enough to escape. She dropped the cigarette and stomped it into a gray heart onto the creamy plush, "left me to raise our girls by myself."

Brenda dropped her lighter on the table. It skid across and knocked over a row of pictures. She reached down, losing her balance and put her heel through the glass in the frame. She pulled up the shattered square and looked down at Oriana's deep brown eyes and crooked smile stared back up at her. It had been her eighth birthday, the last birthday that was going to be happy.

Brenda felt her heart flood with a familiar poison, venom that only a mother can feel from a pain of losing her children. She hurled the picture causing it to smash against the TV, a force hard enough that tipped it over and onto the floor. The table came next and bounced over the bed, rolling over and placing a dent in the wall. It cratered the fall of the TV resting on the night stand and the final one on the left wall. The stacks of remotes made pits and all the history in the photos slid across the floor and lay in a scattered and crushed display on the floor.

By the time that Remi pried open the door and pushed through the mattress, Brenda had fallen asleep curled into a fetal position under the window.

Chapter Thirty Eight
Mexico- Eulojo's Compound

Eulojo watched Lena and the children disappear, listening to the feet fade on the gravel. Charlie kept his head low, staring at the fluff of the penguin stuck on the hay, its carcass staring blankly at him. His mind was spinning and heart pumping furiously at what was going to happen next, he didn't hear Eulojo's question.

"Do you know Judge Andersen?"

"Not personally," Charlie said, quickly thinking about the name.

"But he is a customer at your club?" Eulojo asked, moving off his throne and sitting level with Charlie.

Charlie shrugged. There were so many important officials that came to the club. The federal court was just blocks away so it was possible. He looked toward his feet when Eulojo moved next to him on the bale of hay. Eulojo's scent was familiar, Charlie recognized it was from one of the endless glass bottles of cologne that Lisa bought for him. The pungent musk stood out because it was called Conquest. He never wore it because it reminded him of all the smooth talking assholes wanting him to invest all his money. He didn't think he could hate Eulojo more.

"Judge Andersen is also your neighbor," Eulojo continued, placing his arm around Charlie as if they were old friends, "he lives just a street down from that market."

"I work nights...I don't know my neighbors." Charlie said, gritting his teeth. "What do you want with him? You want money to bribe him?"

Eulojo gripped Charlie's shoulder and his head shook as if he was suppressing a joke, "I don't need your money. I make more in a week to buy all your clubs. You should know better than anybody that it isn't money but power that keeps people in line and their fear to please you when they realize you own them. Once they understand that, they do not think for themselves, they think for you."

"So if you have all this power and money what do you need me for?" Charlie asked, unable to stop the words from sounding sarcastic.

Eulojo's arm pulled Charlie back and wrapped his hand around Charlie's throat. The straw stabbed into Charlie's back as he flew backward off the bale. Eulojo squeezed and Charlie instinctively swung his arm striking Eulojo's cheek. Eulojo swore at him but didn't release his grip.

"You better be praying I need you. If not, we've got nothing to discuss and that boy of yours is going to get gutted. Oh, and your *wife and daughter*? I'll turn them over to my men as party favors until they get bored." Eulojo screamed, his face flush-red as his voice echoed through the rafters. He released his grip on Charlie's throat and spit on him, kicking him to the side as Charlie gasped for air. "Can you get into Judge's house?"

"You want me to rob it?" Charlie asked, his fear was confusing him.

Charlie felt Eulojo's blade pressed against his chest. He stared up at Eulojo straddling him, his eyes blazing, "Would the Judge welcome you into his home or not?"

Charlie tried to remember if he really knew Judge Andersen. There were so many people that pretended to know him that were only interested in getting connected with the Thibodeaux name. A social climbing "connect the dots" that Charlie never played. The name did sound familiar. Had he shaken his hand before? Seen him driving to work as was driving home? Or had Charlie only seen Judge Anderson's name on a voting ballot? It didn't matter if he couldn't place the face.

"You're useless," Eulojo said as he stood up and headed for the barn door, tossing the blade in his hand, "I'm going to slit your son's throat."

Son...Son... Judge has a son. The kid Charlie saved from a beating the night Max left. Jesse... Jesse Andersen.

"I know him...I know him!" Charlie said, his voice barely above a harsh whisper, his throat still raw from being crushed.

Eulojo kept walking. Charlie struggled to sit up, gasping, "His son Jesse comes in all the time!"

"I told you what happens when you lie," Eulojo said, his pace starting to quicken.

Charlie's arm collapsed and he fell flat on his back, the air suddenly filling his lungs. "If you touch any of them. You get nothing. I know Judge Andersen. I could walk into his house tonight but if you hurt any of them, just kill me right now because you won't get shit from me."

Charlie closed his eyes and listened for foot fall. Was Eulojo still deciding He heard nothing until a voice broke through the silence.

"I believe you."

The crunching of feet came closer. Eulojo appeared at the door and charged over to Charlie. He put his foot on Charlie's chest and pointed the blade at him. "Tonight, you are going to walk into the Judge's house and blow his brains all over his pristine white house."

"You want me to kill him?" Charlie repeated the words twice. It didn't sound like what real people say. "Why?"

Eulojo extended a hand to Charlie but pulled him up by the arm when Charlie refused. Eulojo was smaller than Charlie but unexpectedly strong.

"Not for you to ask," Eulojo said, his tone had stopped being pleasant," I tell you what to know."

"Why can't your men do it?" Charlie argued, trying to find some reason why he was expected to kill a federal judge, "They're trained killers. I'm just a—"

"He's a federal judge for fuck's sake. You are a respected member of your community," Eulojo interrupted, running his hair through his hair, "you're no threat to anyone. Get inside and kill him."

The thought sickened Charlie. A man's death meant Max and Lena and Giselle's lives. It wasn't complicated, for their freedom, another man's life was going to be shortened.

"And when that's done," Charlie asked, slowly, "you'll get them across the border."

Eulojo shook his head. "You will come back here and I will release them."

"How do I know you'll let them go?" Charlie asked.

"You don't," Eulojo barked.

Charlie stood up to face Eulojo. "They need to be safe."

Eulojo's eyes narrowed. "You don't get to negotiate."

Charlie took another step closer to Eulojo, his heart racing. "I could get killed, and then what?"

Eulojo laughed, "Then nothing is going to matter to you, anyway."

Charlie took two more quick steps and grabbed Eulojo's arm. "I need to know they're safe."

Eulojo moved the blade to Charlie's side. Charlie took a deep breath and tried to calm his voice.

"I can pull the trigger if I know it means they're not going to be hurt. Please."

Eulojo leaned into Charlie's face. "Do you still say that the girl and her mother are your wife and daughter?"

Charlie paused. If he answered wrong it could all be over right now. He matched Eulojo's gaze. "No."

"And yet you still want them to be safe?" Eulojo asked.

"Yes."

Eulojo didn't believe him. "Why?"

"Not for you to ask," Charlie said, surprised at the gruffness in his voice.

"Fair enough," Eulojo said, giving a tight smile as he moved the blade from Charlie's side, "They will be released when-if you don't come back."

Eulojo walked through the entrance and he waved his arm. Paulo appeared and motioned for Charlie to follow behind. Eulojo scraped the knife along the wall making Charlie's ears hurt. "If you don't kill the judge you can add three more that you killed. I'll drive to La Jolla myself and make that little daughter, pretty sister and mother of yours wish they were dead too."

Chapter Thirty Nine
La Jolla- Charlie's House

After viewing the carnage in Brenda's room, Remi found her on a pool lounge with her eyes glazed like a donut. He stood in front of her until she finally recognized him.

"Do you want anything? Remi asked, "Another cup of coffee? Perhaps the chef can prepare you a light dinner?"

Brenda held up her coffee mug and let it slosh. "I got what I need."

Remi wanted to break off her head, drop-kick it down the hill and let it bounce off the cove and into the ocean. He gripped the railing tightly for fear he would have separated Brenda's head before he knew what he was doing. "The room is uninhabitable. The TV's and bed will need to be replaced and a hazard-material team to give it a thorough cleaning. I'll have them removed this afternoon and new ones will be here tomorrow."

"Leave them," Brenda said, straightening herself up on the lounge.

"The materials are toxic," Remi said, irritated, "I can't just leave them."

Brenda put her coffee mug on the ground making a loud clang. "Nola can bring them to the trash."

"Brenda look at me."

Brenda turned her attention to Remi's face. It was pale and his eyes sagged with blue pockets. "You need some sleep. You look like you aged twenty years."

"I came back to find Nola almost pissing herself in the corner, Orrie crying in her room and you curled up in a fetal position in the fucking earthquake that used to be your room. I thought someone had raided the place." Remi yelled, taking his hands off the rail and pressing them on her lounge chair, "There are shards of glass embedded in the carpet. Nola is not your personal cleaner and not equipped to handle that kind of clean up. No one is going in that room until its clear, do you understand?"

Remi looked into the house. The TV was off in the living room and no light coming from the kitchen. "Where did Lisa go?"

Brenda clicked her teeth, "Went to bed."

Remi checked his watch, it was only eight thirty. "This is hard on her."

"She's a lucky girl."

"Jesus, can you just give her a break?" Remi sat on the edge of the adjacent lounge chair and reached for Brenda's mug. She had moved from black coffee to something clear and brown. The smell burned his nose as he drained the cup to the bottom. Brenda made no attempt to stop him.

"She is lucky," Brenda chuckled at her own thoughts, the whisky made her words soft and slushy, "She can close her eyes and nothing fills her empty head. I can't close my eyes without getting my own horror picture show."

Remi sunk down into the lounge cushion next to her. He felt his body weigh down, pretty sure he wouldn't be able to get back up again. "You may not like her but she's with Charlie."

"No, you may not like that Charlie is with her."

Remi felt the jab like a knife in his ego. "Really know how to cut people in half don't you?"

"Oh, I'm on your side. She's a girl that can't think past the shine on her wrist and Charlie's got the right kind of money that sparkles," Brenda said, trying to pat Remi's arm but only comforting the air, "He's got more money than the state of Texas but that doesn't make them a sweetheart couple. He buys everyone. He pays you to lay down the laws that he lives behind. He pays Kier to keep his security. Charlie's paying you to be a man for him but he can't pay anyone to actually be the man he needs to be. He's smart. Got my brains and his Daddy's slow charm and sweet smile but love requires more than picking up the check."

Remi was beyond justifying his feeling for Lisa or picking apart his best friend. He decided to steer in a different direction. "I don't think you've ever said anything nice about Charlie's dad unless it was joined with a four letter curse."

"Do you need to wake up Sleeping Beauty so we can start talking about what you found out from the Mexican lawyer?"

Remi spun the cup in his hands and looked up at the heavy cloud hanging above him. "The Ranch was attacked. He says they found Mariana and her family."

Brenda's hands gripped the metal on the lounge. "And?"

Remi stood up, unable to say the words. "They didn't find Max or Charlie."

"But she and her whole family are dead, right?"

Remi's silence was all she needed. Brenda sniffed hard and rubbed her eyes. "Well that settles that."

"That proves nothing."

"What more do you need?"

"Why do you want to be so sure that means they're dead?" Remi said, looking down at the empty mug and wishing it was bottomless, "I can't talk to you without a lot more of this," Remi said, turning the mug upside down and heading toward the door.

"Bring the bottle."

Remi felt a drop splash on his arm.

"Come inside and we'll talk."

"We've got nothing to talk about anymore." Brenda whispered. More splashes started to come down but Brenda didn't want to move. The drops were cooling on her skin which felt like it was on fire.

Chapter Forty
Mexico- Eulojo's Compound

Paulo took Charlie straight from the barn down a dark pathway to the left. From the corner of his eye, he could see the lights on in a house just up a hill. A figure passed in front of the window he hoped was Lena. At least she and the kids were out of the cold. The pathway dead ended into a line of simple door, Paulo pushed open the second one and it opened to a single cot, sheets folded with military discipline. Two stacked crates provided a bed stand balancing a sterile office lamp glaring down on a bent back book of matches and a crumpled pack of cigarettes with a lonely smoke peeking out.

There was just enough light for Charlie to see the detail of a bathroom door. Paulo pushed Charlie through the opening.

"Get cleaned up."

Peering from the bathroom door, Charlie noticed a toilet and single white sink joined the bathtub. A sharp poke in the back pushed him onto the cold tile.

"Clean up." Paulo said again.

Charlie pushed the bathroom door to close but Paulo tapped the wall as he sat on the bed and rescued the lonely cigarette. "Keep the door open."

"I can take a shower by myself." Charlie asked.

Paulo, unfazed, lifted his leg and farted loudly. "Eulojo says the door stays open. Throw out your clothes."

"What am I supposed to wear?" Charlie protested. He felt more bold dealing with Paulo who hadn't shown any hostility toward him. He felt his ear sting as something whizzed past his head and clatter into the tub. He leaned over to see a bar of soap broken into three jagged pieces.

"What the fuck you care, cabron? Facundo is getting you some clothes," Paulo grumbled, the friendlier image fading, "Hurry up. We got to go."

Charlie peeked out the door to see Facundo entering the room and slipping clothes onto the bed from a dry cleaning bag. He spotted Charlie's stare and clutched the plastic in his knuckles almost like he was trying to decide to put it over Charlie's head. If Paulo hadn't been there, Charlie knew Facundo wouldn't have had a problem. Charlie quickly ducked back into the bathroom and turned the water on.

The shower head was small but the stream was steady and hot. It felt like silk on Charlie's skin. He allowed it to splash over his hair, the drips streaming down his face only once. There was guilt in the joy of a simple shower. Were Lena and the kids allowed to clean up? He took a few minutes longer and stepped onto the cool tile, a thin mat slid beneath his feet. He wrapped a heavily bleached towel around him.

In the bedroom, Paulo was nowhere to be seen. On the bed Charlie saw a precisely pressed white business shirt and dark tailored pants. A folded pair of socks and Kier boxers stacked neatly beside. They knew Charlie couldn't walk into Judge's house not looking every inch the typical US business man.

Charlie looked over to see if Paulo was watching from outside. He saw a trail of smoke curling into the entrance and guessed Paulo was in the courtyard. He slid on the underwear and socks, still uneasy that Paulo was going to pop back in any minute. He pulled on the pants and wondered if the expensive suit belonged to Eulojo.

"I'm dressed, what now?" Charlie called out the door as he reached for the shirt and began to slide out the buttons.

"I liked you better standing in your underwear."

Charlie's heart lifted the second she spoke. He looked up to see Lena standing in the doorway, her eyes asking permission to come inside. Charlie didn't give an answer, he quickly moved toward her and pulled Lena close to him. He inhaled her body, filling his senses with the scent of orange blossoms. Her curves fit snugly in a dark fuchsia dress and a lemon-colored scarf tied at her waist. He felt relief to know they were being treated well. He glanced down at her face looking up at him.

" The kids are safe," Lena said, "We're up in the farm house. They let us clean up there and gave us food."

Lena pulled him back toward her and he pressed her tightly against him, preserving the moment in his head.

"Max is safe with me." Lena whispered, she pulled away and looked back at the door. Paulo's smoke was no longer in the corridor. "If you get there and you cannot get back..."

Charlie stepped closer to her, not wanting the smell of orange blossoms to fade. "I won't leave you here."

Lena picked up Charlie's hand and intertwined them. Her fingertips were icy. Charlie pressed them against him to warm them but she still shivered.

"When you get there and their back is turned- run. Do not kill this man," Lena whispered, glancing back at the door, "find your lawyer friend and talk to your government but do not come back here."

"I don't have a choice, Lena."

"No harm will come to them."

"You were telling me just a few days ago that children are currency down here," Charlie argued, "That was you, right?"

"But not Max. I won't let it happen." Lena said quickly.

Lena moved toward the door but Charlie grabbed her arm and pulled her back to him. He buried his face into her hair and squeezed her tightly. "That is the only way I can do this. Look toward our future. I'll take you anywhere you want to go. Please don't lock yourself to this land. Don't push me away. I can't kill anyone unless I know it's for us to be together and the kids to be safe."

Lena shoved away from him, wiping a tear from her eye. "Stop saying "us." I am never going to leave this place. I promise you that I will keep Max from harm and find him back to you. Stay in California or we'll all die."

Before he could say another word, Paulo appeared and Lena pushed past him out the door.

Chapter Forty One

Charlie pressed himself into the leather of the back seat supporting his forehead with his hand. The darkness was comfort after the prickly hay. He looked down at his clean hands. He almost felt guilty for feeling refreshed from the shower. His head hit the cold pane of the window and it brought him back to the two figures in the front, Paulo and Facundo. After Lena had run out, Facundo pulled him from the room and threw him in the back of a black car with all the branding removed. They had been traveling for a few miles on unpaved roads. Occasionally, an outline of buildings clustered into view and would fade. Charlie wanted to close his eyes but tried to keep alert for any markers of where they were. It was hard to keep his mind off what he was expected to do.

The car weaved into a cluster of industrial shops and then stopped with a jolt awakening Charlie's adrenaline. Paulo turned off the car but left the headlights staring at the door to a large hanger bay. A fresh red and green sign above the door read, Neumatico Mercado de Lopez. Charlie didn't know why he was surprised to see a tire shop. As if he expected the sign to read, Lopez Drug Shop instead. Three stacks of tires stood seven feet high on each side of an office door. Opening the door swept wind inside and Charlie recoiled. Paulo grunted from the cold and motioned for him to hurry out of the car. He tried to close the thin coat around him but he still felt the sting on his neck. Paulo cursed down the driveway, the wind was blocked by the building across but the beginning of an angry rain started to spit at them.

"I thought we were going across the border."

"Shut up." Facundo growled.

The office door to the shop creaked like a carnival haunted house and the smell of rubber and grease greeted them. Facundo pushed Charlie's back and soon Charlie was walking in a void darker than the one he had just left. Boots scuffing on the floor and hands prodding his back told him to keep moving in the dark. Instinctively Charlie put his hands in front of him and soon felt a wall flattening on his palm. His hands moved along until the tips were blockaded by a door jamb.

"Keep walking."

The command was not for Charlie. A heavy bulk pushed past him and he heard a sharp click echoing through his ears. A fluorescent light blinded him temporarily. Once he adjusted there was a large loading bay with clear gray metal walls and a large processing hangar looming above from a quick eye view it looked like any loading bay until stepping onto the floor. It was hard, paved earth and gravel crunching under his feet. The ground was imprinted with tire tracks of industrial wheels that disappeared when they met a large cavernous pit. Two men climbed out wearing orange jump suits and carrying tools. If it had been any other night he would have thought they were part of a construction crew on a San Diego freeway. The sound of an engine roared behind Charlie causing him to jump.

The constructions workers laughed as they watched Charlie dance around and then disappeared to the front of the store.

Paulo grabbed Charlie's arm and pulled him backward toward a blue, late model Honda with California plates. Facundo was already in the driver's seat and cursing as he tried to find the controls for the heater. Paulo shoved Charlie in the back seat and wedged himself into the front seat, howling as a cold air blasted through the compartment.

"Pendejo!" Paulo growled at Facundo and smashed a switch on the dashboard until the air began to warm.

The Honda lurched forward toward the pit. If felt like a roller coaster as the Honda tilted up the lip and Charlie had no idea what to expect on the other side. The Honda tilted downward and the bright, fluorescent lights were swallowed after a few jolts of dirt, the Honda soon leveled out onto a concrete path. They moved quickly through walls of smooth dirt with a light attached every hundred yards. It reminded Charlie of the tunnels that Max and Orrie dug on children's beach with their plastic shovels. Whatever made this tunnel had more help with shovels. It was a massive effort on an industrial scale and clearly big enough for a small car to travel through.

"How far down are we?" Charlie asked.

Facundo grunted. "It's not a fucking field trip."

They car continued in silence for ten minutes. The tunnel narrowed and made several slow turns at times the panels scraped along the wall. Facundo stopped once and Paulo squeezed out of the car to remove fallen debris from the windshield too heavy for the wipers to carry.

The digital on the dashboard said it was early evening. Orrie and Nola would be curling up on the couch to watch one of their favorite shows. They were all the same with something to do with a heartbroken girl and a clueless guy. Brenda would be up in her room, sneaking a smoke out of the window because she was too lazy to go out of the balcony.

In a perfect world, Max could be playing nearby the couch launching Penguino over the couch in an attack on the girls. They would complain but in the end, Max would be curled up between them until he fell asleep and Brenda would come up to bring him to bed.

Charlie felt a sickening feeling in his stomach for promising never to leave Max and then letting Lena take him. A stranger to act as his mother and a child struck as a zombie-like replacement for his sister, yet Lena was the only reason that Charlie could even let him go. She was there to watch over Max no matter what happened.

Charlie had to focus on what to do when he arrived at Judge Andersen's house. Would he be allowed inside? How would he get the judge alone? What if his son was there? Could Charlie kill a man in front of his son in order to save his own?

Trapped in the tunnel, Charlie was starting to feel suffocated, he felt pressed into the seat from a thud in front. The Honda came to a halt and then began to incline sharply making its way up a metal ramp. Light shot through the windshield and suddenly they were inside a loading bay just a little smaller than the tire shop.

Facundo honked a few time and a steel garage door cranked slowly upward with just enough room to allow the Honda through. Whoever had allowed the gate to open was not visible but in the shadow Charlie could see the outline of the guardian of the gate.

The car cleared the driveway and moved onto a paved road with as much ease as leaving from an oil change. Charlie recognized immediately they were on US soil. Passing salvage yards and construction companies just across the border near Chula Vista. They were soon whipping a corner onto Interstate Five heading northbound. Could it really be that easy? It shouldn't be that easy. After three days of struggle and a short rollercoaster ride through a tire shop brought him back to his home.

San Diego's downtown skyline came into view and Paulo pointed to the familiar crescent curve of a bridge.

"Does that go to Coronado Island? "Paulo asked.

"I thought we weren't playing tourist." Charlie said.

"Does it?" Paulo said, ignoring the snipe.

"Yes."

"I got a cousin who's stationed in the Navy out there." Paulo announced to nobody. After the downtown buildings slid by Paulo turned his shoulder and threw a bag onto the seat. Charlie felt the hard metal through the plastic.

"You ever use one? "Paulo asked

The plastic bag crackled as Charlie pulled it back and the gun slid onto the seat. It was so small that Kier would have called it a pee shooter.

"Yeah, I've shot a couple times." Charlie lied. The last gun that was that visible was the one that Sam held when he raised it to Jackson's face and pulled the trigger. He hated the sight of them.

"Okay, stick in the left pocket of your jacket," Paulo said turning his body around to look over the seat. He held up his jacket pocket. "Don't forget the left. If they check you they'll miss there."

It was clear to Charlie that getting him inside had already been arranged. "If there is someone on the inside, why can't they kill this judge?"

"Eulojo says, he can't. So he don't." Facundo mumbled.

"Get Judge Andersen alone in his office, it's off to the right on the first floor, raise the gun and shoot him in his neck," Paulo made an exaggerated gesture at Charlie's throat, "When he goes down, tap another bullet in the head and walk out through the balcony door to the garden. Go to your left out the side gate.

The Honda slid onto Garnet Ave and began to make that familiar climb up the hill on Mount Soledad Road toward his home. Charlie could feel the sweat pool on his neck.

"Where are you going to pick me up?" Charlie asked, as they quickly moved up.

Facundo laughed. "Like you gonna get out of there."

"Don't freak him out," Paulo said punching Facundo's arm causing him to steer across the lane and almost into a dog park. Eulojo say this has to work or we don't come back."

Chapter Forty Two
La Jolla- Charlie's House

"Stay and drown in the rain for all I care," Remi thought as he left Brenda outside and headed inside to the kitchen. He reached behind a box of crackers on a top shelf for a bottle of Macallan Single Malt that he knew Charlie kept hidden for "emergencies."

If there was a time to call an emergency, it's now," Remi thought, scanning the counter for a glass. He found a blue fish cup resting in a dish rack and quickly poured it to the rim. Tilting it back he thought about how tacky it was to even let a fine liquor costing $75,000 even touch plastic, "and yet I'm going to do it again."

Remi filled another cup and stared out the window at Brenda's untanned legs sticking out from the lounge. The rain was plunking onto her blond hair. For a second he thought maybe she was dead because she hadn't moved. Remi felt hopeful that he wouldn't have to deal with her anymore but he quickly dismissed the thought. She may be an incredible pain in the ass but she was still Charlie and Nola's mother and they both loved that mean bitch. He had no idea why but he had to respect that. No one is perfect and yet they can still be loved. He loved his own mother and she had sent him a birthday present with his brother's name for three years straight.

Rain hitting the windows was the only sound in the house. It was unsettling without a TV on or the kids bouncing around. He remembered the day Charlie moved to his custom built palace on the cliff. Remi walked into the house and stood at this exact spot in the kitchen which was a perfect view to watch the circus. Mariana, newly pregnant with Max had severe morning sickness and was chattering with the decorator that she was finally happy with the color scheme for the kitchen. She was leaning on Charlie as he rubbed her feet and nodded occasionally. Oriana was clanging pots onto the kitchen floor and howling along with the sound. Movers brought boxes inside, narrowly moving around the three year old and trying desperately to move the boxes in the direction that Mariana wanted. It was loud and messy. Remi felt relief that he was able to escape back to the condo that was sanitized by a maid once a week and he had control of the sound. Right now he wished for that chaos again. The life was taken out of this house, a thought that filled Remi with loneliness and sorrow. He filled the cup two more times.

Remi didn't remember leaving the kitchen until he stumbled on a tile heading toward the stairs. He braced on the railing and closed his eyes for a second. His head was swimming and a tingle replaced feeling in his fingers. For a moment he thought he heard a male voice agree with him. It was faintly echoing from downstairs. Who was down there? Remi stepped down on the first step but missed the second and landed on his back gripping the railing. "God damn it. "

Remi's face flushed hot from embarrassment and he lay there unmoved as he strained to hear the male voice again and then started climbing up the stairs. "I'm losing it."

Stopping at Charlie's bedroom door, Remi tapped his finger, and he walked right to the bedroom.

Lisa lay on her side facing the wall. She was still wearing the red dress from the afternoon disaster from Fashion Valley Mall. He had been a bull in a fighter's ring earlier, angry that she had been so stupid to lose Nola. Now he just wanted to feel that soft, red fabric against his fingers.

The room began to lose focus and Remi allowed himself to sink onto the bed and lay his head next to the nape of Lisa's neck. He inhaled the sweetness of her perfume and closed his eyes as he listened to the cadence of her breath.

"Charlie should be the one lying here." Remi thought, "I need to leave."

"You belong here, baby."

Remi's eyes flew open as Lisa rolled toward him, her arm moving across his chest. Her eyes still closed breath heavy as keeping rhythm. Had he imagined the words that he wanted to believe? She was still sleeping and his head was swimming in his thoughts. Thoughts of Charlie's head lying bloody next to Kier made his stomach lurch and he moved his head to the side before he could taste the scotch come up. He leaned back in the bed and remembered Brenda's words about how nice it was to be able to sleep in peace.

Chapter Forty Three
La Jolla- Judge Andersen's House

Facundo dropped Charlie off around the corner and Charlie walked up the sidewalk toward the white house encased in a brick wall. The house had been for sale years ago and Charlie remembered the realtor had let Charlie and a newly pregnant Mariana have the first view. Charlie liked the stark white building with its long columns in the front. The brick walkways and side gardens reminded him of New Orleans. Of course, Mariana hated the sight but liked the view. She said it lacked any culture and she immediately wanted to hire a decorator. Charlie refused to proceed with the sale if she even thought about painting one wall. They went round and round until he made her happy with buying a much more expensive plot with full views of the beach and city. She could build from scratch if she agreed that the outside was California Spanish Colonial. She could make any changes to the inside as long as he didn't have to drive into a garage painted orange and teal. He didn't want to be *that* house on the block.

The front door opened before Charlie got through the gateway and onto the cobblestone path. A large chested guard in a dark suit and crisp white shirt greeted him with a curt nod.

"Good evening sir," the guard's dark skin made his crisp, shirt glow iridescent. Charlie guessed he might be Somalian. "How may I assist you?"

Charlie swallowed hard and tried to smile. "I have business with Judge Anderson."

Two other men dressed in dark suits walked outside the doorway. Their gaze held a hard indifference toward him.

"Judge Andersen conducts all business during work hours at his office," the Somalian said with a pleasant, clipped tone, "You can call for an appointment."

The guards at the front were now circling and one had opened the entry gate for Charlie to exit. Charlie felt his hands shake and he shoved them in his pockets feigning the cold. "I'm sorry, I was talking about neighborhood business. I live two streets down."

The Somalian's expression didn't change as he proceeded toward him. Charlie moved backward to keep from being stepped on.

"Look, I really need to see him," Charlie said, "It's important."

The Somalian smiled patiently as his firm hands spun Charlie around with cautious precision so Charlie moved on his own weight. The gate grew closer and Charlie could see the Honda slowly approaching from up the hill.

Charlie swung around and tried to put his arm up but the motion was responded by a pain in his elbow as the Somalian swung his left arm behind him.

"Just ask Judge to see me." Charlie said trying to break free from the grip, "Can you just do that?"

"Call his assistant tomorrow," the Somalian said.

"No, I don't have that kind of time, "Charlie said finding himself saying the words he hated most, "Do you know who I am?"

The Somalian and guards chuckled, ignored the question and started to slide him forward. Charlie tried to reach inside his jacket, maybe if he took the gun out, he could force himself back inside or be shot and killed.

Charlie heard an engine approaching. Shit... the henchmen are out in the street. They're going to see him thrown out on his ass.

"What are you doing to him?"

The voice instantly relaxed the Somalian's grip on his arms but Charlie was still held in place.

"Let him go."

Charlie's arms were released and he spun around to see a boy standing at the gate. He looked like a beach comber with loose board shorts and a worn green T-Shirt with the sleeves ripped on each side. His hair waved wildly with untamed curls. It was hard to see the scrubbed judge's kid in the white button down from a few days ago. Charlie only recognized Jesse from the crescent-shaped scab crusted under a cluster of whiskers where he'd been hit with the glass.

Jesse grabbed Charlie's arm and moved him toward the walkway.

The Somalian protested. "He can't go until he's searched."

Jesse scoffed. "What's he going to do?"

"Judge Andersen says everyone must be checked before entering," the Somalian said matching their steps up the walkway.

Jesse spun around and waved his hands in frustration." My Dad tells you to frisk me too? I'm telling you that he's a friend, Marcus."

The Somalian now had a name and a hardening stone expression. "He gets checked."

"Fine," Jesse said, pulling Charlie's arms up, "this guy saved my ass but you think he's got a bomb wired to him. Let's see."

Jesse bent down and whispered to Charlie, "Sorry about this, man."

Jesse patted Charlie's legs and up his thighs. He held his breath when he reached his jacket, scanning over it quickly and reaching into his pocket and pulling out Charlie's wallet. "Look he's armed with a fat wallet. Shall we call the police? Oh, wait he's a fucking millionaire."

Marcus didn't seem bothered by Jesse's attitude. "I am following your father's instructions, sir."

"I live here too," Jesse snapped, "follow my orders and stop harassing my friends."

Jesse moved Charlie through the door and slammed it shut behind them.

The foyer was minimal. It had been remolded since Charlie last walk through. The horseshoe staircase inlaid with wood had been replaced with marble. A crystal chandelier dripped down from the pitch in the ceiling and showcased a granite statue of arms reaching upward and then disappearing into a solid block. Lemon polish from a freshly waxed floor and three stands of fresh-cut roses perfumed the air.

"He's probably upstairs, c'mon." Jesse said, starting up the first steps of the staircase. Charlie looked down the corridor to the right. The door at the end of the hall was opened slightly. He could see the patio door that Paulo had told him was his only escape. He had to keep on the first floor.

"Ask him to come down," Charlie said, "I'd rather talk downstairs."

Jesse started back down. "Don't make me drag you."

Now was the time to use any charm that Charlie had left. Charlie flashed a smile and nodded toward the door. "I'd rather keep out in the open. I don't want to give that guard outside a reason to strip off my skin."

Jesse laughed and scratched his nose with the back of his arm. "Yeah, Marcus is a dick. Wait here and I'll bring Dad down."

Charlie stuffed his hands back into his jacket and felt the metal against his rib. He closed his eyes then opened quickly. The room felt like he was spinning and he couldn't be sure if he was lying on the floor or still standing. It was warm and yet he couldn't stop the cold in his bones.

"Mr. Thibodeaux."

Judge Andersen's voice echoed up the foyer. It conveyed a politeness and formality reserved for his court room.

Charlie had never met him before but he had seen pictures of him. Andersen was an older version of his son. His dark hair cut short was peppered at his temples and a thick mustache that covered his upper lip. His eyes folded with a few wrinkles and tanned skin blended with the light blue shirt rolled at the elbows.

Jesse came down the stairs behind Andersen and stood next to him. There was no doubt they were related but their differences were a splintered branch of the family tree. Charlie imagined they had both spent time enjoying the sun and could be surfers yet was pretty sure they had never shared the same beach. Charlie swore when he got Max back he'd teach him whatever he wanted to learn, they'd master it together.

Andersen took Charlie's hand and gave it a firm squeeze as they clasped together. "It's cold out there."

"Charlie is the owner of that club where those guys jumped me," Jesse said beaming, "He saved my ass."

Andersen dropped Charlie's hand. "Jesse told me. I imagine being a club owner you must encounter many troubles."

"I pay heavily for good security." Charlie shifted his weight, he felt Andersen's eyes analyzing him, and "I want customers to feel safe in my clubs."

Jesse picked up the tension. "Dad those guys had knives and were going to slice me open. I could've been killed and Charlie lit up for me."

Charlie avoided Andersen's glance, acutely aware of the exaggeration. Andersen patted Jesse on the back. "Yes, of course. I am grateful for my son's safety but I'm sure you didn't come to speak to me about that."

"I would like to talk about some concerns I have regarding us," Charlie took a deep breath, "I mean not you and I. I have concerns about the neighborhood. I live off Via Alto."

"Oh yes," Andersen nodded politely, his eyes focusing on a swelling cut on Charlie's hand.

Charlie slid his hand inside his pocket and touched the gun. He thought about pulling it out right now but he didn't want Jesse to see his father die. The office was too far away to run without giving time for the guards to get close.

"Could we go somewhere to discuss some things?" Charlie asked.

Andersen sighed. "I was preparing for court tomorrow."

"It will only take a minute."

Looking at his watch, Andersen began to move to the left. "Yes, of course."

Charlie's heart sank as they stepped further away from the office. They rounded a corner but the judge stopped when they heard loud laughter coming from a side hallway.

"On second thought," Andersen said, "My daughter's cheer squad is here. It will be quiet in my office."

Charlie felt a mix of dread and relief as Andersen moved past him and toward the office door. Charlie worried Jesse would follow but once the boy heard cheerleaders he was going the other direction. Jesse paused and looked back at Charlie. He raised his hands up in victory. "You're saving me, man."

It occurred to Charlie at that moment that Jesse never checked his left pocket.

Judge Andersen's office was smaller than expected and not as flawless as the foyer. A bookshelf climbed the wall behind a mahogany desk with files stacked on top of a computer hiding the monitor from view. A dark red carpet with white stripes disappeared under a leather couch where a worn pillow lay with a blue blanket knotted and worn after years of covering a few moments of guarded sleep. This was where Judge Andersen really lived.

Charlie closed the office door behind him, realizing he had just left more proof that he was there. Not that the scene with the Marcus and the guards or Jesse calling him by name wasn't enough to put him strapped into a chair. He'd be trading his neighbors for child killers like Westerfield and Petersen on death row.

Andersen sat behind his desk and closed a stack of folders to the side. He made no motion for Charlie to sit down.

"I am grateful to you for saving my son's life," Andersen said, his mouth twisted, "I want to make it clear. If you came here expecting some kind of favor like making a DUI disappear, then leave right now. Before you start to ask, you should know I report all bribe attempts."

Andersen leaned back in his chair, his stare boring into Charlie's skull. The sweat started to gather in the back of his neck and his tongue felt too large for his mouth. Charlie wanted to throw up all over the antique mahogany. He looked over at the side door to the garden. It was opened slightly and he could run out right now. Charlie had done nothing wrong and was free to go. He'd be embarrassed but still free to run to the police and tell them everything but there weren't police on the hill. The closest would be in

Pacific Beach and he'd never make it that far. Before he reached the parking lot, Eulojo would be told and torturing Max. Lena and Giselle would be raped. He would cause their death. The police weren't going to understand why he didn't come to them sooner. Charlie couldn't live knowing he'd run off with Lena and the kids only chance to live.

"Mr. Thibodeaux..." Judge Andersen sighed, looking through a drawer and flipping papers onto the desk.

Charlie took the distraction to pull out the gun. "Forgive me. I don't do this for me but I can't save us all."

"What did you say? " Judge Andersen asked, looking up as Charlie pulled the trigger.

The trigger remained frozen in Charlie's hand. It couldn't be that hard to shoot a gun if the drug addicted Sam could figure it out. Charlie squeezed again.

Your gun has the safety on," Judge Andersen said quietly, pulling his own gun from under the desk, "but mine doesn't."

Charlie lowered his gun and stared at the Judge Andersen's finger on the trigger.

After ten minutes of silence, Charlie could no longer stand to know what was going to happen. "Why haven't you called Marcus?"

Judge Andersen steadied the gun and moved it into a better vantage. "Put your gun on my desk."

Charlie lowered the gun onto the desk. He looked at the side door. He'd be dead before he got one foot outside.

"Do you have any more weapons on you?" Andersen asked.

"No."

Andersen relaxed his gun but kept the barrel in position.

"I just pointed a gun at your face," Charlie said, "how can you believe me?"

"I spend a lot of time with liars, Mr. Thibodeaux. Some come before me to be sentenced and others represent them, "Judge Andersen said, pointing his gun toward the couch, "It gives me an accurate measure. Sit down."

Charlie waited for Marcus and his security to burst through the door but the Judge studied Charlie instead.

What did you mean when you said you can't save us all?" Andersen asked.

Charlie leaned forward and Andersen brought the gun back to attention. "I don't know."

" I think you do," Judge Andersen snapped, "You're a respected businessman who doesn't have any dealings in federal court. We've never met and you have money so this isn't a robbery. You have no reason to kill me so who has their claws are in you?"

Charlie ran his hands through his hair and started at the floor. He was tired of lying. "I have spent the last four days in Mexico. My son, a woman and her daughter helping us are being held down there. Killing you is the only way I can save them from a man who is part of the cartel."

"They are with Eulojo."

Charlie and the Andersen locked eyes. The tan had drained from the Andersen's face, the wrinkles on his temple deepened their crevices.

"So this isn't random," Charlie said, hopeful when someone else recognized the name of the devil, "You've done something to piss him off and he wants you dead?"

Andersen started to speak but paused when heavy footsteps approached the door. He waited until they faded before he began.

"The reason Eulojo wants me dead isn't as tragic as the alliance he has created," Andersen said, "He is working with someone on this side. Someone let you into my house so you were unchecked by my guards. It's not a coincidence."

Andersen lay the gun on the table, "Mr. Thibodeaux, you are trying to save your son's life while my son is trying to take mine."

Charlie couldn't believe his ears. Jesse was a typical college kid from California. He was smart but too nervous and inexperienced to be an accomplice with a devil like Eulojo. Despite knowing how wrong Jesse sounded to be a mastermind, the fact that he got Charlie inside without inspection had been predicted. Perhaps Jesse allowed everyone to dismiss him as a kid while the man inside had freedom to roam into darker places.

"My son looks just like me as a boy," Judge Andersen's eyes softened, "Inside Jesse is his mother's son. She was free-spirited and idealistic about the world, both traits I admired in my wife but have not been so easy to understand in my son. We differ greatly on how drugs should be handled. Jesse thinks we should legalize the drug trade. Eulojo has filled his head with ideas that he could be a founding father of the next California gold rush."

Judge Andersen grabbed a picture from his desk and handed it to Charlie. A smiling girl about twenty was holding up a slice of apple pie toward the photographer. She was bundled in a dark blue coat and a knitted cap that sat dangerously close to falling off her thick, bouncy curls. What made the picture stand out were the bright, blue eyes on her heart-shaped face. They were beaming through the camera at the photographer.

"Beautiful girl." Charlie commented.

"I took my wife, Helena, up to the mountains in Julian. She just thought we were going to get a piece of apple pie but I was there to propose, "Andersen smiled at the photo as he placed it gently on the desk, "It was so cold but she wouldn't put back on her gloves. She couldn't stop looking at her ring.

We lived in Riverside when I started out in the district attorney's office. It was a lot of hours but Helena kept busy with our house and Jesse. When my daughter Carin came along, Helena had a difficult recovery. They prescribed two more weeks of Vicodin.

Several months later, I was packing for a meeting in Washington DC. I needed some aspirin and noticed her prescription bottle for Vicodin in the medicine cabinet. It was full and I assumed she never finished them so I disposed of them and went on my trip.

When I came home three days later, I walked in the house to find Carin crying and struggling to get out of her high chair. She was in a soiled diaper that hadn't been changed in days. Jesse was cowering under an overturned couch. I thought an intruder broke inside. I grabbed the kids and took them to the neighbor, told them to call 911 and I went back."

Andersen took a deep breath as he returned to the memory.

"I thought I would find Helena dead. I flashed through all the cases I prosecuted. Was this an attack from a parolee that wanted vengeance? Was this a warning from a gang? My imagination couldn't prepare me for what I saw when I got to the second floor. I found Helena scrounging under our bed, her eyes like a wild animal searching for her Vicodin bottle.

I tried to coax her from underneath but she was irrational and sprang at me. She scratched my face with the very ring that she wouldn't conceal on the day I proposed. In the three days I had been gone, she went into full withdrawal.

A doctor friend, now former, started writing her a prescription for Vicodin two weeks after her own ran out. After eight months, my wife's addiction had built so much in her system she was only satisfied with a dose you wouldn't give to a professional football player. Helena weighed only 110 pounds.

She would never admit she had a problem."

Judge Andersen took a moment to rub his eyes before he continued.

"She got better at hiding her addiction that ended the fatal day she combined them with a bottle of wine.

The thing is Mr. Thibodeaux...Charlie... our society can't handle the use of our own prescription drug. The bulk of users aren't the junkies in crack houses and alleys. They're the ones picking up their kids in a minivan and going back to their office jobs after their half hour lunch. The casual users that hide in their prescription bottles and deny they have a problem. If they can't handle what is legal, how can we expect them to ever handle what isn't?"

Charlie stared at the twenty minutes lost on his watch. "Everyone's got a story about drugs. You lost a wife, I lost my brother to a drug addicted father. I'm sorry about your family but right now I am losing time to save mine."

"You marched in my home and raised a gun in my face," Judge Andersen leaned back in his chair, "and you don't want to know why?"

"I don't care why."

"Well you're going to listen," Andersen yelled, "You say you lost a brother and carry your cautionary tale like a badge you think you've earned? You think we are veterans from this war? We turn our backs because we don't have to serve anymore. I left the duty to my son and he listened to the only one talking. Eulojo has convinced him that I am holding him back from a future.

There is a decision coming up in the courts that would open the door for the public sale of marijuana nationwide. I intend to rule against legalization which has upset pro-marijuana activists. They call me the Father of Modern Day Prohibition."

"Keeping marijuana illegal means the cartel won't lose money," Charlie argued, "so Eulojo should be your best friend."

"The cartel is a well-funded corporation that keeps an eye on our moral dilemma like the US is an upstart company with too many uncommitted investors. Our disorganized mess doesn't interest them right now but it's the ambitious ones like Eulojo who see opportunity in our mistakes and want to start their own business."

"Mariana told me once that you don't quit the cartel unless you want to die," Charlie said, "why would Eulojo want to sign his death warrant?"

"Eulojo wants to be the silent partner so the cartel doesn't know his plans. He convinced my son that he wants to be a legitimate business man and needs Jesse to be a partner and the face of the new drug trade," Judge Andersen said shaking his head, "a criminal never has a noble intention unless it disguises their purpose."

"I don't have the time to debate with you about legalizing drugs," Charlie said sliding off the couch and lunging at Judge Andersen, who tried to bring the gun up but Charlie grabbed his arm and pinned it down with his knee to the chair. His hand circled firmly around Judge Andersen's throat, "I can't allow my son to die because I was too weak to protect him. "

The more Judge Andersen struggled to move, Charlie squeezed as he got a stronger hold, pushing away from the desk with his knees and forcing the chair over on its side. He gasped as Charlie lunged for the gun and grasped the handle. It was easier to hold now. Its weight fit like an extension of his hand as he aimed it at Andersen's head. Andersen threw his arm up and dove around the desk.

"You don't have to do this!" Andersen forced out between ragged coughs.

I don't have a choice." Charlie said, trying to steady the gun.

"Charlie, you do have a choice." Judge Andersen said, anchoring himself on Charlie's leg, "Listen to me, please. You aren't a killer. "

Andersen edged himself against the desk and sat up. He looked squarely into Charlie's eyes, "I promise you if you put down the gun, I will show you a way that saves us all."

Chapter Forty Four
La Jolla- Judge Andersen's House

There was more rustling outside the door. Charlie picked up the gun from the desk. "Are you ready?"

Andersen took a deep breath and positioned himself behind the couch, "Are you?"

"No." Charlie said, pointing the gun to a stack of books, "What if you're wrong about this?"

"I wish I was," Andersen said, "but I'm not."

Charlie squeezed the trigger and this time the shot felt like it rang through him, the noise puncturing his ears as Jesse burst through the door.

Jesse gave a quick glance to Judge slumped on the couch and Charlie holding the gun.

"Son of a bitch!" Jesse yelled, grabbing for Charlie's middle as they crashed to the floor, a flurry of papers and the computer monitor tipped onto Jesse's back, giving Charlie a change to swing the gun into Jesse's jaw. Jesse howled and flipped over on his back. Jesse's eyes widened as he stared in horror as Judge Andersen had moved from the couch and was now standing over him with his gun clicked in his face.

"Dad? You are okay?"

"Shut your mouth," Judge said, his voice cracking, "Don't say another damn word."

"But I saw you... lying on the couch," Jesse whimpered, "I heard the shot. Charlie... the gun..."

"A real hero stopping my attacker," Judge shouted, grabbing Jesse's shirt and pulled him within inches of his face, " when you're the one who let the killer inside our house!"

Marcus came through the door and paused as he surveyed the scene. Judge let go of Jesse and motioned for Marcus to pick him up "Put him in a closet for now."

"Dad, I don't know what this guy has told you, Jesse said, sounding like a whining child, "I don't understand what the hell is happening."

Judge Anderson's vein on his forehead popped as he gritted his teeth and pulled his gun from the couch. He grabbed Jesse by the neck.

"I told you not to say another word," Judge said shoving the gun into Jesse's mouth. The boy began to scream as Judge cocked the hammer back.
Marcus drew his own gun and touched Judge's shoulder. "Let go sir."

Judge stared into Jesse's wide eyes and took a deep breath. He released his grip and handed the gun to Marcus and allowed Jesse to collapse onto the floor bursting into tears. His arms went slack as two of Marcus' men started to pull Jesse out of the room.

"Wait a minute, "Judge stopped them and began to search Jesse's pockets. He pulled out a cell phone and threw it on the desk. "Don't put him anywhere that has access to a phone, computer, anything. Put him in the dark. And Marcus?"

Marcus swung Jesse around, him head hanging low like a rag doll. "Call an ambulance and say that I've been shot. Then come back here. Don't let anyone in this room, understand?"

Judge picked up Charlie's gun and pulled off his wedding ring. He tucked them into Charlie's pocket. "In case you need proof that I'm dead."

Charlie didn't know what to say to him. The Judge's face looked like he had just aged fifty years since he met him half an hour before. Charlie rested his hand on the handle going out to the courtyard but paused. Judge Andersen read his thoughts and waved his hand to the garden door, turned out the desk lamp and settled into his chair in the darkness. "Go. We're not going to let you lose your son too."

Charlie pushed out to the night air, shivering as a gust of wind blew from the Pacific. His feet began to move as soon as he heard the siren in the distance.

The courtyard let out into an alley, Charlie searched for the Honda. Nothing there but the recycle container for tomorrow's pick up and a chubby cat startled by his quick entrance.

Goddamn them.

A red glow appeared over the trees in front and the siren was approaching the front street. Charlie pressed against the wall and headed for the other end of the alley, crouched behind the recycling.

Just wait a few more minutes, Charlie thought, he heard shouting in the courtyard. A black and white passed the gap and swiftly around the corner. It was too dangerous to stay long. Charlie shot out from the alley and moved quickly to a side street to figure out his location. He was in a cul-de-sac that he didn't recognize. Charlie never walked his own neighborhood. It never made sense to walk around homes. There wasn't anywhere to go. If he had been downtown in San Diego or New Orleans, he would meet Lisa at a restaurant or head with Remi to a game or a bar. There was a purpose to walk around. On the residential hills of La Jolla, there wasn't anywhere to go unless it was a church or a French school. The only other businesses were in a hidden strip mall holding a market, hair salon and the Mount Soledad memorial office. It had a small, poorly lit parking lot and might have been a good waiting place for Facundo and Paulo to hide. He couldn't just walk around without having a purpose unless he travel three miles down the hill to hit Garnet and blend into the traffic feeding into Pacific Beach's bar scene.

Standing by himself on the sidewalk was making Charlie a target so he started to walk. How long could Judge Andersen keep from being discovered? The window was closing to get back to Lena and the kids. He had to find Paulo. Had they left him? Maybe it was true that he wasn't supposed to come back.

When Charlie reached the corner, he saw a sign for Kate Sessions Park. A public place. Close enough to walk but far enough from the Judge's House to wait without immediate suspicion. More sirens stopped him in his tracks. Two more patrol cars rushed past on Mt. Soledad road and turned off toward Judge's house. Charlie kept his head down and pressed his hands in his pocket. A couple walking a Labrador started up the hill nodded to him as they watched the glowing lights. Cars started to line up on the road as the intersection was clogging with emergency vehicles.

Charlie looked toward the glow of red, looking like a sun set in the west and noticed the familiar red tile of his roof. He heard a screech in front of him and felt a thud as his hands braced against a car cutting off his path. He looked at one hand resting on black paint and the other one white. His face rose toward the windshield and he gazed directly at the police officers sitting inside. "Shit."

The passenger window rolled down and a white arm stretched out of the police car and waved Charlie over.

"This is it. It's all over," Charlie thought, leaning down to see the arm belonged to a burly cop with a large nose. The second cop, younger and agitated, sat at the driver wheel, his fingers beating a rhythm on the steering wheel.

"You okay?" The burly cop had a rumbling growl that matched his appearance.

"What?" Charlie felt his face feeling hot despite the cool wind.

The burly cop frowned. "Are you okay, sir? You stepped off the curb and we almost ran you over."

Charlie's thoughts couldn't catch up with him. Go back to Judges and confess everything. Maybe they could get some connection to the south. Capture the Honda before they left the hill.

"I-I'm Charlie Thibodeaux."

The burly cop nodded. "We know."

"You're going the wrong way," the younger cop said, pointing toward a side street, "take that one back and wait in the alley by your house."

The words didn't register to Charlie. The burly cop flicked his arm impatiently toward the street. "It's not safe for you to be out here. Head toward your house and they'll pick you up."

Charlie stepped back on the curb and turned into the side street. As soon as he was covered back in darkness he broke out running and didn't bother to look back. He knew the cops were watching every step.

Chapter Forty Five
La Jolla- Charlie's House

The front of Charlie's house was dark, the timers had not synced with the time change. Charlie hesitated as he walked along a clump of oleanders. He shrunk behind a bush and watched the quiet street. No head lights passing. Cars always parked in the side alley which meant only one thing, they had left him. He made his way to the side of the house where he could still have a clear view of the front door and street. A square outline of light came from the living room so Charlie stopped at the edge of the light's border and peeked upward to see Nola standing at the window, Charlie instinctively turned his face away even though he knew she couldn't find him in the darkness. He watched her like she was a mannequin in a store window.

Nola was the most innocent soul Charlie had ever known even beyond his own children. If she hadn't been damaged who could she have been? Would she be hardened like Brenda or could Nola's sweet spirit have broken out of the cycle? Could she have a husband and kids of her own? With a fighting chance could she have carved out her own place in the world?

Charlie knew that if she even had the chance for a normal life, he would be dead or in prison by now. His success was directly related to her downfall.

About a dozen times, Charlie tried to find a reason they could both be happy but the scenario always played the same. If Nola hadn't been taken to the hospital then Brenda would have kept Charlie with her. Charlie would never be placed in foster care where he was taken in by Professor Hemsley and his wife who made him focus on school. He spent the time crafting his love for jazz and getting a scholarship to Loyola. He wouldn't have met Remi and built their empire. Had Nola been released the next day from the hospital, Brenda would have taken them back to live in that shitty janitor closet. All of Charlie's dreams came true because Nola was robbed of her own.

The front door cracked open and Charlie ducked further out of sight. Nola was out the front door scanning with the same blank stare. Had she heard him? He was so close he could have easily slipped back inside into the warmth of insulated walls. He would head upstairs and crawl into bed. He would bring Oriana with him and fall asleep until he could wake up from this horrible dream, but he wouldn't have Max with them. He had to stay in this nightmare to protect Max. And now Lena and Giselle needed him. He couldn't rob one more person of their future.

I won't let this happen to anyone else, Nola.

Charlie couldn't stop himself from calling out Nola's name. He only needed to watch her lift her head to know he had made a terrible mistake. The Honda was now pulling into view.

As the Honda turned around the corner, Charlie tried to catch a look at Nola. He could only see the curve of the driveway. He felt Paulo's thick hand on his neck as Charlie was pushed him down against the upholstery.

"Head down," Paulo said, his face staring out the passenger side window, "you didn't let no one see you, did you?"

"No."

Facundo growled. "He's lying. We already know he talked with the cops. He was talking to the girl on the driveway."

Charlie tried to move but Paulo's hand had him pinned. "She came out but she didn't see me."

"You sure?"

"I didn't talk to her," Charlie shouted, "Why would I give myself up like that? I'm not supposed to be seen."

Facundo slowed the car, "You want me to go back and get her?"

Charlie pushed upward. Paulo's fingers tightened around Charlie's neck. "Jesus Christ, we need to get off the hill. Why would I risk everything to talk to anybody?"

Paulo's grip relaxed. "Keep moving. We're supposed to be back by now."

Five minutes passed and Charlie was able to move up, catching a glimpse of the Hilton on Mission Bay. They were headed south on Interstate Five. Charlie felt a flood of relief that they had escaped the hill and that Nola was safe.

It was silent for the next twenty minutes until Facundo broke the silence. "He hasn't called."

"He'll call," Paulo said, "Just drive."

"You weren't in the alley." Charlie said, starting to feel more bold.

"We got you," Facundo said gripping the steering wheel, "and you can't get far from us."

"We could have gone sooner if you hadn't lost me." Charlie said.

"We never lost you," Paulo chuckled, "we've got eyes everywhere."

Chapter Forty Six
La Jolla-Judge Andersen's House

Judge Andersen stayed still as someone paused at the door and moved quickly away. From the bedroom he could see a flashing cop car and a road barrier with a crowd starting to form.

"Half of them just want to see a dead body and the other half are irritated at the inconvenience," Andersen thought with disgust. For a judge, you would assume he liked being a voyeur into someone else's tragedy but he never cared about the drama of it all. The people standing before him were never as important as the question they presented him. He cared about the law and how it applied to the facts. It's what made him successful, to take the emotion out of it all and find an answer within the law.

Now sitting in the darkness, he was swept up in the drama he detested. All he could do was thinking about Jesse sitting in a closet, a prisoner just like him. His own son aligned against him as if the only option for his happiness was the death of his father.

Judge Andersen could hear Marcus trying to console his daughter, Carin, but she was growing worse. The girl lost her mother and now she thought she had lost him. It was more than Andersen could tolerate. He was losing his son, he wouldn't lose his daughter so he picked up the phone and connected with Marcus.

"Who's here?"

"Two paramedics, five SDPD, and house security," Marcus said, "We're keeping it closed off to the few you approved."

"Carin and her friends?"

"The friends were moved out the back and taken home. I put Carin in the kitchen."

"And the press?"

"Press?"

"The press," Judge Andersen snapped, "Can they hear Carin crying?"

"Yes, sir."

"Who is going out in the ambulance?"

"Mel. He's being covered up and moved in twenty."

"Get him out as soon as possible. Lights off," Andersen instructed, "Make sure the crowd gets a full view that there is not a chance of going to the hospital."

"Sir," Marcus said, pausing, "Carin may need something to subdue her."

"Drug her?" Andersen said, "Absolutely not."

"She is having trouble breathing."

"Bring her here." Andersen said, feeling the guilt flood his heart.

In a few moments, Marcus had brought Carin inside the dark office.

"Daddy?" Carin whispered, she stiffened at Andersen's voice and then broke free and into his arms. "Oh, God what's going on?"

Andersen moved her to the couch. She squeezed him tighter, pressing her head into his chest, her tears felt warm on his shirt. "I thought I had lost you."

"I never want you to feel that pain," Andersen felt the tears in his own eyes start to well as he kissed her face, "I promise I can explain all of this."

When I heard the shots, we all froze. Marcus rushed everyone out. I didn't know what was going on," Carin said, her body trembling, "All they would tell me was you'd been shot and then pushed me into the kitchen."

Andersen kissed her face and hugged her tightly. "I'm sorry you got stuck in there."

"It could have been worse," Carin said, sniffing as she dabbed her eyes with the back of her sweater, "Jesse was stuck in a closet."

Judge sat up. "When did you speak to him?"

"I heard him pounding so I opened the door," Carin said, her voice faltering, "he ran out the back door. We need to find Jesse, he doesn't know you're alive."

Chapter Forty Seven
Mexico

It didn't take as long for Facundo to drive them out of La Jolla and through the mystery tunnels. For all of the military crowding the borders, they passed underneath them and were back in the tire shop in Mexico in half an hour. Charlie sat in the Honda listening to the rain that had started beating a hard pattern on the metal roof. It drowned out Paulo and Facundo as they talked in the corner. Charlie sat in the back seat and watched Facundo pulled his phone out of his pocket and stared at the screen. Paulo grabbed the phone and shook it at him as he pulled back and charged over, opening the back door.

"Get in the truck."

Charlie started outside of the body shop, the rain dropping sideways as he opened the door. He felt breath on his neck and Charlie turned to see Facundo directly behind him. Facundo grabbed him by the arm and yanked him against the wall. "How do we know you killed that Judge?"

Charlie pulled his arm away. "You saw all the police."

Paulo sighed. "Facundo has his huevos in a bunch but he's right. We didn't get the call."

Charlie dug deep into his pocket and could feel the round, smooth ring in the folds of cloth. He pulled it up and let it flash under the single light on in the office. "Here's your proof. He loved his wife and never took this off."

Paulo took the ring and examined it closely.

"How do we know that ain't yours?"

Paulo handed the ring to Facundo. "It's got initials on it. Now shut the fuck up it's done."

Facundo eyed the ring and then stuffed it in his pocket. Charlie held out his hand. "I want it back."

"You don't get it back," Facundo said.

"It's *my* damn souvenir," Charlie said.

Paulo grabbed the ring from Facundo and pushed it back in Charlie's hand. "Get in the fucking truck."

The rain was cascading down like sheet metal making it difficult to see the truck. They sloshed through pools of water that dampened up their calves. Charlie pushed ahead, feeling like there were four eyes poking into his back. Charlie turned around to see that Facundo and Paulo hadn't moved from the stoop, their voices drowning out. Charlie moved toward the truck and looked down the roadway. It was pitch black without the lights and now rain meant he could barely see even his arm in front of him.

Charlie felt a pain above his left ear as the mirror on the truck shattered. They had shot at him. He turned to feel a punch into his stomach, his lungs tried to grab the air as it left his body. His knees buckled and he knelt before Paulo.

Paulo dug his boot into the muck and kicked upward, spraying Charlie's face so he sputtered and spit out the wet clumps. Charlie raised his arm to deflect the boot which now swung toward his face. The heel dug into Charlie's arm and pushed him onto his back.

A pain seared around his ear, he brought his hand up and felt a meaty pulp where the skin had been on his lobe. He stumbled over his feet and rolled into a watery crater on the side. The pool of water was deeper than he expected forcing him to tilt his head out of the water. It was soothing to his ear at first but then began to sting. He tilted his ear out of the pool as he searched for Paulo.

Above him, he watched Facundo move into the driver's side of the truck and slam it shut.

Paulo stood at the driver rear bumper and wiped the water from his face.

"Stand up. "Paulo shouted.

Charlie pushed himself deeper into the water. The pool allowed him to submerge himself if he lay flat allowing him to keep his mouth just high enough to breath.

Paulo slid down into the embankment and cursed as his shoes filled with water. "You make it hard and I'll make this hurt."

"Stand up." Paulo yelled again.

Charlie pushed himself further into the mud, his knees creating islands in the black water. The darkness and rain, protected him from Paulo's eyes.

"You know this isn't coming from me," Paulo called out, "Eulojo says they need to find your body. In case you start giving them the bullshit about saving your kid."

"You know it's not bullshit," Charlie yelled out and then pushed toward the other side of the hole.

Paulo turned his face to the direction of Charlie's voice and raised the gun. "Don't matter if it's true or not. Eulojo wants to make a point. You get in the way."

With only Paulo's voice to guide him, Charlie felt like an echo calling back to four days ago when he clung with Max to a cliff on the beach. The voice was the same one afraid of demons haunting him but had no trouble to kill an entire family in minutes. Paulo was at the Ranch.

"You don't want to kill me, I'd come back from the grave and haunt you," Charlie said, moving toward the south end, closer to Paulo was a gamble but it was enough proof that Paulo couldn't see him. Charlie pushed closer.

Paulo's head turned, confused at the direction. "What did you say?"

"The people you kill, they will always stay with you."

"Bullshit." Paulo spat and brushed water from his face, "ghosts aren't real."

"I grew up with ghosts walking down the streets of New Orleans," Charlie called out, "Soldiers missing their legs but still moving on. Lost, no eyes, hollowed out. Sometimes you'd hear a baby crying from a cemetery or slaves burned alive because they're chained to a stove."

Paulo splashed into the hole, gaining his footing right before he started to slide. Charlie pushed to the side and crouched behind Paulo's right leg. Paulo shot the gun into the heart of the pool, the bullet's destination disappeared with a splash. "Shut your fucking mouth."

Charlie lunged at Paulo's waist forcing him down into the water. Charlie used his weight to pin Paulo's right arm against him, forcing the gun to stay horizontal from his chest. Paulo shot again, the bullet zinging into the darkness. Paulo's elbow swung upward, trying to wedge the gun in between Charlie's chest and his own. Charlie's feet slid as he tried to straddle Paulo and he suddenly found Paulo's weight pushing down on his legs and his face plunging into the water.

Charlie's mouth filled with gritty liquid, his nose stinging. Paulo's hands pushed down on his shoulders.

"I'm not dying in a mud hole," Charlie thought, he grabbed hold of Paulo's leg forcing it under the water. Charlie heaved forward, his face reached the surface, and he spit out the water into Paulo's face and gasped for air into his lungs. They ached, unable to be filled enough before Paulo grabbed ahold of Charlie again and shoved him above the lip of the pit. His face leaned close, the water dripping onto Charlie from a gutter formed in the matted hair hanging down his face.

Charlie opened his eyes and stared up, only able to look at Paulo's nostrils. The man was different but the same feeling of helplessness was like he was a kid, cowering from Sam under Brenda for cover, his heart beating, tears running down his cheeks as Jackson lay by Sam's feet, his right eye staring at Charlie but twitching. The wail of Nola filled with pain and confusion. There was only one thing that was saving Charlie right now. He knew Sam had been wrong. Through all of the tragedy and bad streaks of luck, life always found a way for the good to survive. There was no way that Charlie had come this far to not see that through.

Charlie balled his fist and struck inside Paulo's mouth, pushing him backward. Charlie pinned Paulo's arm and pried the gun from his fingers. He pushed it into Paulo's ribs.

Paulo's eyelids widened in surprise and his body scrambled to move away but Charlie kept pushing, trying to keep his finger from slipping on the trigger.

"You're going to take me back. I'm going to get my family and you'll drive us to Tecate. After that, I don't give a shit what you do." Charlie yelled over the rain. "I just want to go home."

Paulo shook his head. "Facundo's not going do it."

"Convince him," Charlie said, trying to pull the gun higher but it caught on Paulo's jacket, "no one else has to die here. Now, stand up."

Paulo moved onto all fours, Charlie steadied himself and helped Paulo move up.

Charlie opened his mouth to speak but Paulo slipped his full weight against Charlie, knocking them both over. Charlie felt a thick hand cover his and press down to unlock his fingers on the gun. He instinctively squeezed the trigger and Paulo fell over into the water, clutching his stomach. Charlie froze in his spot, staring down at the gun.

"If he dies," Charlie thought, "I don't know how to get out of here."

"You think a little bullet will stop me? I got no problem killing you. You think killing you is hard?" Paulo continued to squirm and bellow, struggling to move back to his knees looking like a turtle struggling to get off his shell. "I killed a whole family this week. If a bunch of little kids and women aren't going to haunt me, why the hell would I care about you?"

"You killed women and children?" Charlie felt his throat burn. Images of Mariana dying had plagued him for days but now he could only see her begging Paulo for her life, "don't you worry about your soul?"

"Slit their throats." Paulo said, moaning as he tilted on his side, "and I'd do it again.

Paulo's leg kicked up narrowly missing Charlie's face and he grabbed Paulo's knee pushing it below the water. Paulo's face disappeared under the water, his arms reaching upward. Charlie sat on Paulo's legs, feeling a strange surge of power, he put his full weight against Paulo as he struggled, his arms splashing above the surface trying to grab anything to raise his face. His fingers slipped off Charlie's shirt weakening their grasp with each passing moment. Charlie let go of Paulo's body long after the struggle was gone. Charlie's arms quivered with adrenaline, clutching onto Paulo's body. He never felt empowered with such a feeling of control. He thought about Sam and that look in his eyes when he was shooting his brother. His eyes had been lit with a fire that he couldn't understand until now. It horrified Charlie how good it felt.

Chapter Forty Eight
La Jolla- Charlie's House

Nola thought it was just the weather. When it howled and rained like tonight, sometimes it sounded human. She thought she saw Charlie on the lawn and could have sworn she heard her name. There was a little blast of wind that blew around her as she opened the door and felt a chill run straight through her. Gazing into the darkness, Nola saw only shapes of the lights on the lawn.

Oriana spilled the popcorn and let out a yell for Nola to help her pick it up.

"You spilled it. You pick it up." Nola yelled inside. Sometimes it seemed that Oriana was more like a little sister than her niece and she liked that she could boss her around. Oriana was the only one that Nola got to scold.

"Ew, I think I spilled your soda too!" Oriana whined. "Why did you leave it next to the chair?"

Nola began to quickly move back inside. She'd be the one that was yelled at if there was a stain, "Get a towel before it spreads!"

Nola started to close the door when she heard her name coming out of the darkness again.

"Nola."

It was just a whisper but it was definitely not the wind. Nola took a step outward to get a better look into the bushes.

"Nola, it's me!"

The voice was closer and now from the lawn, a dark shadow was forming under the eucalyptus tree.

"Who is me?" Nola called out, quivering in her voice. Nola's heart was beating out of her chest.

The faceless man whispered hoarsely, "I need help."

"Help? What's wrong with you?" Nola called out. "And who needs it?"

"Nola, it's Jesse."

Nola had met Jesse once at Mount Soledad Market down the street. Charlie waited in the parking lot so she could go inside to buy a sandwich. Jesse was standing in line in front of her and was arguing with the owner, Mark, because he refused to sell him a case of beer without his ID. Jesse noticed Nola and put his arm around Nola and said she was his girlfriend and would buy it for him. Mark got mad because he was friends with Charlie and knew Nola very well.

"I know Nola isn't your girl, Jesse," Mark growled, motioning for Nola to step away, "give me an ID or get out."

"Nola... that's a sexy name," Jesse whispered as he brushed against her arm causing her whole body to blush. He gave her a wink and left the market but didn't leave her mind. She'd thought about him every night for those five months but was frozen that he was actually standing at her own house. He looked the same as in her dreams. She remembered the same dark, curly hair, deep brown eyes and tanned skin. Jesse's eyes weren't smiling, they looked frightened and he was holding his arm, she noticed a trickle of blood that was spiraling down his shoulder.

"What happened to you?" Nola asked, running to the tree.

"My dad..." Jesse started but his voice broke, "tried to kill me."

Nola hesitated. She'd met Judge Andersen once

and he had been nothing but nice to her. "Your dad hurt you?

Jesse nodded, motioning toward the shelter of the tree. "I can't let him see me. He's out there looking right now."

"We need to call the police." Nola said, pulling him toward the front door but he grabbed her arm.

"He's too powerful. He'll just throw down some money and I'll just disappear," Jesse whispered, "you don't want me to disappear do you?"

Nola shook her head. She started to feel scared that she didn't know how to help him and it was overwhelming. "What can we do?"

"Can I hide here?" Jesse asked, his eyes so soft and pleading, "Just for a few hours."

Nola smiled. She imagined him sitting next to her on the overstuffed leather couch. "Of course you can! We're getting ready to watch a movie."

Jesse shook his head. He made her face him. "Nola, this is really important. No one can know I'm here."

"But-" Nola said frowning. The vision of him sharing popcorn with her was fading.

Jesse glanced into the vacant entry way. "What would your mom do if she found me here?"

Nola now had images of Mama seeing Jesse sitting with Nola. That would make her furious. "She'd call your Dad."

Jesse's eyes lit up. "Can I hide in your room?'

"My room?" Nola asked stepping back with a little surprise. No one was allowed in her room and especially not a boy.

Jesse watched her pull back. "Never mind, I'll go hide at the park. I thought I could trust you but I'll be okay if my Dad doesn't catch me."

"Okay, you can stay," Nola said grabbing onto his hand as he turned his back, "Go around the garage and wait at the side door."

"You are my beautiful butterfly, so gentle but so

strong as you flutter in to save me," Jesse said, gently kissing her forehead. Nola felt her face flood with heat.

As Nola headed back toward the front door, her heart thumping so loud she was sure Oriana could hear. She had to send Oriana to brush her teeth and get Jesse inside her room before she got out of the bathroom. What if Mama walked out of her room and saw him the hall? Nola would be in a lot of trouble.

"Butterfly?"

Nola peered into the dark to see Jesse was looking at her from the edge of the lawn. He looked so sweet standing there.

"I need one more favor," Jesse said.

"Anything, Jesse." Nola said, trying to keep her voice down so Oriana wouldn't come out.

"I need you to bring me a phone."

Chapter Forty Nine
Mexico

Facundo was growing pissed at the thought of getting out of the truck to help that fat slug kill one weak American. If Paulo had let Facundo kill him they'd be done by now. He was about to get out and kick Paulo's ass as well when Facundo finally heard the passenger door open.

"Shut the door. You're getting rain inside." Facundo said putting the keys in the ignition but stopped short of turning it over. The door slammed shut and out of the corner of Facundo's eye he saw the gun pointed near his cheek.

The American was sitting inside the truck trying to look like he was in control. "Take me back to that farm."

Facundo took his hand slowly off the key. He had hoped to slip into his actual bed tonight and grope his wife. Get up and meet his mother for church, now that was over. He leaned back and surveyed the American. He was caked in mud and dripping water all over the cab. This would be a funny story over a few beers one night but right now it was pissing him off and this cabron might have put a bullet into Paulo's skull, now he had to kill this one and find Paulo's body. He wasn't getting in his own bed tonight to touch his wife. He'd be apologizing to his mother that he missed church and she'd make him go to confession.

The American tapped him on the temple. "Start moving."

Facundo leaned back in the seat and stared down his options. He could take him back to the compound. The American would open the door and Facundo would pull his head back and stick a knife in his neck. He'd wanted to cut the son of a bitch the second he saw the American running down the beach like a bitch. When Eulojo gave the order to kill him, Facundo wanted to make it hurt but Paulo felt sorry for him and wanted to make it quick. Facundo had learned since he made his first kill at twelve that a mercy kill wasn't real. They know they're still going to die and you're the one killing them.

The only problem with bringing the American back was Eulojo wanted the body left dumped on the border. Facundo would get shit for botching it up and losing Paulo. He'd end the American right here. It meant longer in confession but only for taking pleasure in the kill.

Facundo reached for the keys and pulled them out of the ignition. "Fuck you."

The American looked rattled. "Start the truck. I don't have any trouble with you."

"Well, you've got trouble with me, asshole," Facundo said evenly, "You kill Paulo?"

"He didn't give me a choice," the American said staring down at the gun, "I had to kill him."

Facundo turned his body and leaned against the driver door, "You just got lucky."

"If you don't get moving, I've got no use for you." The American's hand began to shake, "start the truck."

Facundo moved closer, leaning his arm against the back of the seat. "Did you really kill that judge?"

The American moved slightly back, "You saw the police at his house."

"I didn't see a corpse."

"Did you expect me to drag him out for you to see?" the American shouted.

Facundo laughed. "Are you suddenly some bad ass killer now? You shoot a couple bullets and you think you in the same level with me? Just because you draw a stick figure you think you're fucking Picasso."

The American's face reddened. He was easy to upset which meant it was only a matter of time before Facundo had the gun.

"Not really an art to being a murderer."

The American had a mouth on him. Facundo inched closer.

"I think you closed your eyes to shoot that Judge, you got the best of Paulo because he felt sorry for you. The only thing I care about is cutting open your head because I need to take a piss." Facundo said, licking his lips as they drew back in a snarl. He pressed the barrel of the gun to his throat. "So, why don't you pull the trigger?"

The American stared him in the eyes, the gun shaking slightly. Facundo grabbed his hands and pushed the barrel tighter, deeper under his jaw. "C'mon, I'll make it easy for you."

"I'm not a killer," the American said, trying to pull back the gun.

"No shit," Facundo said, pulling back and leaning against the seat.

"I did what Eulojo asked," the American said, now pleading, realizing that he wasn't going to threaten Facundo, "I just want my family safe."

"Forget them. They don't belong to you anymore." Facundo said.

"I won't leave them."

"Eulojo isn't going to let you have them," Facundo said, pausing to look out the driver side window, "even if I get you there, you'd be dead before you get out of the truck."

"I've gotten this far." The American gave a half smile and was starting to get bold. Facundo knew it was time to crush his spirit.

Facundo pulled the keys from the ignition and tossed them under the dashboard by the American's feet. He pushed against the driver door and it cranked open.

"Get back and drive!" The American yelled after him, climbing out over the driver's seat, "What are you doing?"

Facundo could hear the American splash down from the truck.

"Get him out into the open," Facundo thought. Blood and brains were a pain to clean from upholstery. It was Paulo's truck but they'd make him clean up the mess. He rubbed the handle of the knife in his pocket and stifled a smile. Facundo hoped the American would get scared and start running. If he was going to be late, he could at least have some fun with a hunt.

Facundo's pocket started to vibrate and he glanced at the glow of the screen. It was an 858 area code he didn't recognize but figured it was the judge's kid confirming the judge was dead. He tried to slide it open but the rain pooled on the screen causing his finger to slip. He started to walk to the overhang of the tire shop.

"Stop!" the American yelled.

Facundo put the phone to his ear before he heard the pop and felt the pain in his spine. He fell forward, hitting his face on the body shop stoop. The momentum rolled him over and he stared up at the American holding the gun over him. His eyes were crazed, almost bulging from their sockets. His chest heaved and he let a wail that broke over the rain. "Why couldn't you just drive me?"

Facundo knew something was wrong with his legs. They were folded backward and he wasn't feeling what should have been horrible pain. He spit out a tooth, allowing a spray of blood to fall back onto his face. "You shot me in the back? Fucking coward."

The American pressed the barrel against Facundo's forehead. "Two shots to the head to make it count, right?"

Chapter Fifty

Facundo's eyes tilted up at the sky with the same hardened stare they had in life. Anger had not left Facundo even when he faced death and Charlie put a bullet in his forehead.

Charlie leaned against the building, gun lying against his thigh, letting the rain soak him.

Charlie had never lost control before but he was pushed so far beyond his mind that he killed two men without thinking. He could justify that they were the lowest of maggots. They were killers who didn't discriminate if their orders are to kill a child or the competition. They got pleasure at doing their duty. It didn't matter who he killed when all the thoughts came back that he was no better than Sam. They now shared something in common aside from the same blood and last name. They both killed when desperation had lost control over their lives.

Lena and the children would be dead soon, Eulojo's men were all around, Charlie would be killed and even La Jolla was within Eulojo's reach.

Charlie tapped the gun on his leg. His hands no longer shook but were calm. The first time since Kier dropped him down onto the beach. Charlie raised the gun to his left temple while he thought about pulling the trigger.

A large thumb pulled open Charlie's eye lid, forcing him to look up at a boy no older than twenty. His face was fresh, almost baby faced with rounded cheeks and eyes fanned by thick lashes. He was scanning the area, peeking over at the body shop and then frowned at Charlie.

"Give me the gun," the boy said, his hand reaching down and prying it out of Charlie's fingers. "You hurt anywhere?"

It took a minute for Charlie to understand the question. Time didn't seem like it had passed but the surroundings were changed. The rain had stopped and there was a small truck moving away behind Paulo's truck. "It's cold."

The boy prodded Facundo with his foot. "Is Paulo dead too?"

Charlie nodded over to the watery pit.

The boy surveyed the pit and came back after a few minutes. "It's deep enough we can fit them both in there. Help me drag him."

The boy grabbed Facundo's leg and started to pull him toward the pit leaving a watery trail of muddy blood. After a few feet he dropped the leg and stood over Charlie. He nudged Charlie's arm with his foot. "Come on. We need to get rid of them before we go back."

Charlie started to overcome the numb and feel a familiar fear. Eulojo had sent someone to bring him back. He felt himself be pulled to his feet.

"Go back." Charlie repeated.

"Yeah, grab his arm."

Charlie bent down and pulled at Facundo's hand. It slipped from his grip and flopped to the ground. The boy looked back in irritation. "Get control of yourself. She said we only got another hour."

"She?"

"Lena."

Charlie felt a loud bell ringing in his ear and his heart started to beat faster. "Are she... the kids.."

"They're safe for now," the boy said focused on pushing Facundo's body forward.

Charlie reached down and they moved the body closer to the pit. "You're here for Lena."

"Yes."

"Bullshit." Charlie said pulling back, almost stumbling on his heels, "you work for Eulojo."

"If I was with Eulojo, your head would be fed to his dogs right now," the boy paused to roll Facundo into the water, the body made an unceremonious splash, his arm striking up a wave, "Damn, I thought he'd fit."

"Why are you helping her?" Charlie asked.

"That's between me and her." The boy said, wading into the pit and pushing Facundo's arm forward but it continued to bob on the water.

Charlie tried to think what Lena would have done. "Did you have sex with her? Is that why you're helping me?"

The boy scrunched his nose, "she said you'd be a pain in the ass and to give you a message."

"What did she say?"

"Let's get this done, first," the boy grumbled, "if we can't hide him we have to pull him out and put them behind the shop. When the patrols run, they can't see a hand sticking out."

Charlie's heart was beating faster. "No, tell me now."

The boy sighed and waded further into the pit.

"Tell me, god damn it!"

"Don't rush me," the boy yelled, "she said I had to say this right and we've got a lot to do before the first patrol comes by."

The boy closed his eyes and tapped his fingers on his leg. "My feet are unlocked from the land. Let me follow you in the river."

Charlie smiled.

"You okay now?" the boy snapped, "can you help me now?"

Charlie jumped into the pit and stuck his hand into the water looking for a better grip on Facundo's collar.

"When we're done maybe you can tell me what the hell that means," the boy muttered.

Once Facundo's body was no longer visible, the boy reached into Paulo's truck and pulled out a soft red hat. He threw it at Charlie. "Put on Facundo's truck and get into the truck, Charlie."

Hearing Charlie's name surprised him. "What's your name?"

"Rolando, now get in the damn truck so we can get you floating down the river in a raft or whatever you want to go."

The truck rolled in silence. In the darkness, Charlie would never have found his way through the fields. Rolando made quick turns and rounded corners with ease. He occasionally stole glances at Charlie.

"Keep your head down so they can get a look at your hat, they'll think Facundo fell asleep."

"I don't know what to say," Charlie said starting to say but Rolando raised a hand to stop him.

"Don't start with that," Rolando said, "This probably won't work and you'll get everybody cut up."

The thought of getting everyone out was overwhelming to Charlie. What was he going to do? Walk in with guns blazing like a damn cowboy?

"I told her this was risky but it might work. When we get through the gate, I'm supposed to bring the kids and Lena into the truck," Rolando said, grinding the gears, "You get out and walk them out instead. Get in the car and I'll drive you to Tecate. You can cross over from there."

"How will I know where to find them?" Charlie asked.

"Keep your head down, we're hitting the first gate," Rolando said, pulling down on Charlie's arm, "make sure they see the hat."

The gate looked like a basic wire gate but as they got closer, Charlie could see from under the hat there were three men sitting in a truck with the lights off. Rolando nodded at them and hissed from the corner of his mouth, "Move your hand from the window."

The glint of Judge's ring on Charlie's right finger was gleaming off the light. Charlie quickly moved it away. He'd forgotten that his hand was bracing him. They moved past the gate and back into the darkness as they started up a steep incline. Charlie relaxed a little but Rolando's hand tightly twisted on the steering wheel. A familiar set of buildings came into view on the left and then the farm house that Charlie had seen was now directly in view.

"Keep your head down. They'll be in the front room so bring them out and get back in the truck."

Charlie stared at the front door. It looked quiet but he had no idea to know what waited on the other side. "Wouldn't it be better if you get them?"

"I need to stay here to make sure no one decides to use the truck," Rolando said, looking through the rear view mirror, "If the truck is gone or if Eulojo changes his mind then they might pull me to do something else. So be real quick."

Charlie absently checked his pants for his wallet. Rolando stared at him. "Lose something?"

"No, I'm sorry," Charlie said, feeling foolish as he reached for the door, "I don't know what the hell I'm doing. I'm looking for money to give you like some damn valet. I feel like I should give you something," Charlie said quickly, "but all I can say is thank you."

Rolando looked insulted and waved his hand to push Charlie out the door, "you ain't home yet."

Chapter Fifty One
La Jolla- Charlie's House

Nola opened the door but shut it quickly so it stayed dark. Jesse had closed the shutters and was lying between the corner of the bed and wall. Unless you looked, you wouldn't have seen the gap was a little wider than normal. From down on the floor, Jesse had a limited view of Nola's pictures on a white dresser. Since she had left, Jesse had found her softest pink blanket that was embroidered by tiny roses. She slid carefully on the bed and looked down at him. His eyes opened at the creaking of the springs and smiled up at her. He reached up and gently touched her face.

"There's my pretty butterfly princess," Jesse whispered.

Nola felt a charge run through her body. Jesse looked at her the way Charlie looked at Lisa. He didn't seem irritated or want to run. The warmth of his hand on her face caused her heart to beat happily. She hated to move away but she wanted to show him the gifts she had brought him. She pulled out the food and lowered an apple onto his chest.

Jesse shifted weight so he could sit up and let the apple roll into his hand. He winked as he gently polished the apple up her arm; carefully brushed the fruit across her breast causing her to pull back.

Jesse moved toward the wall and took a bite out of the apple. Nola was afraid she had made him angry. She reached down and touched his hand. Gently she picked it up and Nola swallowed nervously as she placed his hand under her shirt. The warmth of his flesh felt wonderful on her stomach. He patiently allowed her to move his hand where she wanted, eventually resting his hand on her bra and then let his hand go. He kept his hand there for a long time.

Jesse traced the embroidery on the strap and then Jesse lifted himself up so that they're faces were almost touching. She felt her breath grow quicker as he tilted her head and pressed his lips against hers. They felt so warm and firm. The first kiss lasted only for a few seconds before Jesse moved away and smiled. Nola began to feel a need grow inside. She wanted to feel that charge again. Nola moved toward him again and this time she kissed him back, firm and insistent. Jesse responded back and wrapped his arms tightly around her. He raised himself up and moved next to her on the bed. She slid her arms around him and pressed against him. His hand slid down her stomach and rested on the top of her jeans. Jesse began to tug on the top button.

Nola gasped as the button slid open and the zipper easily slid down. Jesse looked at her and smiled with amusement. "What's wrong Nola?"

"Nothing, I just-" Nola felt the heat burn on her cheeks and began to pull away.

Jesse chuckled. "Is my butterfly a virgin?"

Nola shook her head and pulled away. "No, I just don't want to right now."

Jesse pulled her arm around her and drew her thigh over his leg. "Someone so beautiful must have been with so many guys."

Nola pulled herself and slid off the bed. 'I should check on Orrie."

Jesse quickly grabbed Nola's arm and pulled her toward the bed. "Nola, don't leave. I'm sorry. I didn't mean to scare you."

Nola tensed her shoulders. "You didn't scare me. I'm just supposed to be watching her."

Jesse gently nipped her chin. "You didn't tell anyone that I'm here, right?"

Nola looked at his eyes, they were so gentle. "No one."

"If my father finds me here, he will take me away from here," Jesse said tracing his fingers on her leg, "that might get you in trouble."

Nola knew he was right. She thought about Mama's face if she knew that there was a boy in her room. Mama rarely hit her unless she was really upset but this would get her smacked for sure. Nola leaned back to Jesse's face hoping for another kiss like the first one but he pulled back down to the floor.

"Did you bring me the phone?"

Nola shook her head.

"Nola, if we're going to be together," Jesse said, gritting his teeth, "I need the phone, my love."

Nola's heart soared. "I know where I can get one."

"Then go," Jesse said moving her off the bed. Nola reluctantly moved away and reached for the door. She turned to look at him but he already closed his eyes closed and curled back under the blanket.

"I love you too," she whispered and carefully closed the door.

Chapter Fifty Two
Mexico- Eulojo's Compound

Charlie opened the front door expecting to find a henchmen waiting but was surprised to see Lena and Giselle sat at a round kitchen table. Giselle lay with her head on table, eyes closed. He had walked into a kitchen that could be from anywhere. A simple lamp hung down from the ceiling over the table, leaving a soft glow to the dark blue cloth. On the wall next to the stove stood shelves neatly stacked with boxes and jars of spice. To each side was a darkened hallway. The trim over each painted with twisted green vines and yellow flowers. It gave him a comforting illusion of safety when he knew they were in serious danger.

Lena's eyes had been closed until she heard the scuff of his shoe on the floor. She gazed up, her eyes starting to water.

"He found you," Lena whispered, her voice causing Giselle to stir.

Lena stood up as if she was going to embrace him but hesitated as she looked down at Giselle. Lena lowered her arms and put them around the girl. "The things I said to you... if that had been the last thing you remembered of me."

"It doesn't matter," Charlie said brushing away a tear that fell on her cheek and kissed its trail.

Lena smiled and grabbed his hand. "Max is sleeping in the next room."

"Lena moved into the dark hallway. Charlie could see Max lying on a small cot, his eyes squeezed tightly as he clutched a green blanket.

"Lena what is this place?" Charlie started but Lena quickly kissed his mouth and placed Max into his arms.

"Eulojo will be back soon," Lena whispered, "If we leave now, he will think Rolando has taken us out of here."

Charlie looked down at his son who didn't stir when Charlie shifted him in his arms. He only leaned his weight onto Charlie's chest. He started to feel hope that this could be done. He balanced himself, keeping Max on one arm and the knife down to his side.

"The truck is parked on the left side," Charlie opened the door but stopped when he saw Lena's face. She was frozen, her eyes staring past Charlie, clutching Giselle to her like a statue.

Charlie could smell the overpowering cologne fill the room. It made the hairs on his neck stand up like a hot breath blowing behind him. A reflection on a side mirror in the hall showed surprise on Eulojo's face as he stood next to the table. Charlie could tell it was not a look that Eulojo carried very often. He was always the one in power, giving the commands that made people live or die depending on his moods. It filled Charlie with an adrenaline that turned him on like a generator. Hate so powerful to replace the fear and all he could hear were Lena's words in the first moments that they met. 'Don't stop until you've killed him."

Charlie turned his shoulder and plunged the knife at Eulojo, embedding him deep in his eye.

The next few moments were a blur for Charlie. He remembered the knife catching in Eulojo's skull but he was able to pry it free and lodge it into the flesh on his right shoulder and chest. Eulojo screamed out as he braced against another attack. Charlie would have struck him again if Max's voice hadn't centered him back to reality.

"Daddy!"

Charlie sprang back at Max's cry. He gained his balance, pushing off with his foot in Eulojo's stomach as he made his way to the door. He didn't bother to look back when Eulojo began to scream like a raging giant awakening the farm. He pushed Lena and Giselle and stumbled out the door, along the path trying to adjust their eyes to the darkness.

Charlie could barely see the outline of the truck, the driver door hung open, the driver seat vacant.

Where the hell was Rolando?

Reaching the door, Charlie could see the keys were not in the ignition. He reached on the floor to see if Rolando had hidden them. He felt the barrel of a gun and quickly put it inside his jacket.

From the farm house, shadows were forming in the windows and footsteps crunching on the gravel just to their left.

Charlie pressed them to the driver's side. Their legs flush against the rear tire. The footsteps grew louder, passing on the right side of the truck. Two thin boys holding knives passed on the right side of the truck and hurried toward the farmhouse.

"Get inside," Charlie whispered, he helped Giselle up so she could scramble up, immediately heading for the back seat. Lena moved past him and slipped inside. She reached for Max and nestled him in her arms as her eyes darted to the passenger window."

"More are coming," Lena whispered.

Charlie's head scraped on the floorboard, "We don't have the keys."

Flash lights were starting to dance on the ground and voices shouting between the buildings. The gravel crunched next to the driver's side door and sprang open. Charlie pulled the gun from his jacket and started to squeeze the trigger in the shadowed face.

"Rolando!" Lena cried out, grabbing Charlie's arm.

Rolando pushed Charlie over and cranked the engine. "Keep down. I'm supposed to go down the hill and meet up with a crew to find you. We've got to get ahead of the other trucks and got one chance to do this."

The rain had started again. Rolando struggled to keep the truck from swerving in the mud. He moved the truck into position and directly downhill toward another gate. Charlie put on Facundo's hat and sat with his head tilted away. He was able to see the gate was full of men, each agitated and nervously pacing. Rolando nodded at three henchmen standing at the gate with a pack of dogs, hungry and barking to be unleashed.

"There are others that will follow, but I can get a lead. Down this hill, the road curves to the right, with the rain, it gets muddy so it will make sense for me to slow down," Rolando said, motioning to the right, "When I hit the curve, jump out into the arroyo. It's full of water so stick to the side and wait under the bridge. When you see three trucks pass over, head the other direction. In five miles, there's a group of houses. Do you remember where Senora Mendoza lives?"

Lena nodded and grasped tightly to Max as the truck hit a hard bump and pushed her against the window.

"I'll head south but we'll be circling back in a few hours," Rolando turned sharply, narrowly missing a boulder that had rolled into the roadway, "Stay there until the sun comes up and I'll send someone to get you inside Tecate."

"Come with us. I'll do what I can to get you across." Charlie offered.

Rolando jerked the wheel and ignored the offer, "Get ready, the corner is coming up."

The truck tilted and Lena grabbed the handle, clutching Giselle when she recoiled.

"It's going to be okay," Lena yelled, her hands grasping Giselle's head to keep her from looking at the roadway

Giselle dropped her eyes and went limp into Lena's arms. Lena looked up at Rolando. "Be careful."

Rolando avoided her gaze and looked into the rear view mirror. "I'm going to slow at a red post and you jump."

"You aren't stopping?" Charlie shouted, realizing the danger they were in. Pushing out of a speeding car around the corner in the pure black and driving rain was a blind jump off a cliff.

"If I stop, they'll see the brake lights. They might think I saw something," Rolando said, nudging Charlie's arm, "Grab the boy because it's going to be fast."

Charlie clutched Max in his arms, positioning him with his head cradled against his chest then changing his grip. What if he landed on him? Broke his neck? What if he didn't hold him tight enough? He looked toward Lena, she was moving her arms the same way over Giselle, her eyes locked on Charlie, lips trembling, repeating the same words over and over with no voice. "God protect us, God protect us."

The red post came into view and Rolando struggled to keep the truck steady as it skid on the gravel. The door swung open, wind pushing rain into the cab. Charlie grasped Lena in his sight for a second more and she disappeared into the night, like a vortex sucking her away.

"Now!" Rolando's voice was the last words he heard before he felt the rush of air and felt a sharp pain against his back. Max pinched his neck as he clung to him.

Charlie heard himself yelling out. "God protect us. God protect us."

"Charlie!"

Hearing his name snapped Charlie back. Max was lying face down, his head resting on Charlie's leg. Charlie reached down to touch his hair. He felt the pain shoot up his arm almost paralyzing his neck. He only grasped a lock of Max's hair and gently pulled. Max struggled to pull away and Charlie released in relief.

"Charlie!"

Lena was calling him but it felt like she was down a long hall. He was able to turn his head and he could see her and Giselle clinging to the side of the hill. When he turned, he could see her relief.

"Are you and Max okay?" Lena called.

"How long have we been here?"

"I don't know. I saw the trucks pass. We need to get out of here before they start looking on foot."

Charlie could see they had landed in a ravine, water streaming through like a tiny rapids just under the roadway. If it had been daylight, they would have been visible but the rain and night protected them. Slowly Charlie sat up, his body aching with every push. Max moved as he shifted and sat up, rubbing his eyes as if he'd woken from a nap. He looked at Charlie, his lip quivering.

"We're not going to make it home are we, Daddy?" Max's voice broke and his little chest began to heave.

Charlie moved so he could see Max's face. "Look at me Max. We're going home. I promise you that."

Max nodded and wiped his eyes again. "Did you kill Eulojo?"

The question made Charlie's heart ache. "He was a bad man and was hurting everyone."

"I'm glad you killed him," Max said, standing up, turning his back as he headed toward Lena and Giselle.

Charlie realized he would bring his son back home but his innocence was never leaving Mexico.

Chapter Fifty Three
La Jolla- Charlie's House

"Where the hell is it?"

Remi opened one eye cautiously and then quickly shut it. A shaft of sunlight aimed directly at his face beamed through the east window. He grabbed a pillow and buried his face to escape. His head split open and tongue was a cactus pricking the sides of his mouth. He forced his eyes to re-open. "I just had a horrible nightmare."

"Finally you're awake." Lisa called from her dressing table. She was furiously digging into her purse, and then threw it on the surface, knocking over a row of nail polish bottles. Gone was the silky seductive red replaced by the conforming cotton of her chef's coat, buttoned partially up but still exposing the thin strap of a teal bra.

"What time is it?" Remi groaned, rubbing his face.

"It's morning."

"I need to talk to you," Remi said, sitting up carefully and balancing him on the side. He eyed a bottle of water on the side table and picked it up, "but first I'm finishing this off."

Lisa stood up and disappeared into her closet. She surfaced with a pair of white athletic shoes and a large gray purse. She dropped the shoes on the floor and absently slipped inside them. "I don't have time right now."

"Where do you think you're going?"

"I need to confirm the menu for the Garamendi party tonight."

Remi sat up and then immediately lowered himself back onto the bed. "Can't Dylan work on that? You really shouldn't-"

"-Dylan doesn't know what he's doing" Lisa interrupted, reaching into a pocket on a jacket draped on the chair, "A sous chef isn't using my reputation to practice."

"Lisa," Remi said, "working isn't the best thing right now."

"I don't think you're in a place to tell me what's the best thing," Lisa growled, "I woke up with you lying next to me stinking of scotch."

Remi forced himself to stand up, his stomach still swishing right to the bottom of his feet. "One too many kiddie cups."

"Is that why you drooled all over my arm?" Lisa asked.

"I had a nightmare some guy came into the bedroom and watched us sleep. It looked real." Remi said, trying to still shake the image, "we need to talk about Charlie and Max."

Lisa raised her head, nodded and picked up the first purse again, "There's nothing to talk about."

"Lisa..."

"Please don't ask me to sit here and wait for news." Lisa whispered, "I can't just sit here."

Remi wanted to tell her it was going to be okay and take the pained look from her face. Instead he picked up a purse from the floor and carefully laid it on the bed. "What are you looking for?"

"I need to confirm an order of salmon and I can't find my cell phone."

Chapter Fifty Four
La Jolla- Charlie's House

Jesse had just finished leaving a message when she walked into the room holding a banana and a glass of orange juice like she was serving him breakfast in bed. He moved the phone underneath his shirt and let the harden crystal case press against the small of his back. He rolled over on it putting his hands on her hips as he pulled her toward him. Nola gave a soft sigh and rested her chin on his chest, her eyes wide and curious.

It wasn't a hard decision to take Nola with him. There was a lot of money for a virgin of legal age. She had a body under those kindergarten kiddie clothes, put her in a lace thong and a baby doll. Jesse fought to not damage the merchandise and gave her a smirk so wicked that Nola's cheeks burned with a blush. To think what control he had over her virginity gave him a rush of power that made him hard. Jesse could take it all away from her right now and she wouldn't even know how to stop him. Too bad she was going to be a present for Eulojo.

Nola could be that distraction to take Eulojo's mind off the fact that his dad was still alive. Jesse just wanted a chance to explain it wasn't his fault.

Eulojo was the one that sent someone as weak as Charlie. If he had been asked, Jesse could have told Eulojo how Charlie let Jesse get his head slammed for five minutes before he broke it up because his bouncers didn't block for him. Jesse had to give credit to Eulojo that if Charlie had killed Dad it would have been a genius move. A rich, white guy wouldn't have ties to a cartel and they wouldn't suspect that this had anything to do with the legalization of marijuana. He wasn't going to get a chance to explain anything if Facundo didn't pick up his phone and get the message that his dad was still alive.

Nola was useless to find a phone but it wasn't that hard. All he had to do was slip out when the house was quiet. He walked straight into the upstairs bedroom and watched Charlie's woman sleeping. Too bad she wasn't a virgin too. You could tell she had wrapped those lips around a lot of guys. She'd still be worth something, someone would want to hurt her. He saw it in the eyes of that drunken attorney who made a bee-line for her bed and snuggled up after puking all over the floor. He only stirred once to look at Jesse standing above him and then rolled over to sleep.

Nola had moved close to him and was starting to settle when that old lady started screaming for her. Nola's eyes turned toward the door and she almost flipped off the bed in a panic. She got off the floor and put a finger to her lips as if Jesse was going to suddenly start shouting. She opened the door and peeked her head into the hallway.

"Nola!"

The old lady yelled again and made her jump every time. Jesse watched like a comedy routine as Nola hit her elbow on the doorknob, rubbing the joint as she moved out the door except she didn't close all the way. Jesse rolled off the bed so he wasn't in clear view but not before the door was pushed open and Jesse could see a small pair of eyes staring at him. A little girl around eight had moved inside the room.

340

Jesse froze in place and tried to figure out his next move. What was she going to do? Would she start screaming and call for help? She hadn't run yet. Maybe the same tricks that got Nola to bring him inside would work. What the hell, why not try? Jesse gave her a smile and waved.

"Hello," Jesse whispered, "do you remember me?"

The little girl didn't look happy but she didn't look frightened either. "You're not supposed to be in here."

"Nola said its okay," Jesse said slowly moved up so he was sitting level with her. He was far enough that she wouldn't scatter easily but close enough he could shove her down by the neck if she tried to get away.

The girl looked as if she had caught him in a lie. "Nola doesn't get to say anything is okay."

"She can't have friends in her room?" Jesse said, giving her a big smile.

"Nola doesn't have friends."

"I'm different," Jesse said, lowering his voice when he thought he saw a shadow in the hall, " I'm Nola's boyfriend."

Jesse could see that he wasn't winning any favors with her. This one wasn't smarter but she had a street sense. She actually listened to all those "don't talk to stranger" videos in school. She had put one leg behind the door and it would be more difficult to grab her without calling attention.

"I'll bet you have a lot of boyfriends," Jesse said, "you're very pretty. Like a butterfly princess."

Jesse watched her ears perk up at the word *butterfly*. He'd played enough poker to know she had just given herself away. "Does the pretty butterfly princess have a name?"

"Oriana." Her voice was starting to soften.

Jesse looked up in surprise for her benefit. "You're not Oriana Thibodeaux are you?"

Again, Oriana perked up on her name. Jesse had grown up with his sister and her friends. He knew enough to know they liked when attention was paid directly to them. "I'm good friends with your Dad you know what that means, don't you?"

"What?" Oriana asked now moving her whole body inside the room and relaxing her grip on the door. She was already in his control the second she asked him.

Jesse smiled and relaxed on the wall. She wasn't going to run. "Well if I'm friends with your Dad that makes us best friends too."

Chapter Fifty Five
Mexico

Three times, Lena stopped them because the
rain beating on the path sounded like feet pounding
on the ground behind them. The wind howled around
them, as if surrounded by hundreds of angry voices.
Clothing sagged with the weight of water. Shielding
from the rain was no longer possible and Charlie and
Lena were resigned to trudge with their feet sucking
back to the earth with vacuums of mud.

Charlie didn't remember when they moved
from the ravine to the cluster of houses clinging to the
hillside. The unformed earth gradually came together
to form a hollowed road winding between homes.
Lena guided him between narrow alleys and into a
walkway that appeared to be a dead end. Seven
houses piled unevenly on top of each other. She lifted
a splintered plank in a fence and they squeezed
through one by one. It led into a small flooded yard
with a strip of flowers next to a small folding table
and a metal chair.

Lena pulled a key from her pocket and moved
them inside. The living room was square and sparse
with a couch and little table. In the corner was a stack
of cabinets and beyond was a tiny door to a closet
with a bed frame squeezed to fit the space. The air
inside the room wasn't much warmer but immediately

the children stopped shivering and dropped onto the floor and huddled together. Charlie and Lena struggled to separate them out of their clothes, heavy and soggy. Eventually, giving up, Lena stripped the bed of the blankets and pillow and placed them over them. Soon they were asleep.

Lena unzipped her dress, lowering the cloth over her hips and put it on the table. "Remove your clothing."

Charlie looked down at the dripping shirt.

"Come on, they need to dry," Lena said, now standing in a thin, white camisole. It clung to her like a second skin and he averted his eyes to a cluster of pictures on a cabinet. He was startled when she began to pull at his pants, "now is not the time to be shy."

Charlie's pants slipped easily to the floor as she quickly moved her fingers to the buttons on his shirt and moved the sleeves around the shoulders. The wet material gathered at his arms. The more she struggled, it bound them together until the weight pinned him. Charlie burst out laughing. "Shouldn't we choose a safe word first?"

"I'm sorry." Lena moved quickly backward but caught her feet in his pants.

"Now who is being shy?" Charlie whispered, his right arm loosened far enough to grab around her waist. Constricted with the left he held her thigh so she wouldn't fall, Lena let out a soft sigh.

Charlie's left thumb moved up her thigh to keep a better grip and was now sliding the camisole above her hips. The camisole's strap slid down her arm and she pressed herself against him to keep it from slipping off. It pushed up her breasts and Charlie no longer averted his gaze. His right fingers circled the strap and pulled it further down her arm until the material was gathered in his hand at her waist.

Lena's breath grew heavy as Charlie guided her gently to the floor. His left hand moved between her legs, his lips now touching the base of her breast. She opened her mouth and moaned as Charlie moved up her throat to her lips and kissed her. She moved her fingernails down his back and pulled at Charlie's shirt so that nothing separated their skin.

"Look at me," Charlie said, softly nudging her face with his cheek.

Lena opened her eyes and Charlie braced his hands to hover above her.

"I want this to happen," Charlie started, "But if you-"

Lena pulled on Charlie; her weight forced him to lay on her.

"Don't move away," she whispered.

Lena and Charlie lay down on the couch and covered themselves with the last remaining thread of a blanket.

"Watch the window," Lena pointed to a small sliver concealed by a thin, orange cloth, "keep looking for any shadows. They won't come here but they might check the house above."

"Where are we?" Charlie whispered.

"Senora Mendoza was a friend. She would watch Rolando from time to time."

"Is she dead?" Charlie asked.

Lena smiled. "She's visiting her grandchildren in California."

Charlie started to laugh but groaned as a sharp pain hit the side of his chest. "Lucky woman."

Lena moved her hand to his side, the heat of her hand eased the pain. He moved her hair from her neck and nestled his lips at the base.

Charlie hesitated. His body would force him to sleep soon but his mind wanted to know answers. "Lena-"

"We need to sleep," Lena whispered, "We'll be moving in a few hours."

"Too many questions," Charlie said, stroking her hair from her face, "I don't understand that farmhouse. I thought I'd find you and the kids tied up or in cages but you weren't. And that kid, Rolando, why did he risk his life?"

Lena was quiet for so long that he thought she had gone to sleep. Her head turned and he could see her eyes staring at the window. "I know there are many things to explain. When things are quiet, I can give you more answers...but for now, we need to rest."

He moved his hand to her hip. She put her hand on his wrist but didn't move him away. His fingers traced a rose tattoo that's stem curved her hip. "Why do you have one petal colored and the rest are empty petals?"

"When Giselle was born, I filled the first one," Lena said, squeezing his wrist. "Antonio and I imagined a big family and I planned to fill each one."

"There are four empty ones here!" Charlie exclaimed.

"I imagined if we had more I would grow the rose." Rose murmured, she nestled into the crook of his arm.

"More petals?" Charlie asked.

"Didn't you and Mariana plan a family?"

"Yeah," Charlie yawned, fighting to keep his eyes open, "but she never wanted more than one."

"And you?"

"I wanted a bigger family," Charlie said, reminded of the very night Mariana told him he was in the wrong century if he wanted her to have more than one, "but I was thinking more like three."

Lena's hip shook with laughter," That must have locked you out of your bedroom for a few nights."

"No, I agreed to only one," Charlie said.

"But you have two?"

Charlie smiled as he leaned back so he could see his son's face. "Max was a bottle of tequila after the party when Mariana passed the bar."

"We need to sleep." Lena fought off her own yawn, "we don't know what time Rolando's help will be here."

Charlie had so much more he wanted to ask. "Just a few more questions."

"One more." Lena said, turning to lean her face into his chest, her eyes already closed.

"How do you know Rolando?" Charlie asked.

"Rolando is my nephew."

"Nephew?" Charlie's questions now filled him with so many other questions but Lena had already fallen asleep.

Chapter Fifty Six
La Jolla- Charlie's House

Remi followed after Lisa down the stairs, his
eyes burning into the back of his head from the
sunlight. Regret wasn't strong enough word to define
his hangover. The queasiness in his stomach churned
when he saw Brenda waiting for them at the landing.
The damp bathrobe and the disheveled bird's nest
built up by her hair meant only one thing. When Remi
had left the balcony, she had never gone inside and
slept in the rain.

"Couldn't wait until Charlie's in the ground?"
Brenda fumed, "And in his bedroom?"

Lisa ignored Brenda and was pulling her keys
from the purse when she froze. She looked over
Brenda to Remi. "Is she telling the truth? Is Charlie
dead?"

Remi managed to leave the stairs and lean
against the wall hoping to keep his head from
spinning. "We don't know anything yet."

Lisa's shoulders relaxed and she started to
absorb Brenda's accusation and shoved a finger in her
face. "No matter what you say, I'm marrying Charlie.
Get over it."

"No way he'd have married you." Brenda
snapped slapping away Lisa's hand.

Remi rubbed his temples and debated whether he should get in the middle. It might be less painful on his head if they tore him to shreds but he didn't get a chance to decide. Lisa had pulled back and was looking behind her toward the stairs.

"What was that?" Lisa asked.

"What a backward way to change the subject." Brenda grumbled, "Do you think I'm stupid?"

"No, she's right," Remi said, holding his hand up, "I hear something downstairs."

"Of course you do," Brenda said pointing the stairs, "the girls are down there."

"Shut up, Brenda, it's a man's voice." Lisa said, moving toward the stairwell, "maybe Charlie came home."

"Charlie's dead," Brenda's voice was filled with gravel as she grabbed Lisa's arm. "And the next time you talk to me like that, I'll stomp some respect in to you."

Lisa raised her hand to strike Brenda but Remi put his hand up to block the blow, their anger was put on hold when they heard a creak coming from the stairs below. Peered through the slats, they could see a head come up toward the landing.

"It's just the damn maid," Brenda growled, "told you we shouldn't have a stranger just walk into this house."

Remi looked over the railing at the first landing to see a petite woman he recognized as Victoria Casillas, the owner of the cleaning service. He'd forgotten he called her to help with cleaning Brenda's room. Remi motioned to her to stop. "Stay there, and I'll show you the bedroom."

Remi took three steps down but stopped when he saw she wasn't alone. Someone was holding a gun to her back.

A large, expressionless man dressed in a dark suit stepped onto the landing with Victoria.

"Are you Remi Parrish?"

"What the hell are you doing in this house?" Remi yelled. He motioned behind his back for Lisa and Brenda to move to the kitchen,

The man ignored Remi's question and moved his eyes to Victoria's purse. He pulled a leather wallet and produced a driver's license from the folds. "Do you know this woman?"

The cocking of a gun answered his question.

"She's the maid," Brenda said, positioning the barrel of a magnum through the railing, "she's supposed to be here but you ain't. Pull the god damn gun away from her back or she's going to be cleaning up your brains first."

The man looked up in surprise but did not seem concerned. He lowered the gun and handed Victoria back her wallet. Her hands shook as she grasped the wallet and tripped heading up the stairs. Remi's arm braced her and he pulled her quickly behind him. She immediately reached for Lisa who pulled her into the kitchen.

The man gave a curt smile and nodded in apology. "We saw her trying to enter through the garage and had to be sure she wasn't involved."

"You better start giving your name and some answers," Remi said, praying that Nola and Orrie didn't exit their rooms. He looked back at Brenda who still had a gun aimed at the man's head, "she'd really love to shoot someone right now."

The man looked behind him and then stepped back toward the wall to allow an older gentleman join him. His eyes were weary and his clothing was disheveled. Remi knew him instantly as a man that was supposed to be dead.

"Remi Parrish," the gentleman said giving a slight nod and then looked up at Brenda.

"Ms. Thibodeaux, my name is Judge Andersen."

"I don't care if you're Judge Judy," Brenda snarled, "Who said you could come into my house?"

"I am here with a message from your son."

Judge Andersen turned from hostile intruder to the most important man in the room.

Brenda wanted to check on Nola and Oriana but Judge insisted they stay in their rooms until they heard what he had to say. The living room soon filled with ten men in dark suits all led by the larger one that the Judge called Marcus. Lisa and Victoria looked on from the kitchen, but didn't join the crowded living room.

Remi motioned for Judge to sit down on an overstuffed chair and got Brenda to join him on the couch across the way. Marcus silently went into the kitchen and came back with three sterile glasses of water that he strategically put on the coffee table between them like setting up pieces of a chess board. The living room settled into a strained and surreal calm.

"You're all over the news," Remi said breaking the silence, "it was the only time the news had broken from the coverage of Mexico. You look real good for a dead man."

Judge sighed heavily and stretched his hands across his thighs, "There is no real easy place to start."

"Start with the message from my son." Brenda said, glaring at her gun lying on the table that Remi forced her to surrender. He had given no reason to trust this man sitting in her living room.

Judge Andersen took a sip of water. "Last night, Charlie was at my home with the intention of killing me."

351

Remi and Lisa stared at each other in disbelief.

"Charlie couldn't kill anybody," Lisa said, prying her arm from Victoria's grip and moved gracefully to the couch, allowing the men in the room to catch a glance of her.

Brenda rolled her eyes more from the fact she agreed with her than her model runway entrance. "Bullshit."

Andersen shook his head. "I know it sounds unbelievable. I had never met Charlie Thibodeaux until last night but he has a reputation as an honorable man. While in Mexico, he was taken with your grandson by a leader in a cartel. If he came here and murdered me, they would all be released."

Brenda snorted. "You're so powerful that someone needs my Daddy Long Legs of a son to kill you?"

"This isn't a joke, Brenda." Remi said unable to control his irritation.

"I think it's funny as hell," Brenda's voice broke, "I have heard that Charlie is dead. Now I hear that he's an assassin on hire? I know my son. He's not capable of getting his hands dirty."

"Brenda-" Remi started but Brenda cut him off.

"It's easier to believe he's dead," Brenda shouted.

"Desperation can make you do things beyond your capability," Judge said, the only one not affected by Brenda's anger, "a man will do anything to save his wife and kids."

Remi's head turned sharply. "What did you say?"

"I said that desperation-"

"No," Remi interrupted, "about the wife and kids? Did Mariana make it out?"

"I don't know about her," Judge Andersen said, "there is a woman and her daughter traveling with

352

Charlie. He's trying to get them across posing as his family."

Lisa's lips twisted. "Who is this woman?"

I didn't have a lot of time to discuss the details," Andersen said, "I know that their lives depend on the news reporting that I am dead until we can get them home."

"And you come over here?" Remi said, "That was too dangerous. What if you'd been seen?"

Andersen shifted uncomfortably. "Someone catching sight of me is not as big a concern as my son knowing the truth and alerting the cartel."

Remi was in disbelief. "Your son would cause the death of innocent people?"

"My son is only thinking about saving his own skin right now. He's gotten himself in over his head," Andersen said, picking up the glass and stared at the water, "and may already be Mexico."

"How do we know he isn't lurking around to get revenge on Charlie?" Brenda said, eyeing her gun left on the table.

"We don't," Andersen said, causing Brenda to look up in alarm, "until last night, I could never believe my son was capable of harming anyone. Our sons continue to keep us guessing about the men we raised."

Chapter Fifty Seven
Mexico

Rolando is my nephew.

The words rang in Charlie's mind through all the night. As soon as he opened his eyes he prepared to ask her again but he heard the sound of broken glass cracked in the backyard. Rolling off the couch, Lena had already reached the children and moved them into the closet with her finger at her mouth. Charlie noticed the shadow in the window and moved to the far end of the couch.

The door knob jiggled and from the backyard, the heavy splash of boots stopped. Without pause, the door cracked open and armed with a gun directly at his head, a soldier with his face covered in black entered the room. Two more entered like cloaked bandits and crowded the small room.

Lena stood slowly from her position, hands raised. The taller of the soldiers motioned his gun toward the door. She pointed to her clothes next to the table and the soldier nodded. Charlie stood up and suddenly felt all the guns train on his middle.

"I'm just standing up, I'm not attacking."

A smaller soldier gave a muffled laugh and lowered his gun. Soon another was stifling his laughter.

"Why don't you put these on," Lena said, throwing Charlie's underwear in his direction.

Charlie slipped them quickly on and felt a thud as his pants hit him in the chest. At that moment, the entire crew began to laugh. Charlie smiled weakly. "I didn't think this was going to get worse."

The clothes were still damp and caked with mud but there was no choice but to use them. The sun was already up and the soldiers loaded them into the back of a van with ten other people.

"We can slip into the crowds, they will drop us off at the border." Lena whispered as Charlie eyed three men jamming up against the door.

"And you feel safe like this?"

"Rolando did well."

"What's with all the ski masks?"

"This is a government raid. Looking for anyone connected with the assassination. They can't risk showing their faces. If anyone retaliates, they won't just kill them but their whole family."

"Jesus," Charlie muttered, his stomach growling kept his mind distracted. He glanced over at Max who was holding his stomach as well. When the van started moving, Lena moved a bulky cloth by her feet and unwrapped three hardened pastries and a ripe mango.

"It's all I found in the house. I'm sure Senora Mendoza won't mind."

Lena rubbed the juice from the mango onto the pastry and handed one to Max and Giselle. The cake had hardened like a cracker, slightly softened by the juices. They didn't notice as they gnawed hungrily at them. Lena handed Charlie the last one and brushed her hands.

Charlie broke the pastry, crumbling into two halves. He put out a piece in front of her. Her brow frowned.

"If you don't eat then I'll throw it all away," Charlie warned, tipping his share toward the floor. Lena smiled and grabbed her share.

"Thank you."

"I'm glad you took it," Charlie said, clipping off a piece, "I was starving, how long until we get there?"

Lena took a bite and thought about their distance. "We should be ten minutes away. They'll release us by the entry into their compound and we'll move into the customs office. Then it's your turn."

Charlie felt a slight panic until he felt the outline of the passes in his pocket.

"How are we going to explain that we're covered in mud?" Lena wondered out loud, looking down at her blouse.

"I think it's actually a good thing," Charlie said, "easier to explain that we were caught across the border and had to walk our way back in the rain. It will cover up anyone looking at the pictures for details."

Lena nodded, now she nervous. He grasped her hands. "Pretend you are irritated at the inconvenience this has caused you. You know act... American."

Lena smiled and picked up Max who snuggled into her arms.

"So last night you said that Rolando was your nephew."

Lena's expression froze. She looked down at Max and began to pick caked mud from his shoe. "Yes."

"How can you let your nephew work for that monster?"

Lena sighed. "He is a man and must make his own choices."

She smiled as the van came to a stop and the engine turned off. "Just a little longer and this will be over."

"We're close, just let me do the talking and we'll be eating at a MacDonald's in Disneyland,"

Charlie said, pushing the kids toward the doors as they opened, "it's just a little longer now."

Charlie stepped down from the van. He felt a spark of hope when he saw they were facing the US border crossing, its entrance heavily fenced but he could see a familiar US flag on a tank in the distance; a trickle of people were moving through a short corridor. He adjusted his eyes to the border station in Tecate and he felt his mouth fall open. The door to the station was wide open with a crowd five deep spilling out and rounding across the block. The line was so congested with refugees, the end was not visible from where they stood.

Chapter Fifty Eight
La Jolla- Charlie's House

Nola saw her door open and worried that Jesse had left without saying goodbye. As soon as she saw Oriana standing near the foot of the bed, Nola's worries turned to fear that Oriana would tell Mama and that meant trouble. Nola felt tears bubbling up. She wanted to speak but she stood there with her mouth gaping.

Jesse looked up and smiled at Nola. He pointed to Oriana. "Another little butterfly fluttered into your room."

Nola's lips trembled as Jesse took Oriana's hand and pulled her to sit on the bed next to him. She felt an anger building toward Orrie and possessiveness to Jesse. "You said I was your butterfly!"

"There are many butterflies, Nola," Jesse said, patting Oriana's leg, "we're just waiting here for my friends to pick me up."

The look of concern on Nola's face alerted Oriana that something was wrong. She started to shift away from Jesse but he put his arms around the girl and brought her close to him.

"You said you were hiding from your father," Nola said, swallowing hard as she reached for Oriana's hand. Jesse grabbed her arm and pulled him on top of him. He pushed her face toward him and kissed Nola hard on her mouth. His lips stiffened as he bared his teeth, "I thought you weren't as stupid as everyone said you were."

Jesse gave her a hard shove and Nola stumbled onto the floor.

Orrie cried out, trying to move toward Nola but Jesse gripped her waist and kept her firmly on the bed next to him. In the struggle, Orrie scratched his face and Jesse struck her with a hard slap. "Little bitch."

Oriana pushed herself into the corner of the bed sobbing. Jesse took a deep breath.

"We're all going to stay in this room and you're going to be good butterfly princesses," Jesse said patting Orrie's leg, she pulled it away as if struck by electricity. He looked down at Nola crying on the floor and rolled his eyes as she hid her face, "now shut up so I can make a phone call."

Any number Jesse dialed when straight to voice mail confirming the cell phone receptors were jammed or down with the trouble in Mexico. He gave up and threw the phone on the ground. He'd need to find his way down to a house down in City Heights that was serving as a contact point. With Nola and Oriana with him, traveling was going to be a pain in the ass but he could play them off each other. It was much better to show up with two flowers in his hand.

Jesse tugged at the hem of Oriana's dress causing her to shiver and she tried to push further into the wall. He eyed Nola sitting defeated on the floor. He'd need her to get the keys to the Mercedes parked in the garage. "Nola, my love, are you sorry for making me angry?"

Nola looked up at him and sniffled. She nodded and looked up with wet eyes. Jesse wanted to laugh at how easy this was.

"Good, there's a way you can make it up to me."

Chapter Fifty Nine
Mexico- Tecate Border Crossing

The sun was now midway in the sky and Charlie felt like a fried egg on the sidewalk. They had moved a block in over three hours and stood exposed in the middle of the street. Lena and Charlie stood in front of the children, pressing them to the stucco to give the appearance it was only the two of them. Eulojo's men were still out there searching for them. Until Charlie could get them inside, anyone could spot them, raise a gun to their heads and they would have nowhere to run.

Lena had left them in line and was slipping through the crowd to get information. She had only been gone twenty minutes and Charlie felt the sweat drip down his temple. Max and Giselle sat with their backs to the wall and moved to keep in Charlie's shade. He tried to keep as still as possible but the sun was already making him feel exposed like an ant under a magnifying glass. He tried to keep himself sharp so he could spot any of Eulojo's henchmen. It was difficult to know where what direction they would come from. He was still standing out but felt some relief that he could blend a little easier. The line was filled with a mix of people. He was able to fade into the background. Closest to him was a family with kids running under their feet causing three weary business men in wrinkled suits to brace against the wall so they didn't trip over them. A girl wearing a red Aztec shirt leaned against a slightly older boy whose eyes were red and puffed. She occasionally whispered into his ear and he would answer; his voice shaky. A tall woman in a white dress with large magenta flowers folded her arms huffing every minute that the line grew longer with no movement.

"Here."

Lena pressed a cold bottle of Coca-Cola in Charlie's hand. He admired the curves of the glass like a fine bottle of wine.

"Where did you get these?"

"There is a Mercado opened around the corner. There are quite a few places on the main street that are open for business. Tecate has not had violence like Tijuana," Lena said, giving each of the children, "The owner said this crossing has long lines but it has been peaceful."

Max's eyes lit up as he quickly drank the bottle back. Giselle gently took the bottle from him and tipped it upright.

Lena let out a soft sigh. She looked back at Charlie with tears in her eyes as she handed a soda to Charlie. He stared at the bottle and smiled.

"I'm glad you enjoy sharing with me." Charlie said as he offered her the first sip.

Lena winked and pulled another bottle from her side. "I bought my own this time."

The sidewalks were congested with people that spilled out onto the road so it had been closed off from traffic but a truck rounded the corner letting out a large squeal as it pushed through the people. Charlie pressed himself against Lena and pushed everyone toward the wall. The truck slowed beside them.

"Keep looking forward," Charlie whispered. Out of the corner of his eye he saw one man leaning toward the windshield. The second was talking rapidly into a cell phone.

"This road is closed."

A round soldier cut Charlie's view as he approached the passenger's window. He kept his hands on his side arm.

"We've got a delivery for Carvajal." The passenger said pointing to the customs building.

The passenger's defiance did not impress the soldier and he pounded on the hood. "Back up and move to the west side."

The truck pulled into reverse so fast that three people almost fell underneath the back tires. The truck met with a huge roar from the crowds and pounding on their windows but that only caused them to increase their speed and leave the street. Lena pressed herself against Charlie's arm. "They know we're here. We've got to get inside. Now.

Charlie wasn't listening because he had heard the passenger say one name that could save them. He needed to act quick before it was too late. The round soldier started to turn up the street until Charlie caught his attention.

"I have a meeting with General Carvajal."

The soldier approached them and frowned at their mud-caked faces. "You?"

Charlie stood upright. "My family and I have been through hell to get here. Tell the General that Charlie Thibodeaux expects to be inside immediately."

The soldier scoffed and spit onto the road. "I don't think so."

Charlie turned to Lena. "Do you still have my watch?"

Lena lifted her shirt to show a bump in her pocket.

"Give it to me."

The diamonds on the band caught in the sunlight and the soldier's eyes widened. He quickly grabbed the watch and put it in his pocket. "You crazy? That's not real."

"It belongs to General Carvajal," Charlie said with as much irritation as he could attempt with the crowds now focusing on him, "I know he'd be very upset to lose it. Tell him I'm here so he can thank me."

The soldier shook his head as he moved toward the entrance and then disappeared around the corner.

"You just lost your watch, Pendejo." A woman muttered in front of Charlie.

Lena looked at Charlie with a gleam in your eye. She leaned in and kissed him hard on the mouth. "My impatient American hero."

"Let's hope this works," Charlie whispered in her ear, his eyes catching sight of the white truck slowly moving down a cross street.

Chapter Sixty
La Jolla- Charlie's House

Andersen finished his call and rubbed his temple with the corner of his phone. He had an audience sitting around the living room waiting for news and he had nothing good to give them.

"There's a man shot to death in a car in Otay Mesa matching the description of the one that took Charlie over the border," Judge said, picking up a picture of Charlie holding Max as a newborn, "someone needs to go view the body before it's taken to the morgue."

Andersen's words were drowned out by Brenda pulling out an empty cigarette carton and crumpling the wrapper. He picked up the picture of Charlie and Max and clattered it on the table in front of Brenda.

"This man," Andersen said tapping the glass in the photo frame, "was in my house. He was risking his life for his family. In my heart I don't think he's gone. But if I am wrong, I will not let him lay there without a name. You will go down and identify him."

"I'm not going anywhere," Brenda hissed, "I don't need to see what I already know."

"I'll go," Remi said.

Andersen pointed a finger at Brenda. "No, *she* goes. I need you to help cover the border crossings. Those documents are worthless and we don't know where Charlie is going to cross. He's going to need someone to vouch for him on this side."

"I'm not looking at a bullet filled body to tell you he's my son. " Brenda snapped.

"I need you to confirm he's not your son." Judge said.

"I won't do that," Brenda said, her voice gravelly, "I know it's Jackson's body."

"You mean Charlie."

"What?" Brenda looked up startled at Remi.

"You said you know its Jackson's body," Remi said.

Brenda threw the empty carton in Remi's face. "His name don't matter. Nothing changes the fact that I have two dead sons."

Judge tried to grab Brenda's arm but she pushed past him and disappeared into the kitchen. He gripped the couch and looked toward Lisa.

Remi slapped him on the shoulder and muttered under his breath. "Don't even bother."

Marcus nodded. "Marcus will send someone down to confirm."

Lisa realized she was being dismissed before she'd been considered. "I can't see Charlie that way."

"No one asked you anything," Remi's voice sounded angrier than he had wanted. He took a deep breath and grabbed the remote control. Weary, fearful faces of refugees flashed on the screen with a streaming ticker tape ran underneath them with the latest updates about the clashes in Mexico, all the attention now focused away from Lisa.

"Why am I the bitch in all of this?" Lisa's voice was being drowned out by Marcus rushing in with another phone for Judge. The noise in the room grew louder, the bustle becoming the hurricane in the room.

Lisa stood in front of Remi, blocking his vision of the TV. "Remi, I would fall apart."

"Lisa," Remi said, turning his back to pick up a tablet, "it's not about your right now."

"I know it's not about me," Lisa whispered and moved behind Marcus and into the kitchen.

Lisa hesitated as she entered. She looked back at the crowd of men that were all talking on phones, scanning the TV and arguing among themselves. Inside the kitchen she was alone with Brenda and Victoria. Victoria was sitting at the kitchen table, staring out at the balcony, obviously stunned at how she got involved. Brenda sat apart on a bar stools at the kitchen counter staring down at her empty coffee mug.

"What the hell am I doing?," Lisa muttered picking up the coffee carafe and held it in front of Brenda.

Without looking up, Brenda slid the mug in front of her.

Lisa stacked three sugar cubes in the center and carefully poured the coffee onto the side and then moved it back under Brenda's fingers.

She pulled a bottle of water from the fridge and sat next to Victoria. All the women sat in silence watching the circus of chaos growing in the living room.

Brenda took a loud sip and then put the mug slowly down. "You know how I like my coffee."

Lisa shrugged. "I've seen Nola make it a dozen times. We should get Nola."

"Keep the girls in their rooms," Brenda said, eyeing Marcus' pulling out two guns and putting them on the counter, "this'll just scare them."

Victoria fidgeted in her chair. "Am I being held prisoner?"

"I'll sneak you through the garage," Brenda said between slurps of coffee, "but I need you to get me into first."

Chapter Sixty One
Mexico- Tecate Border Station

The air inside the office was worse than waiting outside but they were out of sight and inside an office behind a dozen of soldiers.

Charlie had pried the passes from his pocket, muddied and curled around the edges, and they now sat on a desk with a sweaty agent staring at the crumbled papers.

The soldier picked them up with two fingers and studied the official seals and expired dates. He looked up at Charlie and Lena several times and then threw the papers on the desk and went search for help.

Max leaned his head on Lena's shoulder. She stroked his bangs from his sweaty face. "I'm hot, Mama."

Charlie and Lena exchanged glances. It wasn't the time to correct him but was he old enough to know this wasn't real? Charlie feared that Max was already forgetting his mother. When they were safe in California, he'd get the best therapist. Oriana will need to go see one too. The thought of telling her, going through the heart break would be tearing at a fresh wound.

Returning to La Jolla was leaving one hell for another. Charlie had forced himself to push it back in his mind but answers would be expected. What happened to Kier and Mariana's family? Did he cause their deaths?

Charlie moved his arm around Lena. Their arms sealed together in the heat but Charlie didn't move. Time was short and he wanted to keep her close.

"When we get out of here," Charlie whispered in her ear, "I'm going to get you both into a hotel and we'll figure this out."

Lena's eyes looked down at his hands and grasped them, "we don't need you to do that."

"*We* includes more than just you and Giselle." Charlie said, forgetting his tone, "You didn't think we'd cross and leave everything with a handshake, did you?"

Lena grasped his hand, her eyes conveying a sadness that Charlie recognized as a look that preceded every bad memory in his life, "What do you think "we" and "everything" means?"

Charlie swallowed hard. "Us... everything is us."

"You are engaged," Lena said.

"Don't tell me you're married," Charlie interrupted, "that doesn't change how we feel about each other. I know I'm not the only one."

Lena's eyes filled with water. She moved her arm from Charlie and caught the tears with the back of her hand. "I am thankful that God brought you to me, but-"

"Lena," Charlie started to say but Lena kissed him and placed her head on his neck.

"I care for you, "Lena whispered, "but that doesn't change that I am married."

Charlie noticed soldiers starting to step aside and the General's burly frame came into view toward the office.

"This isn't over," Charlie whispered back, "Let's just get past this and promise me that you'll hear what I have to say."

"I promise."

What do you promise, Mrs. Thibodeaux?"

General Carvajal's frame blocked the light from the doorway.

"My wife has been through hell the last four days," Charlie said, moving his shoulder to protect Lena's face, "If you have any questions, direct them to me."

Carvajal hesitated and then squeezed into what space was left in the room. He sat on the desk causing it to groan. He coughed and stared at the children sitting in the corner. He gave them a thin smile before picking up the papers. "I was glad to see you were safe. We didn't know anyone survived. What happened to Senor's family was a tragedy."

"No help from your government," Charlie said, trying to keep on the verge of irritated and anger, "we had to find our own way back when you promised us safe passage."

Carvajal's expression remained unchanged. "We had no way to know you had survived. It appeared from the carnage that all were dead."

Max began to whimper and grabbed onto Giselle's hand.

"We don't want to discuss any of that," Charlie said, quickly looking over to Max, His heart started to pound, "we're going home right now."

"Yes, I am sorry that was insensitive of me," Carvajal said, shuffling the papers and observing their condition.

Charlie's heart started to pound. "They're the same papers we showed you. Let's just get this over with."

"Things are not the same," Carvajal said, his eyes looking up from the papers and directly at Giselle, "you were coming back with one child and now you have two."

Chapter Sixty Two
La Jolla- Charlie's House

Opening the door to her bedroom, Brenda let a plume of dust and debris float into the hallway causing Victoria to step back but Brenda plunged inside and made a bee-line for her closet. She kicked the bottom of an overturned nightstand to hedge the closet door a few inches wide enough to step inside. A flurry of boxes flew at onto the floor unsettling the dust.

Victoria looked impatiently at her watch. Remi had asked her to find a crew that worked on toxic clean-up and she'd offered to come down to evaluate the damage. Some of her staff had worked on hazardous materials in the past and she could get the job done. Instead of doing her job, she was in the middle of a hell storm.

The old lady convinced Mr. Parrish to let her take Victoria down to assess the damage in her room and he consented as long as Victoria kept an eye on her. Everyone had demands they were putting on her. She didn't want to be there and especially didn't like the mean, old lady that kept one glaring eye on her employees like they were going to clean her toilet and then clean out her jewelry box. "What are you looking for?"

Brenda ignored her and after a few more minutes, emerged from the closet holding an overstretched, men's sock bulging with an object like a digesting cotton snake. She let the sock's mouth dangle and it expelled three bullets onto the floor.

"You're going to get us all killed," Victoria muttered, backing away from the door and checking how far the stairway was if she needed to make a quick run for all the security upstairs, "Didn't Mr. Parrish take your gun?"

"One of them," Brenda responded, producing a .38 Special from the stretched fabric, "you can never have too many friends to back you up at a party."

Victoria silently watched Brenda load the gun, cutting herself on a small shard of glass. Brenda sucked on her finger and threw the shard on the floor with all the other debris.

"It looks like you had a bar fight instead of a party. "Victoria said thinking Brenda would get angry with the remark but instead she caught her holding back a faint smile, "Why the hell did you do this to your room?"

Brenda disappeared back into the closet. "Just push your broom back onto your side of the border and mind your own business."

The old lady was always spewing racist crap and normally Victoria ignored her sewer for a mouth because Charlie Thibodeaux was a loyal customer and Nola was so sweet. Today, however, she was in no mood to take anymore. "You got a problem with me being a maid or being Mexican?"

Brenda reappeared out of the closet wearing a zippered red hoodie and a pair of jeans. Victoria had never seen her out of the bathrobe and she looked almost formal. Brenda might as well have come out wearing a ball gown and tiara. "I got a problem with you Mexicans coming over and taking jobs from Americans."

"Lady, I am American," Victoria shot back, "the only borders I crossed were the ones when I moved from Michigan fifteen years ago. I don't even speak Spanish."

"I've heard you speak with your girls," Brenda said, eyeing her suspiciously, "and you aren't talking English."

"Some of the staff don't speak any English so I know enough to explain what needs to be done," Veronica said, "why the hell am I explaining this to you? To you, I'm just a maid."

Brenda looked up from the gun. "I've cleaned my share of toilets. I don't have a problem with maids."

Victoria almost detected a soft belly under a rough shell. "Wow... a white maid. I thought those were imaginary like unicorns. I'm surprised no one's shot and mounted you on their wall."

"I like you," Brenda said, a raspy chuckle came from her smoker lungs, "we could have been friends."

Brenda shoved the gun into her left pocket and Victoria made a mental note to call Mr. Parrish when she got clear so he could disarm her. She appreciated that Brenda has pulled a gun against the Judge's security but she knew it wasn't really about saving her life as it was protecting her home. The old lady reminded Victoria of her Aunt Francis who always had a cigarette in one hand and a look as if she'd smelled something rotten. There was bitterness in their words but it was just to keep people at a distance. A kind word was never appreciated and was quickly swatted down with an insult. The old lady and Aunt Francis only responded to resistance and bitterness because it's the only thing they could trust as sincere. "You and I could never be friends."

The old lady started up the stairs but stopped Victoria when she tried to follow. She pointed down the hall to the garage door at the end of the hall. "Go back the way you came. I'll say you snuck out when my back was turned."

Victoria started down the hall but then paused. "This still doesn't mean we're friends."

"Not very smart, are you?" The old lady motioned for Victoria to keep going but shook her head, "If you were then you'd know you always stay friendly with the one holding the gun."

Chapter Sixty Three
Mexico- Tecate Border Station

Charlie's mouth went dry. He knew the longer he didn't say anything about Giselle the harder it would be to explain. "You didn't hear us. As you can see there are papers there for two children. My two children."

"There was no misunderstanding," Carvajal interrupted and threw the papers on the desk, "That beast you hired, who I am not sorry to say was killed, said you'd pick up your son and wife and be right back before I could order a burrito."

"Damn Kier," Charlie thought, "I'm always apologizing for you."

Charlie leaned forward, allowing his anger to direct him, "I don't care what you think you heard. You can see my daughter is sitting right there."

Carvajal picked up the papers, "Oriana... Oriana Thibodeaux."

"I've only got one daughter!"

The General snapped his fingers at Giselle. "I am calling you, Oriana."

Giselle's face turned away from the General. He folded up the papers and threw them in the trash can.

"That is not your daughter," General said, pointing at Giselle and then at Lena, "And I personally saw Mariana Thibodeaux's body pulled from a pile of corpses. This show is all very entertaining... for you. If this was a few days ago then you would have passed through this line with your little family. But these passes are expired. They are useless. I don't have to do anything for you anymore. And that is very entertaining...for me. You will need to find another way into your United States."

"We're American citizens, you can't do this!" Charlie roared, standing up but the General pushed him back down and moved directly into his face.

"No, you and the boy are American," Carvajal growled. The woman and girl are Mexican citizens."

Carvajal leaned onto the wall and folded his hands.

"Direct your concerns to the US Embassy. There is a possibility that they may return in a few years after our little *disturbance* is settled. That's what your president called the killing and destruction of my people, a *disturbance*. If you don't want to wait the three to five years for them to return, you can try to cross the border on your own. I should warn you, there are bandits robbing and killing anyone that tries to reach the other side. They are easy targets with all they own strapped to their bodies. If you do get past, all US soldiers have been given orders to shoot without question, anyone trying to cross over.

Perhaps you can walk further inland, maybe Arizona. I hear that there are vigilante death squads that are covering any gaps in your little wall. I'm sure they won't shoot your Mexican wife in the head before you explain that you are all Americans."

"You son of a bitch," Charlie yelled, "men out there are trying to kill us! If you release us, we won't survive an hour."

"That is no longer my problem."

"You would let children die?"

Carvajal's face was already sweaty and red but now it turned crimson. "Fifty children are dying every fifteen minutes in my country! Are you going to do anything for them?"

"Yes," Charlie shouted causing Max to flinch, "I would do whatever it takes. No one should lose their child."

The room grew silent except for Carvajal's heavy breath. "You only say that when your own children are about to die. But I am not a monster. You can wait here until it gets dark and we'll release you out a back entrance. I will not do anything else to help you."

Carvajal turned to leave when Lena touched his back. She began to speak in a low, rapid Spanish that Charlie couldn't keep up with. Carvajal didn't seem too concerned until Charlie heard the name "Eulojo" in the quick spurts of Spanish. The General turned around, his expression going from indifference to fear and then anger.

Carvajal raised a gun and pointed it directly at Lena's face. "You are going to die today."

"No!"

The room was startled by Giselle's scream. Giselle ran toward Lena and put her arms around her. It gave Charlie enough time to pull the knife from his pocket and press it on Carvajal's scrotum. The offices outside began to buzz with alarm at the strange positions in the tiny room.

Charlie put pressure on the blade causing Carvajal to grimace. "Put the gun down. We're going to walk out this office and you're going to get us home. If you don't let us through, I'm taking a piece of you as a souvenir."

Lena began to speak again in Spanish so fast that Charlie was lost at the conversation between them.

Carvajal listened reluctantly, his face still puffing with anger, but with every word, his chest started to heave quickly and then he now looked afraid. Carvajal lowered the gun and glared at Charlie. Slowly Charlie moved the knife away.

Carvajal put out his palm. "Give me the knife."

"I'll give it to you," Charlie said, moving the knife back at Carvajal.

Carvajal grabbed the knife out of Charlie's hand and threw it on the floor. "You can't have any weapons when they check you at the crossing. Now let's go before I change my mind."

Chapter Sixty Four
La Jolla- Charlie's House

It didn't take Brenda long for her to recognize that old feeling that something was wrong. It started with Nola moving from shadow to shadow. She didn't look interested in the crowds of security moving around the impromptu headquarters set up in the living room; normally large groups of people made her curious. Brenda watched Nola keep her eyes in front, slinking behind busy men unobserved and move up to Charlie's room. The only reason she'd go up there was to find Lisa but it was obvious Lisa was sitting in the living room begging someone to pay attention to her. Nola had returned and looked straight at Lisa before she quickly slinked back downstairs clutching something in her hand. Brenda might have let it go but when the time turned closer to lunch, Nola never returned. No one was interested in lunch but Nola hadn't come back up to ask.

Brenda expected the girls were squabbling and Nola was pouting in her room but she wasn't prepared for what she saw when she stepped off the landing. Oriana's door was wide open which was not like Baby

Girl who always kept her door securely closed in defense of her own space.

There had been many strangers running around the house in the past few hours, but Brenda observed the man standing in the hallway was not like the career men upstairs. He was younger and not dressed in the pressed suits of the Judge's men. What had they called him? Jesse. The scraggily goon had a sunbaked hand holding on Oriana's neck and he was pushing her toward the garage.

"Like hell that's going to happen," Brenda thought, not feeling any fear. Fear is a luxury when you justify being someone's victim. She allowed herself a moment to congratulate herself that she was smart enough to get the second gun and let her heart heat with the anger that kept it beating. A lot of good those pressed suits did when Jesse was already inside and heading out the door with her Baby Girl. She kicked the wall to get his attention. "Step back real slow."

Jesse turned around and picked up Orrie protectively covering his chest and nuzzling her cheek like a doll. "She smells like berries."

Brenda remained unmoved. She carefully kept her aim, steady and direct as she stepped further into the hallway.

"Maw Maw," Oriana began to sob and reached her arm for Brenda.

"You're going to be just fine, Baby Girl," Brenda said hardly moving any muscles in her mouth.

Jesse dropped Oriana to the ground and put his hands around the sides of her head. "All I have to do is twist and her neck is going to snap. Put the gun down and slide it over to me."

"Why am I going to do that?" Brenda snapped, "So you can turn it on us?"

A whimper came from the side and Brenda noticed Nola standing timidly at her bedroom door. Jesse followed Brenda's gaze and winked at Nola. "I don't want to hurt anyone Ma'am. In fact, I'm in love with your daughter."

Nola's eyes widened and her fingers trembled as she tried to raise her hand toward Brenda. "He means it Mama. He's not going to hurt anyone."

Brenda's stony face stared at Jesse. "Keep down Nola."

"Mama, don't!" Nola whimpered.

"Keep down girl!" Brenda's voice snapped like a bear trap, "Don't have enough sense to know when you're being fooled!"

"That's not true, Nola," Jesse said, shifting his weight so he could look toward Nola. His soft-honey voice was easier to listen to the vinegar coming out of Brenda's lips. "You know I have to do this so we can be together."

Nola looked at Jesse's eyes, so soft and encouraging. She hedged from the door and dropped to her knees in front of Brenda, "Mama, this is a mistake, Jesse needs our help."

"Jesse needs help alright," Brenda said, she nudged Nola so she shifted to the wall.

"Mama, listen to me!" Nola said grabbing at Brenda's leg, "His Daddy wants to kill him!"

"I know the feeling," Brenda muttered causing Jesse to clutch Orrie harder.

Tears were falling freely down Nola's face, "You can't let them hurt him, Mama!"

Brenda took a deep breath. "He won't get hurt if he slips his grip from Baby Girl."

Jesse kissed Oriana's head. "You're just fine, aren't you my Butterfly?"

"I don't want you to hold me," Orrie cried, she tried to wiggle out of his arms but Jesse only closed tighter around her chest. "That's up to your grandma."

"You hide behind little girls and promise to make love to slow ones?" Brenda snorted, "You're a coward."

Jesse grew agitated as Brenda took two steps closer. He twisted Orrie's chin until she cried out again. "Crazy bitch, stop moving!"

Nola stood up, jolted by Orrie's cry, her mind was swimming in confusion, and the changes in Jesse were so hard to understand. "Jesse, please don't hurt her."

"You want the little girl then let me slip out the garage," Jesse said to Brenda, ignoring Nola's pleas, "I'll leave and everyone gets to stay alive today."

The front door slammed and Remi's voice was heard calling for Brenda upstairs. She gave a tight grin. "You aren't going anywhere."

Jesse increased his grip on Oriana's head. "I'll snap her neck."

"Why are you acting like this? Please let her go," Nola sobbed.

"That bitch is forcing me to hurt her!" Jesse shouted, "Do you think I want to do this?"

By now, there were feet coming quickly down the stairs. Nola could see three men with guns drawn slipping toward them.

"Just let him go!" Nola clung on Brenda's arm and pulled down on the gun.

"Stupid girl," Brenda's feet stumbled and she tilted off balance, the gun now aimed at the floor giving Jesse a chance to grab Oriana by the waist. The little girl lurched toward Brenda but Jesse picked her up and moved toward the garage door.

"Maw Maw!" Oriana choked.

Brenda anchored herself against the bedroom door and steadied the gun again. "Last time I'm telling you to let her go."

Jesse struggled to hold onto Oriana as he pulled on the garage handle, cursing as Oriana bit down hard on the soft flesh of his arm and he lost part of his grip. Oriana let her body go limp and slid down his leg.

"Drop on the ground, Baby Girl!" Brenda shouted as she took her aim and squeezed the trigger.

The next few seconds passed in years to Nola. Pulling herself upright she heard a sound so loud she was forced to cover her ears. She watched Jesse's body stand upright, his arms dropping in surprise like a marionette being summoned by his strings. Orrie crumpled to the floor, her hands covering her face. Jesse suspended in air and then in a twisted pirouette, he descended to the floor, his head smashing against the wall, bending his neck back toward the ceiling. He folded on top of Oriana.

Nola scrambled toward him, Brenda pulling at her leg to come back but Nola kicked her away, reaching Jesse and grasping onto his arm. It twitched and slapped against her thigh as she gently reached down to touch Jesse's face, eyes staring upward at her, surprised and frozen upon her. She searched for help from Brenda but she was miles down the hall.

Oriana's face appeared from under Jesse's arm. She pulled up onto Nola and then ran passed her, only turning to stare back once she reached the safety of Brenda's arm. In the distance, three of the judge's men gathered behind Brenda. Soon they were joined by Remi and Lisa; all with their eyes fixed on Nola, a scream like a wild and primitive animal was coming from her throat, she was lost in the grief of betrayal.

Chapter Sixty Five
Mexico- Tecate Border Station

Several soldiers were waiting outside the door but the General pushed them away. "Move those kids along. Hurry, I want this done."

Carvajal moved ahead into a line of refugees. Charlie picked up Max so they wouldn't lose sight of him. Lena moved behind them, Giselle's arms glued to her middle.

"What did you tell him?" Charlie whispered, a feeling of relief washing over him as he could see a gate ahead with five soldiers watching as three men disappeared into the opening of the concrete tunnel he had seen outside the building.

"I told him I knew he worked with Eulojo. I told him if we get released into Tecate I would make sure everyone knew," Lena said, "he was furious until I told him that if Eulojo found me first, I would tell him that Carvajal had been holding out with bribe money you gave him to get down here."

"I didn't bribe Carvajal," Charlie said.

Lena shrugged. "Eulojo doesn't know that. He'll torture Carvajal for holding back."

"Remind me to never get on your bad side," Charlie said, his arm circling around Lena. She moved away, looking at him nervously, "We're almost there."

Charlie looked ahead, Carvajal was talking to a soldier monitoring the gate and pointing in their direction. They were getting close enough Charlie could start to pick out words of their Spanish... Release... contact... woman...

A breeze cut through the stale air and Charlie began to smile. He felt like he was breathing air that had traveled from the US to greet them. Carvajal moved his arm in an exaggerated gesture like an usher sending late patrons in after the concert had .started. Charlie moved Max forward, excitement growing as the stepped onto the concrete. He moved Giselle past him and reached for Lena but she still stood by Carvajal.

Charlie tried to reach for her and was stopped by a soldier's gun pointed at Max. "Let her through."

Lena tried to speak but her lips trembled. She heaved a huge sigh and pushed Giselle toward Charlie. "Promise me that you'll take care of my sweet girl."

"Move that gun from my son's head," Charlie shouting, putting his body between them, "what have you done, Lena?"

"Carvajal agreed to let you all go if he can turn me over to Eulojo."

"Why would you do that?" Charlie shouted, "he'll kill you."

Giselle moved past Charlie and tried to re-enter the door but Carvajal shoved her with his arm causing her to stumble. Charlie's arm grabbed her before she fell to the ground. Lena began to push on Carvajal.

"Let me explain to my daughter," Lena said, her arm reaching around him, "I need to tell her goodbye."

Lena's cries were muffled as Carvajal pushed her back inside and trained a gun on Charlie's chest.

"Turn around and start walking."
Carvajal barked.

Charlie could still see Lena standing behind Carvajal, a soldier holding her by the arms. "I'm not leaving without her."

Carvajal put his finger on the trigger. Lena screamed out, "Don't kill him! He'll go! Please Charlie!"

A shot echoed through the concrete barrier. A cluster of refugees instinctively dropped onto the ground and covered their heads. Charlie fell back, staring at Carvajal who still had the gun trained on his chest. Charlie didn't have time to look for the shooter when another shot cracked the sky and Carvajal slumped forward grasping at his throat as blood ran rivers over his hand. The soldiers, stunned, tried to take cover but barely turned when a blast of fire exploded through the offices. Screams and more shots erupted from behind them as the refugees struggled to find safety.

"Eulojo's men are here," Lena shouted. The soldiers pushed past Lena and ran toward the front of the building. She jumped over Carvajal's body twitching and grabbed Giselle's hand.

Charlie picked up Max and began to run inside the corridor toward the US. The chaos behind them was growing louder, explosions bounced off the walls and a rapid exchange of bullets. He didn't look back, keeping his eyes on Lena in front of him. A metal gate on the other side was getting closer. A line of soldier positioned their guns warily watching the growing storm in front of them. The entry was still closed.

"We're Americans!" Charlie puffed, Max slipping down from his waist. He grabbed Max's arm and pulled him forward.

Charlie heard another shot. This one was closer. "Faster!"

Lena cried out and fell to the ground clutching her leg. Charlie reached her as she screamed out again. She fell onto her side, blood splattered onto Charlie's arm. He grasped her waist and pulled her toward him. She cried out and pulled away from him.

"They're coming," Lena gasped, "take the children out of here."

"We're so close," Charlie pleaded, trying again to move his arm around her but she fought his arm, "we can make it."

Lena shook her head as she glanced back through the corridor. Shouting and the pounding of boots grew closer. She pulled Giselle toward her. "Giselle, go with Charlie."

Giselle dropped to the ground and grabbed onto Lena. She buried her head in Lena's chest causing her to gasp in pain.

"Charlie," Lena cried again, trying to pull Giselle's hand from her and put it in Charlie's arm, "If you love me, you'll do as I ask. Bring Giselle to Antonio."

Charlie reached down and grabbed Giselle by the waist, pulling her away from Lena. She struggled but couldn't break his grasp.

"I'm not giving up," Charlie said, struggling with Giselle, "I'm coming back."

Charlie turned toward the gate and pulled the children forward.

"No, no, no," Giselle cried, biting hard on his arm.

The gate swung open and Charlie pushed Giselle and through. A soldier took hold of them and pulled them through a hall. Charlie turned around and headed back for Lena. A soldier tried to grab his arm.

"Sir, we cannot intercede. You need to pass the gate."

"I'm not leaving her."

Charlie turned back around to see three of Eulojo's men pulling Lena back. Her head slumped over, body sagging. One of the henchmen looked up, a sneer on his face as he pulled out a cigarette and sucked back the smoke.

"Eulojo has a message for you" the henchman's voice echoed on the concrete corridor, "there is no place you can hide. He's going to kill anyone you love."

Charlie's heart exploded in his chest with rage and he started toward the henchmen who lifted a gun in his direction.

"Sir, step back into the gate." A voice came from behind Charlie that stopped him in its familiarity. He turned to see Marcus standing on the other side of the gate. "Your children have lost their mother. Don't let them lose you."

"I've got her."

Charlie turned back to see Rolando holding Lena. He nodded quickly to Charlie before moving her swiftly out of sight. There was just a small bit of hope that she would be protected.

"I will find you, Lena!" Charlie yelled, his voice broke as it echoed through the tunnel. Marcus pulled him backward and he stepped into the gate. He stood frozen staring at the pool of Lena's blood.

"I won't leave you locked here," Charlie whispered before they forced him to turn away.

Chapter Sixty Six
Durango, Colorado
One Year Later

"No snow on a damn palm tree," Charlie muttered as peeked out the back door toward the gazebo.

"No one is looking for you in Colorado," Remi said, putting a cooler on the kitchen table, "I don't know why you're complaining. I brought you California burritos from Santana's, you stream DSC's morning show on the internet, and you watch the Chargers play on satellite. You're practically riding bikes in Balboa Park."

Charlie pulled open the cooler and peaked inside. "Is Torrey Pines in here so I can play a round of golf?"

"It's the closest you're getting to San Diego," Remi said sitting down on the chair across from Charlie and tilting back his beer, "I can't say I blame you, it's damn cold here."

San Diego became a hunting ground for the family. The clubs had weekly disturbances from thugs looking for Charlie. The house in La Jolla was almost burnt down by an arsonist. Eulojo had unleashed all the henchmen from hell trying to find him which forced Charlie to pack up the family and banish them all from California. The US government offered to put them in witness protection but Charlie wasn't willing to disappear, he wanted to return to California someday and he wouldn't give Eulojo the satisfaction.

For Charlie, he was taking control of his destiny. Against the advice of border patrol and the military, he hired his own bounty hunters and vigilante mercenaries to find Lena. Charlie declared his own personal war against Eulojo and had plenty of money and hate in his heart that couldn't be exhausted.

Charlie had dragged the family to all parts of the country, moving every few months or at a sign of suspicion. In the last year they had moved seventeen times, the remote cabin home in Durango, Colorado had been the longest with three weeks.

A snowball smashed against the window, blocking Charlie's line of sight in the garden. He saw Oriana duck behind the gazebo and looked for security that was assigned to watch the perimeter. There was a time when he would trust the guards to stay at their post but now he couldn't rest easy if he didn't make sure they were still doing their job.

It took Remi a month to convince Charlie that keeping the family in the same room with him twenty-four hours a day wasn't giving anyone quality of life. Charlie would start shaking if they were in the bathroom too long. In the last year he grew stronger but still had nightly panic attacks, waking to check the children were in their beds three times a night.

While Charlie struggled with the night demons, the best medicine for the girls was having each other. The day that Charlie brought Giselle to the house, Oriana cried for Mariana and latched on to Giselle like a souvenir doll. Giselle never left her side, absorbing her grief while she dealt with losing Lena. Both girls found each other in the loss of their mothers.

Giselle was slow to move out of her shell which was fine for Oriana who chattered in Spanish and was delighted someone would listen. After six months, Giselle was speaking in full sentences and Oriana was teaching her English. They were like sisters separated at birth and happy to make up for lost memories.

Max wasn't interested in sharing tears with the girls, in fact he avoided them. His son, the sweet, gentle boy who clutched a stuffed penguin now had sudden outbursts of anger and screaming. There were unexplained broken toys in his wake of destruction. Charlie was ill-equipped with the patience to deal with the tantrums but Brenda was limitless in her understanding.

Charlie thought about her patience as he sat in the kitchen and watched Brenda sit with Max while he ate dinner. She hadn't been interested in him as a baby but now she was a protective mother bear.

A clatter came from the living room causing Brenda to jump. The door swung open and a rat-nosed woman peeked her face inside and flinched when she caught Brenda's glare. "Sorry to bother you but do you have any extra extension cords?"

"This isn't my home, darling," Brenda said, "why the hell would I know where they keep the damn cords?

The woman looked confused but then quietly closed the door when she realized Brenda wasn't going to help.

"She's just an assistant, Mama, she's not here to attack you," Charlie said.

"If you were going to commit suicide, why did you drag us all over the country?" Brenda said, glaring at Charlie as she wiped milk off Max's chin, "why the hell would you let that wretched reporter come here?"

"With the anniversary coming up, we need to get Charlie's story out," Remi said, "then those media vultures won't invent things and pick at his dead carcass. We don't need them poking at Eulojo."

The day that Charlie and Lena reached Tecate, there were hundreds of hungry media lenses thirsty for some new angle to sell the Mexico story. Charlie's eyes were not the only ones that captured the memory of Lena, weak and bleeding, dragged into the tunnel. Millions of eyes watched at the moment that he failed to save Lena. Within the hour, stories appeared that Charlie and Lena were star-crossed lovers, there were writers clamoring to write the story and producers wanting to buy the rights.

Charlie imagined the publicity was a constant reminder to Eulojo that Charlie had put a knife in his eye and escaped in front of the world. His reputation as bloodthirsty and cruel was replaced with a fool. It gave him nightmares to think that Eulojo's fury would be taken out on Lena every time he was provoked. Charlie remained silent hoping the story would be forgotten but it only got worse.

Charlie's homes and clubs all over the country had the media swooping down from every corner of the planet, all trying to catch the next exclusive and capture the next picture of the heroic millionaire and the motherless girl with the mournful eyes.

Charlie's banishment meant he needed a link to make arrangements for money and housing and that was Remi. It was a lot to ask of one person, to be the mouthpiece or to stand silent when necessary. Remi never hesitated to take risks that put him in danger but kept the family safe. He had his own security detail to look around every corner and moved out of his condo.

Remi and Charlie reacted the same in crisis, always trying to make things humorous. He played games with ambitious reporters trying to get an exclusive with Charlie. He had been offered seven figure deals, his own show, and in a few cases there were promises of sex. Remi did admit he had dinner with one producer but she wouldn't continue without a signed contract and the romance ended when he explained he wasn't a prostitute.

There were plenty of stories that Remi shared with Charlie about the journalists but Nadia Murphy-Hayman was the one that Remi enjoyed the most to torture. Her producer, Barry Waters, hounded Remi every day for an exclusive interview with Charlie. Barry's dramatic pitches to convince Remi ended in whining and pleading that were ridiculous for a grown man and Remi told him every day that is why he was hanging up the phone. Two weeks ago, Remi arrived in Durango and rather than a joke he told Charlie that he had met with Barry and agreed to set up an interview.

"Forget it," Charlie said, "if we do an interview at least make it with a reputable journalist."

Remi took a moment to respond. "Nadia claims to know Lena's whereabouts."

"Bullshit." Charlie said, there are twenty investigators, trained bounty hunters, and trackers searching every inch of Mexico, "what did a tabloid sleaze queen find?"

"You're doing this interview." Remi said, something in voice closing the subject from discussion.

Now Nadia Murphy-Hayman was sitting in the living room with a team of make-up artists, production assistants, glaring lights and cameras at every angle. He could barely look at Nadia Murphy-Hayman who beamed at him with her iridescent teeth and overemphasized cheek bones from too much plastic surgery. Rather than ripping the blonde extensions off her head, he focused on her big mouth bass of a producer, Barry Waters who was sweating in the kitchen and talking on one of three cell phones he carried. It could be thirty below zero and Barry would sweat like he was baking in the sun. He was like a greasy stain large enough that Charlie would need to re-paint the whole kitchen. Barry caught Charlie staring at him and he rolled over, slapping a meaty palm on his back.

"I know we agreed to not mention your location, but can't we put the fireplace in the background?" Barry said, his voice an octave higher than you would expect for a large man, "It gives a family vibe and it doesn't give your location away."

"You don't negotiate with him," Remi said, startling Barry as he approached from behind, "I won't warn you again to stop bothering my client."

Barry held his hands up like he was being held hostage and gave a high-pitched squeak, "Can't blame me for trying."

"What did a tabloid reporter uncover that all the paid professionals couldn't find?" Charlie asked.

"All will be revealed," Barry said, distracted by an assistant running passed him, "now come inside the living room and we'll get started."

Barry disappeared into the living room and Charlie turned back to Brenda. "Are you ready?"

Brenda nodded. "The girls are packed and I'm almost done with Max."

An interview in an "undisclosed location" was no longer anonymous when you brought a camera crew, make-up artists and an entourage for a diva journalist like Nadia Murphy-Hayman. The risk of a desperate assistant wanting to make a little money by leaking their hiding spot was too much. For that reason, Remi arranged for a new house on the beaches of Gulf Shore, Alabama. If Charlie was going to move again he wanted somewhere with an ocean.

Marcus, Judge Andersen's former head of security, would take Brenda and the children tonight. Remi and Charlie would decide what path to take when they heard the information that Nadia had uncovered about Lena. He hoped they could narrow the location in Mexico. He hired so many mercenaries to canvas every inch of the country but Lena had disappeared that day she was dragged from the Tecate border station.

Charlie had not been a praying man but since he got back from Mexico, he asked God every day to help him find Lena even if that wasn't alive. Nadia was the first clue they had found in months, as much as Charlie felt like this was a hoax, there was a part of him that wanted to be wrong.

Brenda and the children left once the sun went down and the house was now vacant except for Charlie, Remi and Nadia's crew.

The living room with the open windows and high log fireplace was no longer a peaceful snow lodge but was transformed into a studio in Hollywood. The windows were blackened and two wooden chairs sat under glaring lights that felt like a prison interrogation room.

Sitting to the side, surrounded by several assistants and a make-up artist fixing her lips sat Nadia Murphy-Hayman, the queen of tabloid media. She reminded Charlie of Estrella with her mean eyes and tough exterior. If paths had been different, Estrella could have been sitting in her place. Nadia spotted Charlie and flashed a toothy-smile with large, silicone lips.

"We're giving up the perfect hide-out," Charlie whispered to Remi, "this better be worth it."

"You hated this place," Remi scoffed, "by tomorrow you'll be walking on a beach in Alabama."

"Charlie!" Nadia screamed as if they were at a college reunion, her shrill voice causing the film crew to jump, "Come sit down!"

Nadia tried to hug Charlie but he avoided her step and glared at Remi as he sat down on a wooden chair. Nadia gave up and sat across from him as an assistant put a plush pillow behind her back.

"I am so glad you could meet with us!" Nadia said, giving a girlish giggle.

Charlie fought back the desire to leave. This wasn't a social visit and they were not friends. "What news do you have about Lena?"

"After we get the interview done, we will have a big reveal, okay?" Nadia said patting his leg as if they were going to have brunch. It made the hairs on the back of his neck bristle that Nadia's "big reveal" was leading toward bullshit.

The fact that Remi was convinced this would bring him closer to Lena was the only thing keeping him from dropping their camera equipment in the snow. He moved the chair further from her reach, "It's your extortion but it's my time so let's get this going."

Nadia ignored the jab and leaned in for a quick brush of powder from a fidgety make-up artist. "Move your chair closer to me."

Charlie raised an eyebrow, "Ms. Murphy-Hayman, are you even listening to me?"

"Oh please use my first name, Charlie, it will sound more intimate," Nadia said, adjusting her jacket, "we'll start with a brief introduction and then I'll begin with the questions."

Charlie glared at Remi who sent him a cautionary look to stay seated.

Nadia looked directly in the camera and her light voice was now deep and syllables over-pronounced for effect.

"We are here in an undisclosed location for our safety and the protection of our host and his family who are hunted by the cartel. Every three months, Charlie Thibodeaux must move his family to a new house in a new state to protect them."

Nadia straightened so high in her chair that Charlie thought she was going to salute the camera.

"A year ago, the country was riveted to the TV watching our southern neighbors erupt into civil action. While our cameras were turned toward Mexico, San Diego entrepreneur, Charlie Thibodeaux was waging his own war to get home. Our hearts broke as we helplessly watched Charlie holding his son, Max and clutching a young girl only known as Giselle running toward the border gate in Tecate while being chased through gunfire. Once he knew they were safe, he returned to save Giselle's mother and his lover, Lena, who lay bleeding to death only 100 feet away. He was too late and could only watch her be dragged away. While the civil action quieted in Mexico in less than a month, we've had no answers about the fate of Charlie and his beloved, Lena. Tonight, Charlie speaks only to me. He will tell us how his life has changed, his desperate search for Giselle's father, and tonight, will learn the fate of Lena that has been exclusively obtained by my staff."

The word, 'fate' made Charlie nervous. Was it a sensational word for effect? Charlie felt his stomach twist at the speculation and he had to get through so many questions to know the answer he'd been seeking.

Nadia's practiced face of a hard journalist, now turned to Charlie and melted into a concerned neighbor. "Charlie, how are you doing?"

"How am I doing?" Charlie said, straightening his tie, "if you're going to waste my time then I'm going to end this interview right now."

"You're nervous. We'll edit that out," Nadia said, reaching out and patting Charlie's leg again. She looked up at her director and nodded, "we'll work on streaming the questions together in post-production. We'll just ask the direct questions."

The camera came back on and the questions started again.

"Your fiancée Lisa Guinto watched from your home. It must have been hard for her to see you risk your life for Lena," Nadia said for the audience's benefit, "How has Lisa been?"

"You'd have to ask her," Charlie said, "you'll probably find her sitting on a beach in Jamaica with an umbrella drink and a cabana boy in her hands. She left me a month after I returned."

"I'm sorry to hear that."

"Why?" Charlie asked, "It's the media vultures that caused her to run screaming for the Caribbean."

Nadia pursed her lips, "You don't think it had anything to do with the fact you were seen declaring your love for another woman? The public have been supportive of Lisa as a victim in this tragic situation."

"You have never met Lisa, have you?" Charlie said, glancing at Remi who shifted his position on the wall. Without Charlie's version, the media cast Lisa as a heart broken fiancée with a heart of gold. Lisa wasn't heartbroken. She was furious that she was painted as the simple girl who was losing the love of her life to another woman. Lisa wasn't supposed to be that girl. She was the woman that men left their girls at home to worship at her feet. She woke up to the news calling her *heartbroken* and *dutiful* and began to scream that Charlie's little "vacation" made her look naïve and stupid. She grabbed her passport, a dozen designer bathing suits, drove straight to Lindbergh Field and boarded a private plane to Jamaica. Charlie didn't know she was gone until she called him upon arrival and said she couldn't marry someone who wasn't faithful.

Charlie let her break things off without another word. He didn't bother telling her that Remi had admitted he had slept with Lisa three days after he returned. Charlie knew he was supposed to be angry but he had his own guilt. He hadn't thought about Lisa in Mexico and she wasn't on his mind when he was lying naked on Senora Mendoza's floor with Lena. The fact was that his relationship with Lisa was over before he left for Mexico and there was nothing to forgive. It would be more tragic to lose his twenty year friendship with Remi.

"On the same day of your return, your mother was arrested for shooting your sister's boyfriend."

Nadia's voice broke through Charlie's thoughts. He was back in the present forced to defend the past.

"Jesse was not my sister's boyfriend. He broke into my house, threatened the lives of my family and was shot as an intruder by my mother," Charlie said, repeating what Remi had rehearsed with him. It had taken several tries for him to get the anger out of his voice, "Brenda...my mother was cleared of all charges."

"Your poor sister, Nola Thibodeaux, watched her boyfriend die and had a nervous breakdown," Nadia said, pausing as a make-up artist blotted her forehead, "and was institutionalized?"

"My sister didn't have a breakdown." Charlie lied, visualizing the last time he saw Nola, her eyes glassy and the disoriented. Without heavy medication, she would wake up screaming and start accusing Brenda of killing Jesse to deny her happiness. When news came that Eulojo had put a bounty on Charlie's family, it was apparent that the strain would be one more thing that might break Nola. She needed a calm environment and Charlie needed to keep the family moving from place to place. With a heavy heart, Charlie brought her to a secluded rehabilitation facility in Minneapolis. He swore it was temporary but Nola cried as if he was dropping her off at her first day of kindergarten. So many times, Brenda wanted to go see her but Charlie kept her location a secret. He couldn't take the chance that someone might be watching and Brenda was so stubborn she would sneak away. Charlie wasn't about to tell Nadia anything that might give Eulojo's men an idea where to search.

"Wasn't the man killed, Jesse Andersen, the son of the federal judge murdered in January?"

Charlie bowed his head. Judge Andersen didn't want to be put in federal protection either. After losing his son, he was more determined to strike down legalizing marijuana but he never got the chance. Andersen sent Marcus to secure Charlie's family in the first of many safe houses. He disappeared one week later and was found floating in Mission Bay with his daughter Carin. Charlie would never get over the guilt that he had caused another family's destruction.

Nadia waited for more details but when Charlie's silence she gave a polite cough and forced a smile. "You're going to need to help me here. I ask questions and you give me details. It's called an interview. How are the little girls, Oriana and Giselle?

"They're fine for girls who have lost their mothers."

Charlie gave Nadia a dramatic sound bite so she could have her sensational story but that was all she was going get out of him.

Nadia looked into the camera. "This is a good time to send a message to Giselle's father. We understand you are living illegally in the United States. We want to reunite you with your daughter and arrange a private meeting, free of prosecution. There is a number that will be on the screen, please call us and we will make sure that we bring you together."

Nadia looked back at Charlie and flashed a smile. He didn't think he could hate Nadia more right now. Lena's last wish was for Charlie to find Antonio but in the last year he hadn't hired anyone. He knew that was breaking his promise to her but he couldn't separate Giselle from the family. It was cruel to separate her from the kids and even Brenda had grown attached. Charlie could give her a better life and he personally didn't want to lose her. It would be like losing Lena all over again. Now, Nadia was putting him in a position to look for this mystery husband. If Charlie had his way, Antonio would never be found.

"And what about you?"

"What about me?" Charlie said, leaned back and folded his arms, "My family has been torn apart, we move like gypsies always wondering if someone isn't waiting to kill us and you're holding information from me so you can profit from my personal life. How do you think I feel?"

Nadia was losing her own composure. "You make me sound like the villain and all I want to do is help you with closure."

"You're a media whore who capitalizes on people's pain," Charlie said, watching the words stun her, "but don't worry, your people can edit that."

"You want to know why your people couldn't find Lena?" Nadia snapped, leaning toward him, a gleam in her eyes, "They couldn't think like someone wanting to cover their identity."

"I want to know about Lena," Charlie growled.

"Lena is short for Inez Magdalena Cortez. She's the daughter of a prominent business man and his wife, both deceased, and the youngest surviving sister of twelve siblings," Nadia said, pausing to make sure she had Charlie's attention, "and sister to Eulojo Cortez, member of the Sinaloa cartel."

Nadia looked satisfied that she had stunned Charlie and motioned to her assistant to bring something to clear his throat. He took a large gulp of water but his mouth was too dry to speak. He stared down at the glass and wished he could drown inside.

"You're lying."

"We were contacted by her nephew, Rolando Cortez, who gave us the story," Nadia said, taking a moment to sip her water before continuing, "We checked the footage at the Tecate border crossing and confirmed he is the one that places her in a truck after she is dragged from the Tecate border gate."

Charlie swallowed hard. "Where is she?"

"I think we've told you enough to prove we have found Lena," Nadia said, reaching for her satchel, "let's get a few more questions on camera first."

"You don't get anything else from me." Charlie interrupted, "stop the cameras."

Nadia took another sip of water as she looked at Barry and motioned to keep the camera rolling. "Rolando brought her back to his father, Eulojo. Despite her danger, Lena, was at peace, knowing she could be brought before the judgment of her brother and suffer his rage if she knew that you and the children were safe."

Charlie's stomach felt sick. She was talking about Lena in the past tense.

Nadia's eyes dropped down and then after looking direct into the camera, she took a deep breath and looked back at Charlie. "Eulojo's anger was savage after the loss of his eye. After three days of torture, he brought her to a Rosarito beach and slit her throat. Rolando came back for her but it was too late."

Charlie felt like he'd been hit with a stun gun and he started to see the world in slow motion. The words didn't process right away and he struggled to understand.

Nadia reached out and grabbed Charlie's hand, trying to console him in a well-choreographed motion for one final shot before Remi had them blocked, "I'm sorry for your loss."

"You're sorry for my loss? You tell me on camera that Lena has died and that's all you can say? Was the pain on my face real enough?" Charlie asked, grabbing her hand and squeezed it tightly. "Did you get my reaction? Do you want to shoot it again?"

"What the hell is this? Stop the cameras now! This is a goddamn ambush!" Remi yelled, moving toward the camera man who dodged him and kept the camera focused on Charlie and the look of horror on his face.

"You have the entire world concerned about you," Nadia said, glancing at the camera and trying to pull her hand away, "don't you think you owe them to share this moment?"

Sympathy was thick in her voice but in Nadia's eyes, Charlie saw a glint of excitement. She was preparing to lay out his pain in front of the world and trying to hold back her joy at the situation. Anger shot through him and before Charlie could stop himself, he hurled his glass at the table breaking it into shards that flew toward Nadia's face. He let her hand go in enough time to cover her eyes but she cried out at a slice on her cheek.

"We're filing assault charges!" Barry said, pointing a finger at Charlie.

"Get out of my house," Charlie said, throwing a napkin at Nadia and headed toward the kitchen, "pack up and drive back to hell."

Charlie could hear Barry's shouting as he followed behind him but there was a scraping of a chair across the floor.

"Now that I've got your attention, you son of a bitch," Remi said, blockading the producer, "let's talk about the restraining order I'm filing if you come near my client."

The kitchen was dark except for a night light near the sink and it was too bright. Charlie charged out the back door and felt a blast of November air go through him as he headed to the gazebo. The night sky radiated with too many stars and he wanted a black hole to suck him into a void. He leaned against the gazebo wall and waited for hypothermia to take control, hoping that freezing to death would cool the pain in his heart. He squeezed his eyes shut but images of Lena lying dead wouldn't leave.

Revelations that Eulojo was Lena's brother was the piece of the puzzle he was missing. It explained why Eulojo knew that Charlie was lying about being married to Lena. Charlie had wondered if Eulojo might be Giselle's father. He now understood why Rolando worked for an evil monster but was loyal to save his aunt. Charlie hated that so many answers were leaving him with more questions.

The only true answer was that he had loved women in his life but never someone that he didn't think he could live without. As long as he searched for her, there was hope that they would find each other again but with Lena's death, he was lost.

Charlie heard soft, crunch of snow coming closer and stopped at the gazebo steps. "How could you bring that bitch here?"

"I haven't finished telling you her story."

Charlie's eyes flew open to see Nadia standing outside the gazebo in a thick, fur coat.

"I told you to leave." Charlie said.

"It's beautiful up here," Nadia said, moving inside the gazebo, "but I hate snow."

"Great, we have that in common," Charlie growled, "I also like football and jazz concerts. I hate sleazy reporters that don't know when to get the fuck out of my life."

"Ouch." Nadia said, but continued to stand, unfazed, "I prefer beaches. My boyfriend has a yacht that we sail to Puerto Vallarta the minute the temperature drops below seventy."

Charlie stood up with some difficulty, his torso was freezing. "Are you going to film when I have security throw you out on your ass?"

Nadia turned toward him. "Not before I tell you about my vacation."

"How dumb are you?" Charlie said, looking for Remi at the house but no one was coming.

"The day we arrived in port, I went shopping and was approached by a Mexican who insisted that I speak with him," Nadia said, coming closer to Charlie than was comfortable, "I told him to go away but he wouldn't leave until he gave me a gift."

Nadia unrolled a yellow scarf revealing the green covered book of poems from the hotel in Rosarito and forced it into Charlie's hands. His numb hands grew heavy as he cradled it from fear of dropping the book into the snow. Shuffling his grip, the book fell open to the Landlocked poem marked by a photograph of Nadia in a tiny, striped bathing suit with her arms around a man with a tan deeper than a leather couch.

"That was taken on his yacht in Puerto Vallarta." Nadia said, tapping the photo and bringing it close to his face, "he brought the crew to celebrate the show picking up for next season."

In front of Charlie's eyes there half-dressed people surrounding the deck and he was about to rip the photo in half when a woman sitting under an awning in the background caught his eye. Her olive-green dress made her look conservative compared to the party-goers. Her long, dark hair was blowing around her, eyes rimmed with thick lashes that stared straight into his soul, and on her neck was the same yellow scarf in Nadia's hands partially hiding a long, red cut across her throat. Just behind with a hand on her shoulder was Rolando. For the rest of his life, Lena's beauty would take his breath away.

"Eulojo thinks she is dead. Rolando used her death as a reason to break free from his father and gave his aunt a chance to have a peaceful life," Nadia said, gazing at Charlie, no longer looking big and bold, "but for your love she risks everything to find a journalist on holiday and asks for help."

"How did she know you weren't going to take advantage and exploit her?" Charlie asked, his heart wanted to believe but he couldn't be sure this wasn't a trick.

I make money capitalizing on sensational stories but I come from a long line of respected journalists and authors and my parents don't approve of my career choices," Nadia said, taking the book from Charlie, "but as long as I use an alias and don't disgrace the family name, they let me visit for Christmas every few years. I have been Nadia Murphy-Hayman so long that I barely remember the name my mother gave me."

Nadia took a deep breath as if she was about to make a confession. "Elijhun Cann-Saez was my great-grandfather."

Bullshit!" Charlie said laughing out loud, "you aren't related to a famous poet.

"It's true," Nadia protested, pulling her fur coat closer, "but no one would accept my public image as a hard-nosed journalist if they know I'm the granddaughter of a national treasure."

Charlie snorted. His mind was running through the spectacle of the interview. "Why the big act? A decent person wouldn't put someone through that."

"I wanted to prepare you for the interview but Remi said you couldn't fake that kind of shock. It's important the world sees that you are broken." Nadia said and then smiled, "your grief will make better television and I'll make a lot of money."

"Remind me to thank Remi after I kill him," Charlie said.

"It's more serious than that," Nadia said, her smile fading, "my show broadcasts in North America and parts of Central America. With all the publicity, Eulojo must see that you have been crushed. He must think you will stop looking for her."

Charlie looked down at the picture of Lena and spotted a US flag on a hotel off shore. Had Nadia brought Lena to the US?

"She's not here," Nadia said, anticipating his question taking the book back and folding it back in the scarf, "but she's close. For her safety, we don't move her in the daylight."

"Take me to her," Charlie demanded.

"Not yet," Nadia said, shaking a finger, "you need to come back and answer a few more questions. We'll edit them so they look like they're the beginning of the interview."

"Take me to her and you can ask me all the questions you want," Charlie said, growing angry, "You brought her to the US and now you're holding her prisoner?"

"She is not a captive. She has Rolando with her for protection," Nadia said, moving back toward the house, "she is perfectly safe in a hotel in Santa Fe."

"I want to talk to her," Charlie pressed, following after her, "get her on the phone."

"You know we can't get phone reception out here," Nadia scolded, "finish the interview and I'll give you back the book. I've put the address on the back of the picture. You're not going to drive five hours in the snow tonight. You can send someone to get her in the morning."

Charlie stopped. "Why would you say that?"

Nadia stopped on the steps of the house. "You're the kind of man who can afford to have things brought to him."

Lena was hours within reach and once again he had to play with someone else's rules. It didn't matter to him if it was Mariana, Eulojo or Nadia. Charlie was tired of the ones he loved always being held hostage.

"Allow your soul to be free."

Charlie stared up at her. "What?"

"It's the last line in the Landlocked poem." Nadia said, "You'll be free once you sign an agreement to give me another exclusive interview in a year, I've already got Lena's signature and as soon as your name is on that paper, I'll give you the book and you can live happily ever after."

Charlie had waited to hear Nadia's real motive. She might be related to a respected poet but she wasn't doing anything that didn't help beat her competition. She was saying that Lena and Charlie would be free as long as we played by her rules, and that was just putting their souls in a cage to sing on her command. After all the hell they had endured, Charlie had learned that true freedom was making your own choices and he was about to make one. His legs loosened but instead of heading up the stairs into the house, he snatched the book from Nadia's hand and began running for the garage.

Nadia started after Charlie but grabbed the rail as she slipped. "Come back here!"

Charlie could hear Nadia's voice growing faint as he put distance between them. He pried open the door to the Jeep and slid onto the cold leather, his body shivering with excitement and cold. He didn't have a jacket, no money and no idea what highway to get to New Mexico but he knew he couldn't step back into the house without someone trying to stop him.

"Where the hell am I going?"

The book was poking in his rib and he yanked it from his side catching the scarf on the gear shift and unrolling the book onto the passenger seat. The picture of Lena fell out and flipped over. On the back of the photo, he stared at words scrawled on the back:

La Posada Hotel
Bring me where I belong

Charlie couldn't stop smiling, pulling the key from the console and firing up the engine. Once again, Lena was right about that book of poems, it always found a way to bring them together.

Charlie moved the Jeep forward and headed toward the road. He was plunging into darkness, unafraid that he couldn't see where he was going but with every moment he was closer to Lena and both had waited long enough for life to begin.

Acknowledgements

This book couldn't be written without your help:

Mark Sanchez for believing in the dream
Rebekah Tuttle, for your objective and nurturing eye
Thomas Sanchez for working out plot ideas
Matthew Sanchez for being my marketing guru
Aviva Layton for taking a look at the whole picture
Brian Fahrner for making the digital media come to life.
Elyse Jewell for keeping me grounded.
Patricia Lopez for your angry voice
Barona Resort and Casino for your beautiful hotel
 and excellent room service (especially the albondigas soup at 2am)

I am grateful and thankful for all of you!

www.ingramcontent.com/pod-product-compliance
Lightning Source LLC
Chambersburg PA
CBHW060341260626
47160CB00006B/2163